CRITICS RAVE FO

BEHOLD A RED HORSE

"Paperback Pick. Cotton Smith…a genre fiction favorite."

—*ReadWest*

"From his vivid descriptions of a prairie night to his hoof-pounding action scenes, Cotton Smith captures the look and feel of the real West."

—Spur Award Winner Mike Blakely

PRAY FOR TEXAS

"[Cotton Smith's] stories are centered around the wonders of the human spirit in overcoming life's obstacles."

—*True West*

"It is impossible to read *Pray for Texas* and not come away changed."

—Spur Award Winner Loren D. Estleman

DARK TRAIL TO DODGE

"One of the Top 25 books of the American West."

—*ReadWest*

"Cotton Smith has taken the traditional cattle drive to Dodge and breathed new life into it with interesting characters, clever plot twists and great descriptions."

—Spur Award Winner Dan Coldsmith

A SHADOW WITH A GUN

Rios's patience paid off as a dark shape loomed where none should be. It flickered across the far wall and disappeared again behind a boulder, twenty yards to his right. Whichever outlaw it was had guessed where Rios might be and was trying to get an angle to determine if his hunch was correct. Without waiting, Rios rolled away again. When he stopped rolling, he was parallel to the last boulder, the one where the outlaw had gone. Slowly Rios brought his rifle into firing position. He was still twenty yards away but hoped the outlaw would show himself just enough for a good shot.

A gurgle broke the silence. It came from the direction where Abe had been. It was the sound of a man dying. From a knife. Rios couldn't worry for the moment if it was Abe or one of their enemies, but he had to wait for the outlaw to step away from the rocks.

The shadow emerged. Slowly. Gradually. Linked to the boulder, yet separate. In an instant, Rios knew it was two outlaws. Just behind the first was Gee himself....

Other *Leisure* books by Cotton Smith:

DARK TRAIL TO DODGE
PRAY FOR TEXAS
BEHOLD A RED HORSE
BROTHERS OF THE GUN
SPIRIT RIDER
SONS OF THUNDER
WINTER KILL

COTTON SMITH

DEATH RIDES A RED HORSE

LEISURE BOOKS NEW YORK CITY

A LEISURE BOOK®

April 2005

Published by

Dorchester Publishing Co., Inc.
200 Madison Avenue
New York, NY 10016

ISBN 0-8439-5260-1

Printed in the United States of America.

DEATH RIDES A RED HORSE

Chapter 1

Three armed men charged into the busy McKeon General Mercantile Store and every customer knew they were not there to buy anything. Wild-looking and filthy, their unkempt appearance was less significant than their cocked revolvers. Most realized they were part of Victorio Gee's feared outlaw army of renegades, desperadoes and killers.

Within the last month they had swarmed into this part of Texas like angry hornets from the border. Four small towns in the region had already been hit, leaving them with dead citizens, empty banks, ransacked stores and raped women. Just hearing about their violence was enough to bring fear to the throats of most. Now they were a lot more than some other town's nightmare.

Each outlaw wore a tightly rolled black silk neckerchief tied around his upper left arm. Many also wore black hats, taken from the ambush and massacre of an unsuspecting Union infantry company near the end of the War of Northern Aggression. The place of the massacre had become known as "Kill Creek" and the name "Kill Creek Gang" followed them wherever they struck. They seemed untouchable by local or state law. Hitting swiftly and disappearing just as quickly. Days ahead of exasperated Texas Rangers. Some thought the state police didn't want to catch up with them.

The sudden manifestation of the three outlaws was the gang's honed manner of attack. Fear was always magnified by surprise. Their entrance was met by surprised gasps and a swirl of the aromas of freshly ground coffee, leather, tobacco, bacon, spices, salted fish and vinegar. Everywhere in the store, customers froze in place at their shopping tasks, examining kegs, sacks and barrels of cooking staples and chosing groceries, dry goods and hardware. Store owner, Jeremy McKeon, always eager to assist, was helping the mayor's wife select a bolt of cloth for a dress.

A tall woman beside them, coveting a set of crockery, screamed and fainted. Immediately, the courteous store owner sought to comfort her. Angry at this distraction, the mayor's wife threw down the cloth and spun to leave. For the first time, she saw the three outlaws at the front of the store.

"Get out of here or my husband will have you arrrested!" She huffed and folded her arms.

Spitting a thick brown stream of tobacco juice in response, the apparent outlaw leader's face looked almost presidential. Definitely Germanic, his thick, light-brownish beard accented a very square jaw. His upper lip was clean-shaven, however. That's as far as the presidential look went as wide suspenders held up torn pants struggling to handle cross-belted guns.

His faded blue shirt had a hole just above where the right pocket had been. A dark circle surrounded it. Food stains and trail dirt decorated the rest. Two black bands decorated his upper arm, one above the other. An indication of rank.

On either side of him stood two equally dangerous-looking men gleefully studying the terrified townspeople, ranchers and farmers shopping for supplies.

In a swirling mixture of English and German, he growled orders, "*Guten morgen, meine damen und herren*. Do not to be moving. *Nein. Wir* to get *kost* . . . ah, food . . . *und der* gold. *Ja, und der* bullets." He stopped and studied the store filled with unmoving customers. Pleased with the reaction, he continued, "*Ja, wir* taking *der gut fräuleines Ja*, only so *der gut* . . . pretty . . . young . . . ones." His laugh was guttural and filled with phlegm.

Chuckling at his broken German manner of speaking and his mention of taking women, the other two brigands resumed their examination of the ladies. Instinctively, some men stepped in front of their wives to shield them. Both outlaws were taller than the stocky German. Their clothes were similarly filthy, strange combinations of range and town wear.

The tallest of the two, a mule-faced man with long, curly sideburns, wore a cavalry jacket that had once belonged to a Union army officer. His black hat was too big for his head, resting against pushed-down ears.

The outlaw to the German's left was either part Kiowa, part Mexican or both. His stringy black hair lay across humped shoulders; a gold tooth glittered from a smile that appeared to be locked into place. Shoved into his belt was a long knife and a second pistol. Kiowa leggings, up to his knees, were layered with old mud and older horse dung. Black eyes darted along the rafter beams holding heavy cooking pots, slabs of bacon, sides of mutton and large hams, deciding on what should be taken. His gaze dropped to the room to search for a woman he would take with him. His examination came to rest on a woman in a wrinkled gingham dress and white shawl.

Realizing what his attention meant, her bosom rose and fell with her gasp and she stepped behind her farmer husband, holding tight to his arm. Their eyes exchanged fear. The lanky farmer swallowed; his Adam's apple raced back and forth before resettling. At his sides, his hands clenched into fists but the color slid from his face.

The mayor's wife glanced down at McKeon. "Mr. McKeon, you get rid of these ruffians—or else."

A sunburned rancher in a new stiff shirt and coat turned toward her. "Mrs. Lovington. You'd best be quiet."

"What did you say?"

The rancher's wife spun toward her. "Shut up before you get us all killed, you fool. Those are Victorio Gee's men."

Mrs. Lovington's face shattered as each word slammed against her mind and clung there.

In the back of the room, two brothers—Ethan and Cole Kerry—stood quietly next to a large barrel of coiled rope. Although blind, Ethan was selecting lariats while Cole waited patiently for his older brother to caress each rope to make certain the texture and strength was what he wanted for their ranch. Details like that were always left to his careful attention.

Along with their oldest brother, Luther, the three men owned one of the biggest cattle spreads in this part of Texas. Fall gathering started two days ago but a need for more lariats and a few other supplies had brought them to town along with their wives and Ethan's children.

With the two Kerry brothers was Eli, Ethan's ten-year-old son. His face was peppered with freckles and topped with light brown hair plastered into what passed for combing. His blue eyes were wide; he loved being with his father and, especially, with his Uncle Cole.

"Who are they?" Ethan whispered, continuing to work with the rope in his hands.

"Must be part of Victorio Gee's bunch," Cole responded. "Heard they hit a string of towns south of here. Wonder how many are in Uvalde?"

The tautness in the younger Kerry's face couldn't hide the boyish charm. Or the deep cleft in his chin. Or the once-broken nose, courtesy of Ethan when they were boys. Cole had immediately returned the favor and his taller brother had a matched Roman nose above his thick mustache.

"Damn, if they are, you can bet some of them are across the street at the bank." Ethan's eyebrows twitched above unseeing eyes. "A lot of our money's there, Cole." He was a hard man who had built the Bar K ranch up from wild Texas prairie and was dealing with the much more terrifying aspect of not seeing it anymore. At least, most of the time he was.

"Yeah. So are our women—and Maggie."

Eli gulped and whispered, "Whatcha gonna do, Uncle Cole?"

"Sh-h-h. Wait here. If shooting starts, duck behind this barrel. And stay there." Cole patted the boy on the shoulder as he watched the German outlaw walk over to the kneeling Jeremy McKeon and demand he get money from the cash register.

The other two outlaws busied themselves stuffing food and tobacco into large burlap sacks. To each other, they discussed which women they would take along. The halfbreed stopped once, pointed at the farmer's wife, snickered and continued putting cans in a sack.

The Kerrys were dressed for ranch work, wearing

trail-worn chaps and long coats. Cole never wore his two-gun rig when they worked cattle. Only Ethan and Luther knew of his one-time reputation as a gunfighter and an outlaw after the war. One of his ivory-handled, silver plated Colts, however, was shoved into his waistband. The gunbelt and other Colt were in his saddlebags, as usual. Ethan carried his revolver the same way. More out of desire to remember the old days when he could see than expected use.

Before leaving for the roundup, their oldest brother, Luther, advised them of a shortage of lariats and leather for harness and saddle repairs. The Kerry women—Ethan's wife, Claire, and Cole's new bride, Kathleen, and Ethan's daughter, seven-year-old Maggie—were happy to use the excuse to come to town. So they all came in the buckboard with Claire driving while Ethan and Cole rode horses alongside. Eli asked if his dog, Blue, could come along. Approval was reluctant, but given.

Ethan would have insisted on riding a horse even if there had been room in the wagon. It made him feel closer to the old days—when he could see. Cole always rode beside him, just to make sure Ethan's well-trained horse didn't stray or act up. He made certain Ethan wasn't aware of it though.

Of course, the roundup cook added a few other things to their list, before leaving for the first camp: another sack of flour, another of beans, more coffee and a jug of molasses. It bothered Ethan that everything wasn't in place for the roundup, even after Luther and Cole told him they had taken the same number of lariats and leather into last year's fall gathering. Rain had caused an increased number of problems with both. That and someone had left several lariats next to the branding fire the first day. The roundup was a joint gathering with other area ranchers, as usual, but none had rope or leather to spare. Their steady hand, Harold DuMonte, was in charge while the Kerry brothers were away.

Of course, Cole could have gone to town alone but he rarely went anywhere without his brother. This wasn't out of pity. He valued Ethan's judgement. An untamed sorrel, the magnificent horse Cole now rode, may have blinded him but the kick didn't take away his savvy. Or his attention to detail. Or, ultimately, his ability to lead. Of course, anywhere Uncle Cole was, Eli wanted to be there, too. Eli's dog, Blue, had to stay in the wagon, however; the ugly dog wasn't the best around a lot of people. The only person he loved was Eli and the only other person he ever made up to was Cole. Not even Ethan tried to pet him.

Ethan had insisted on Claire going to the bank to withdraw some cash for paying his men after the roundup. It was a tradition he had established from the beginning of their ranch. That was always followed with a few days off for the tired crew. Kathleen and Maggie had gone with her. They planned on joining their men in the store to look at housewares and bolts of cloth. Ethan had reminded her that they needed to get their supplies to the roundup camp as soon as possible. Claire had just smiled. Not even Ethan dared to tell her what to do.

Rolling his shoulders to relieve the tension, Cole turned toward the rope barrel so his movement wouldn't be noticed by the outlaws. He quickly laid down the handful of black Spanish cigars he was getting for his friend, Miguel del Rios, a small rancher who was helping with the roundup. Next, he drew his gun and shoved it into his right-hand coat pocket.

"Stay here, Ethan." His light-blue eyes studied his brother and, just for an instant, once more wished Ethan could see.

"Alright. Be careful. When this is over, maybe we should get some more of those 'good 'noughs.'"

"Yeah."

Cole walked away, shaking his head and tugging on the wide brim of his dust-laden black hat. Only his brother would mention ready-made horseshoes at a time like this. Strolling toward the front of the store with his hands in his coat pockets, the young rancher tried to act as if nothing was going on. The music of his spurs accompanied his stroll.

He stopped at a filled cracker barrel with a scrawled sign that read "For customers only." Taking a cracker with his left hand, he nodded at the three men sitting in chairs around a coughing potbelly stove, the customary meeting place for some men waiting on their wives. Their collective gaze was a mixture of surprise, fear and annoyance.

He walked on, munching on the cracker, and passed startled customers who whispered for him to stop. He eased along displays of tools, hats, boots, spurs and gloves. Pausing again, he stood beside a table laden with flat irons, stoneware water jugs, coffee grinders, copper boilers and clocks. One clock was carved with intricate designs and he wondered if Kathleen would like it. He ambled on, keeping an eye on the three outlaws without appearing to do so. As he past a long shelf of canning jars and supplies, he cocked the Colt inside his pocket. The noise was muffled but it still sounded loud to him.

"Hey *der*, cowman! Vhere *dost* ya be going?" The German outlaw swung his gun toward Cole.

The young rancher walked on, running the fingers of his left hand along the shelf. Ignoring the command, he studied an adjoining shelf of canned goods as if trying to make a decision about what to select.

"Cowman, I said stop. *Jetzt*. Ah, now."

Stopping, Cole looked up at the outlaw. His voice matched the feigned surprise in his chiseled face as he pointed to himself. "Are you talking to me?" He turned toward the German, now only a dozen feet away.

"*Ja*. Ya be to stand *der*—vhile ve to take care of our needs. Maybe ve let you live. Maybe ve give ya one of *der fräuleins*." He chuckled at his joke.

"Sure."

Orange flames snarled from Cole's coat pocket and the German outlaw was slammed backwards against a display table. Boxes of cigars, tobacco plugs and sacks of shredded Durham tobacco flew in all directions. His pistol stayed behind with them for a breath, then thudded to the floor. The jar of the gun sent a bullet slamming into the east wall. The outlaw's out-of-control body bounced off the table, landed awkwardly on the floor, gurgled once and moved no more.

From the back of the room, Ethan's voice was a command that took over the room, belying his blindness. "If you move, you're dead."

Cole wondered how his brother knew Cole had succeeded, then decided it was simply the warrior in Ethan. If Cole was dead, Ethan was going down, too.

Cans crashing to the floor preceeded the jerky response of the outlaw in the cavalry jacket as he dropped his sack and straightened. Cole wanted to pull the gun from his pocket but was concerned it might not come out smoothly, so he left the weapon where it was. The recocking was muffled.

Cole pointed with his left hand at the mule-faced outlaw trying to decide whether to challenge him. "Drop the gun. Now. Or join your friend."

The outlaw stared at the gun in Cole's hand.

"I take that as a no." Cole fired and the hole in his coat pocket was a bigger one, smoking at the edges.

Grabbing for his wounded arm, the outlaw cursed

through clenched teeth. His revolver remained in his hand. He gasped in agony, realized he still held the weapon and threw it as if it were poison.

Taking advantage of Cole's focus on the other outlaw, the Kiowa-Mexican outlaw stepped to his right, behind an older woman with a green parasol. Without hesitation, she jammed it backwards into his stomach. He doubled over to hold back the pain and the pistol in his fist discharged into a shelf. A hole appeared in a can of peaches, quickly followed by a long string of peach syrup.

Cole chuckled and said, "You quit moving, too, or I'll let that nice lady hit you again."

She smiled at him but the corners of her mouth trembled, giving away her nervousness.

Snarling, the halfbreed raised his hands.

"Take that other pistol—and that knife—and drop 'em on the floor. Pull them out real careful-like," Cole demanded. "I'm a real nervous person. Might think you were trying something if you don't do it right."

His eyes never leaving Cole's face, the halfbreed lowered his right hand and slowly withdrew the weapons one at a time, and dropped them at his feet. The woman cocked her parasol to strike again, if needed; the halfbreed glared at her but she seemed oblivious to his posturing. Cole thought she badly wanted to hit the outlaw again and withheld a grin.

Satisfied with the situation in the store, Cole turned toward McKeon watching from the cash register. "Jeremy, do you still have that long-nosed revolver under there?"

McKeon nodded eagerly and reached under the counter, reappearing with a long-barreled, double-action Smith & Wesson revolver in his hand.

"Watch these two for me. Can I borrow one of your Winchesters?" Cole was already headed toward a rack of rifles against the east wall, five feet from the German outlaw's bullet hole. He left his pistol in his smoking, black-holed coat pocket.

"Of course, Mr. Kerry."

The farmer, whose wife attracted the halfbreed's attention, blurted, "Give me that gun, I'll take care of these bastards."

His wife chided him for swearing.

At the rifle display, Cole quickly pulled one from its setting, worked the lever and eased the trigger back in place with his thumb. Several saddles and bridles lay across empty barrels with an opened box of "good 'noughs" horseshoes next to them. He glanced down at the box and decided Ethan was right about needing more.

"Where are your cartridges?"

"To your left. On top of that display case." McKeon sounded like a clerk advising someone where to find sugar or flour.

"Thanks."

Crash!

Ethan had overplayed his ability and walked into a stack of umbrellas, knocking them across the room. His revolver skidded along with them. Cole's attention went involuntarily toward his brother's clumsy sprawl. So did McKeon's.

"Ethan? Are you alright?"

Ethan's response was laced with embarrassment. "Oh, yeah. Just wasn't paying attention." He didn't want to tell his brother that he didn't know where his revolver was.

Out of the corner of his eye, Cole caught the movement. He swung toward the halfbreed's fierce lunge at him. Stepping to the side, Cole clubbed the outlaw with the barrel of his Winchester. A soft groan followed. Then the young rancher instinctively sought the third outlaw, who, gripping his wounded arm tightly, mouthed, "I ain't doin' nothin'."

"Got 'em, Jeremy?"

"Yes sir, Mr. Kerry."

"Good."

Cole Kerry stepped toward the doorway, shoving bullets into the rifle.

"Everybody stay inside. They're trying to rob the bank." He spoke quietly over his shoulder as he headed out. It sounded like he was advising customers about the weather.

Chapter 2

Across the street, outside the Bank of Uvalde, an armed man was handing two large sacks to another outlaw on horseback.

"I'll stay here." Ethan Kerry's response from beside the overturned umbrella stand was that of a strong man resigned to the reality he would only get in his younger brother's way.

The three words summed up a long journey from the uncontrollable anger that sprang from the day he was blinded by a wild horse's kick. But he couldn't resist adding, "Don't let those bastards take any of our money, Cole. Claire will fight them. You know she will."

Rushing outside, Cole glanced in the direction of Eli's dog, Blue, sleeping on the porch next to the door. The large brown-and-black animal raised its head in response to the movement; he had strayed from the wagon to a position closer to Eli.

"Stay, Blue. Stay," Cole said.

The ugly dog's ears perked up. He was definitely

Eli's pet. Not even Ethan or Luther dared to mess with him. Cole was a different story; the two had hit it off immediately. Obediently, Blue slumped back down.

Standing in the store doorway, Cole raised the Winchester and fired. The outlaw on horseback grabbing for the sack of bank money straightened and slid from his horse. The sack slammed into the hitching rack and splattered coins and certificates into the muddy street. Cole's mind raced inside the bank as if it could see through the walls. *Where were Kathleen . . . Claire . . . Maggie? Were they all right?*

The only way to make them safe was to eliminate Gee's men. Cole hoped the three Kerry womenfolk were standing aside and not trying to stop the outlaws. *Claire, this isn't the time to argue,* his mind shouted. Taking another step forward, Cole fired again at the outlaw handing off the bank's money. And missed.

His bullet thudded into the adobe wall of the bank building. The outlaw had been watching the money spray along the street, paying little attention to his fallen comrade. Cole's shot made him realize what had happened.

The outlaw's eyes were hot and red. A downward curve to the right side of his mouth had been made years before with a knife. He spun his own pistol toward Cole and fired twice wildly. Bullets chipped pieces from the beam supporting the store's overhang, a foot from the moving Kerry.

Another outlaw emerged from the bank, wearing a sombrero and firing rapidly with a revolver in each hand. From down the street came a dozen Kill Creek riders shooting and leading saddled horses for their companions.

Selecting his targets, Cole felt the presence of his older brother behind him. "Ethan, stay down."

"Here, thought you could use this." Ethan held out a box of cartridges in Cole's direction.

"Where's Eli?"

"Told him to stay back at the barrel, like you said."

Bullets ripped along the planked sidewalk, creating a line of destruction in the wood. Cole took the box, shoved it into his left-side coat pocket, beside his pistol, and urged his older brother again to kneel behind a barrel. There was no use asking him to crawl back inside. Ethan might be blind but he wasn't going to crawl for anyone.

"Do you see Claire an' Maggie . . . an' your lady?"

Cole never said anything about it, but his brother seemed to have a problem accepting the fact he was married. Or maybe he just didn't like Kathleen. The ranch house was big enough that they certainly didn't bump into each other too much. Maybe it was just Ethan trying to protect his little brother.

"Not yet. I hope they're inside. Being quiet."

Ethan wiped his mouth. "That won't be Claire's way, Cole."

"I know."

Townsmen were beginning to return gunfire as the rest of the gang tried to mount fearful horses. In the doorway of the store, the farmer was shooting with the halfbreed's pistol.

"Get down!" Cole shouted without looking.

"I'm gonna—" The farmer stiffened as striking bullets lifted and shoved him back into the store.

Cole fired and one of the outlaws crumpled as he tried to pick up one of the bank sacks. He felt something nudge his hip. Blue had inched over to be close to him. Cole stroked the dog's head, worried that a stray bullet might hit him.

"Go find Eli inside. Blue, go inside." Cole turned back and fired without aiming.

From the store, he heard Eli yell, "Come here, Blue."

"That's the way, get inside," Cole encouraged and fired again. "Ethan, tell Eli to keep Blue in there. Until this is over."

Blue disappeared into the store with his long tail wagging.

Through the opened bank doorway came the gang's leader, the infamous Victorio Gee.

Cole grunted. He would have known the fierce prairie pirate anywhere. Like some buccaneer, the right-side brim of Gee's black hat was turned up and pinned with a gold brooch to the crown. Dancing on his chest was a necklace of wolf fangs mixed with human teeth, supposedly taken from his victims. Long, stringy brown hair flopped across the shoulders of his black frock coat. Gee looked every inch the mad leader he was proclaimed to be.

On his left sleeve were double black armbands, one above the other. Knee-length black boots were edged at the top with beadwork. Silver Mexican spurs flashed in the autumn day's sun. A sheathed machete hung across his back on a beaded sling. Although tales persisted of his being the son of a Mexican whore and an Apache warrior, he was actually of Italian descent, born in New York City as Victor G'Abrisso.

From the bank's darkness Gee yanked a sobbing woman in front of him, controlling her with his left hand by grasping a fistful of her dark crimson hair. He fired a double-action Smith & Wesson revolver in his right fist. In the red sash around his waist were three more handguns.

"Oh, my God! Kathleen!"

The words snapped from Cole's mouth as he realized Gee was holding his young wife.

"Cole, be smart. You ain't gonna do her no good gettin' yourself killed," Ethan's voice was low, almost gentle. "Cole, you listen to me. Think, boy."

The young rancher aimed at Gee but the renegade leader was wisely keeping himself behind the terrified Kathleen. His face hissed contempt as he emptied one revolver, shoved it into his sash and drew another. His chin was long and pointed, matching an elongated nose that looked like a pink butter knife. Intense dark eyes studied the street, locked onto Cole's face for an instant, laughed and fired at him.

Does Gee know she's my wife?

"Cole! Cole!" Kathleen blurted his name. Her plain freckled face was white with fear; her large brown eyes searched for her beloved husband.

Gee laughed at her pleas, dropped his hand to her right breast and held her in place next to him.

Cole fired, carefully aiming a foot above Gee. It had little effect but the young rancher felt he had to do something. Levering a new round into his Winchester, he tried to concentrate on what he should do.

Staring directly at Cole, the outlaw leader bit Kathleen's ear, bringing blood and a scream. She struggled to free herself and he cuffed her head with his pistol. He laughed and fired at Cole. *Victorio Gee knew. He had to know*, Cole told himself. *But how? Had Claire said something? Had Kathleen?* It didn't matter. What mattered was getting Kathleen free of this devil.

Gee's men pulled up beside the bank with four unmounted horses. The effect was to keep Cole from seeing what was happening. He didn't remember deciding to charge at Gee, only that he was now in the middle of the street, running furiously toward the gathered outlaws. Kathleen glimpsed him through the swirling horses and yelled. Bullets spanked the dirt around him and nipped at his clothes. A shattering instant of light and sound within the fog of battle was all that registered in his mind. He didn't feel the bullets slicing along the sides of his stomach and across the calf of his leg. He levered and fired the Winchester as he closed in, dropping two outlaws before they could turn toward him.

Three riders spun away from the gathered band and rode directly at Cole, firing as they thundered toward him. He threw his empty rifle and yanked the half-loaded Colt from his coat pocket. Bullets tore at Cole's sleeve and the gray air around him, but his own found the closest rider. The one-eyed outlaw jerked and slumped in his saddle.

Unaware of anything except getting to Kathleen, Cole ran directly at the second rider's horse. It reared in fright, pushing the rider's aim beyond Cole's head. Cole hammered the remaining three shots into him and he slid off the back of the rearing horse. Wildly, Cole spun to avoid the riderless animal as the third horse's shoulder caught his left arm and he stutter-stepped sideways. The Colt in his hand freed itself. He felt the thud of a glancing blow against his head. A bright light. His fierceness vanished as fast as a fist becomes a hand. He went down and didn't see the third outlaw spill from his saddle as bullets from hidden townsmen found their mark.

At the front of the bank, the other outlaws fired in all directions while three jumped down. Several held large sacks of garnered treasure; one carried a large ham. Another tall outlaw had stuffed his own saddlebags with bottles of whiskey and cradled four more in his right arm.

Two grabbed Kathleen from Gee, shoved her onto one of the open horses and remounted themselves. The third grabbed one of the money sacks and returned to his horse. Gee swung onto a magnificent pinto horse held for him. The remaining outlaw outside the bank made a foolish attempt to retake the remaining sack and bullets found him from several locations.

Cole staggered to his feet. Blood slid down the side of his head and stung his eye. *Where was Kathleen? Where was Kathleen?* Cole spun toward the sounds of the fleeing Victorio Gee and his remaining men. Other bullets from town followed them but the firing was sporadic out of fear of hitting the captured woman. Kathleen's screams reached Cole's ears as he sought a shot at Gee.

Gee slid to the far side of his running horse as smoothly as a Comanche warrior in battle. Cole picked up his Colt and aimed at Kathleen's horse. She was barely in sight. It was the only way to save her. Pointing at the back of her horse's head, he squeezed the trigger slowly. He squinted to keep the blurriness from returning.

Click. Click.

His gun was empty. He had no bullets for it, only for the Winchester. *Where was the rifle?*

He turned back and the movement made him kneel. He saw the gun and forced himself to run for it. Grabbing the Winchester, he stood. Too quickly. He was on his knees before he realized what had happened. He pointed the gun in the direction of the fleeing outlaws, only vaguely remembering it, too, was empty.

Gee's sick laugh stayed behind as the outlaw returned to the top of the saddle and his thinned army disappeared into the horizon. Kathleen wasn't in sight. Her screams were only an eerie memory ringing in Cole's ears.

"Did you get Gee? Is Kathleen all right?" Ethan's voice boomed from behind a post. Cole knew his brother already realized the answers to both questions.

"No. They've got her."

"Should'a shot his horse."

Cole started to explain he was going to shoot Kathleen's horse but his gun was empty. He knew it would only draw the observation that Ethan had brought him a box of bullets. He dropped the empty Winchester.

Wobbly, Cole ran for the hitching rack where his red sorrel waited. He tried to shove the empty revolver back into his coat pocket. The gun slid away and fell to the ground. It was two steps before he realized what had happened. He stopped, retreated and picked up the gun, reminding himself it was empty.

"Did they get our money?" Ethan yelled.

"I'm going after them. They've got Kathleen."

"What about us?" Ethan yelled. "Where's Claire an' Maggie?"

"In the bank, I guess." Cole sprung into the saddle. "Get a posse coming behind me."

"Load your rifle, Cole."

"I'm taking mine." Through his mental haze, Cole realized it would be like his brother to know the gun wasn't loaded.

"Don't forget the money, Cole." Ethan's defiant response as Cole spurred the sorrel into a run.

Patting his saddle-seated Winchester, Cole knew his brother was right about reloading, though. He must force himself to take the time to ready his Colt. A fire fight with Gee's men could happen fast. Opening the saddlebag, he removed his gunbelt with its two holsters. The right-side holster carried the matching revolver to the empty one in his bullet-ravaged pocket. The empty gun was usually held in a sidewinder holster, on his left side and tilted sideways so the butt almost touched his belt buckle. He eased the gunbelt around his waist and buckled it in place.

Fighting off dizziness, he reined in the sorrel he had grown to love. The shiny barrel of his Colt had slipped through the burned hole in his coat pocket. He withdrew the weapon, rejected the shells and replaced them with fresh cartridges. His head was clouded with the aftermath of the blow and the swelling anxiousness to return Kathleen to the safety of his arms. But Ethan was right; racing after her with empty guns was tantamount to riding to his death, and hers. He returned the loaded pistol to its sidewinder hoslter, slipped the tie-down over the hammer and stepped into the saddle.

Halfway down the street, he was aware of a man riding from an alley and coming alongside him.

"You riding after them?" A tall, lanky man on a dark bay yelled. Pinned to the collar of his long coat was a Texas Ranger badge. Sunlight touched it timidly and darted away.

His opened coat didn't quite hide a gunbelt with a second pistol shoved into his waistband. He held a smoking rifle with his right hand, casually pointed at Cole's midsection. A faint smile settled in the corner of his chapped mouth for a moment and vanished. His left eye twitched twice. Cole assumed it was from the tension of the battle.

"Yeah." Cole glanced at the ranger's pointed gun. "You intending to do something with that?"

Looking down at his rifle, the ranger grinned through clenched teeth. "Sorry. Didn't realize it was aimed at you." He lowered the gun and held it at his side with his right hand, brushing his horse's flank with the barrel. His face turned slightly to the left. As if speaking to someone else, he said casually, "He's a little jumpy. Been lots to be jumpy about."

"'Jumpy's' one word for it." Cole glanced toward

the empty horizon and slapped his reins against his sorrel's well-muscled shoulders.

The ranger spurred his own horse and the two men raced down the street and beyond the town's last structures.

Leaning forward in the saddle, the ranger yelled, "I'm Ranger James Bartlyn. I'll ride with you." It wasn't a question. "Be a little while before a posse gets going."

"Yeah. Figured they might see somebody trailing 'em . . ."

"An' let the woman go." Bartlyn interrupted. He turned his head again to the empty space on his left. "Do you know her?"

"That's my wife." Cole spurred his horse as a punctuation mark.

Bartlyn jerked his head away and said to no one, "What did I tell you?" Turning his attention back to Cole, Bartlyn swung alongside him as the wind continued to cut into his words. "Just happened to be in town. On my way to San Angelo. Got a war brewing down there."

"Got one here, it looks like." Cole was trying to keep his mind away from recollections of what he had heard Gee did to kidnapped women.

"Deputy Logan's bringin' a posse. Shouldn't be too far behind us."

"Good. If we keep after 'em, they won't have time . . ." Cole didn't finish the statement as he glanced in Bartlyn's direction. The ranger was looking to his left as their horses bolted into the prairie. In the distance, a cloud of dust signaled the direction of Gee's escape.

"I'd just as soon not catch up with 'em before we get some help," Bartlyn said, whipping his horse with his reins to keep within two strides of Cole's sorrel. "That was Victorio Gee himself, ya know."

"Yeah." Cole had already made up his mind to catch up and make Gee pay. Hard. Real hard.

Chapter 3

In minutes, the horizon took the two riders while the town was torn between caring for the wounded and trying to assemble a posse to join the chase. All along the main street, townsmen and cowboys erupted from hidden places to assess damage to property and lives, determine the breathing status of downed outlaws and seek their horses.

Through the gathering crowd of concerned citizens came a terrified man in a new suit. From the dirt on his knees, he had evidently been hiding somewhere across the street. His voice was shrill and he coughed to rid his voice of the lingering fear.

"My word, what a terrible ordeal! My God, where is the law around here?" He pushed through the crowd, looking for the town marshal or anyone with a badge.

"They shot him, Goddard. He's dead." A shopkeeper glanced down at Goddard's knees, then back to his face.

"They got our money, Joe. We've got to go after 'em."

"Cole Kerry an' that ranger are already ridin' after the bastards. That's Kerry's wife they took."

"Where's the rest of the rangers? That's two against an army. Come on."

Another store clerk with a bloody arm shouted, waving a pistol in the air. "Those bastards killed my brother at Kill Creek. Somebody give me a horse!"

"They dun wiped out my cousin's whole family in Needles. I'll ride."

"The marshal was a friend of mine. Who's got a gun I can borrow?"

A wave of appreciation—combined with sad recitation of known victims—slid along the group as Ethan yelled for Eli to come and help him. He knew his brother had gone after Gee and, now, that Ranger James Bartlyn had joined him. What he didn't know was where his wife and daughter were—or how they were.

Through Ethan swelled a ball of anger and frustration. He was useless. As useless as a child. Useless. During the war, he had fearlessly led men into battle and after it had lived by his ability with a gun. He had built a great ranch from Texas wilderness and had killed a Comanche war party by himself when they attacked the ranch in the early days. Now he stood, unseeing and waiting for his young son to escort him to a store, while his youngest brother chased hell's heathens. His lips trembled and he fought for control of his mind.

"Where the hell's Deputy Logan? Where's that posse?" Ethan shouted. With his feet spread apart, he blocked the planked sidewalk in front of the store.

To his right, he heard a man telling others what he knew about Victorio Gee's band of former war guerillas. A savage bunch, like a pack of wild dogs, they had raided, raped and killed throughout the southwestern rim of Texas. They had also kidnapped numerous women and taken them to Mexico, where they were sold into prostitution. Or traded them to Comancheros. Occasionally, they also took children; no one knew what had happened to them. So far, the Texas Rangers hadn't been able to catch them.

The conversation infuriated Ethan. Why wasn't a posse being formed? He yelled again, swinging his arms for emphasis, "Come on! Get movin', men! Dammit, my brother's expectin' help. That's his wife they took."

"Hold your horses, Kerry. We're getting ready. Not everybody had a saddled horse waiting, ya know." The response was from a bespectacled man in an ill-fitting suitcoat and an oddly shaped derby. He was astride a paint horse with a Henry repeating rifle cradled in his arms.

Ethan took a deep breath. "I know. I know. It's just . . ." He turned around. "Where are you, Eli?"

"I'm right here, Dad." Eli ran through the doorway with Blue at his side and took his father's arm.

"Come on, son, we've got to find your mother—an' Maggie. They're inside the bank. Come on."

Back on the street a stout businessman sought answers to the town's attack. "How much damage did they do?" It was clear he had no intention of joining any posse. "I was upstairs in my office when I heard the shooting. My Lord, couldn't anyone stop them? I heard they robbed the bank."

"They did. Not all our money, though. Got some food, too. Whiskey. More guns, I think, from Layman's up the street. Marshal Jacobs is dead." A tall businessman fiddling with his silver chain fob recited. "They rushed his office first thing, I heard. Got one of his deputies, too. Lennie Bensted." He paused, inhaled his cigar and took it from his mouth. "Heard there's a clerk down. Maybe even one of the town council. Justin Heustan. I haven't seen him today, have you?" He returned the cigar to his wet lips and puffed again. "We've got to get the rest of that money back. The whole town's depending on it, Henry."

"Yeah, a real shame. Where are the rangers when you really need them?"

"Good question. Heard one was in town."

"What good is one?"

"He rode out with Cole Kerry."

"I expected more from Jacobs, for that matter. This is terrible."

"Heard they stole loan papers too. What do they want with those?"

Questions were followed by a green-faced banker in a vest and sweated-through white shirt, but no coat, emerging from the doorway. Beads of sweat populating his face, he glanced around, saw the remaining money sack and immediately picked it up, along with three stray gold coins and scattered certificates. Without a word, he vanished again inside the bank.

The stout businessman grinned. "Well, some of the money's safe. That'll be Picklewhite. I think he counts it every hour."

A short man ran past them, barely pausing enough to report the news. "They've got one of them bastards on his feet. He wasn't dead, just wounded. Right over there."

The exclamation stopped the gathering of men with weapons and horses. Two men left to get a closer look at the outlaw.

"You gonna stick around for the hanging?" the stout businessman asked, more interested in watching four men half drag a wounded outlaw than the answer.

The second businessman exhaled a thick cloud of cigar smoke, ignoring the few other men still standing near him. "Wonder who they'll pick for the new marshal."

"Don't know. Plenty of good men around."

"How about that Cole Kerry fella?"

As Eli led his father across the street to the bank, the boy's eyes were wide with appreciation at his uncle's daring. "Uncle Cole went after them, Dad. A ranger went with him."

"I know. Let's find your maw."

"Dad, th-they came at Uncle Cole. A-a bunch of them. They hit him on the head. I-I thought . . ." Eli's expression changed from wonder to worry. "Dad . . . I wish you were with him. You were good with a gun. Uncle Cole told me so."

Ethan couldn't hide the smile for an instant. "No, your uncle's joshing you. I'm just a blind ol' fool."

Two men hurried past and Ethan jumped back from the sound.

"Uncle Cole told me about the time you, Uncle Luther and him were part of General John Bell Hood's Texas Brigade." Eli looked over at his father, unseeing but drawn to the past. "He said you were the toughest man he ever knew. He said you still were."

"After we get your maw an' little sis, we can ride to camp an' send some men after Cole. We sure don't want a bunch of riders standin' around because we didn't bring enough rope," Ethan interrupted, abruptly returning from a daydream and hoping Cole hadn't mentioned his brothers following him as guerilla fighters, briefly carrying on their own private war, or as outlaws for a spell.

His wife, Claire, kept a folded wanted poster as a remembrance of how she met Ethan. It was while the gang was robbing a small border town bank. She was there with her father, transacting business. Ethan quietly asked her name and said he would return to see her. He did, and one month later they were married—after he promised to settle down. Cole Kerry, six years younger than Ethan, was so angry about his big brother's decision that he left and didn't return until after Ethan had been blinded.

Three men ran right in front of them, on their way to see what was happening with the captured outlaws. Blue growled and Eli held out his hand to keep his father from colliding with the excited men. Ethan ignored Eli's touch on his chest or didn't understand it and banged into the closest man.

Jarred by the collison, the townsman stumbled and fell. Ethan stutter-stepped to the right. Jumping to his feet, amid chuckles from his continuing companions, the man turned angrily toward Ethan. "Why the hell don't you watch . . ." He stopped as soon as his mind registered on what his gaze told him about Ethan.

"Don't let my being blind stop you, partner," Ethan growled. "Go ahead and take a swing. You weren't tough enough to fight them Kill Creek boys so I reckon you won't cause me much trouble."

Ethan's remark surprised and embarrassed the man. He mumbled something about "next time," and hurried to catch up with his friends.

"How'd you know he didn't fight, Dad?"

"Just a guess. I can see more than you think, little man," Ethan said. "Do you see your maw?"

"Y-yes, she's in the doorway. There's Maggie, too."

"Good. Good. Are they all right?"

"I think so." Eli bit his lower lip. "I'm worried about Uncle Cole—an' Aunt Kathleen. What will they do to her?"

"Don't worry about your uncle Cole. He knows how to handle himself." Ethan's face was a contradiction to his words. "An' he isn't going to attack them. Just keep close so they decide to drop the money to stop anyone from followin' them. If not, he an' the ranger will keep 'em in sight for the posse."

"What about Aunt Kathleen?"

"Her, too."

Claire rushed from the bank doorway to Ethan and Eli. Crow's-feet danced around her widened eyes. She held him tightly and tried to hold back the tears that wanted to come. Ethan's hand sought hers and squeezed it. Immediately, he wanted to know what had happened.

Swinging her pigtails excitedly, Maggie explained that her mother had shouted at the outlaws and one of them had held a pistol at her head while Gee grabbed Kathleen and kept the gun there until they left. Maggie's voice choked back fear as she asked what would happen to their aunt Kathleen. Then she saw Blue beside Eli and frowned. Blue was not her favorite thing and the feeling was mutual, although the dog had never done anything to her. Except once. He growled when she approached with an old shirt for him to wear while she was playing pretend. That had ended any thought of his participation.

"Are you all right, Claire?" Ethan asked, holding her at arm's length.

"I'm fine. But Kathleen . . . where is she?"

It was Eli's turn to explain. He wanted to hug his mother but wasn't certain if he should. Claire took away the indecision by stepping over to him and giving him a long hug. Eli hid his face in her arms so no one would see his tears.

A long-haired man wearing a floppy-brimmed hat and sporting a deputy badge on his soiled suitcoat slid alongside them. He was nearly out of breath and his face was lit with excitement.

In a loud whisper intended to be heard, Ethan asked, "Who's this?"

"I'm Deputy Logan, Mr. Kerry." The deputy crossed his arms and tried to act nonchalant but his eyebrows kept jumping skyward, giving away his agitation. "Just came to tell you we'll get your sister-in-law back."

"Where's your posse, Deputy?"

"I'm gathering men now, sir. I deputized Jimmy Maynard. He's going to stay in town an' help with things."

Cocking his head to the side, Ethan growled, "You got two men chasin' an army. How long before you get at it?"

Annoyed by the remark from a blind man, Deputy Logan sputtered, "Well, ah, I'm tryin' to get organized. Ah, there's a lot goin' on, ya know."

"What'd the ranger say before he left with my brother?"

"Ah, told me to get a posse together an' follow him." Deputy Logan looked at the assembled horsemen on the street.

"Victorio Gee's got some of our money, too. You get it back."

"Right. I . . . we will, sir." Deputy Logan said, almost apologetically. He wasn't certain why he was intimidated by this blind man but he was.

Ethan cocked his head to the side. "There's nothing we can do now but wait for Cole an' Kathleen to get back. In the meanwhile, let's get our supplies. We kinda got interrupted."

Claire grabbed his arm but said nothing, then shook her head.

"Come on, then. Claire, everything's gonna be fine."

Chapter 4

Cole Kerry and Ranger Bartlyn pushed through the hole between the hills and could see the dust of Gee's bandit army ahead of them. Above, the sky was losing its battle with a string of dark clouds. Rain was definitely coming sometime today. A good autumn rain. Cole's wounds were slight and he ignored them. His head pounded from the blow as he tried to concentrate on Gee's gang ahead of them somewhere. Bartlyn's continuous talking to himself was a distraction. So were the images of Kathleen smiling at him.

Just this morning, before dawn had yet decided to assert itself, they had made love. When he was with her, everything was good. All his loneliness was gone. Even when she was in a different room than he, that empty ache crept into the shadows of his mind. She wasn't beautiful by most men's standards, but he had never seen anything so wonderful as Kathleen smiling at him. He thought he had lost her back in Dodge when her weak father was coerced by a town merchant into making her marry the rich man's son. But she had rejected the idea, and her father's demand, and followed Cole to Texas—and his life was all new again.

And now she was in the hands of a madman. He squeezed shut his eyes for an instant to drive away that thought. To help give him something else to think about, he pulled his Winchester free of its scabbard and laid it across his lap, holding it with his right hand.

Stretched out along the curving trail, Cole's sorrel led the way and was suddenly alert, ears cocked, straining to determine the extent of something only he sensed. Bartlyn was three lengths behind and jabbering.

Cole's voice calmed the big horse. He rolled his neck to relieve the tension. He was happy to see he was gaining on the outlaws; Kiowa's blistering pace was producing results. If Cole could see their dust; they could see his and the ranger's. That's what he wanted. Of course, if they guessed it was only two men in pursuit and turned to fight, the duo would quickly be in danger.

Hopefully, the bandits wouldn't guess their numbers and think it was a much larger posse in pursuit. He didn't know this ranger but he had certainly responded to the need to keep after Victorio Gee. If he was like the other rangers he'd known, Ranger Bartlyn could fight with the best of them—and would, if it came to that. If they were really lucky, Gee would decide to leave Kathleen behind; she had served her purpose as a shield for their escape. He didn't care what they did with the money. He would gladly accept that trade. So far there was no sign of a posse trailing them but he knew it was too soon to expect that. Anyway, the terrain made it difficult to look back and see very far. The wobbly land was taking them around tree-lined ridges, over hiccuped hills and along rock-lined ravines. Above them in the distance was the mysterious Ghost Mesa, where no one dared to go. Looming against the gray sky like a bad dream, *Anaabi Nanjsuwukaitu* was the Comanche name for the forbidden landmark. Hill of Spirits. Some men had started calling it just "Anaabi" but most referred to it as "Ghost Mesa." At first, he thought it was a surprising route for the outlaws but realized how difficult it would have been to track them on the hard, uneven ground if the posse was by itself and so slow to get started.

Behind him came a question he only partially heard, "Part of our job . . . why not now?" Followed by a chuckle. What was so funny? He turned toward the ranger. In a heartbeat, bullets erupted from Bartlyn's rifle. Cole's head jerked sideways, followed by a red line popping across his left temple. His hat flew away with the bullet. His turning had momentarily saved him from a bullet through the head.

As if yanked by strings, the impact spun him halfway around in the saddle. A bullet ripped across his upper right arm. He lost the reins, along with his balance and his Winchester, and flew flailing from the saddle. His sorrel reared in fearful surprise as a bullet grazed its flank. The great animal spun and galloped back toward the shooting Bartlyn, leaving Cole dazed and disoriented in a swale beside the rain-darkening trail.

He didn't hear Bartlyn yell to himself, "Kill the bastard!" Followed by his nervous assessment, "The damn horse is in the way!" All Cole heard was his brain screaming at the pain while demanding he escape.

Only the momentary disruption of the horse passing between him and his surprise attacker was keeping him from being a helpless target. Blood was in his eyes. His mouth. His hair. His right coat sleeve was a widening ball of crimson. Fighting off the shock of being hit, he pulled the Colt from his sidewinder holster and fired two random shots in Bartlyn's direction.

Wildly, he looked for somewhere to hide. Why had the ranger shot at him? Was it Bartlyn—or had Gee's men somehow slipped behind them? It didn't matter. Only escaping mattered.

A downed oak tree twenty yards away was the closest cover. He scrambled toward it, firing once more. Sickening thumps of bullets striking trees around him were matched by the sounds of lead ripping through the branches of a nearby stand of trees.

Another shot grazed the top of his right shoulder and bounced him off a tree. Blindly, he stumbled for cover in the uneven shadows, clutching his Colt in his fist. Too late to catch himself, he stepped into an unseen cleft in the ridge and fell helplessly toward the bottom of the slope. His arms and face were clawed by branches and rock edges as he plummeted down the fifteen-foot granite crack. A screaming hot pain shot to his temples as he slammed against the ground. Blood sprayed his face and arms as he bounced and rolled over on his stomach.

Intense pain cleared his head. Dazed, he studied the area for any kind of protective cover. He realized his pistol had been ripped from his hand during the fall. But a glance down at his feet gave him a false relief, for the weapon was lying inches from his right foot. He picked it up like he was in a slow-motion dream. Next to the cleft was a small cave, nestled underneath a rocky overhang. It would have to do. He dragged himself inside and lay down, gasping fiercely for air that would not come fast enough. His right arm would not respond, tangling at his side. He was badly hurt and knew it.

Now he was trapped. Trembling, he broke open the pistol to replace the emptied shells. He jerked a handful of new bullets from his coat pocket. Four. Only four. His gunbelt was with his horse. One cartridge fell from his shaking hand and pinged against the rock floor, echoing a tiny metallic song inside the narrow opening. He propped the seemingly heavy gun against a rock to keep it from falling to the cave floor, too. Nothing was in focus. The ground was moving. His head was roaring. He might pass out any minute now and they would come and kill him as he lay. Turning his head swiftly to look for more cover was a mistake. Sudden movement made him very dizzy. He vomited.

Five minutes passed before the ugly sensation stabilized in his head. But he had seen where he must go. The cave was deeper than he first thought. It was made so by an internal spring that had slowly eaten away at the hillside. Cole dragged himself back into the cave another twenty feet. A small pool of water was a welcomed sight. Face down, he drank; then struggled to pull his face from the water. It took all of his evaporating strength to lift himself. He could see no other exit than the way he came in, but he hadn't expected that luxury. Panic left him and recognition of the end took over. He would die soon.

"I love you, Kathleen," he whispered. His right shoulder spasmed and the fury of it jerked him down. Falling more than sitting, Cole positioned himself behind a row of pointed rocks and waited with his pistol in his left hand. Through his mind marched a fury of color and pain. Throbbing, unforgiving pain. His head was leaving the cave. Spinning. He must grab the rocks to keep from flying away. He was unconscious. The handgun rattled against the cave's floor as his hand followed his mind.

Above on the ridge, Bartlyn was confused. He couldn't figure out what had happened to his unsuspecting prey. He had gone from cocksureness to uneasiness. He dismounted and wrapped his reins around a struggling young tree.

It had seemed so easy.

Killing Cole Kerry had been a spur-of-the-moment decision by Bartlyn, Gee's advance man in town disguised as a Texas Ranger. A standard procedure with Gee, Bartlyn had come to town first to make certain it was ripe for attack. His secondary assignment was to lead any town posse into a prearranged ambush. But he knew Cole must be eliminated first. The young gunfighter was actually gaining on Gee and apparently had no intention of waiting for help.

Bartlyn's habit of talking to himself was agitated by his uneasiness. He told himself aloud that Cole was dead and lying somewhere nearby. His snarled response to himself was that he was alive and could be hiding anywhere. Cole's disappearance down the break in the ridge had been sudden, reinforced by the difficulty of seeing him in the wooded shadows. So far, Bartlyn wasn't aware of the existence of the cleft and wasn't eager to pursue too quickly, in spite of his own one-sided, continued assurance. Finally, he stood and walked with confident quick strides toward the area where he last saw Cole.

"Hell, I nailed him in the head. That boy's lights is out." He jerked his head to the side, then wiped his forehead with his sleeve to remove a layer of sticking sweat.

"Not so," Bartlyn responded to himself, warily deciding to track after Cole. His eyes sought every downed pine tree and rock as he eased along the lumpy ridge. "Hell, you probably only nicked him. Anyway, Victorio will want his body. Better if he's still alive. He'll like skinning him—alive. Eating his eyes. Pulling out his teeth."

He jerked his head again to the left. "Cut that out, you're making me sick. You're wrong. I got 'im. I'm sure of it. I saw 'im fall. Right in the head."

With a face juggling disgust and fear, Bartlyn pushed through the underbrush, looking for signs. He carried his rifle like it was getting heavy, moving it impatiently from one position to another.

"Have you found anything yet?" He blustered to himself. "Blood. There's blood here."

His head turned again to the side. "Keep looking. Victorio will want his body. Nobody kills his men an' gets away with it." Bartlyn waved his gun more enthusiastically than he felt.

He didn't like this. Shooting Cole Kerry in the back was one thing; tracking after him in this woods was another. He found the cleft in the ridge, catching himself just before duplicating Cole's fall.

"Here! He went down here. See? He's down there. Somewhere. Dead as can be." He pushed his hat forward on his head to punctuate the statement, glancing over at an imaginary companion.

Bartlyn swallowed and edged even closer to the open ledge. "He mighta found some cover down there. Mighty long way down, though." He swallowed again. "You go that way. I'll go along the ridge. Be careful."

"Don't worry. He's dead. Shot in the haid." Bartlyn assured himself with his head tilted toward a silent tree. "You wait an' see."

He straightened his back like a rooster about to crow. "Well, you can be havin' him for yourself," Bartlyn muttered. "I saw the fire of hell in his eyes. Damn. So did Victorio."

Below the ridge, an aging panther meandered back to his home, the cave where Cole lay. The catamount had spent the day hunting. Field mice were his only find; awareness of a coming rain had pushed his potential meals into places of hidden warmth. He paused at the cave's entrance. The smell of blood was in his home. And the smell of man! These unexpected signs disturbed him. He had grown old by staying away from man.

From above, the big cat heard a man approaching. The man moved slowly, pausing to check out possible hiding places, and was still talking. He was coming down a slanted rock shale trail. Both panther and Bartlyn saw each other at about the same time. Snarling, the big cat sprang directly up the crease where Cole had fallen. A quick shot followed the muscled blur. The bullet splattered against the rocks as the cat climbed out of sight.

"Damn! That's all we need—a catamount," the nervous Bartlyn said, and shook off the shiver that tracked along his spine. He glanced to the left. "Damn cat must've been in that cave yonder. Glad I didn't go in there a' lookin'." He shook his head for emphasis.

Bartlyn studied the enclosure and pronounced, "No way he's hiding in there anyway. Would've heard him an' the cat fighting." He paused and spoke to the empty air. "Wouldn't that have been something?" He stared up at the darkening sky. Rain splattered lightly on his face as he tried to recall any such sounds of a struggle.

"I bet he's hunkered in that buffalo grass. Probably crawled over there an' died." He pointed. Looking to the side, Bartlyn snapped, "I don't see any blood." He folded his arms around the rifle and stood. "Well, I'll bet he's there." He looked down at the ground, then back to the invisible associate who was always with him. "This is silly. We're just gonna get soaked out here. The man's crawled somewhere an' died, I tell ya."

Bartlyn walked wide of the cave and stared down the rock-structured incline, "We've got to find him. Victorio won't let it be."

After a few minutes of searching, Bartlyn tired of the effort and decided that he should take care of his first priority, the posse. Cole Kerry wasn't going to be a problem now, dead or wounded. Besides, his mind had shifted to receiving his share of the bank's money—and taking a turn with Cole Kerry's young wife—after the posse was dealt with.

"Hey, that gal looked real ripe, didn't she. Maybe I can have a turn, huh?" He grinned and took off his long coat, holding it in his right hand. "Victorio'll want to keep her for himself—an', later, for trading," Bartlyn said as he returned to his horse. "Maybe just a little bit, huh?" He climbed on the horse and rode away, slapping the animal on the flank with his rifle and telling himself that Victorio Gee would be pleased.

He rode to the highest point on the ridge, stopped and waved the coat over his head toward the valley below. He waited. A blur of white finally answered. Gee and his men were waiting as planned. Bartlyn smiled and turned to his left. "Just like we arranged. Victorio and me." He spurred the horse back toward town. Somewhere back there, a group of determined townsmen would be coming.

"I'll tell 'em the money and the woman are waiting. The gang left 'em and kept running. That'll make those town clowns relax an' ride right into it."

He turned toward the left. "Better say Cole Kerry is with them."

"Good idea."

Bartlyn's right cheek bobbed up and down. "You think Victorio's gonna wipe 'em out?"

"Of course. Nobody shoots up his men an' gets away with it." Another raindrop hit his hat brim. He remembered his coat resting in front of him on the saddle. After putting it back on, he straightened the badge pinned to the coat lapel.

"Victorio'll want to find Kerry afterwards—an' make sure he's dead."

"I know."

Chapter 5

The Kerrys watched quietly as the posse roared out of town, full of loud, vigorous declarations of what they would do to Victorio Gee and his outlaws. Their weapons were mostly breech-loading rifles with a few Winchesters, a Sharps buffalo gun and three muzzle-loaders mixed in.

As the last man rode past, Ethan turned to no one in particular and said, "Hope those fools don't shoot my brother." Then he laughed.

Standing next to him, Claire whispered, "Don't say things like that."

"Will they get Aunt Kathleen, Daddy?" Maggie looked up at her father's blank face.

"Sure they will, honey, if Uncle Cole doesn't already have her."

"Are you sure, Daddy?"

Claire patted Maggie on the back and looked around to locate Eli. The young boy saw the Winchester Cole had borrowed lying in the street. Pointing in the direction of the gun, he asked for permission to retrieve it.

"Yes, but come right back," Claire advised, trying to regain some sense of sanity within this mad happening. "Keep the gun pointed to the ground."

"It's probably empty. That's why Cole dropped it," Ethan advised as he crossed his arms. "He didn't use the bullets I gave him."

"I thought you taught him to handle every gun as if it's loaded." Claire watched her son race from the planked sidewalk to the rifle and pick it up. He held the gun, barrel slanting down, as if it were made of solid gold.

"Of course I did. Just telling you what's what. Details make the difference—in gunfights," Ethan sputtered, annoyed at her comment.

Smiling proudly, Eli returned with the gun.

"Give it to your father, Eli."

Eli held out the weapon to Ethan, who touched it with his fingers before taking it from him. He held the Winchester with both fists out in front of him. Around the corners of his tense mouth were the faintest of trembles. For the first time, Claire understood what was truly troubling her husband. The gunfight. He had been useless. A tall, proud warrior, who had led men into many battles and won, had not been able to help his young brother. Or keep outlaws from escaping with his brother's wife. The only way he could handle this mental pain was to act like the whole thing wasn't much at all, a minor distraction from more important things, like the roundup.

Claire touched his arm. "You didn't let Cole down. Or Kathleen."

Ethan's face hardened. He jerked his arm away, nearly hitting her with the barrel of the gun.

"Come on, Eli, let's get those ropes we need." He spun around and walked stiff-legged toward the store doorway.

Hurrying, Eli took his arm and redirected his steps, just before Ethan would have slammed his left shoulder into the door frame. Claire and Maggie followed. This time, Eli told Blue to wait outside and the big dog reluctantly refound its resting place in the back of the Kerry wagon.

Reentering McKeon's store, they saw several customers tending to the severely wounded farmer. With Claire's nudging, Eli went past them to the counter, leading his father by the hand. Ethan held the Winchester with his right hand, down by his side. Ethan asked his son if the dead outlaws remained in the store. Eli told him their bodies were gone.

Pausing beside the group, Claire realized the man wasn't going to last the day. Eli had shared with her what had happened inside the store earlier. She tried not to think how foolish the man had been but realized her own actions could be judged that way as well. The only thing that saved her from being shot was Victorio Gee himself. He didn't want the noise of a gunshot alerting the town at that particular moment. Later, he was preoccupied with Cole's counterattack from across the street.

A well-dressed customer with a freshly lit cigar stepped next to Claire and, in hushed, self-important tones, said someone had already gone for the doctor, adding, "Should'a gone for the preacher." His slightly amused eyes sought Claire's face for agreement. In his fist was a souvenir of the day, the removed black band from one of the dead outlaws.

The farmer's frightened wife glanced up and her gaze asked Claire to respond.

"He was a brave man. He helped save the town," Claire said and walked on.

Thumping against the counter, Ethan held out the gun and asked the polite storekeeper about the two dead outlaws.

"Jimmy Maynard, Mr. Barnes and Mr. Kelso were here a few minutes ago. Had shotguns. They took both of them. Gonna hang 'em, I reckon," McKeon responded nervously. "The other one . . . the one Cole shot . . . is dead." He rubbed his hands together. "I-I think Deputy Logan . . . ah, deputized Jimmy before he rode out with the posse." He rubbed his hands more vigorously. "I'm . . . real sorry about Cole's . . . wife. Real sorry."

"They'll get her back."

"Yes, I-I ho . . . think so. Would you tell Cole that I'd like him to keep that Winchester . . . as a thank-you."

"That's real nice o' you, McKeon. I'm sure Cole'll like that." Ethan's expression couldn't quite mask the envy that drove at the corner of his mouth. He returned the gun to his side and told Eli they should complete the selection of ropes.

Loading their wagon took a half hour. At first, Ethan insisted on carrying loads out himself; Claire quietly advised him to let Eli lead him so he wouldn't bump into something and look foolish. The latter advisement struck and the tall Kerry reluctantly did as he was told. It would have been faster to let Eli carry out the supplies himself, but Claire knew Ethan needed to feel in control. Claire and Maggie joined in with loads of their own; Maggie's consisted of one or two cans each trip. Claire felt it was important that she learn helping early.

Sensing rain wasn't far away, Ethan insisted on having the supplies covered with a tarp he kept in the wagonbed for that purpose. Eli didn't want to mess with the task because it took away Blue's resting place. Claire thought the dog would be just fine under the wagon and they would make room for him in the bed when they left. Blue wasn't eager to get down but obeyed his young master and took up residence beside the back left wheel.

Several hours passed.

Each hour was a day in Claire's mind with fear for Kathleen always near. Claire was a strong woman. She would have to be, to live with Ethan. Tough-minded and controlling, even in his blindness. In some ways, more so. Yet, she loved him more than the day she had met him—robbing a Union bank after the war. And she loved him from the moment she saw him. It had been mutual. Ethan had come over to her as the bank robbers left, asked her name and said he would return to see her. She wasn't surprised when he showed up at her parents' ranch two days later. She had barely slept during that time, wondering if he would come—and then worried that he would.

They were married a month later. But only after he promised to leave the outlaw trail. It was the first—and only—time she had met Cole Kerry, before he returned to Uvalde a little over two years ago. As fiery, or more so, as his older brother and six years younger, Cole had left as soon as Ethan told him the news of his marriage. He couldn't believe his brother would give up the cause. It didn't help that Ethan told him the cause was dead and they were just outlaws.

Luther came to live with Ethan and Claire after his family was destroyed by disease. A few years went by and Ethan decided his younger brother was dead. Claire believed Cole was alive but kept her thoughts to herself, until the day he rode back into their lives. In doing so, he saved the Bar K after Ethan was blinded.

Her recommendation to her husband convinced him that he should make Cole a partner.

She had watched Cole and Kathleen together and knew they were meant for each other. The young Irish woman had turned her back on her weak father and come to Texas to find Cole. Their wedding had been held at the ranch. It was a glorious, happy day with friends coming from everywhere to share in the joy.

And now this. It didn't seem real. What had started out as a joyful trip into town with their husbands had become a nightmare. She had tried not to worry after hearing of the attacks on other towns in the region but that was difficult to do. Images kept curling into the corners of her mind when she least expected.

A light rain slipped into the region, adding its own sense of dread to the waiting. Claire tried to take her mind off the awful situation by taking Maggie on a comprehensive tour of McKeon's store, pausing to examine and discuss everything from pots and pans to bolts of fabric to patent medicine bottles lining one shelf.

She didn't spend much time at the small jewelry case; it wasn't good for Maggie to get excited about such things. Claire's actual purchases were few: simple remedies of quinine, cod liver oil, epsom salts and castor oil, plus three pressed soaps. Her own instinct—as far as medical treatment was concerned—was to let nature take its course. She didn't believe many of the so-called "cures" were beneficial to anyone except the manufacturer. The new miracle drugs of opium and cocaine were things she distrusted the most. A friend of hers had become mad after taking a medicine containing cocaine for a year.

Maggie was caught up in the giddiness of so many items, so many aromas, so many things to touch and feel. Only once did she mention her Aunt Kathleen: When she was examining the pressed soaps and Maggie told her mother that Kathleen always smelled like flowers.

Claire's response had been a short gasp, then as controlled a statement as she could make about Kathleen being very clean, someone Maggie should look to for guidance. She had turned away so her young daughter wouldn't see her brush away a tear that wanted release.

Quickly bored by the wait, Eli had gone to play with his dog under the wagon. Claire had let him buy an apple for Blue. The ugly beast was more than a pet, however; he was a fine cattle dog and his negative disposition worked in his favor around the big animals.

From under the vehicle, Eli watched water beads create a curtain of rain around the wagon as he fed slices of the apple to Blue. Cuts from the apple were made with a pocketknife his uncle Cole had brought him from Dodge City. Staring at the knife made him want to cry. Blue seemed to understand and licked his face with a rough tongue.

Earlier, Ethan had retreated to one of the chairs around the stove at the back of the store. He sat silently, smoking a cigar. If he was worried, he didn't show it. The new Winchester for Cole lay on the floor at his feet. On the other side of the stove a farmer with long dark sideburns and a heavy overbite tried to engage him in conversation. Ethan's one-word answers kept it mostly a monologue as the farmer droned on about the Victorio Gee gang and what they had done to the town.

Hawking up phlegm as a prelude to a new subject, the farmer looked around for the spittoon. After leaving most of it in the brass container next to the stove, he asked Ethan what he thought would happen to "that thar lady they took wi' 'em," then proceeded to tell Ethan that he thought she wouldn't be seen again.

Ethan's face erupted into crimson as he jumped to his feet. "Find someplace else to jabber. Do it now."

Surprised, the farmer mumbled an apology and slipped away to the front of the store where his wife was shopping. She looked back at the still-standing Ethan as her husband recited what had happened.

"Excuse me, Mr. Kerry. Ah, this is Jimmy Maynard. Ah, I'm a deputy now. Too. Logan appointed me." The awkward voice was that of Jimmy Maynard. His young gaze was a mixture of excitement, fear and acne.

"I heard."

"I was wonderin' if'n ya thought I should be a'telegraphin' towns around 'bout Gee an' all." The deputy crossed his arms and tried to act nonchalant. His eyebrows kept jumping skyward, giving away his agitation.

From across the store, Claire had seen Ethan send the farmer away and now watched the exchange with the deputy. She couldn't hold her curiosity any longer and walked toward them.

Cocking his head to the side, Ethan growled, "If I were you, Deputy Maynard, I'd wait 'til the posse gets back. They'll be ridin' in soon, I reckon. Might have Gee in tow. An' there'd be no need for worryin' other folks."

Deputy Maynard looked like a great weight had been taken from his shoulders. "Thanks. Ah, that makes sense."

"Yeah, that posse may come rippin' back here any minute now—with that sonvabitch in tow." Ethan repeated the phrase, liking the sound of it.

Maynard hesitated, licked his chapped lips and said,

almost apologetically, "A couple of folks told me some of the shooting—at us—came from inside one of the buildings. What do you make of that?"

Ethan rubbed his chin. "Deputy, I would go back to them an' find out exactly what they saw—and where. In battle, some folks can imagine all sorts of things. If they're right, there're either traitors in town—or some of the gang got inside. May be hiding still. Better take a few men with you. Anybody left who can use a gun?"

"A few. I guess." After glancing at the advancing Claire and seeing Ethan didn't intend to add to his remark, Maynard touched the brim of his hat, muttered his thanks and hurried away.

"That's reassuring," Ethan snarled.

"What was that all about, Ethan?" Claire asked, her eyes bright with worry.

"Oh, nothin' really. That new kid deputy wanted my opinion on whether he should wire ahead to some of the towns around." Ethan shook his head to reinforce his statement.

"Did he think the posse would be coming back soon?"

"No. I told him it would—and he should wait until they did. Hell, it'll all be over soon. People just get too riled up over things."

"An' you don't? What if that was me with them—instead of Kathleen?" Claire's voice was heated.

"Oh, come on, Claire, don't talk like that." He started to sit back down but stopped halfway.

"Well, quit acting like it's nothing then." Claire's expression was stern, her eyebrows laid against her eyes. "My God, Ethan, they've got Kathleen. Th-they might kill her. Th-they might . . . take her."

"I was just sayin' what I thought would happen. Gee's just like any other outlaw. He's gonna run like hell. He isn't gonna want to be slowed down by no woman. He'll let her go . . ."

"What if he doesn't?"

Ethan shrugged his shoulders. "Claire, I'm not gonna argue with you 'bout this. I think it's gonna be fine. Cole an' that ranger were right after 'em—and the posse that rode outta here . . . was full o' good men. Men who carried their weight in the war."

From outside, shouts rattled through the store.

"Bet that's the posse comin' back right now," Ethan said. "Let's go see." He smiled as the word "see" slid from his mouth. "Well, you can."

Along with everyone else in the store, Ethan and Claire hurried to the windows and door. Ethan held on to her upper arm for direction. Maggie was more interested in a doll she had discovered and stayed in the corner where there was a small display of toys.

"Do you see her . . . Kathleen? Where's Cole?" Ethan asked, barely masking his anxiety this time, as they stood inside the doorway with another couple.

Claire didn't answer.

"Claire . . . what is it? Claire?"

The first words out of her mouth were cloaked in a gasp that made them difficult to understand. "Th-there's . . . only six. K-Kathleen . . . isn't with them. Neither is Cole."

"What?" Ethan squeezed her forearm.

"One of them is wounded. It's Mr. Clarkson."

From down the street, Deputy Maynard came running, spurting up water gathered in low pockets of the sidewalk. The six riders were white with fear and their horses, lathered. Rain had soaked their clothes and fear had drained their manhood.

Pushing back her emotions, Claire told Ethan she was going to have Eli go inside and stay with Maggie, and that she would return. His nod indicated his understanding. When she reached the wagon, Eli was standing beside it, watching the posse. Blue was lying at his feet, his head on the boy's boot. Claire told him what had happened and that she wanted him to stay with his sister in the store.

His eyes filled with trouble, Eli asked about his aunt and uncle. Claire bit her lower lip to keep from reacting and told him as evenly as she could that no one knew anything yet. Claire didn't believe in keeping bad things from children; bad things were a part of life. But it made no sense to speculate either. However, she told him not to tell Maggie, that she would do so later. After instructing Blue to stay, the boy left for the store and Claire returned to Ethan's side.

As she approached, a balding man without a hat, wearing a torn, long coat, waved his arms as he talked. "B-bullets were comin' from everywhere. Oh God, everywhere. L-like this . . . rain. From every direction. Down on us. I-I saw Mitchelson get it in the f-face. Right beside me. Th-that's his blood on my c-coat." He didn't yet realize that he had dropped his rifle in the escape.

She touched Ethan's arm and he sought her hand.

As the bald man spoke, the rest of the harried group spouted further details of their ambush by the Victorio Gee gang. They were the only ones to get away; the rest were slaughtered, including Deputy Logan. Claire and Ethan listened to the agitated reports in stunned silence. Two helped Clarkson from his horse. Apparently his upper arm was wounded; the shock of it had removed all color from his face.

"Did you see my brother . . . Cole Kerry?" Ethan took a half step toward the terrified men. His face was white; his jaw locked to hold back the trembling that rumbled through his body.

All of the posse turned from the gathering townspeople, many holding umbrellas, to see who had questioned them.

"N-no. They must've killed him. The ranger said he had gone ahead to keep watch on the gang. They must've killed him," the hatless man said, looking up at Ethan and ignoring the rain splattering on his face. Unspoken was what would happen to Kathleen. It didn't need clarifying.

Behind him, Claire's gasp struck hard at Ethan's soul. *How could I have been so wrong about all of this?* he asked himself and let agonized air escape through clenched teeth.

"Where's the ranger?"

"Hell, I-I don't know. Shot down like the rest, I guess."

To himself, Ethan muttered, "No." Pulling away from Claire, he took another step toward the battered remnants of the posse, now stepping down from weary horses. Rain shoved its way onto his face as he cleared the short overhang. "If everybody was shot, how'd you boys get away?" His voice cut through the rain like a beam of sunshine.

The half-dozen riders froze as if they had reentered the ambush. This blind rancher had become something more than a curiosity-seeker; he was, in effect, challenging their courage.

A youthful clerk, still mounted, looked away, then back to Ethan. "W-we was all at the back—when we rode into that valley. Not far from Ghost Mesa. Ain't that a place for it? W-we turned an' ran, Mr. Kerry. We ran like hell. I-I'm sorry but we did."

The bald man slapped his reins around the hitching rack angrily. "What would you have done, Mr. Kerry?"

"I would have been expecting an ambush."

The bald man laughed and turned to the others to get them to do likewise. "Hell, you can't even see."

"No, but my brother can. An' he wouldn't have ridden into an ambush like that."

"What are you sayin'? If you wasn't blind, I'd . . ."

"Don't let that stop you, friend. I don't need to see to handle the likes of you." Ethan took another step forward, pushing out his chin as he moved.

From behind him, Claire whispered, "Don't, Ethan. They did their best."

A hand touched Ethan's arm. Ethan swung in its direction, readying himself to be hit.

"It's me, Mr. Kerry. Deputy Maynard." The young deputy was breathing hard from running.

"What do you want?" Ethan's voice was hard, challenging.

"I want your advice. What should we do next? I-I guess I'm in charge."

Claire watched her husband, barely able to hold the sob that filled her throat. If the posse had failed—and Cole was dead—Kathleen was doomed. How could this be happening to them? First, Luther's family dying; then Ethan being blinded. And now this. It was too much. She stared at Ethan, wondering how he would react. The morning had already brought him to a state of near dejection. What would he do? As she watched, it was as if a layer of frustration cracked and fell from his face. In its aftermath was the man she remembered. No sign of remorse. No whining of what might have been. Only resolve. Rock-hard resolve.

There was something about him that drew men to his leadership. It was as if he wasn't blind. Not really. At least not for the moment. Ethan Kerry was in charge. Totally and completely. And every man close by knew it. He stood with his arms crossed and told the deputy and the huddled townspeople they should plan on the gang returning; the outlaws would expect little resistence since most of the posse had been destroyed.

"Every man—and every woman—must stand ready to fight. If you don't, you will die. Those who can use a gun, take places throughout the town. High an' low. You arrange 'em for the best firin' patterns." Ethan motioned with his outstretched hand to no place in particular. It didn't matter, the knot of scared townspeople got the idea. "Those that can't shoot well will load." Ethan paused and turned back toward the store. "McKeon, we're going to need every gun you've got. An' every bullet. The bank will pay you, won't you, Picklewhite?"

The banker was surprised the blind rancher knew he was standing at the edge of the crowd. Everyone turned toward him.

"Well, I . . ."

"Just say yes, Picklewhite. That's the town's money. Not yours. Some of it is mine."

"Ah . . . yes, of course. Yes." Picklewhite tried to smile but it was more like an unseen hand had pulled the corner of his mouth away from his teeth.

"M-maybe they won't come back." It was the well-dressed customer from the store. He shoved the black armband into his coatpocket as he spoke, hoping no one would notice.

Ethan's response was more gentle than Claire—or anyone else—expected. "You might be right, mister. Victorio Gee's a hard man to figure. I don't think there're any dishonest neighbors around either, but we still brand all our cattle." He cocked his head to the right. "A savvy man'd be ready. Your choice, though."

"Mr. Kerry's right. We need to be ready." Deputy Maynard didn't want his voice to crack in the middle of the statement but it did anyway.

A swirl of activity followed his pronouncement as

men and women scurried to secure weapons. A dozen people jammed into the store, demanding guns.

Ethan quietly told the deputy where to place his best marksmen and how to prepare the town for an attack. He suggested putting six steady men inside the bank, behind the counter so they could surprise the gang if they got into the bank. He was certain Gee would return.

Maynard listened intently, without interrupting. When Ethan finished, the young deputy told him that he would do as Ethan said and then asked how long he thought the town could hold against an assault. Ethan said he thought they could hold out long enough for him to go get his men from the roundup camp and return. Maynard's face brightened at the news.

"Steady everybody down as best you can. There are still some men here in town who've fought. Check the saloons," Ethan finished. "I'll be back—with our bunch. I promise."

"I don't know what to say, Mr. Kerry. Th-thank you."

"Don't thank me. I've got a score to settle with Victorio Gee."

For an instant, as Deputy Maynard stared at the calm, chiseled face of Ethan Kerry, he actually felt sorry for the outlaw leader.

Leaning into Ethan, Claire whispered that they needed to tell the children what had happened, and that they were both in the store. She couldn't read his expression but thought it was an indication that she would be doing the talking.

Chapter 6

Gunfire in the valley beyond stirred Cole Kerry from painful sleep. He was cold. His head ached. His whole body was stiff. His right arm would not move. Nor would his left leg. He had to try to get away, though—or die here. His mind finally registered that concern. The longer he stayed in this cave, the less likely he would be found. That he knew.

When he sat up, the spinning of the cave was so great he vomited, then vomited again and again, until there was only empty gagging. He slept again for a few minutes but awoke in a scared sweat. Finally he dared to move once more. He didn't know how much time had passed since he was shot. Was it the same day, he wondered, or was he hallucinating? Things were blurry every few minutes.

He cleaned the caked blood from his head with cave water, then drank from the cooling liquid; its color was almost red. Blinking to force concentration in spite of a mind-numbing headache, he realized it would have been smarter to drink first. A deep, raw line across the left side of his face was painful even to the slightest touch. He had been very lucky. He vaguely recalled turning to see what the ranger thought was funny and that had saved his life. Or maybe just prolonged it. Was he pushed? What a stupid thought. Of course he wasn't pushed; no one was behind him. Why had Bartlyn tried to kill him? He couldn't be connected to Victorio Gee, could he? His mind didn't want to explore anything further.

At times like these, he knew a Comanche warrior would sing his death song. Cole didn't feel like singing and didn't have a death song anyway. But he did ask for help; his short prayer echoed within the cave's walls. His mind brought Kathleen to him and he ached to hold her. Just once more. He could die happily if she were with him. But she was with Victorio Gee and the agony of that fact ripped into his aching mind.

His calf wound was swollen, hardened in pain. Any pressure brought an immediate response of teeth-gritting torment. Slowly he removed the cloth fragments and dirt from the blackened mess on his arm. The wound began to bleed again. He took some moss from the base of the cave wall and dabbed it over the oozing hole. Only his left hand and arm were usable so movement was awkward and slow. His shoulder crackled with pain, too, but he was certain the wounds were slight. He laid some moss across them anyway, but decided not to put any on his forehead. It made him dizzy just to touch the gunshot crease and his head pounded from the earlier clubbing.

Examining his body to determine if he had been hit elsewhere, he felt along his stomach and discovered a tear in his belt but only a slight cut. There was one long scratch on his left arm that needed attention but he couldn't do anything except rest it in the water. Feeling faint again, Cole laid down by the discolored pool and drank one more time. The cool water encouraged him. He tried to stand, began shaking uncontrollably and fell to his knees. The motion sent shivers of shock through his bad leg as it slammed into the ground. He did not move again for minutes, letting the dizziness dance through him unchallenged.

The young gunfighter tried to stand again; this time, very slowly. He stood at last and thought he was going to pass out. He knew to do so was to die. Someone would find him here and that someone might not be a friend. After a minute of trying to breathe evenly and not gasp, his head stabilized. But he was heaving for air like a man who had run up a mountain.

Slamming into his aching mind came the realization that Kathleen had been taken from him. It sucked the wind from his chest and he bent over, unable to breathe for an instant.

He had to get to her! He had to get to her!

Dragging his stiffened leg, he edged himself toward the entrance. It seemed like hours before he reached the cave's opening. Sweating and panting, he leaned against the rocks and looked out at the darkness.

A soft wind, singing of rain, brought more chill to the afternoon. He wanted to cry out but there were no sounds in him. With a long, shallow breath, he began the slow ascent along the shale trail Bartlyn had taken earlier. But his leg wouldn't cooperate. Cole could think of only one thing. He must make it, at least, to the far ridge or Gee's men would find him in the open and kill him easily. He was not going to die. He was going to live and save Kathleen. And make them pay. He was. He was. He w . . .

Somewhere near the middle of the rock trail, he passed out. A nosey squirrel chattered in his face and woke him. The little animal was furious at having his walkway blocked and let Cole know it. Groggy, but determined, he started up the slide again. Fifteen minutes later, he rested at the top of the ridge, where he had been earlier. He was drenched in sweat and bleeding. His left pant leg was torn to the knee.

Waves of nausea rolled through him almost rhythmically. Finally, he found his Winchester. Rather, it found him. He crawled over the gun before realizing what it was. Squatting, he pulled the gun to him and laid it across his lap. His wounded arm found a large knuckle-shaped rock beside him to rest on.

He wanted to sleep. His body cried for rest. Just a little rest. Just a little. But to sleep was to die. He would go on. He would not die. Could he walk back to camp? To town? Where was the posse? Where was Kathleen? The gunfire in the distance didn't register as anything except annoying sound.

A few minutes later, there was a rustling to his left. Something was moving through the trees. He clumsily pulled his Winchester from his lap with his left hand. He struggled to cock the weapon. The lever wouldn't cooperate but he finally jerked it into place. He tried to hold his breath and wait for the movement to get closer. Panic ran through his mind, trampling on the last of his resolve. He wanted to fire . . . at the trees. At anything! But he waited. There would be only one shot from him: He didn't have the strength to recock the gun, at least not fast enough to stay alive.

Leaning against a large outcropping of granite, he looked into the graying day, trying to determine the extent of his unknown problem. How many were there? His eyes kept losing their focus no matter how hard he tried to keep them steady. A low whinny cut through his fear.

It was Kiowa!

Cole hugged the sorrel's neck and it nuzzled him

gently. Dried blood marked a bullet wound on the horse's right flank.

Cole led the animal closer to the big rock he had been leaning against. His strength was rapidly leaving him and he questioned whether he could remain in the saddle long enough to get away. A thought passed through him as he steadied the horse: he would tie himself to the saddle. After easing the hammer back in place, he shoved the Winchester into its saddle sheath and moved awkwardly to his saddlebags.

He sought some leather thongs that should be pushed into a corner. A box of cartridges was packed away along with some old corn dodgers but he was too nauseated to consider eating anything. Only the leather thongs were of interest now.

Vomiting was held back only by gulping the moisture-laden air. He struggled to mount the patient horse and finally wrestled himself into the saddle. Both his head and leg were bleeding again. For the first time, he realized his hat was missing. He couldn't recall what might have happened to it. Leaning over, he tied one long thong around the upper thigh of his right leg and the stirrup strap. He repeated the same containment on his left leg to hold his balance in the saddle. Sharp jabs of pain followed each tug.

Pushing the straps of his canteen, looped over the saddle horn, out of the way, he tied his right hand to the pommel as best he could with his left hand. Then he wound his left hand around the remaining leather thong to give a restraint to both hands if he passed out during the ride. For the first time, he heard distant gunfire and realized what it might be. Gee's men could be anywhere. He imagined the evil face of Victorio Gee and knew the outlaw leader would come after him if he could.

"K-Kathleen, I'm coming . . . I'm . . ." His words were little more than mumbled sounds.

A quiet urging brought the horse into an easy walk. The fine animal seemed to understand. He was carrying his master away from danger.

"F-find Kathleen. F-find K-Kathleen."

As the rain began its assault on the land, Cole Kerry lost consciousness. But his red horse kept plugging on, climbing higher and deeper into the craggy wilds of Ghost Mesa, southwest of town. His rider was a rag doll in the saddle, flopping against the horse's dark, sweaty neck. Occasionally the horse stopped to make certain his burden was still in the saddle and to breathe wearily before resuming the journey into the safety of the high, eerie plateau. Shortly before nightfall, a heavier rain began to bound the jagged land.

But the wounded gunfighter felt none of it. And the only sound matching the rain was the delirious repetition of "Kathleen, I'm coming."

Chapter 7

Silent and reflective, Ethan Kerry and his family were lost in their own thoughts as their wagon bounced along the afternoon plains. Maggie and Eli had finally run out of questions for Claire to answer and she was too busy handling the wagon team to worry if she had answered them well.

Claire had agreed with Ethan's plan to get men and return; she made no attempt to express how she felt about the situation. She knew Ethan didn't want to hear it. Not now. Later, when it was all over. That was the time to mourn. But not now.

The only thing she insisted on was his riding in the wagon, and not on his horse. It was one thing to ride with Cole or Luther; quite another to ride by himself. Even if it was just behind the wagon. He was too filled with planning for the counterattack on the outlaws to complain. So his horse trailed behind the wagon with a rope halter tied to the end gate.

Uvalde was initially in a state of panic, but gradually became a purposeful frenzy. Deputy Maynard was doing the best job he could getting men—and some women—ready for a return assault, taking firing positions throughout the town. Ethan had stayed long enough to give the young deputy a few other ideas about preparing for the attack. He recommended placing two-man scout teams beyond the sight of town; their objective was to "fire and fall back." Ethan thought it would delay Gee's attack somewhat, yet draw him closer because he would think it was just an accidental encounter. The firing would, of course, serve as an alarm. But Ethan warned Deputy Maynard not to use any inexperienced men for this purpose; they would only die quickly.

The Kerry's two-horse team didn't need encouragement but Claire was pushing them faster than she should have normally. There was nothing these animals liked more than covering a lot of ground fast. Four farm houses zipped by and Claire acknowledged each working family with a wave and told Ethan to do the same. Long rows of wheat and corn looked endless. Ethan gave her directions as if he were seeing every corn stalk and every house.

After Ethan's observation about going too fast, she eased the team into a lope that led them through a mile-long string of trees lining a fat creek, past a spongy swale of slick, wet grass and over three broken hills. Trying hard to remain calm, her mind swirled with the possibilities of what could happen to her new sister-in-law. She, too, had heard the stories about Victorio Gee and kidnapped women. And now she was worried that Cole had been shot as well. Yet, she was calm; a reflected attitude from the way Ethan had reacted. He was determined and focused.

A man-high jutted rock passage was the prelude to a heavily wooded area, trees looming like large, dark sentries. On the other side, the land opened into wide expanses of pastureland. Bar K land.

As the wagon was absorbed by shadowed forest, Ethan said laconically, "Hey, we're almost there now, Claire." He could tell major differences in light and knew, anyway, they were entering the treeline.

Once a courageous and gifted fighter, he was slowly adjusting to the blackness that surrounded his life. With the help of Cole, their oldest brother, Luther, and the ever-steadfast Claire, Ethan had settled into a life without sight but one filled with activity. Only occasionally did he express frustration with his situation, but nothing like the early days when he challenged Cole to a gunfight on a trail drive to save his ranch. Except for this morning, when he was drowning in frustration about not being able to help in the town fight. Hearing that his young brother might be dead had snapped him out of the mental malaise.

"I'm sorry, Dad." Eli wasn't certain how to respond.

Ethan chuckled and reached into his shirt pocket for cigarette makings. Both Kerry brothers had marveled at Ethan's acquired dexterity in rolling a cigarette without seeing. Quite an advancement from his first attempts, when he spilled a complete sack of tobacco.

A match snapped to life on Ethan's belt buckle and he inhaled the smoke, let it encircle his head, slide across the wide brim of his hat and disappear. His manner was that of a man fully in control of his feelings and his surroundings.

An owl saluted as it flew across their path in search of dinner. To their right were the remains of an old campfire. They surprised two cows, each with a calf.

"Hey, ladies—you get out of here. We need to brand your young 'uns." Ethan shouted and waved his arms in their general direction.

Annoyed, the animals lumbered toward the daylight at the far side of the forest.

"How many?" Ethan asked, taking the cigarette from his mouth.

"Two cows. Two calves," Maggie pronounced precisely.

"Thought so. Should be a lot more in here. They like these woods for some reason. We'd better get some riders to work it—as soon as we get rid of Gee."

Claire looked at him and wondered what was going through his mind. Both Eli and Maggie wanted to renew their concerns about Victorio Gee, their uncle Cole and aunt Kathleen, the ranger and the posse, but didn't. Their mother was preoccupied with driving and their father obviously didn't want to talk about the events in town. He didn't seem worried about Cole at all. And barely seemed cognizant that their aunt had been kidnapped. Ethan leaned forward on the seat, eager to get to the roundup camp.

"Don't come chargin' into camp, Claire. Might scare the beef." Leaning over, Ethan crushed the used cigarette against the wagon's belly.

From the back of the wagon, Blue moved up to nuzzle against the boy. Eli shrugged his shoulders to get him to retreat while his mother pulled back on the reins without commenting to Ethan that she hadn't intended to come running into camp. She never did.

When they broke through the forest, a great valley opened to them, dotted with cattle and riders. A great brown lake of cattle ebbed and flowed below them, drowning out most of the green. All had been nudged from hills, ravines and hedgerows. It was a good holding place for the gathered herd, with enough grass to keep them comfortable while they were separated and, if needed, branded. Around the branding fire was a swirl of activity as sweating men brought calves for branding and castrating. Severed testicles were tossed into a bucket for frying as a suppertime treat. A circle of riders kept the herd settled and in place.

At the edge of the flattened prairie was the chuck wagon. Two men were hovering around the opened apron shelf. Another was drinking from one of the water barrels on the side of the wagon. Two outriders were switching horses before returning to their assigned land to search. The rest were long gone, working specified areas to assure no land or animals were missed. The banded-together cowboys from the four major outfits were currently working Bar K land and would eventually cover the entire region.

At Ethan's urging, Claire reined in the wagon team to let the sounds of the gathering reach them. Just for a moment. Agitated cattle. Angry horses. Creaking saddle leather. And demanding cowboys. All squeezed into a wonderful song that made the day right again even when it wasn't.

"That's some sight, isn't it." Ethan's comment wasn't a question.

"Yes, it is." Eli glanced at his father. No matter how often he heard a statement like that, he always wondered if his father actually saw anything. "Dad, aren't you worried about Uncle Cole and Aunt Kathleen?"

"Where's your Uncle Luther?" Ethan responded.

"He's over there." Eli pointed to two silhouettes huddled around a horse's rear leg a few feet from the remuda string. "That's him with Loop. Looks like they're studying Loop's pony. Back leg."

"Figures. Where else would he be," Ethan snapped and reached again for his cigarette makings, "unless he was checkin' out supper."

Even as a shadowed shape at this distance, Luther Kerry was a distinctive figure with extremely bowed legs, a tall crowned hat and a way of walking that looked like the earth was moving around underneath him. Luther might be slower-witted than his two brothers but neither had his way with horses. Or his caring.

Steadying the horses, Claire turned toward Ethan next to her. "Your son asked a question, Ethan."

"Huh?"

"He asked you about Cole and Kathleen."

"I don't know any more than you do, Eli. I know your uncle is a savvy fighter. I taught him," Ethan rubbed his unshaved chin. "Right now, the best thing we can hope for is that the gang *does* attack the town. That's our best chance for getting Kathleen. Might be our only chance."

Claire reached past Ethan and warmly patted Eli's knees to reassure him. Her smile was forced and Eli knew she was worried, regardless of how she acted.

"I wonder what's the matter with Loop's horse?" Eli wasn't sure he wanted that blunt of an assessment from his father. He would ask Uncle Luther; the bow-legged growl of a man always had time to discuss anything with him.

"Don't know, Eli. But if anybody can figure it out, it's your Uncle Luther," Ethan acknowledged, happy the subject had changed. "Loop's turnin' into a real hand, ain't he?" He completed the cigarette roll, ran his tongue along the unflapped edge of paper and sealed it with his fingers.

Brown hair lying on his shoulders, a short, intense cowhand fingered a lariat as Luther ran his hands up and down the horse's rear left leg. Not yet eighteen, Loop had been on three trail drives to Kansas already. His first was when Ethan was blinded and Cole led the drive. Loop hadn't been called by his Christian name, Josiah Bryanson, for a long time. Probably wouldn't think the person using it was addressing him.

There weren't many times when the lad didn't have

a rope in his hands or was asking an older cowhand about some aspect of roping. During the roundups and on the drives, he usually ate with a lasso in his hand. Of course, that attraction—and his growing prowess—had led to his nickname. All three Kerry brothers liked him, especially his determination to do things well.

"Let's go on down and get our boys headed for a fight," Ethan said, lighting his cigarette and flicking out the match.

With a click of her tongue and a gentle roll of the reins, Claire urged the wagon team forward. Maggie took the moment to ask her mother if they would ever see their aunt and uncle again. "Are Uncle Cole and Aunt Kathleen going to Heaven to live with Uncle Luther's family—and our brown horse Jake?"

The question struck Claire's heart and she pulled back instinctively on the reins, jerking the wagon to a stop. Ethan winced like he had walked into a door. Her mind swirling with gray, ominous clouds, Claire urged the team to move again while she tried to find words but couldn't.

It was Eli who responded, exasperated at his little sister. "Maggie, Uncle Cole and Aunt Kathleen will be home soon. Now quit it. We all have work to do."

When Maggie started to complain about her brother's response, Claire found the words to tell her that he was right; there was work to be done and no questions would speed up the return of their loved ones.

Harold DuMonte was the first to see them coming. He stood up beside the fire and waved with a branding iron. A quiet black cowboy steady with animals and men, he was the Bar K "rep" for the roundup, in charge of the Kerry herd. Beside him was fat-bellied and marble-faced Zeke Ferguson with another iron.

Ignoring the advancing wagon, he placed it against the tied calf's hip and the acrid smell of burning hide snaked through the air.

Claire maneuvered the wagon through the herd and next to the fire as Ethan told her to do. Ethan's horse whinnied at the smell of burning hair and the sight of working horses; the older black horse had been a part of many roundups, especially after Ethan was blinded.

The brim of his high-crowned hat flopping in front of his unlined face, DuMonte walked from the branding fire to the wagon. He removed his hat and bowed slightly toward Claire and she addressed him formally as "Mr. DuMonte." Removing his glove, he walked to the front of the wagon and held out his hand to Ethan, brushing it against the man's stomach so Ethan would know where it was. Immediately, Ethan sought the extended hand and shook it vigorously.

"Where's Cole?" DuMonte said. He carried himself with the assured poise of a college professor. "An' his missus?"

Unable to hold the news back any longer, Maggie blurted out what had happened in town. Ethan and Claire sat quietly while Eli added more details, even the farmer getting shot in the doorway of the store and that the store had a new supply of candy sticks.

A devout Christian, DuMonte folded his hands together as if in prayer as he listened to the terrible news.

Finally, Ethan interrupted, laying a hand on Eli's shoulder, and told DuMonte what they were going to do. The roundup would have to wait. Every man would be asked to ride for town. Not just Bar K men, but all of the ranches' men involved in the gathering. It would be every man's own decision, however, whether to go or not. Staying behind would not be a disgrace—or cause for losing one's job. At least not for Bar K men. He couldn't speak for any other ranchers.

But he made it clear that he felt it was time to put a stop to Gee's violence. Ethan said he looked at it as preservation. The blind rancher reached out to put his hand to find the lip of the wagon but couldn't find it and waved in the air awkwardly, before he returned his hand to his side. He paused and added, with a smile, "Think we got everything on the list though."

DuMonte waited but no more details came about town. He glanced at Claire, but she was fiddling with the reins and not inclined to talk, so he changed subjects. "Good a time as any, I guess. We've cleaned out the whole north side, except that long stretch of hedgerow. Got riders working it now. Mostly our stuff. Some Double B—and a few Lazy R."

"Good work, Harold. Sounds like we're ahead of schedule," Ethan responded.

"Think so."

"Must be your good standing with the fella upstairs," Ethan folded his arms and forced a grin. "We're gonna need that today."

DuMonte smiled but didn't respond. It was well known the black man read the Bible daily, prayed on his knees before sleeping and never swore or raised his voice. He had been a point rider on Bar K trail drives for a long time now. His fellow hands called him "Preacher" but neither Ethan nor Cole ever did. The nickname was received with patient understanding; as a black man, he had been called much worse over the years. The dependable cowhand had been chosen again to be the "tally man" for the roundup. It was a major responsibility, keeping the count of calves of the various ranches as they were branded. Only a man of considerable honesty was ever selected. Of course, it didn't hurt that the Bar K was the largest outfit, by far, in the region.

This was DuMonte's second year at the job. If there

was any concern because he was a black man, no one mentioned it to any of the Kerry brothers. No one dared to.

"Better assign some boys to hit that ridge after we get back. Saw a bunch of ours comin' through." Ethan motioned toward the hillside behind them.

Eli hunched his shoulders and said, "We saw four."

"More'n that in there," Ethan said, squeezing his son's shoulder to indicate he shouldn't interfere.

"Will do, Mr. Kerry." DuMonte cocked his head to the side. "How long you figure we'll be gone?"

"Hard to tell. I figure Gee will hit the town hard an' quick," Ethan stared unseeing at the sky. "I want Abe to start lookin' for Cole. Gonna ask Rios to ride with him, if he'll do it."

Eli glanced at his mother and Claire nodded that he should remain quiet. Maggie stuck out her tongue at him and he mouthed, "Quit it."

"Rios would be angry if you didn't ask him. They're good friends, Mr. Kerry." DuMonte rubbed his chin. and added his assessment, "The beef'll drift."

"Can't help it. If we don't go, Gee'll put a torch to Uvalde." Ethan shook his head. "They already ran through some towns nearby. Uvalde's our town too. When the outriders get in, they can help some with the beef until we get back."

"How many men does Gee have?"

Ethan wished he hadn't asked. He twisted his face. "Oh, I reckon we'll be outnumbered."

DuMonte listened with a strange expression on his face. "We got a new calf—one of ours—that won't suck. Gonna need help or it'll die before it learns."

"You sure it's not the mother pushing 'im away?"

"Don't think so, Mr. Kerry. We've helped the little fella get right up there, but he doesn't . . . get what it's all about."

Behind them, a portly rider cleared the ravine to the south and loped toward them. Ivan Drako owned the ranch to the south, one of several that had once been a part of the Winslow empire. Russian born, according to the stories, he had come from Houston a year ago, after selling his riverboat company, and invested in land. It was also rumored that his original name was Drakorski. Ethan considered him a worthy enough neighbor and had invited him to join the roundup. Drako and his three riders had been there at the beginning. According to DuMonte, they were always first in the saddle and last off; the black foreman always respected hard work.

"How you to be this day, Mr. and Mrs. Kerry? Master Kerry . . . Miss Kerry. I did not expect to see you out here." Drako shouted as he reined the horse, jumped down and strutted toward them, leading the bay. His speech was somewhat formal and somewhat stilted, with traces of a Russian accent. Luther had snorted it was the Yankee in the man, not the Russian, that made him speak that way.

Claire returned his greeting before Ethan did. Maggie made a move to climb down but Claire quietly told her to stay on the buckboard seat.

Narrow eyebrows, high-arched lips and closely cut, steel-gray hair made Drako's pumpkin face appear even larger. A stub of a cigar was shoved into the corner of his mouth, unlit. No one had ever seen him actually smoke a cigar, only chew on them. Constantly. He wore an old dark-gray suit coat and matching vest, a clean white shirt without a paper collar, stovepipe chaps and a center-creased Stetson with silk trim. Even in roundup attire, he looked like a city man, but one without a gun.

"Not so good, Ivan. Just came from town. Victorio Gee was there. We're going back—with men. As many as will go." Ethan proceeded to brief the rancher on the situation.

Drako's expression yielded little emotion as he listened. He was an intelligent man, Ethan thought, and consistently wary. Nothing wrong with that. Ethan wasn't certain of the man's cattle savvy but no one would ever accuse the new rancher of not working hard or trying to learn. He and his wife, Evangeline, had spent several evenings at the Kerry ranch with most of the conversation about cattle and the area. Ethan liked the man and encouraged his efforts. Luther thought Drako was too hard on his horses and Cole hadn't paid the man much attention. Not with Kathleen near him again.

"Will not the herd scatter?" Drako asked, his thin eyebrows running at each other to make a frown. "Why do you think these renegades will go back there? It would appear to myself they will keep running." The cigar stub in his mouth moved from the right side to the left without any assistance from his hand.

"You an' your men don't have to go," Ethan said. "Fact is, you can help keep the gathered stuff close while we're gone."

"I am of the roundup, Mr. Kerry, so I will to do what I am told to do."

Ethan smiled. "You can do what you want. I think it's a chance to put an end to this wild man before he tears up more towns." He liked Drako, as much for the fact that the man had never mentioned his blindness as for anything. Ethan's hand slid from his son's shoulder and patted him on the back. Eli studied his father, then looked at the Russian rancher, silently comparing the two and pleased with his review.

"I understand." Drako glanced at DuMonte. "But I am not soldier. I will to stay and watch the herd. I will tell my men they can do what they to wish."

"That's fine, Ivan. You and your riders should stay here." Ethan swallowed, folded his arms and turned toward DuMonte without moving from the wagon seat. "We'll leave Rommey an' Stevenson here as well. They can watch over the camp 'til we get back. Ivan and his men can hold the beef." He cocked his head to the side as if responding to an unasked question. "Yeah, I'm goin' with you. In this wagon." He raised his chin. "Tell the men to each take his best horse, rifle an' a box of bullets. I brought extra. They're here, in the wagon. We need to get it unloaded—and we need fresh horses." He outstretched his left arm to point in the direction of the wagonbed and continued, "I'll get Rommey to have somethin' for 'em to take along to eat. Kinda hungry myself. I want to be ridin' outta here in ten minutes."

"What about the outriders?"

"How many're workin'?"

"Eight, including Abe."

Ethan had figured the halfbreed Abe was one of the outriders working the land. Half-Sioux, the men called him "Abe" because his Sioux name, *Ablakela Sunkawakan*, Calm Horse, started with that sound. He, too, had ridden the death trail with the Kerrys two years ago. Ethan—and Cole—were especially fond of the men who had been with them through that Kansas drive when Sam Winslow and his men tried to destroy them with ambushes, even with a well-placed prairie fire. They had lost good riders overcoming Winslow's evil desires.

The Kerry brothers' intent was to leave well-marked graves so they could pay their respects each year on the way, but wind and weather had other ideas. No sign of their markers were anywhere to be found on their first trip back. They had taken some solace in Du-Monte's words: "Our friends are not here. They are with God in heaven." Luther had asked about his dead wife and children at that time, then spent an hour riding alone with his memories.

After listening, Drako straightened his back. "Mr. Kerry, it is to me clear that you are a man of soldiering."

"Some. On the losing side, though. My brothers, too."

Pawing the ground, the left-side horse tugged on the harness to indicate its desire to move. Claire pulled on the reins and the animal returned to a quiet position. Ethan patted her knee to let Claire know he knew what she had done and approved. Claire smiled in spite of herself.

"My reading tells the Confederate military made much of little."

"We had Marse Robert. That evened things out—for a while."

Drako turned back to his horse and put a boot in the stirrup. "This General Robert Lee was the exceptional . . . tactician, I believe is the word."

"Yeah, he was. And then some."

It was Claire's turn to respond. "Mr. DuMonte, I'm quite capable of helping with the cattle, too—an' informing the outriders when they get in. I'll also stay—an' so will Maggie and Eli."

Maggie grinned and looked at Eli, who chose to stick out his tongue at her, returning the earlier favor.

"I couldn't ask you . . ."

"You didn't. I volunteered. We'll tell the outriders what's happened and see if Abe will start . . . tracking Cole."

"I'm gonna ask Rios to go find Abe an' start tracking," Ethan interjected.

"For Cole?" Claire asked.

"For Cole—or Gee. If I'm wrong an' they don't hit the town again, we'll have to go after 'em."

DuMonte shook his head. "Outriders won't be happy at being left behind, boss." He watched Ivan Drako lope toward the ravine where he came from; the heads of his three riders bobbed from behind the crease. In seconds, the four horsemen disappeared into the brush to continue their search for cattle.

"That's the way it has to be. They'll be helping by keeping the beef close. Drako and his men can't do it alone."

Switching subjects, Ethan told Maggie and Eli that they would have to milk the cow with the slow calf and help get it to drink. It was a good way to keep them occupied, mentally and physically. Immediately, Maggie wanted to start. Claire thought it best to wait until the men were gone. Eli stuck out his tongue at her again. This time Claire saw it and told him to stop.

Excusing himself, the black man went back to the branding fire and began giving orders. Just as quickly, the roundup's rhythm changed into readiness for battle. Although black men were common among cowboys in many regions, few had achieved DuMonte's leadership status. If anyone thought of him as just "a colored man," it was kept out of earshot of the Kerrys. Of all the men working, only Drako seemed to be annoyed by DuMonte's presence.

Taking a break for water, John Davis Sotar walked over to the reined-in wagon to greet the Kerrys and ask where Cole was. His standing horse was left beside the water barrel; reins curled loosely around the rope holding the barrel in place. A compact snarl of a man, Sotar was immediately ready to ride for Uvalde. His silver-studded pistol belt was no ordinary cowhand's. A cutaway holster lay on his left hip; walnut handle forward with an inlaid silver star on each side.

Although years in Texas had softened it, his voice definitely belonged to the Missouri hills. He was proud of the absence of his left ear lobe, one of several gunfight reminders. Early in their relationship, Sotar had threatened Cole because of an incident with one of Sotar's cousins. That tension had become a solid friendship: gunfighter with gunfighter. He was genuinely worried about Cole.

Remembering his manners, Sotar touched the brim of his hat in a delayed greeting to Claire. "Good to see you, Mrs. Kerry. Sorry to hear about this trouble."

"Thank you, Mr. Sotar. We can only pray all will end well," Claire said.

Sotar put his left hand on the side of wagon next to Claire and directed his concern at Ethan. "Shouldn't we be riding to find Cole first?" The thumb and forefinger of Sotar's right hand rubbed together in a continuous tiny circle, a habit long past correcting.

"I'm as worried about Cole as you are. More," Ethan said, "but he would tell you himself that we have to stop Gee first. That's our town, too—an' our best chance of getting Kathleen back." Ethan straightened his shoulders, not daring to add finding Cole to the list.

Sotar withdrew his hand, realizing it was too close to Claire to be polite.

"Uncle Cole was hurt." Leaning toward Sotar, Eli's eyes were saucers. "He was bleeding from his head—an' his leg. I saw it."

Chapter 8

Abruptly, Ethan told Claire to wrap the reins around the long brake handle and climb down, so that he, too, might get out of the wagon. She quietly told him the reins had already been tied. After she climbed down, with Sotar's polite assistance, Ethan eased his way over the edge of the planked seat, found the wheel with his right boot for balance and jumped free.

Only someone who knew the situation would catch the careful placement of Ethan's hands a foot from his face as he released. The Missouri gunfighter knew, from past experience, that the rancher would not want assistance from anyone. He glanced at Claire and she shook her head to assure him that Ethan didn't want help. Still, Sotar couldn't help watching to make certain he didn't misstep.

Eli and Maggie took their parents' move as approval for them to get out of the wagon as well. Eli jumped down on the other side; Maggie followed, using her own perfected descent in three awkward-looking, but effective, stages. Eli pointed at the horses tied along the remuda line and told her that he liked Rios's gray horse the best. Maggie responded by saying she favored the "pretty horse with the spots." It was a horse in Loop's string.

"Wish I'd been there, Mr. Kerry," Sotar said to regain involvement.

Ethan straightened himself. "Me, too. We'd have gotten a lot more of those wolves."

Smiling at the compliment, Sotar nodded, realized the blind man couldn't see his response and said, "That'd bin alright with me."

"Would you ask Rios to come over here for a minute?"

"Sure." Sotar gave an excusing nod to both Ethan and Claire, then headed back to the chuck wagon. After getting his rifle from the wagon, he pulled the loosely wrapped reins from the water barrel roping and remounted his horse. Easing the animal into a lope, Sotar rode past the group of men listening to DuMonte and headed toward the northern edge of the milling herd. Barely visible in the dust, Miguel del Rios was keeping cattle from straying before they could be sorted and branded if necessary.

From the chuckwagon to their right, William Rommey, the cook, laid down a big knife and waited for someone to unload the Kerry wagon's supplies. Rommey was actually wearing a fresh white shirt. He usually did. Rommey was definitely a good cook but Ethan wasn't certain the man had ever been part of a cow camp before. Hiring him was Luther's idea.

Walking alongside their supply wagon, touching it with his left hand for direction, Ethan came to the back, opened the end and began pulling out lariats and tossing them on the ground. With Claire's direction, Eli brought over a box filled with food packages and cans; he greeted the cook and Rommey bowed slightly.

Formally. Eli thought the man was a bit silly, but resisted grinning. Blue followed from the back of the Kerrys' wagon. Claire gave two cans to Maggie to carry over and she took on her assignment eagerly.

Watching the boy and his dog advance, Old Ben Speakman leaned against the opened chuckwagon apron while he talked. He was talking more or less to Rommey but the cook was paying no attention. Speakman's scratched pipe poured out smoke as he rambled on. Finally Eli let a smile spring to his face. As usual, the older man was likely recounting some war battle. That was his subject of choice. But Eli enjoyed hearing the tales, even when they were repeated. Often.

The gray-haired man stood up and saluted as Eli approached. A former Rebel captain under Longstreet's command, Speakman had lost his left arm in the great battle of Gettysburg. His thinning buttermilk pants were all that remained of his uniform but he continued to wear them proudly. Eli's approving gaze went to Speakman's belt where an old Walker Colt was kept. He knew his uncle Cole had offered to give him a newer, more dependable weapon but Speakman politely refused, saying he just felt more comfortable with the heavy gun.

"I'd lend a hand, Sergeant Kerry, but one's all I got. The Stars and Bars dun got the other'n." Speakman dramatically held his empty arm socket.

"No problem, Mr. Speakman. Thanks, anyway."

"Well, you are growing into quite a man."

Over his shoulder, Rommey merely said, "Put it around front."

Eli's back straightened and he proudly carried the box toward the front of the wagon. "Come on, Blue."

The big dog wagged its tail and followed. Behind them several steps came Maggie with her arms full and a frown of concentration on her face,

Claire watched from the wagon, sensing a scene that wasn't consistent with what was going on in her mind. Around her, men were preparing for a war they hadn't expected, while, somewhere, her dear sister-in-law was in the hands of vicious outlaws and her husband's brother, likely, lay wounded—or dead. She wanted to scream but took a deep breath instead. Her ample bosom rose and fell slowly. This was a time for thinking, not fearing.

From beside their supply wagon, Ethan called out, "Rommey, we're riding out. Victorio Gee's attacking Uvalde. You get somethin' for the boys to eat while they ride. Now. Anythin'."

Folding his arms for emphasis, Rommey's chin rose in concord with the movement. "What do you think I can serve them? I haven't even started dinner." His recitation sounded like he couldn't believe such a request was even being made.

"I don't give a damn, Rommey." Ethan held out a hand to locate the wagon, then leaned against it. "Give 'em a potato. Jerky. Somethin'. They're riding to war. I don't want 'em hungry, too—an' I don't want any excuses from you."

Claire moved across the wagon seat and climbed down as she said, "I'll go help him, Ethan."

"Good. I'd appreciate that."

Returning from the front of the chuck wagon, Eli chuckled at the cook's frantic search for food in response to Ethan's command. He glanced at Speakman who was biting hard on his pipe. The boy turned to Maggie and told her to put her two cans in the back of the chuck wagon. She strutted past him, but one can slipped from her arms and bounced on the ground. She stopped and waited for Eli to come back, glancing down at the runaway item. Exasperated, he picked up the can, stomped to the back of the chuck wagon and laid it inside with the other goods. Smiling, she followed and placed her remaining can in the wagon, clearing away other cans so that hers would set in a space all its own.

Back at the supply wagon, Ethan turned to the new sounds of Stovepipe Henderson, who had come over to take care of the wagon horses. Last year, Eli had asked why the man was called "Stovepipe" and Ethan had been thankful for the man's lean, bullwhip frame—and told Eli that was the reason. It wasn't. Actually, the size of his manhood had been the reason for the nickname and it was first applied by a whore, but Ethan had no intention of telling his son that story.

"Sure do like these new gloves, Mr. Kerry. Smooth as a baby's behind. Look at 'em." Like many cowhands, Henderson was fond of gloves and eager to evaluate them, along with lariats, horses and women. The realization of his statement about Ethan "seeing them" made him choke and sputter. "I-I'm . . . d-didn't . . ."

"Yeah. Too good for you," Ethan teased and smiled.

"Reckon so, but don't tell nobody." Henderson's face splintered into relief and he forced a laugh.

Ethan told him what was happening and the lanky cowboy's expression changed into granite. The rancher told Stovepipe to take his black horse with him and to switch the wagon to a fresh team of horses. It was going with the riders to Uvalde. Ethan wanted it empty, too, except for the three boxes of cartridges.

Before Claire headed toward the chuck wagon, she noticed Eli was trapped, listening to Speakman begin his standard—and long—speech about duty and ending with a gruesome description of losing his arm. Maggie was standing a few feet away, studying the older man's empty sleeve.

"Hey, Eli, come and give Mr. Henderson a hand, will

you?" she yelled. "Keep Blue away from the horses though. Maggie, you come, too."

"That's all ri't, Mrs. Kerry. I don't need no help." Henderson said.

"I know—but Eli does."

Henderson glanced toward the chuck wagon and chuckled. "He sure does." Clearing his throat, he said loudly, "Sure could use ya, Eli."

"Thank you, Mr. Henderson."

With Eli's assistance, he finished unharnessing the team; then untied Ethan's black horse, and led them toward the remuda. Maggie got to walk beside her big brother, thanks to Claire's insistence. Eli didn't like the idea much but let her do so as long as she stayed a step behind him. Her initial attempt to hold his hand was rejected. Blue remained under the chuck wagon, as the boy directed. Ethan heard the boy ask Henderson about Speakman's missing arm; he could only hope Eli wouldn't ask about the cowhand's nickname directly. Henderson would be proud to tell him.

"Luther's coming, Ethan," Claire advised.

"Has Sotar talked with Rios yet?" Ethan growled.

Claire turned to watch Rios loping toward them. "Mr. del Rios is headed this way."

"Good. Hand me that bunch of cigars, will you?"

She reached down, lifted a small paper-wrapped bundle from near her feet and held it out for him. With a few whispered directions, Ethan could locate the cigars and took them. She glanced away for an instant and pushed her fingers against her forehead to hold back the tears; hearing her cry wouldn't help Ethan.

But Ethan was concentrating on the advancing sounds of the Mexican rancher. Rios carried himself more like a Spanish nobleman than a rancher, but his manner was warm and friendly. He wore a short Spanish-styled vest with ballooning shirt sleeves; a tooled shoulder holster held a black-handled Colt. Under his sombrero, a silk bandana covered his head.

His English often got lost among flowing Spanish but there was no doubt of his ability with horses and cattle. Right now he was riding a rangy bay but his top horse, a magnificent gray, was a descendant of one of the legendary "Spanish pacers" that had roamed wild throughout the land. The father, also gray, had been known by many names and the great stallion could supposedly run forever and was never caught. *Bailarin*, Spanish for "Dancer," was the name Rios gave his horse.

Miguel del Rios had bought a small ranch adjoining the Bar K spread last year and quickly become close friends with Cole. His family and ranch had been destroyed by raiders along the border. He had come north looking for a new life. The friendship between Rios and Cole had begun with the realization that the Mexican's Bailarin and Cole's Kiowa were related to the same bloodline of great mustangs. It had quickly turned into one of mutual respect and admiration. And strong friendship.

Determination flashed across Rios's narrow bronze face with its graying goatee, as Ethan told him what had happened and what he wanted the Mexican rancher to do, if he would.

"*Señor* Ethan Kerry, et weel be *mi* honor to ride for Cole an' hees *señorita*," Rios answered. "Abe, he ees in ze north, along ze trees. I find heem. We go. *Mucho* fast."

"Thanks. I knew I could count on you."

"*Si*. Victorio Gee an' hees devils keeled *mi familia*. *Dos* years back. Near the beeg river."

Ethan stared with blank eyes but his face registered surprise. He hadn't known the reason for Rios's arrival; the Mexican rancher had shared that only with Cole. Then he remembered the bundle in his hand.

"Oh, I almost forgot. When we were in the store, Cole had set these aside for you." Ethan held up the cigars.

It was Rios's turn to stare. He looked at the gift as if it were gold. "Your brother, he ees *bueno amigo*. I find heem—or I die."

With that pronouncement, he wheeled his horse toward the remuda to switch to his gray pacer.

"He isn't on Bailarin today," Claire observed. Admiration laced her words. She knew horses well. Almost as well as Luther. She glanced at the remuda string and saw the gray horse standing quietly at the far end.

"Good as Kiowa?" Ethan's mouth edged upward at the right corner. "Wonder if Rios's horse can kick?"

She didn't respond.

"You didn't think that was funny?" Ethan found and squeezed Claire's arm.

"I'll go help Mr. Rommey."

As she started to leave, Luther yelled out as he approached. "Well, would ya look at that. All them handsome folks. Now that's a sight fer ol' eyes." Luther stood and crossed his arms. He shook his head, turned to the side and sneezed. Then sneezed again.

Eli burst away from helping with the wagon horses and ran to Luther, grabbing him around the waist. Maggie had followed, just as eagerly, on her stubby legs. Luther's eyes were bright and warm as he returned the greetings with an enthusiastic bear hug. A toothy grin, underneath a long, droopy mustache, filled his wrinkled face. Actually the right side of his face was more lined than the other. Mostly, the result of years of squinting only with his right eye while spending days in the sun.

"Better not stay too close, kids, your uncle Luther's got hisself branded with a cold." He rubbed Eli's hair affectionately and patted Maggie's cheek as gently as he could. "Don't wanna give ya none o' it."

"It's good to see you, Luther," Claire said warmly and excused herself. "I need to help Mr. Rommey." Her eyes avoided his as she left, taking Maggie with her.

"What's up, li'l brother?"

"Looks like you've been sleeping in your clothes again, Luther," Ethan chirped, moving closer with short, choppy steps. His hands were outstretched to provide an early warning to any obstruction.

The remark surprised Luther. Of course, it always looked like he slept in his clothes, even when they were brand-spanking new. Running his hands through his suspenders, Luther cocked his head to the side. His eyes were red with cold and a stray mucus dribble wandered down his mustache from his nostril. Without saying anything, he nudged Eli to return to helping with the horses. Loop was already assisting several riders who wanted to switch mounts before leaving for Uvalde.

"Now, Ethan, yo-al didn't go an' start seein' agin, did ya?"

Luther meant to be playful but the grimace on Ethan's face was a clear indication the remark hurt.

Luther knew it the instant the words hit the air. Stepping toward Ethan, he blurted, "I . . . I didn't mean that . . . that way, Ethan. I . . . I'm s-sorry."

"That's all right, Luther. I asked for it."

Rubbing his reddened nose, Luther changed the subject, uncertain of what was happening. "That be one lucky hoss. Went down in one o' them damn sink holes. Along that ridge, thar's a bunch o' 'em. Could'a snapped his leg in two. Sur 'nuff." Luther spat for emphasis and judged the brown stream as a bit thin, so he spat again. He continued his assessment, indicating he planned to rub liniment on the horse's leg and let it rest for the duration of the roundup. He studied Ethan as he spoke, aware now of the riders headed for the wagon and weapons.

Handling the horses was always Luther's job, whether on the trail or breaking new mounts. He might be a slow-witted man, but no one could match his understanding of horses. This was an irony his two Kerry brothers had long ago accepted. But it was Cole who had come up with the plan to break the wild sorrel he now rode.

"Bin lookin' like we're gittin' ready fer trouble," Luther finally said. "Whar's Cole—an' his little lady?"

Ethan told him what had happened in town and Luther reacted as if he'd been hit in the stomach. "What? They took Kathleen? OhmyGod! Ya don' know whar Cole be? Ethan, we gotta go. We gotta go. Goda'mighty, this be awful." He sneezed, barely turning his head away in time.

Luther's questions came faster than the man could breathe. He wheezed and sneezed twice between his need to know what happened. Or what had happened to their brother. Ethan wasn't interested in replaying the details of the gun battle, or Gee taking Kathleen, or Cole and the ranger going after Gee's gang. He wanted to tell him what they were going to do next.

Listening to Ethan's staccato description of the planned counterattack and the sending of Abe and Rios, the oldest Kerry studied the hurrying men and suddenly interrupted with news about a rather humorous nightmare. "Last two nights, I bin a'havin' a dream 'bout a chicken chasin' me. A big'un. He's dun bin comin' after me, a'flappin' his wings and peckin' at me. Last night, the chicken got me. He dun got me." He sneezed to the side. "Think that means sum'thin'?"

"Only that you have stupid dreams."

Both Ethan and Luther burst into laughter. Luther's was forced; his stomach wouldn't let him do otherwise.

"Ethan, that thar Gee's a bad 'un. Hear tell he's dun some mighty bad things to womenfolk," Luther blurted, rubbing his reddened nose as he did.

"I know, Luther." Ethan's voice was edgy. His older brother was beginning to get on his nerves. He tried to remind himself Luther had just heard the awful news that had been bouncing around in his own head for hours. "This is a chance to stop 'em. Now. An' get Cole's wife back."

Luther caught the awkward phrase describing Kathleen but it wasn't the time to chastise his brother for not appreciating Cole's finding someone. "I reckon so but . . ."

"I'm going to split our men into three squads," Ethan interrupted. "DuMonte will head one; Sotar'll have the other. Another bunch will go into town in this wagon—with you an' me. Each'll have an assignment. I'll give 'em when we get closer." Ethan was paying more attention to the sounds of readying men than to his brother. "I may be blind—but I can still lead men into battle."

Luther stepped closer and put a large, sunburned hand on his brother's shoulder. "Nobody thought ya couldn't, 'ceptin' Sam Winslow an' ya dun showed him. But jes' whar ya be figgerin' I'm gonna be durin' all this here warrin'?"

"Beside me. In the wagon."

Luther shook his head, then realized his brother couldn't see the physical reaction. "Nope. Won't look ri't fer us to send our boys into it, whilst we be a'settin' back. What 'bout Loop? He's too young to be warrin'."

Rubbing his chin, Ethan agreed, "Just hold on, we'll be the first ones in town, big brother. Loop'll have the job of holdin' the horses we don't need. Outside of town."

Luther nodded affirmatively this time, then quickly said, "That'll do." But he had more questions about the wagon, their brother and sister-in-law.

"I'll tell you later. Cole is fine, Luther. Hell, he's probably ridin' this way now." Ethan looked away, adding that Ivan Drako and his men, Claire and Eli, and the outriders should be able to keep the assembled cattle from straying while everyone else was gone.

At the wagonbed, Sotar had returned and was handing out boxes of cartridges to the riders after they retrieved their rifles and gunbelts from the chuck wagon and received some jerky, hardtack—and tobacco, if they wanted it—from Rommey and Claire. She had a warm salutation for each rider, using their proper last names, preceded by "Mister." The rest of the supplies had been removed, as Ethan requested, and adorned the autumn grass. Putting them away would be a good task for Eli. And Maggie.

Henderson brought a new team of horses and he and Luther hitched them to the wagon. Neither spoke but Henderson's eyes kept asking the oldest brother why they were taking the wagon. Luther's only response was to shrug his shoulders and continue with the effort.

Minutes later, DuMonte walked up to Ethan, leading his own horse. "We're ready, boss. Every man's going, except Mr. Drako and his riders. All of our Bar K boys—and all the rest too."

Ethan managed a thin smile. "Good. I appreciate it."

"Uh, boss, Mr. Kerry?"

"Yes, Harold?"

DuMonte's voice dropped to almost a whisper. "Ah, the boys think you should stay here. They don't want you to get . . . hurt."

Luther turned away to get his rifle so he would avoid seeing the anguish in Ethan's face.

"Harold, tell the boys . . . that I appreciate that. I really do." Ethan carefully placed a boot in the spoke of the front wheel and pulled himself into the wagon seat. "But I'm goin'. I can't see—except in my head." He scooted down to leave room for Luther. "No offense to any o' you, but this isn't about racin' into town, shootin' and yellin'. This is about war. I know war. I'll make the difference."

"Yes sir, Mr. Kerry."

"Oh, an' tell Roper to bring along my black. Might need that pony later."

DuMonte didn't like the request but knew better than to resist.

"Let's ride. I'll fill you in as we go." Ethan was aware of Claire's sudden presence.

She touched his leg, trying to keep the fear in her heart from reaching her tongue. "Come back to me, Ethan Kerry."

"I always will. Where's my big brother?"

"He's comin' now."

He leaned over and found her face with his hand. He ignored the warm tear that settled against his fingers. She took his hand and kissed it gently.

"Give us a prayer, Harold," Ethan said.

Chapter 9

Leaning over from his horse, the halfbreed cowboy, *Ablakela Sunkawakan,* studied the wet ground in the uneven light. His long black hair flopped forward under a shapeless hat. Light rain popped on the brim and ran down his face.

Beside him, Miguel del Rios squinted toward what appeared to be a mesa, now a black wall in the drizzly dusk. The two men had been on the trail of the gang since an hour after Ethan led the men back to town. Right now, Rios was trying to see which way Gee and the others had gone, right or left. They were certain the trail they had been following for an hour was the gang. Dropped cigarettes, even a black scarf, added to the scuffle of hoofprints. It was their best option and they took it. Maybe Cole was a prisoner. His wife surely was.

Claire had told them what Ethan expected and they read the signs as an indication he was right: the gang had doubled back to hit the town again. Rios saw clearly that the gang had regathered themselves in the shadow of this mesa and headed back. There. He saw the tracks leading away through a close-by maze of rock and a few brave twists of buffalo grass.

"*Bueno*. We follow." Rios pointed.

"No. In mesa. Some go. Damn," Abe uttered, pointing toward the mesa. "*Tunehtsuru*."

Rios wasn't certain what Abe meant. The halfbreed could speak little English and that which he did know was laced with curse words, a product of the saloonkeeper who raised him.

"*Señor* Abe, they go here. *Si?* We follow?"

Abe's eyes widened in frustration, "No. In mesa. Damn. Son-of-bitch." He jammed his finger into the air to indicate riders going straight into the wall of the mesa. Curling his finger, he motioned toward himself, indicating they had come back out. He knew the area, knew it was a small box canyon, not a mesa, but couldn't find the words to explain it. He was certain most of the gang, if not all, had left, perhaps leaving Cole and Kathleen behind with only a few guards.

The only words Rios could understand were "Captun Cole Ker-ry" and a few curses. He shrugged his shoulders to illustrate his problem.

Nodding, Abe straightened himself in the saddle and nudged his horse forward while Rios watched. Swinging down, he led the animal toward a wall of twisted underbrush, saplings and buffalo grass. With a grunt, he pushed a particularly large sapling to one side. Rios realized the tree was dead, just stuck in the ground and supported there by a pile of rock.

As the tree shifted, taking along thick wads of brush, an opening appeared large enough for a man with a horse to walk through. A jagged entrance of sorts was cut clear through the side of the mesa, like a cavity in a bad tooth.

Rios realized what his friend was trying to say: It

wasn't a mesa! Instead, this was a small box canyon with a hidden entrance. Rios marveled at the sight. He wondered how many men had ridden past without realizing what it really was. An excellent hideout, at least for a day or two. He nodded enthusiastically, then stared upward. Should they chance going through the opening or climb the outside ridge and look down inside? It was time to trust his gut: They would climb and see. He made signs as he explained what he wanted to do, recognizing his own broken English would be as difficult for the halfbreed to understand as Abe's version of communicating was to him.

A nod indicated Abe understood. After he remounted, they rode to the left of the entrance, around to the northwest corner of the box canyon, and tied their horses to nearby bushes. Abe pointed at Rios's boots, wanting him to take off his spurs. Abe wore only Apache knee-high mocassins.

After Rios removed and hooked the spurs over his saddlehorn, they began their assault of the slope with rifles in hand. In the uneven twilight, the climb was difficult, with sharp rocks offering many ways for a man to cut himself, as well as deceptive shale patches that could result in a swift slide downward. Both riders were trail careful, avoiding the land traps; Abe reached the top first, sliding into place on his stomach to avoid skylining himself. Rios crawled alongside him a few minutes later.

They stared down into the belly of the box canyon and saw that the entrance crease opened into a dark flat land only two hundred yards long and half that distance wide. Even in the purpling air, they could make out a few grazing cattle and a dozen horses. A wide rock lip around most of the inside of the small canyon provided some cover from the weather and made it difficult to see if anyone was there. Using only sign language, they decided to move closer, easing toward the north, on the opposite side of the opening crease.

Neither wanted to bring up the possibility of finding Cole or Kathleen dead, or her, raped, but both knew either was likely. The opportunity to find the Kerrys was too good to pass up; maybe they could search the canyon floor and get away before the gang returned.

Thick raindrops laced the ground and their backs as they studied the silent canyon floor forty feet below them. Rios examined a shape near the center of the canyon but finally determined it was a tree stump magnified by shadow. He wanted to work their way down but Abe insisted they remain where they were for a little longer.

"Aiieee, *punitu*." Abe whispered through clenched teeth and pointed at the far corner. Rios knew the Comanche word for fire and stared. A flicker of light followed from under the rock ledge. The outlaws were building a small fire within its cover, in anticipation of the coming rain. No smoke ascended from their attempt. Rios pointed to a cluster of hardy plants twenty feet away, guarding some rock. They might be able to see under that part of the ledge from there. Settling into their new position, activity in that corner of the canyon was framed in a tight yellow glow.

Golden streaks sped across the faces of laughing men and onto that of a woman. Kathleen Kerry! Rios shielded his eyes with his hand to study the men more effectively. Barely visible were three shapes on the ground in blankets. He decided they were either wounded or dead. He counted six in all, standing or lying. Shadows were trying to protect the other identities but the Mexican saw the one face that was drilled into his mind. Victorio Gee!

Leering at Kathleen, Gee's face was half-painted yellow by the struggling fire. Light bounced off the brooch pinning the right-side brim to his hat, then played with the necklace of teeth and found the four pistols resting in a red sash.

Rios could make out the handle of the machete slung across the back of Gee's filthy frock coat. He shivered as the evil outlaw leader turned toward Kathleen and pulled open her already torn dress to allow the yellow light to savor her pale breasts. He laughed and said something Rios couldn't make out. For the first time, Rios saw her hands were bound behind her back; her bare feet tied together at the ankles. They had removed her shoes; her dress hung together by two buttons. Her freckled face was streaked with dried tears and her long hair was matted with mud.

Rios hissed and silently cursed. Where was his friend, Cole Kerry? Maybe he was hidden elsewhere along the gray canyon walls. What did the tracks leaving the box canyon mean? He knew well the devilry of this outlaw leader. It was Gee and his men who had destroyed his ranch and butchered his family. Deep inside Rios was a place no one could reach, could ever reach. There, his family lived in memory. And, to no one but himself, he had vowed to someday get revenge. But his early attempts to seek the Gee gang had been futile and one had landed him in jail for a few days when a small town sheriff thought Rios himself was part of the gang.

Cole Kerry was a friend. A good friend. And Rios had learned such friendship was to be honored and protected, especially between two men of the gun. In his heart, he knew Cole would try to free Rios's wife if the situation were reversed. Rios motioned for Abe to crawl back to the other side of the canyon wall where they could plan what to do next, without fear of being seen.

Even with the gaps in communication between them, a simple strategy was quickly determined. Abe would work his way down to the canyon floor from where they were while Rios would go back down and enter through the opening. The best positioning would place the halfbreed to the left of the gathered outlaws and the Mexican rancher at their front. Rios figured they would see him first and hoped they would think he was an early returning gang member.

"*Bueno* luck, *Señor* Abe," Rios said quietly and held out his hand.

Understanding the gesture, the halfbreed shook it vigorously and added a Comanche phrase that Rios didn't know, followed by his standard, "You luck. Son-of-bitch. Damn."

With that, the two riders separated. The more he thought about it as Rios skidded his way down the slope, entering as if he were part of the gang made sense. Laughing. Smoking. Talking. By the time he passed their waiting horses, he was certain of it. He paused there only to check the loads in his shoulder-holstered pistol and add a sixth cartridge to the cylinder, instead of the usual five he kept there.

Holding his rifle in one hand, he pushed aside the dead tree and entered the passage. For several steps, he thought it was going to cave in and crush him. But nothing happened and he continued, picking carefully through the rocky bottom. Horses could easily come and go through here, he observed, but escape would be faster without having to walk one through it. He wondered if there was another way in—or out. Ahead he could see a lighter gray and knew he was nearly through.

Taking a deep breath to let worry have a chance to escape, he straightened his back. He decided to light a cigarillo; it was something a Gee outlaw would do, he thought. The withdrawal of the thin black cigar from his shirt pocket reminded him of Cole. After a slight hesitation, he snapped a match into flame against his belt buckle. If he was wrong, it would bring bullets. Nothing happened. He held the flame to the cigarillo and inhaled the harsh smoke.

A forced laugh followed, then another. He slapped his chest to dramatize a casual entrance in hopes it would appear that he was used to coming and going. Darkness would make him only a silhouette with a sombrero. He had left it on, knowing several of Gee's gang wore them—or, at least, they had. A shudder followed that observation. What if none of them wore sombreros anymore? He took several steps, deliberately weaving to the right, then the left. It would appear as if he had been drinking and made him a little less of an easy target.

"Hey ze camp. Whiskey?" He blurted loudly.

No sound from the far side. Only the tiny glow of the fire.

Without appearing to do so, he was veering toward the tree stump now twenty yards or so away. It was the only protection until he reached the far side of the canyon. Wobbling, he began to sing. It was a happy song about a *señorita* who enjoyed making love. It was the only song he knew, except for a lullaby he had sung to his children.

There was movement near the fire. A voice called out, "Hickman, is that you?"

"*Si*," Rios responded and knew it was a mistake the instant the word slid from his mouth.

Orange flame exploded from three places and he ran and dove for the tree stump, landing behind it as bullets ripped at its uneven top.

He laid out flat, trying to keep himself behind the stump and hearing the sickening thumps as bullets struck the dead wood. Where was Abe? He removed his sombrero and decided he must move, even if it meant exposing himself. With a flip of his hat and his cigarillo toward the right, where he had come, he rolled to his left, over and over, away from the stump. Both drew instant gunfire as the combination of a fleeting lighter shape and sparkling heat appeared like a moving man. No shots trailed his escape.

From the left of the outlaw fire came rifle shots. A groan followed and a shadow staggered toward the fire and fell across it, sending sparks in all directions. The shadow screamed, leaped from the flames and collapsed next to it. Rios wasn't certain but didn't think two of the men in blankets were there anymore.

Rios knew Abe was doing the shooting. If he was right, there were five outlaws left. Four, if the one in the blanket was too hurt to fight. Would Victorio Gee hide behind Kathleen? Likely, he thought, and stared into the growing darkness for a target. He wouldn't fire unless he was certain. It would immediately give away his position—and there was always the possibility of hitting Cole's wife by mistake.

His patience paid off as a dark shape loomed where none should be. It flickered across the far wall and disappeared again behind a boulder, twenty yards to his right. Whichever outlaw it was had guessed where Rios might be and was trying to get an angle to determine if his hunch was correct. Without waiting, Rios rolled away again. When he stopped rolling, he was parallel to the last boulder, the one where the outlaw had gone. Slowly Rios brought his rifle into firing position. He was still twenty yards away but hoped the outlaw would show himself just enough for a good shot.

A gurgle broke the silence. It came from the direction where Abe had been. It was the sound of a man dying from a knife wound. Rios couldn't worry for the moment if it was Abe or one of their enemies; he must wait for the outlaw to step away from the rocks.

The shadow emerged. Slowly. Gradually. Linked to the boulder, yet separate. In an instant, Rios knew it was two outlaws. Just behind the first was Gee himself. Rios exhaled and steadied himself, then Gee disappeared again. Disappointed, Rios adjusted his aim and his finger squeezed slowly on the trigger.

Bam! He levered the gun again and fired a quick second shot. The remaining shadow jerked backwards and its gun fired into the air. Someone who had to be Abe was firing again from near the back wall. Rios found himself lifted by some strange energy and ran toward the bound Kathleen, firing wildly as he looked for signs of the outlaws. There were none.

"*Señorita* Kerry, et ees Rios—an' ze Abe. We come to geet you." He was running full out now, almost stumbling several times in his desire to free her. The ends of the bandana tied over his head were feathers flying behind him. He fired at a shadow and it disappeared behind a rock. Bullets cut into the night around him and he fired back, silencing everything for the moment.

Kathleen's large brown eyes were those of an animal. She cried out, choking with emotion that dared not be shared. She pulled on her wrists but the thongs holding her were so tight that she whimpered from the renewed pain.

"*Señorita*, can you walk?" Rios asked as he laid down his Winchester and drew a large knife from his belt. He tried to ignore her near-nakedness as he cut through the bindings on her hands and feet. His movements were those of a wild animal drinking from a pond, constantly looking around for enemies.

He glimpsed an unmoving Abe lying next to a boulder. Something moved next to the downed Bar K rider and Rios drew his pistol and fired, then fired again.

Kathleen tried to stand and fell into him. He held her, feeling her breasts against his silk shirt. Pushing her gently away from him, Rios glanced in both directions and saw only the groaning body beside the fire. How many outlaws remained? Only Victorio Gee? Where was the madman? Was Cole in the canyon? Where?

Making no attempt to cover herself, Kathleen took a timid step, then another. Rios holstered his pistol and retrieved his rifle, studying the camp for signs of more trouble. To his left, he saw three horses tied to a holding rope. All were saddled. He hurried to the closest one, a bay, and untied its reins.

"*Señorita* Kerry, geet on thees horse." He led the horse to her. "Ride for the other side of the canyon. You weel have to walk through ze opening. Then ride. *Vamos*. Do not wait for Rios. I must find Cole—and bring Abe."

She stared at him as if not comprehending and finally muttered, "Cole is . . . not here, Miguel. He . . . did not . . . come."

"Geet on ze horse. Now." Rios wasn't sure if he should believe her statement or not.

"They . . . took me, Miguel. They took me."

"*Si*. I am sorry, *Señorita* Kerry. Let me help you. Be queek. I must geet Abe. He ees *mucho* hurt."

Dropping his rifle, he removed his short coat and wrapped it around her, then took her hand, holding the reins with the other.

As if in a trance, she moved toward him and lifted her bare foot into the air, toward the stirrup. He guided it into place and lifted her into the saddle. Assured of her balance, he slapped the horse on the rear and it began to gallop toward the far black wall.

"Go, *Señorita*. *Vamos*. Do not wait."

Behind him was a shuffling sound. He reached for his pistol.

Two shots rattled in the canyon, sending their echos all the way to the entrance. Kathleen shivered at their sound, hesitated and then dismounted. She glanced back at the shimmering fire but could see nothing moving. Her breath was shallow, jerking its way through her body as she tugged on the reins.

At first, the horse balked as she stood staring at it, yanking on the reins. Then she remembered Cole telling her to lead a horse by turning away from it. She heard another gunshot, trailed by a groan, and it urged her on. She spun on bare feet and forced herself to walk into the shallow canyon opening.

"Thank you, God," she whispered as the bay walked after her as if it never considered doing anything else. Clearing the entrance outside the canyon, she heard running from inside the canyon crease. With renewed energy, she climbed into the saddle, more naked than not. A kick with bare feet put the horse into a gallop.

Behind her, someone climbed through the crevice. She ducked against the horse's neck, expecting bullets to seek her. Into the night she fled. Only silence followed.

Chapter 10

Only the sky's underbelly could be seen among the thickening storm clouds. Determined riders were black shapes against a graying prairie as the roundup riders neared Uvalde. Ethan's mood was a mirror of the settling gloom, drawn sadly to memories of his younger brother and the realization they may not matter anymore.

DuMonte was concentrating on keeping close to the wagon so he could hear, if and when Ethan wanted to talk. Luther was driving the wagon and keeping up a steady stream of sneezing. His own feelings were also in lockstep with his brother's. Was Cole dead? Could that really be? He had already known the emptiness of death in his life and pushed away deeper memories that wanted to join those of his younger brother.

They stopped far enough from town to avoid being seen. Gunfire in Uvalde came to them in disjointed bursts, as if everyone were celebrating the Fourth of July. As planned, DuMonte led his squad to the left with the assignment of entering the town on the far end. Sotar and his riders were to wait for Ethan's command; they would follow the wagon into town on this side. Waiting until they heard the wagon open fire before coming. A half-dozen riders dismounted, handed their horses to Loop, and climbed into the back of the wagon.

So shy he couldn't look up from his horse, Jaimie Ferrel rode over to the wagon. His appearance surprised Luther. "Howdy, Jaimie, are ya ready?"

"I-I jes' wanted to tell ya that I-I ain't . . . afeared o' dyin'." The bearded cowboy rubbed the saddlehorn with his right thumb. "Y'all's the onliest family I got."

"Thank you, Jaimie," Ethan said. "I'm proud to have you riding with us."

Without further response, Ferrel spun his horse and returned to Sotar's riders.

"DuMonte, we'll give you ten minutes before Luther starts the wagon," Ethan pronounced. "Gee's men wear black armbands. By now, they'll be dug in—if the town has done its job." He took a deep breath. "I want Victorio Gee alive."

"We're ready, Mr. Kerry," DuMonte announced.

"Good luck."

The response was thundering horses toward Uvalde.

"I'll give you the 'go', Luther," Ethan said. "Loop, where are you?"

"Ri't here, Mr. Kerry." The young rider's eyes were wide. He held the reins of seven horses and wasn't particularly happy about it.

"I'm counting on you, son, to keep these horses ready for us. We may have to chase Gee." Ethan's tone indicated the task was an important one.

"I'll have 'em ready to chase them outlaws all the way to hell, if need be, sir." Loop's mouth was a line of determination.

"John Davis?" Ethan turned his head toward where he thought the Missouri gunfighter was.

Sotar leaned forward in the saddle. He didn't like waiting.

"I know you don't like waitin'," Ethan said.

"No, sir."

"That's why you are," Ethan explained. "I think we're goin' to need somebody who can drive right down main street an' finish this thing. You're that man."

"I thank ya, sir." Sotar's Missouri drawl punctuated his response.

"Wait until you hear us open up."

"I'll be ready, Mr. Kerry."

Ethan was silent; his head down against his chest. No one spoke. After several minutes, his chin came up. "Luther, you an' me gotta get in the back, too. I want everybody down. Outta sight. Like it's a loose wagon wanderin' through town. Got it? I want us in the middle of town before we open up."

With that, Luther helped his brother climb over the buckboard and into the back. Luther laid the reins over the back of the seat, then followed awkwardly, his bowed legs having a difficult time vaulting the seat. After the two were settled among the armed riders, Luther turned toward the front.

"Gidyap ya hosses!" he yelled and slapped the reins as best he could. After stutter-steps, the wagon rumbled toward Uvalde.

"Keep your heads down, boys, until I call it," Ethan advised, pulling on the brim of his hat.

"Reckon this'll surprise those bastards real good," sputtered Joel Hawkins, the blond-haired cowboy with the thick nose, hunched down beside him.

"Yeah. Maybe." Ethan nodded, then spoke to the group huddled within the bouncing vehicle. "Don't come up shootin'. Come up lookin'. When you shoot, shoot to kill. We want to end this thing here an' now."

"Yes sir, Mr. Kerry." "You bet."

"When this is ov'r, ya think we might be able to spend some time . . . with the ladies a'fer we go back?" Hawkins's eyes studied the rifle in his lap.

"Maybe so, son. Maybe so." Ethan responded, almost gently.

Orville Miller, the sloe-eyed, long-sideburned German with a liking for fast horses and chewing tobacco, offered his bitten-off square to Hawkins as he vigorously chewed on a fresh load.

Frowning, the blond-haired cowboy said, "No, thanks. You be sure to spit that way." He pointed out the wagon.

"*Ja*. I be sure. Ya sure to be ready to shoot."

Down the middle of the main street, the wagon rolled past wind-beaten buildings on both sides. A light rain welcomed their entrance. On Ethan's command, Luther slowed the horses to a brisk walk.

"Thar's Harrison's Hotel . . . an' Hank's harness shop," Luther documented their advance. "Ain't nobody shootin' at us. Yet." He wiped his nose with his free hand. "Three dead 'uns in the street. Gotta manew-ver 'round them." He sneezed into the buckboard seat.

"Do you see Gee's bunch?" Ethan asked. Around him, men prepared themselves for the assault.

"Nope. Shootin's all ahead o' us. Hard to see through this here crack."

"Don't raise your head. Just keep goin'."

The wagon bounced past Dirard's Fancy Dry Goods store, a combined barber and dentist shop, the blacksmith and livery.

"There's the best saloon in town," someone said from the back of the wagon.

"Stay down, boys. We're getting close," Ethan advised as the sounds of gunfire increased.

"*Ja*, we be down fer sure. Ready we are to shoot."

"You can't spit now, Miller. Swallow it."

"I don't see no . . . thar! Thar they be, the black bastards!" Luther growled, then squeezed his nose with his free hand to keep from sneezing. "Thar's a bunch outside the bank . . . an' some on hosses down the street a bit."

"Get us beside the bank, Luther."

"Comin' up."

A saddled horse with no rider loped past them, seeking freedom from the noise. Gunfire from inside the bank indicated Deputy Maynard had taken Ethan's advice and placed men there. Eight outlaws were pinned down along the street, inside the hardware store next to the bank, against the buildings in the alley and behind whatever protection they could find. The town had been prepared and the initial surprise had slowed Gee's gang, but the outlaws' sheer firepower and tenacity were beginning to wear at Uvalde's collective determination. Luther advised that he now saw at least three pockets of Gee's men spread out along the main street.

"Where are we?" Ethan asked.

" 'Bout ten feet from the bank. Most o' 'em are in Jimmy's hardware store."

"Stop there."

"You got it."

"Alright, men. The first round's yours. They won't be expectin' it," Ethan said; his voice was even and steady. "Luther, after we open up, take us to the next alley an' go down it. Got it?"

"Ri't ya be . . ." He sneezed into the seat back, then pulled on the reins. "We're here, boys!"

"Let 'em have it," Ethan yelled.

Miller rose, fired and levered another round, yelling like some German warrior, "Shoot, *mein lieber Gott!* Shoot! Shoot!"

As if one man, the six riders cleared the wagon side and opened fire with their rifles. Three outlaws jerked backward and another dropped his rifle.

"Go, Luther!" Ethan yelled again.

The wagon jumped and rolled on, with the cowboys continuing to fire at the surprised outlaws. From both ends of town, new gunfire indicated DuMonte and Sotar had entered the battle as planned. Sotar was a bit early but Ethan had expected that.

"Turn 'em at the alley an' go down it," Ethan repeated his order through the sporadic fire of the wagon shooters.

In seconds, it was as if they had never been in a gunfight. The wagon rattled down the narrow alleyway toward the open land behind the buildings.

"When you get the end, Luther, swing back to the right—an' come up that alley."

Luther shook his head in appreciation. His brother had figured this out in his head. The outlaws would be too busy with the advance of DuMonte and Sotar's men in the street to see them coming from behind.

"Load your rifles, boys. Anyone hurt?"

"*Nein*." Miller leaned over the side, spat and grinned at Hawkins.

There was no further answer as Ethan told them to get ready for shooting on both sides of the wagon. In a whisper, one cowboy told another that he saw a sign in the store window that said "Manufacturers' agents for Ladd's Celebrated Sheep Dip . . . The Only Certain Cure for Scabs and Its Prevention. It Destroys Vermin and Increases the Growth of Wool. The cheapest, most safe and effective remedy known. Orders Promptly

Filled." The cowboy wondered why anybody would care about what happened to sheep.

Chuckling at his brother's strategy, Luther swung the loaded wagon around the building, straightened it briefly and turned the horses back into the next alley, the one next to the bank itself. He shifted his body to give some relief to his cramped legs as he knelt on them. After a quick wipe of his nose with his shirt sleeve, he chuckled again and hollered, "Here we go, boys."

At the head of the alley, two outlaws spun around, surprised to see the wagon coming at them. One raised his rifle at the charging horses. Bullets from Sotar lifted him into the air and slammed him to the ground. The second outlaw stared at the thundering horses coming at him and ran for the bank. Miller stood and fired at him, screaming in German. The outlaw staggered and slid across the planked sidewalk.

Riding with Sotar, a Circle J cowboy fired his Henry at the shadow of an outlaw seeking shelter behind a water barrel. His shot splintered a board in the sidewalk. As the cowboy levered a new shot into his gun, it jammed and bullets struck him in the shoulder, driving him from the saddle. He bounced in the middle of the street and laid still as the rest of Sotar's riders galloped past.

"Keep movin', Luther!" Ethan yelled as the wagon was hit with scattered bullets.

"*Ja*, we be gettin' *der* bullets!" Miller said from the back and spat over the side. He grinned at Hawkins, who was green in the face.

Behind Ethan, the sickening thump of bullets preceded a cowboy groaning and sliding against the side of the wagon; his rifle tumbled out and attempted to walk on its barrel before flopping on the ground.

A horse carrying a second dead outlaw charged along the street. Wild-eyed and snorting, it galloped in a wide circle, searching frantically for a place to run forever, before heading for the end of the commercial block. The outlaw's body flopped like a window shutter opening and closing in the wind. Stopping with a jerk, the body spun completely off and bounced on the ground with one leg remaining in the right stirrup. The frightened horse nickered and turned its head to study the unmoving man that had been on its back moments before.

In fifteen minutes, it was over. The seven remaining outlaws scrambled for their horses and rode out of town as a combination of cowboys and tired townsmen fired after them. Deputy Maynard soon joined them, seemingly oblivious to the blood on his right pantleg. The young deputy thanked every cowboy he saw for coming; he wasn't certain the town could have held on much longer.

Luther pulled the lathered horses to a stop beside McKeon's general store and noted that this was where the day had started for his family. He stood up eagerly to let his legs stretch out, such as they could. He looked around and sneezed. Twice.

Ethan also stood, uneven on his feet after sitting cramped for so long. He held out a hand to find the buckboard seat backing to steady himself.

"Good work, men. Good work. Now we've got to backtrack the bunch that got away an' find Victorio Gee."

"*Ist vehr gut*. Ve did this." Miller stood, shoved another chaw in his mouth, jumped out and strode toward a frightened group of townsmen just beginning to surface.

Luther started to speak but had to turn away to

sneeze, then he said, "We need to git a look at Langen. He's been hit, Ethan."

"Of course."

"It's too late, Mr. Kerry." A soft reply came from John Arrisen, a short, stocky cowhand who worked for the Circle J.

"Damn," Ethan muttered. He wasn't aware of the cold autumn rain nipping at the edges of town.

Beside the wagon came hoofbeats as DuMonte reined up. "Boss, I've got some of our men checking the buildings now. Might be a few held up somewhere. Might be some wounded, too."

"Good, Harold. Any sign of Victorio Gee?"

"No."

"Damn. Keep lookin'." Ethan's expression was hard and drawn. "If he's not here, we'll just have to make some of his boys talk."

DuMonte glanced at Luther, then eased his horse around and rode back to the growing crowd of men. Slowly, the wagon shooters climbed from the wagon and lifted the still body of their dead companion and laid it beside the hitching rack.

"Ah, Mr. Kerry, I think 'Pinto' . . . Sheldon Langen," Arrisen spoke softly, his rifle at his side, "he'd want to be buried somewhere out in the prairie. He didn't take much to towns."

Standing in the wagon, Ethan was silent for a moment. "I understand. He was a damn good man. We'll take him back in the wagon."

"Thank you, sir."

Chapter 11

Raindrops were singing to the world but that wasn't what was worrying Luther. Orders from Ethan were to search the town for any remaining outlaws—and, hopefully, Victorio Gee himself. Cowboys and some townsmen were moving swiftly in groups of three and four, but no one else saw the three outlaws slip into the Webster Hotel after it had already been searched.

At least, Luther didn't think so. He told Ethan where he was going and didn't wait for his brother to stop him. A shout in the direction of two Bar K men wasn't heard. With a quick glance back at his brother to make sure he was all right, Luther entered the hotel. The lobby was empty. No hotel clerk was in sight; either part of the fight, or hiding—or possibly a hostage of the outlaws.

After assuring himself the outlaws weren't on the main floor, not even the adjoining restaurant, he headed up the stairs to the second floor. Then stopped as the clank of his spurs reached his ears. They sounded like clarion bells. Squatting on the stairs, he yanked them off without trying to unbuckle the leather straps. He couldn't remember ever removing them before, except at Christmas dinner at Claire's insistence. He laid them on the fifth stair and continued his search.

Sunlight was slipping, releasing control of the building to the shadows. He told himself that he didn't mind being alone. Allowing himself the luxury of several deep breaths and a shiver as he reached the floor itself, he continued his hunt from room to room. This was the hard part. He told himself that he couldn't sneeze. Not now, for God's sake.

Outside, only the sky's pink underbelly remained of the sun, surrendering to the swift advance of the coming rain. The gathering of armed men had quickly dispersed to drier places, dragging wounded outlaws with them. Ahead, the hallway was buckled and gnarled. Sentries made of shadows surrounded the walls themselves, watching over each door.

It was a dangerous place, he thought. A place of quick death. His nose started to run and he sniffed hard to settle it. He jumped at the loudness of the snort in the quiet hallway and swung his gun back and forth to assure himself the noise hadn't alerted anyone. Satisfied, he continued.

Luther's mood was a mirror of the settling gloom, drawn sadly to memories of his lost family and the realization they didn't matter anymore. His only family now was his brothers and their families—and one brother and his wife were in terrible danger. Without thinking it, Luther was ready to die to save them.

Voices! Coming from inside the room just ahead. Then silence.

Unlit gas lamps adorned the walls but this wasn't the time to bring them to life. He raised his Winchester and slowed to a tiptoe. He pulled up alongside a door and listened. Rain delivered a soft susurration against the roof, making it hard to hear. He squinted to screen out the distraction.

A sneeze was coming. Oh, damn! He pinched his nose so hard it brought tears to his eyes. But the sneeze disappeared.

There! Two men were talking off to his left. They were in the next room, not the one he was standing next to. Or had they separated into two rooms?

He turned his head and realized they were coming out. Both were looking back down the far hallway as they cleared the door. He dared not move to see them any better. The movement might alert them. He had learned well how a man could remain unseen by his enemies when actually in plain sight. Ethan had taught him. No movement was the first requirement. Courage was the second. Their conversation was crisp in the rainy grayness.

"Hell, I'd say let's take our chances on gittin' outta here. Victorio can take out his mad on that woman he brought along."

"Let's be careful. Nobody's gonna check this hotel again. Least not for a while. Maybe we could find some other clothes. Ya know, look like we was drummers or somethin'."

"Where the hell did all them cowboys come from?"

"That was the Kerry outfit. Heard Jake say so. He knew that damn Cole Kerry from somewhar. Said he were real handy with a gun. Hell, would Victorio like to get his hands on him."

"I thought Bartlyn said he was dead."

"Victorio didn't buy Bartlyn's story. That's why he sent us to check it out."

"We should'a stayed there, instead of . . ."

"Yeah, but when Victorio wants to get somebody . . . Remember that ranger? You ever see what Victorio did after we caught him? Made me sick."

Both men laughed again. Luther heard a match strike and caught the glow protected by cupped hands.

"Did ya ever look inside that cave?"

"Yeah. Didn't see no he-cat like Bartlyn was a'jawin' about. Plenty o' signs though. Hair. Bones. No Cole Kerry. But thar were blood on them rocks—an' some red water. Could be he were thar—or maybe the cat ate 'im."

"Don't matter now. Victorio's got his woman. That's gotta be good enough."

"Ya think them Kerrys gonna try to find Victorio?"

"They came back to town, didn't they?"

"Let's see if Nance agrees with leavin'. I'd sure like to find some horses. That's too damn far to walk."

"Yeah, me too."

Luther had heard enough to know they hadn't found Cole—and had been sent to find him. He was supposedly wounded—or dead. Where? A cave? Ethan said Cole and a ranger had gone after Gee's fleeing men to keep pressure on them while the posse was formed. Victorio Gee hadn't come to town at all. Where was he waiting?

To wait longer for the third man to show himself would only risk discovery. He would be found soon enough; if Luther was lucky, the oldest Kerry would do the finding, not the outlaws.

Fury, mixed with anxiousness, was climbing alongside his other feelings as Luther stood silently against the wall, barely twenty feet from the two men. Where had Cole gone? Was he hurt?

These men would not see the sunrise. This he vowed. But he would get them to talk first. He might not be as smart as Ethan and Cole but he could damn well fight. A dark part of him had wished for such an encounter and he tightened his grip on his rifle. It had nothing to do with Cole or Kathleen. Even the joy of finding them had paled, for the moment, into something like an unfinished dream.

Luther knew his brothers wouldn't give an alarm. But he knew he would. He must.

"Boys, I've come for my brother Cole. Y'all best be tellin' me whar he be. I might be lettin' y'all live."

Spinning toward the sound of Luther's voice, the stringy-haired outlaw went for one of the pistols in his belt.

Luther opened fire. It felt good. His first two shots ripped through the stringy-haired outlaw with the shoulder-carried bandolier of bullets. The man stiffened and the striking bullets lifted him against the wall like the shadows had yanked him away. He was dead before he slumped onto the floor, dropping against the wall as if sitting. His hat popped from his head and rolled for freedom, but flopped against the ground two feet from his unmoving hand. The black band identifying him as a member of Gee's gang fluttered against his arm and was still.

Luther continued firing as fast as he could lever his Wincester. The second outlaw was long dead before the oldest Kerry brother stopped shooting. Only one remained and Luther knew where he had to be: in the room closest to him. Sliding down the wall to give himself some space from the room itself, Luther pushed new bullets into his rifle as he moved. Where the two outlaws lay, he curled and looked around. Only the dark shapes of their bodies greeted him. What would the last outlaw do? Should he attempt to go into the room?

Without giving it much thought, Luther knelt beside the closest dead outlaw. It saved his life as bullets ricocheted against the wall where he had been. He rolled until he was lying chest down in a shallow pool of blood and fired back at the outlaw crouched in the opened doorway. Blackish blood fed upon his pants. He fired, but his Winchester jammed.

Desperately, he rolled away, grabbing for his belt pistol. Orange flame from the darkness sought his life.

From the stairway behind him, two silhouettes cut against the gray. A blur of flame snapped through the smoky haze and the remaining outlaw winced. In an instant, he raised his arms, letting his rifle fall to the ground.

Sotar's familiar growl followed the gunshot. "Hands up or we'll drop you ri't here an' now." Ethan was right beside him.

Luther grinned. He should have expected Ethan to come. But right now he only wanted to take a breath. A deep one. It was good to be alive.

Slightly wounded and wary, the tall outlaw, Feril Nance, watched Luther stand from his new position. He wanted to see the man who had killed two of his companions so easily. Never mind the two behind him. Could this bowlegged wrangler be Cole Kerry? Or his ghost? If James Bartlyn was right about him being dead. Bartlyn had told most of the gang that the gunfighter was dead, shot in the back of the head. Several of Gee's men had heard of Cole Kerry and questioned the veracity of the claim. But not to Bartlyn's face. The man was not stable, always talking to some imaginary person.

Feril Nance was one of those who didn't believe the story. He'd heard about Cole whipping Sam Winslow and his bunch on the trail to Kansas. Standing there in the hallway with the rain on the roof pounding away the last of his courage, he knew Cole Kerry was alive. Even if they had found his hat and some blood. He was alive somewhere. And it sure wasn't where Bartlyn said his body would be. The three of them had covered every inch of ground, even that damn cougar cave.

"Whar's my brother?" Luther's words brought Nance back to his plight.

Nance's eyes caught the scary stare of Sotar as he was walking toward him. Quickly, Nance looked back to see Luther advance as well. Ethan stood with his hand on the stairway post, oblivious to the fact that the rain had shoved his hat brim into an odd tilt on his forehead.

"Is Victorio there?" Ethan asked.

"Naw, he ain't, Ethan," Luther answered quickly.

"Do they know where . . ."

"Don't know, Ethan. I'm a'gonna find out."

"Yeah. Course."

Both Sotar and Luther reached the surrendered Feril Nance at the same time. They were close enough to smell the rancid odor of the outlaw, layers of old sweat rekindled by new fear. Nance's face was crescent-shaped with a protruding chin that looked like a coat could be hung from it. Arching eyebrows made his face appear even longer and he towered over both of his captors.

"I asked ya a question." Luther completed his approach by jamming his rifle into Nance's back. Tension mixed with his cold made the bowlegged Kerry look older than he was.

Nance motioned with his held-up hands. "Hey, I don't know what you're talkin' about. Me an' my friends were just lookin' for someplace dry when ya opened up on us." He pushed his courage further and pointed at Luther. "Two of them . . . he killed two of them in cold blood. Innocent folk, they . . ."

"Ain't a real good time to be lyin', boy." Luther's uneven teeth glistened through the gray stillness. His nostrils widened as a wave of Nance's smell reached him. He turned his head to deflect the intense odor.

Nance jerked his arm back to the surrender position. Did he know this man? The gristled wrangler looked vaguely familiar.

"Do I know you?" Nance asked. He wanted to wipe the sweat from his face but didn't dare to. His movement might be misunderstood—or just the excuse his two hard-looking captors in front of him wanted.

"Reckon not. I don' spend much time 'round snakes," Luther growled. Sotar's entire face was a sneer.

From the stairway, Ethan yelled, "If he won't say where Cole is, kill him an' let's get outta here. I'm soaked an' tired." He cocked his head to the left. "Cole! Are you here, Cole? Cole!" He tensed and listened. No one dared to speak for a moment, not even Luther. Of course, Cole wasn't here.

Stepping closer, Luther's rifle barrel was now an inch from Nance's stomach. "Whar's Cole Kerry? Y'all be tellin' me—or yur gonna die. Real nasty-like. Ri't here an' now."

"H-hell, I-I don't know where h-he is. H-honest." Nance frowned and wiped the sweat from his cheeks, then realized what he had done and jerked his arm into its upright position. "B-Bartlyn said he was near a cave, not too far from town. Where the trail cuts along that steep ridge. Y-your Cole Kerry. S-said he was dead."

"Who be this here Bartlyn? How do he be knowin' this?"

Shrugging his shoulders nervously, Nance explained Bartlyn was posing as a Texas Ranger in town, as he usually did before a raid.

"So, this Bartlyn feller shot Cole—an' then had the

posse follow him into a trap," Sotar observed, as much to himself as to Luther and Ethan. He glanced around the dark hallway as if to reinforce his conclusion.

"What did this here . . . ranger boy . . . dun tell the posse 'bout Cole?" Luther's hard eyes sought Nance's face.

Nance swallowed and looked at his boots. Luther's stare was difficult to handle. "H-he tolt 'em that your man was a'waitin'. Up close to us."

"So wha' do ya think happened to Cole?" Luther moved his Winchester away from the man in a gesture to induce response and to stay out of range of the man's smell.

Shaking his head, Nance told them that he thought Cole had been wounded but rode away to safety. He and the two others were assigned to check it out. There were no signs of his horse around. Definitely no body, only some blood in the cave. Finally he said, "Billy found his hat. C-Cole Kerry's. He's wearin' it." Nance pointed in the direction of the dead outlaw slumped against the wall.

After studying where he motioned, Luther walked over to the stringy-haired man with the bandolier of bullets. He leaned down and picked up the hat near the still body.

"That be Cole's, alright." He held Cole's hat against his chest as if it were a sacred object.

Sotar thought the slow-witted man closed his eyes but wasn't sure; his attention was on Nance.

Muttering to himself, Luther laid the hat down where he had found it and returned.

Sotar couldn't help staring at the hat, then remembered the situation and quickly looked back at Nance. The outlaw smiled.

"He weren't where Bartlyn said his body would be, I tell ya," Nance declared. "An' it wasn't rainin' when we were there. Hell, maybe Bartlyn never even hit him. There's a he-cat around, lives in a cave close by there. Maybe . . ." He didn't finish the thought.

Luther walked back toward Sotar and put a hand on his shoulder. "Let's take him back with the rest o' them snakes." Luther paused and stared into the darkness. "We kin start lookin' for Cole an' Kathleen. I reckon this fella's gonna tell us whar to look-see."

From the stairway, Ethan yelled impatiently, "What the hell's goin' on, Luther? Where's my brother? Where's that sonvabitch Gee?"

"They's not here, Ethan. They dun found Cole's hat, though. This here boy's gonna tell whar." Luther didn't mention Nance also finding blood in a cave.

Ethan pursed his lips and closed his eyes. "If he won't, bring 'im here. I'll skin him with my knife, right here an' now."

Luther glanced at Sotar but said nothing. The look wasn't lost on Nance; he immediately promised to tell him where they should look for Cole and where Gee and the rest of the gang were waiting with Kathleen.

Nodding that the man had made a wise decision, Luther said, "Don' ya worry none, brother, this here boy's gonna tell us."

"If he lies, I'll still skin him."

"I know. I know." Sotar turned back to Nance and whispered, "Friend, he's a mite *loco,* ya know—from bein' blind." He pointed to his own eyes. "He will kill you. You'd better talk. Fast."

Shoving his rifle again into the man's side, Luther growled, "He dun mean, talk now. A'fer we let my brother have at ya with his knife."

Glancing at Ethan from the corner of his eyes, Nance volunteered that he and his friends were to meet up with Gee and the others ten miles east of here in a small canyon. It was a stopping place before heading south. Gee, Bartlyn and a few others had stayed behind initially; what remained of Gee's outlaw army would return there after being driven from town. Nance and his two friends were assigned the task of finding and bringing back Cole, dead or alive. Or, if they didn't find him, they could join in the revenge attack on the town. He started to say that he wished they had gone to the hideout, but didn't think his captors would care to hear it. At the time, hitting Uvalde again sounded like fun; maybe get another woman or two, as well as food, supplies, whiskey—and the rest of the bank's money.

He said Gee was livid about being kept from all of the other treasure he sought in Uvalde. He blamed Cole Kerry for stopping them and wanted the young gunfighter, or his body, so he could do terrible things to him. Without being asked, he said Bartlyn was actually Gee's half-brother and would be given his turn with Cole's wife while the gang was gone.

Both Luther and Sotar were silent after Nance finished.

As if to clear his mind of the black pictures the outlaw's confession had created, Sotar asked if Luther thought Kiowa would bring the wounded Cole back to the roundup or town. Luther's answer didn't surprise the Missouri gunfighter: The oldest Kerry brother thought a once-wild mustang, like Kiowa, might take him to wherever the horse thought it was safe. That was likely far away from any people. Sotar nodded agreement. Nance stared at the two, not understanding.

After the exchange, the bowlegged wrangler walked back to where Cole's hat lay. Moving too quickly, Luther slipped on the blood on the wooden floor, but managed to catch himself with his extended left arm before landing on his back. His rifle was held upright by his right. Shaking his head at his carelessness, he stood and finished his mission, moving more gingerly this time. He picked up the hat again, studied it and turned toward Ethan.

"Come on, boy," Sotar jammed his gun into Nance's stomach and the outlaw groaned and bent over.

Through the empty hallway, Ethan yelled again, "Cole! Are you here, boy? Cole? It's me, Ethan."

Only the shadows answered.

"Ethan, we'll have to start lookin' tomorry." Luther motioned for Nance to head for the stairs. "We don' wanna go chasin' after them boys in the night."

"No. No, we won't wait." Ethan dropped his hand from the staircase.

"But it's gonna be dark soon—an' it's rainin'," Luther explained as he, Sotar and Nance headed Ethan's way.

"We've been wet before—an' it's always dark for me," Ethan said. "If we've got any chance to get Gee, it's gotta be now, Luther." He cocked his head to the side. "If we wait 'til the mornin', he an' his scum will be gone."

Both Luther and Sotar knew he was right. Unstated was what would become of Kathleen if the gang escaped.

"We dun promised the boys they could enjoy the town . . . after," Luther reminded, pushing against Nance's back with his rifle.

"It ain't 'after' yet." Ethan raised his hand and made a fist. "Bring this piece o' crap with us. You'd better be tellin' it straight to my brother or you'll wish you were never born. I swear it."

"I-I ain't lyin', m-mister."

"I'll be the judge of that." Ethan turned and started down the stairs, holding the staircase with his left hand, then he stopped. "Sotar, tell the boys to get hats an' vests—anythin' that looks real different—an' those damn black scarves from those outlaws. Lookin' like Gee's men might help us get close."

Luther looked at Sotar and nodded.

"Good idea, boss." Sotar wanted to remind Ethan that Gee's men would already be there but didn't know if he dared.

As if Ethan read his mind, the rancher added, "Maybe they'll think some more of their bunch made it. Can't hurt. We only need hesitation." Ethan started down the steps again, using his hand to guide his descension. "Get an outfit for me, too."

Chapter 12

Miles from Uvalde, twelve riders passed some brown willows lining natural stone walls on their way to what they were told was Gee's closest hideout. Weary plants formed a pocket around a small pond of crystal clear water, breathing from a spring whose soul lay deep within the earth and reinforced by the rain. But the storm had finally stopped, allowing a timid sunset to have some time in the sky.

Grumbling of the tired and wet cowboys was covered by the slogging noises of a rain-soaked ground on their horses's hooves. None wanted Ethan Kerry to hear them anyway. Switching to his steady black horse, he rode in front, beside Luther and Feril Nance. The captured outlaw had decided it was smart to be cooperative.

The wagon had been sent back to camp with Loop driving it; Langen's body had been wrapped in a blanket from town. Loop was to tell the others what had happened and what they were doing next. Actually, he was sent to tell Claire. Ethan knew his wife would be worried and deserved to know what they knew. It was also a good way to get the young rider away from possible shooting after holding the horses. The young roper didn't like this assignment either, but kept his uneasiness about riding with a dead body to himself.

As directed, the riders were wearing distinctive attire taken from the outlaws, dead and alive. All wore black scarves tied around their arms, mimicking Gee's men. Luther himself was wearing a sombrero and a serape draped across his shoulders. From a distance, he looked much like a dead man known only as *Cuchillo*, Spanish for "knife," one of the few Kill Creek outlaws who didn't wear a black hat.

Cole's hat dangled from its tie-down thong from Luther's saddlehorn for luck.

Sotar had on a tooled tan-and-white leather vest that he was beginning to fancy and one of the gang's trademark black hats. The vest seemed to go with his gunbelt, or so he had decided.

Wearing a black hat taken from a dead outlaw, a black scarf around his right arm and a bullet bandolier over his shoulder, Ethan also looked very much like one of Gee's men in the weary dusk. Everything in him wanted to push the men harder and faster. In war, victory usually went to the swiftest, everything else being equal, and pursuit was as important as the initial attack. But he also knew the men with him were not soldiers. At least, not anymore. They needed time to regain their edge. Ethan may be blind but he knew men and how to lead them.

Ethan's horse kept pace beside Luther; its nose near his brother's right leg. The animal was familiar, and comfortable, with the arrangement. That let Luther pay attention to the land ahead of them, instead of worrying about Ethan.

Going directly past the posse ambush site was the

fastest route, according to Nance, the captured outlaw who was proving even more eager to provide information. Nothing had been said but he definitely hoped to escape a hanging with his help.

No one disagreed with Ethan's plan, only the need to execute it now. Battle adrenaline had long since evaporated from the men, leaving only a hole that needed filling with whiskey and hot food—and, perhaps, a whore. Ethan promised some free time would come after they found Gee and rescued Kathleen. He didn't say so, but he was counting on Rios and Abe to find his brother or run into the posse and give guidance to the outlaw camp. He hoped for the former but would accept the latter.

After securing Gee and his men, he hoped Rios and Abe would ride with him to find Cole. Luther would take Kathleen back to camp, along with anyone else who wanted to return. The recaptured bank money could go back to town with the riders who wanted to go.

What positive talk there was centered, at first, on Ethan's strategy, a new redheaded dancer several had seen in town, and whether or not they would run into Abe and Rios. Most figured the halfbreed could track anything anywhere and probably was already close to finding either Cole or the Gee hideout. They didn't know much about Rios, except he was good friends with Cole. They assumed he had been asked to go because of that relationship.

Gradually, discussion turned to Luther's lone gunfight in the hotel; few had expected the oldest Kerry to handle himself so well. Most had thought of him as the caring and slow horseman of the three Kerrys, not someone who could handle three men alone. Without his knowing it, Luther was being looked upon in a new light, with a new respect.

Neither brother spoke as they entered a long spoon of land that led to a flat-bellied ravine between tree-covered ridges. It was a perfect place for an ambush. High to their left, arching like some rocky dwelling of evil spirits, was the haunting image of Ghost Mesa, a suitable backdrop for death.

Luther nudged his horse forward; the bay's ears were alert and its nostrils flared as the sense of death reached out. Luther's kick, followed by words of encouragement, convinced the animal to continue in spite of what its intuition was advising. Ethan's horse stutter-stepped sideways, then trotted after Luther's horse. Nance followed the two brothers.

If Ethan realized the animal was frightened, he didn't show it. They rode single file for two minutes, rounded a man-high boulder shaped like a bear saluting.

Reining up, Luther looked back to see that Ethan's horse was following. He grabbed its headstall to assist in the horse's compliance.

"Jes' like I 'membered. Be lookin' like a fine place for an ambush," Luther said. "Anybody down in thar is a sitting' duck from anywhar 'round here."

Ethan straightened his back. "Would Cole ride in there?"

"Nope, don't think he would—if'n he had a choice."

"Well, what do you think happened?" Ethan's head swiveled to the left, then to the right, as if something would suddenly let him see. His face was reddening. "Dammit! This wouldn't have happened if he'd just shot Gee's horse, like I told him."

Luther stared at his brother for more but nothing came.

All of the riders knew it was coming but none were prepared for the sight as they rounded the odd-shaped boulder and entered the ravine. Gasps ran down the line of riders, followed by a prayer from DuMonte and exclamations and swearing from the rest.

After taking another deep breath, Luther explained to Ethan what they had discovered. Ethan's nose had already told him. Fourteen bloody bodies were strewn about the trail. All were naked. What remained of their clothing was a smoldering pile of ashes and cloth fragments. Every posse member had been scalped and mutilated.

Luther whistled. "Whooieee. That's one nasty sight. Looks like a Kiowa war party dun had at 'em. Sonvabitch!"

Ethan inhaled. "Reckon this is one time I'd just as soon be blind." He shook his head. "My brother wouldn't have ridden into no damn ambush. I taught him better."

"Prob'ly so, Ethan, but I'd better check. The boys could use a rest anyways," Luther's face was taut and whiter than usual. With that, he loped away from Ethan and Nance to ride around the death site.

Ethan announced that the men could dismount and relax for a few minutes, then took out a paper and put the rest back. After creasing it in the middle, he sprinkled tobacco along the fold. A few shreds bounced off his hand and he stopped pouring.

Nance watched him, fascinated at his dexterity. "A-are you really blind?"

"Yeah."

"You sure can roll a cigarette."

"Thanks," Ethan said. "I can use a skinnin' knife real good, too."

Nance swallowed. "I-I ain't lyin' to ya. I ain't. Victorio's hideout is . . . oh, maybe two miles ahead."

"It'll be dark before we get there."

"Probably so."

"Good." Ethan licked the flap and closed it with his fingers, and stuck the completed cigarette in his mouth.

Nance watched the blind rancher light the smoke and wished he dared ask for one.

Sotar rode beside Ethan and said quietly, "Ya know, boss, a knowin' man kin see a cigarette from a long piece."

"I know. Don't ya figger Gee's men would come back relaxed an' smokin'?"

"But thar's seven or so ahead of us. Don'cha figger Gee'll be a mite suspicious o' another bunch comin'? Shouldn't we be tryin' to git as close as we can before they start a'studyin' us?" Sotar tried to smile to soften his challenge to Ethan's thinking, then remembered his boss couldn't see and his smile vanished.

Nance found his courage. "I'd like a smoke."

"The hell with you," Ethan growled and blew a mouthful of smoke in the direction of the outlaw. "You'd better hope my brother's all right. His little wife, too." He set his jaw. "You're right, John Davis." Immediately, he ground out the cigarette on his saddle horn and flipped it away.

"I've never seen your brother." Nance's eyes narrowed. "I don't know what Victorio'll do . . . about the lady."

"Yes, you do."

"You can't blame me for that."

"I can blame you for anything I want."

A galloping horse cut off any further conversation as Luther returned. His words came like each was a razor blade against his mouth. "Couldn't find Cole. Nowhere." He gulped for air to counter the anxiety swelling within him. Luther tried to smile to show not finding him was a relief. His attempt was more of a curl on the right side of his mouth. His lower lip shivered at the thought that his youngest brother hadn't been found. In his soul was an ache that hadn't been there since he lost his family. He swallowed but it wouldn't go away. Silently, he wished he were smart like Ethan and Cole. And tough like them.

"Well, let's find Gee," Ethan growled.

Luther told the men to mount up and they rode out with Nance leading. Their advance was mostly in silence, with only occasional muttering rolling through the group. Dusk brought more rain. Rather than making them gripe more, the dampness made them more alert. That and the sight of the horribly mutilated corpses. Talking about capturing Victorio Gee was one thing; it was another to do it, riding through a death ravine and into his lair.

Without asking, Luther knew his brother wasn't pushing the men just to fulfill his need to find Cole and Kathleen. Ethan realized the man they sought would be alert after only a few of his men returned. The coming darkness gave them one advantage: it would make it difficult for Gee, Bartlyn or the others to tell much about the riders coming in. Their distinctive costuming should be convincing. Thanks to the shadows, they might believe some more escaped the Bar K trap in town. They might. At the least, Gee's outlaws would wait until the roundup riders were close enough to identify. That's all he could hope for. Engagement with an opportunity to win. It wasn't much of an opportunity but it was all he had.

Their trail turned eastward into prairie and the rain slipped away. They loped past occasional grazing cattle and even fewer scrawny trees. Luther was beginning to wonder if Nance was leading them on a wild goose chase. Why in the world would Gee hide out here? For that matter, where would he hide?

In the distance, Luther saw movement, or thought he did. It was difficult to tell in the drizzling dusk.

Turning in the saddle, Luther drawled, "My eyes ain't what they used to be, but sumthin' might be a'movin' ahead."

"Mine aren't either, Luther," Ethan snapped. "Are you thinkin' man or coyote? Present company makes them two mighty close."

"Could be either or nuthin'. Jes' caught . . . sumthin'. Hosses, I be a'thinkin'."

"Ask Sotar to take two riders and check it out. Hold the men here until we know," Ethan declared. "Nance, does Gee put sentries this far out?"

"No. Usually closer in."

" 'Usually' can get a man dead."

Luther shouted for Sotar, and the Missouri gunfighter immediately galloped forward, listened to Luther's concern and waved at the first two riders behind them, Ferguson and Miller, to follow him.

Orville Miller, the sloe-eyed, long-sideburned German, spat a stream of brown tobacco juice and spurred his mount into compliance. Thick-bellied Ferguson hesitated, then did the same. As they rode, Sotar explained what was going on and the three men pulled their rifles from saddle sheaths and levered them into readiness.

Luther watched them, felt a sneeze coming and turned away to let it release. He sneezed a second time and wiped his nose with his sleeve. He couldn't remember feeling so tired; the stress of the battle, his lone gunfight and the possible loss of Cole and Kathleen wore on him like a too-tight saddle on a green horse. He wanted to ask Ethan about their brother and sister-in-law and finally did. Ethan's response was terse and hurtful: he said they could be dead, hurt or unharmed, and not to ask again about something no one could possibly know.

Nance snickered and Ethan told him to shut up or they would find Gee without him.

An uneasy silence returned.

Behind them, one of the riders asked another how long it would be before they could return to town and was quickly told by another rider to be quiet.

After glancing back at the exchange, Luther straightened in his saddle, pinched his nose to keep from sneezing again and saw three mounted silhouettes returning.

"Don't look like they be findin' nothin'. They's comin' back," Luther proclaimed.

"Nance, you're sure Gee doesn't have guards out this way?" Ethan growled.

"I-I don't know. W-we never . . . that's a woman in the middle there! That's the Kerry woman." Nance pointed in the direction of the advancing riders.

"Wal, I . . . sur nuff, it be our sweet Kathleen. Hallelujah! Ain't that a won'rful sight!" Luther slapped his horse with his reins and headed out to meet them. "But whar's John Davis?"

Ethan called after him, "Find out if she knows where Cole is."

Miller and Ferguson were grim-faced and trying not to look at Kathleen as Luther pulled up in front of them.

Immediately, Miller said, "Sotar *ist* back *dort. Mit Herr* Rios. He *ist* shot *schlecht. Var* bad."

Turning in the saddle, Luther yelled back, "They dun found Miguel, too. He's been a'shot up. John Davis be wi' 'im."

With her dress wrapped around her legs and barefoot, Kathleen looked forelorn and weak. Rios's two-button jacket wasn't hiding much of her bosom. Her freckled face was drawn, almost white. Terror controlled her brown eyes and fear had stolen her engaging smile.

Luther was disappointed that she didn't seem to recognize him. Her expression was blank. They had become good friends after she came to the ranch, providing her with someone to confide in and learn from about the Kerrys.

"Kathleen, it be me, Luther." His voice was soft. "Ya be safe now, li'l missy. Nobody's gonna hurt ya no more."

She stared at him, blinked and burst into tears. "Oh, Luther . . . Luther, they . . . they . . ."

"I know'd. I be mighty sorry."

Jumping down from his horse, Luther strode to her side and lifted her down. She held him close and began to sob into his shoulder. He took off his long coat and buttoned it around her, then patted her back gently and spoke softly about how everything was going to be good again.

"M-Miguel, he saved me . . . he's been shot. Bad." A long inhalation interrupted her report. "A-Abe . . . Abe is dead. Th-they killed him."

Miller nodded at Luther and motioned for Ferguson to follow him back to their places with the others. As they rode past Ethan, the blind rancher asked him how Kathleen was and Miller responded that she was "*nein gut*" and added "*Herr* Rios *ist schlecht*. Many blood *und* bullets."

With that news, Ethan dismounted and began to walk forward on his own, holding out his hands to give him assistance. He wasn't quite headed in the right direction to reach Luther and the oldest brother was engrossed in trying to comfort Kathleen.

"The boss needs help," Ferguson gulped as he looked back. "Should I . . .?"

"*Ja*. I go." Miller had already wheeled his horse around and was headed toward the wandering Ethan.

Swinging down from the saddle alongside the rancher, Miller said, "*Herr* Kerry, I help. *Ja?*"

"Huh? You think I can't get somewhere without help? Like some little kid?" Ethan's tone was harsh.

Miller bit his lower lip. "Oooch, *ochterlieber, nein. Naucht ist* my thinking. I just be thinking you vant to see Cole's *fraulein*." He winced at his use of "see."

Ethan stopped, realizing what the gentleness of the statement meant. "Why yes, Miller, I would. Give me a hand, will you?"

"*Ja, Herr* Kerry." The German cowboy spat and admired the thickness of his expectorant.

Miller led the blind rancher to Luther and Kathleen. She was now sitting on the ground and he was kneeling beside her, asking questions. Mostly about Cole. Her responses were one-word answers or head nods.

He glanced at Ethan and Miller, who was staring straight ahead to avoid looking at her. "Li'l missy, here comes Ethan. He dun bin worried sick 'bout ya."

"I-is C-Cole with him?"

"No, li'l missy . . . he's not. We . . . ah, don' know whar he be." Luther's wrinkled face was a dried apple.

Her sob was the first answer, then she added, "C-Cole didn't . . . come for . . . me. I thought . . . he would."

Luther bowed his head and wiped his runny nose. "Li'l missy, he did come after ya. They ambushed him. We ain't found 'im yet. But we's gonna. Real soon."

"Oh no . . . is C-Cole . . . ?"

"Kathleen, I'm so glad we found you," Ethan said, standing over her, but not quite sure of what he should do or say.

Beside him, Miller whispered, "*Der fraulein ist* sitting, *Herr* Kerry. You might vant to be . . . ah, kneeling beside her. *Ja,* right *hier.*"

Ethan knelt and Miller stepped away, his gaze returning to the graying horizon. He started to spit but, in deference to the situation, swallowed the bitter juice instead.

Kathleen reached out to touch Ethan on the shoulder, then half-rose and hurled herself at him with a long sob accenting her movement. Surprised, he lost his balance when she hugged him but regained it with his extended right arm firmly on the ground.

"Oh, Ethan . . . w-where is my Cole? H-have they . . ." She didn't finish the question, pushing her wet face against his shoulder.

Ethan slowly brought his left hand to her back and returned the greeting, "Kathleen, we're mighty glad you're safe."

Her gurgled response into his shirt was a statement about being raped. Ethan caught enough of the words to feel a deep rage spark within him. Slowly, she pulled back as Luther came behind her. While the other riders kept their respectful distance, Kathleen told them about Abe and Rios freeing her and that she was certain Abe was dead. Six outlaws were in the canyon hideout, counting Gee; he had sent the others back to town to finish the attack. Both Gee and Bartlyn had raped her; Gee talked of trading her to some Comancheros down south. She and the wounded Rios had hidden when some of the outlaws returned. She didn't know how many or how long ago.

It was a terrifying tale neither brother wanted to hear but knew they had to. Her eyes were dull, her mouth barely opening as she spoke. Luther wondered if her wonderful way of talking and smiling at the same time would ever return. Ethan told her what had

happened in town and that they didn't know where Cole might be. This time she didn't cry, only listened.

"Luther, you take her to camp. Claire's there," Ethan said, but it was more of a question than an order.

"I-I want to g-go with you to find . . . my C-Cole," Kathleen muttered.

Ethan licked his chapped lower lip but said nothing.

"Ya will see 'im soon nuff, missy," Luther said with more confidence than he felt. "First, though, we'll get ya all cleaned up an' in a fresh—"

"Th-they took me, Luther. C-Cole won't ever want to even see me."

"Missy, I never seed my li'l brother so damn happy in my life as when he got yur letter . . . that ya was a'comin'."

"B-but, Luther . . . I've been . . ."

"Shhhh. Can ya ride a hoss?"

She held back a moan. "Y-yes."

"Let's go. Claire—an' Eli—and li'l Maggie—will be so glad to see ya." Luther helped her to stand.

Rubbing his chin and nose to hold back emotions he didn't want released, Ethan said, "We'll find Cole, I promise."

Luther stared at him and frowned. "Come on, let's find that hoss." He led her away with his arm around her.

He glanced skyward and noticed a timid star had sneaked into the low gray horizon. They had an hour before slap-dark. He tried to remember what kind of moon had filled the sky last night but could only recall his dream about a chicken chasing him.

To the others, Ethan gave orders to ride ahead to where Sotar was tending to Rios. To the subdued outlaw, Ethan snarled another threat and Nance apologized for what had happened to Kathleen.

After helping her into the saddle, Luther muttered what passed for a prayer, thanking God for finding Kathleen and asking that Cole be alive, too. When he glanced back at Kathleen, her eyes were shut and she, too, was praying.

"It's gonna be all ri't, missy."

She didn't respond.

"Luther, don't leave yet. Let's see what kind of shape Rios is in." Ethan's command broke up any further prayerful thoughts Luther might have considered.

"Wal, sure, Ethan," Luther replied, rubbing his itching nose. "Ya be thinkin' I should take 'im back wi' us?"

"If he can make it."

Chapter 13

Miguel del Rios lay on the ground with Sotar at his side giving him small drinks from his canteen. Even in the fading light, Luther could see Rios's shirt was heavily blooded; his left sleeve torn with bullet holes. In the Mexican's bloody right hand was a tightly gripped revolver. The other riders sat on their horses in a semicircle around them; one held the reins of the quiet *Bailarin*. Only one spur dangled from Rios's saddlehorn.

With a quick word to Kathleen riding beside him, Luther swung down and lumbered over to Sotar and Rios. He started to reach for the gun but Sotar told him to leave it alone, that Rios "needed it."

A spasm rippled through Rios's wiry frame as if a further response.

"Is he gonna . . . ?" Luther asked, looking closer.

"He's been shot up bad, but he's not leavin' us yet," Sotar replied.

Rios's eyes fluttered open. "*S-Señor* Luther, I not

geet to *Señor* Abe. I want bring hees body weeth . . . I could not. I am *mucho* sorry."

"Ya dun mighty good, Miguel. Ya dun saved our li'l missy." Luther reached over to touch Rios's shoulder.

"I've got 'im patched up best I can, Luther," Sotar said, then returned to giving Rios some water. "Easy now, Rios. Easy."

"Kin he ride?"

Rios's eyes opened again. "*Si, Señor* Kerry. I ride *Bailarin*. Where es Cole?"

Luther shook his head. "Dunno. We jes' dunno."

Rios groaned and his body spasmed again.

"Easy, Miguel. Easy." Sotar held him, both hands steadying Rio's upper arms. The Missouri gunfighter looked up at Luther. "We'd better make a travois. He's tough, but . . ."

"Ri't ya be."

After Luther and Kathleen rode away with Rios resting on a travois behind his gray horse, the riders resumed their task, even more somber than before. John Davis Sotar took Luther's position alongside Ethan. They rode without talking for another mile.

Looming ahead of them was a lone mesa. As far as Sotar knew, it had no name. It wasn't important enough, just another bump in the land. He assumed they would ride around it.

Reining in his horse, Nance pointed at the mesa. "There. He's in there."

"Whatcha mean he's in thar?" Sotar gulped. "That thar's a hill."

"Just looks like it," Nance pronounced with a certain sense of pride. "Bartlyn found it, I guess. Leastwise, he knew about it when we rode in from the border. None of us believed him at first. You know he's always going 'round talking to himself and such."

Nance explained that it wasn't really a mesa after all;

it was a small box canyon with a narrow opening that was covered over with wild brush. The gang had reinforced that appearance after they decided to use it as one of their route hideouts. Food and supplies had been placed there. Even a few horses and several cows, since the grass was reasonably good. A small spring bubbled up from the ground most of the time, giving them water. Enough for the horses anyway.

"I remember it. Luther an' I checked it out once a few years back," Ethan said. "There isn't a second way in or out, is there?"

"No. Just this," Nance said and added, "we've never stayed here long. A day or two at the most. 'Til it's safe to ride again. Or Victorio decides where we're gonna hit next. Sometimes he gets, well, black as all hell. Not even Bartlyn can talk to him. We just have to wait 'til he's ready again."

Ethan waved his arms as if trying to encompass the walls of the camp. "Weren't you worried about anyone riding to the top and looking down?"

"Not really," Nance said, his eyes following Ethan's movements. "If we thought anybody was climbing up to look, we could hide under the overhang an' pick 'em off. There's a wide rock shelf on both sides." He shook his head. "Nobody ever did that, though. Everybody thought it was a mesa."

"Makes sense. Why didn't Gee go with you back to town? Why'd he keep men with him?" Ethan asked, gentler this time.

"Dunno for sure. I know he thought it'd be easy. We've done that before, come back an' the town was a bunch o' scared rabbits. Hickman was wounded. Two others." Nance's eyes pleaded for understanding about the real reason. "Ah, I think he wanted . . . to, ah, be with the Kerry woman too." He saw Ethan grimace and changed the subject. "Victorio's moody, like I said.

Some of the boys think he's crazy. Nobody crosses him. Last week, after we hit Knippa, he put that big machete of his into Pete. Awful to see. Just cuz Pete asked how much gold we took outta their bank. That was it."

"That what you call moody?"

"Well, yeah, He's scary." Nance pushed his black hat back from his sweating forehead. "Saw him take three bullets a couple of years ago. He never slowed down or nothin'."

"Somebody can't shoot very good."

"Maybe. *Cuchillo* said he's got ghosts watchin' over him."

"Why'd you take loan papers from the bank?" Ethan shifted his weight in the saddle. "What good are they?"

"Didn't know we did," Nance said, his forehead layered in frown. "Guess some of our boys thought they was worth somethin'. Some of them ain't that bright, ya know."

Ethan was quiet for a moment, then turned in the direction where he thought Sotar was standing. "Well, John Davis, let's get it done." He motioned toward the outlaw. "Nance, you go first. John Davis, put a pistol on him. If there's trouble inside, put a bullet in his head first."

"Got it, boss," Sotar responded. "Ya think Mrs. Kerry's right . . . about them killin' Abe?"

"If she is, we'll hang 'em all. Right then an' there. This one, too."

"N-now wait! I-I've been tellin' you straight. I've led you right to 'em. But I can't promise what they'll do."

"I know. Pray they'll be surprised." Ethan tugged on the brim of his still-damp hat. "It don't matter who's fault it is. Trouble means you're dead. I'll skin you later."

"You'll have to get down and lead your horses

through." Nance decided the best approach was to continue to be helpful. "I'll go first. It's only a few feet of brush an' stuff. Pretty flat inside. As we go in, everybody should yell, 'To Victorio Gee.' That's a signal it's us comin'. Make 'em think a few more got away."

"You think Gee will believe that?" Ethan asked. "I wouldn't." He was challenging his own strategy to see how the outlaw would react.

"Well, I guess you could wait out here—for them to come out."

"We're goin' in. But wait a minute, John Davis." Ethan's voice was clear but not loud. He turned back in his saddle as he spoke.

It was times like these that made Sotar forget the rancher was blind. Returning to his mind, instead, was Ethan's natural leadership style.

"Yes sir, boss." The Missouri gunfighter's response was hushed.

"Does it look like a man could ride up the outside?"

"There's rock an' such, but yeah."

"Good. Pick out three men an' bring them to me. Handy with rifles."

Nance couldn't hear the rest of Ethan's orders whispered to Sotar. When Ethan finished, Sotar spun his horse around, returned to the group and told three riders that Ethan wanted to talk with them. They came forward, questions in their faces. Ethan briefed them quickly and the threesome disappeared around the northwestern slope of the box canyon and could be heard urging their horses up the slanted ridge.

"Where them boys off to?" Nance asked.

Ethan was happy to respond. "They're gonna get on top of the mesa and wait. An' watch." He turned in Nance's general direction; his head aimed a few feet ahead of where the outlaw was. "They're our three best marksmen, Nance. If you're right, we'll be outnumbered. They'll change that arrangement quick-like."

He motioned where the three riders went. Actually, he pointed at a scrawny tree at the base of the mesa, but Nance understood.

"I told them to shoot you first if anything goes wrong," Ethan said, his lip curling and staring straight ahead. "Gee next."

Nance shook his head, glancing at Sotar for understanding. "Been tellin' you straight."

"Good, then my boys'll only have to shoot Gee." Ethan cocked his head. "Alright, Nance, let's go." He waved his arm in the direction of where he thought the supposed opening would be. "You see where we're supposed to go, John Davis?"

"Nope. Looks pretty much like just rock an' mud an' brush to me. Have never been over this way, boss."

"Watch me," Nance pronounced, swung down from his horse and led the animal toward a wall of twisted underbrush, saplings and buffalo grass.

He pushed aside the large sapling that was simply placed there to camouflage the opening. As the tree lifted, taking with it thick wads of brush, Sotar could see a wide crevice in the land wall that a man leading his horse could pass through.

"To Victorio Gee!" Nance yelled as he led his horse through and vanished inside.

Sotar followed close behind him with his pistol in one hand and Ethan holding onto his other arm. The blind rancher held the reins of both their horses. Behind them came the string of riders, holding their rifles and trailing their reluctant horses.

"Lean hard to the left. There's a big branch in the way." Sotar turned back to warn the rancher.

Ethan complied, feeling the leaves slide along his right arm.

Sotar broke a second branch of shriveled tree that had found roots in the dark soil. He shoved a third out of the way of his trailing boss.

Ethan's horse didn't like the idea at all and balked, jamming its forefeet in the wet ground.

"Come on, dammit," Ethan said and yanked the reins, then remembered what he was supposed to do and yelled, "To Victorio Gee!" The phrase caught in his throat like bile.

Acting like a man-high tunnel, the crease in the box canyon opened into a wide expanse of flat land.

"Could put near all of Uvalde in here," Sotar said in a hoarse whisper.

"Hmmm. Do you see the overhang Nance talked about?" Ethan asked.

Nance started to answer but Sotar rode over his words to assure Ethan that the rock outcroppings were, indeed, there.

Slipping alongside Ethan and Sotar, DuMonte spoke quietly and with great respect. "Mr. Kerry, the boys . . . ah, would like you to stay here. Let us make the first advance. Please, sir."

Ethan's smile was evident even in the settling dusk. "Afraid a blind man might trip on somethin', eh?"

"No sir, that's not it at all," DuMonte countered, shifting his weight to his right leg. "The way I heard it, those Rebel boys used to ask General Lee to stay behind on an attack. He was too valuable . . . ah, to lead that way." He paused. "So are you, Mr. Kerry."

Ethan was silent, then his smile grew. "Hard to argue with a man who invokes Marse Robert. All right. I'll stay. You go with 'em, too, John Davis, but you have the boys fan out. Don't get bunched up. An' be careful. Don't figure we're gonna surprise the bastards. No matter how many show themselves, figure there's more hidin'."

"Right sir, we'll be careful."

"An' Harold?"

"Yes, Mr. Kerry?"

"Please say somethin' to the Lord 'bout my brother—an' Abe. 'Bout Rios, too." As an afterthought, he added, "An' Cole's missus."

"I already have, sir." DuMonte pulled on his right ear. "You should, too, sir."

"Maybe so."

Ethan reached out and brushed his hand against DuMonte and the black man stepped closer so that Ethan could put his hand on his shoulder. Quietly, the blind rancher told him to be alert for a marksman lying on the rock shelf itself, but to remember three Bar K men were on the ridge. He wanted the men to dismount and walk their horses beside them; it would make them less vulnerable as targets and easier to shoot quicker and more accurately if necessary. And, if anything went wrong, to shoot Nance first. The outlaw winced at the last statement but said nothing, glancing at Sotar.

DuMonte thanked Ethan and turned to direct the men. In minutes, the line of armed cowboys had disappeared into the gray with Nance in the middle, beside DuMonte. He had finally secured a cigarette, suggesting it would reinforce the appearance of the gang returning—and make him a greater target.

Alone with his own horse's reins in his hands, Ethan stood a few feet from the box canyon's narrow opening. Nightfall was sneaking onto the land, filling up the the small canyon first.

"Reminds me of the time in Tennessee, remember?" he muttered aloud. It wasn't the first time he had talked to himself, even before he was blinded he had a tendency to do so when alone. It was a way to go over details and he liked going over details.

"I sent my men, just like that, into a Yank camp." He hesitated. "Only I led them." He rubbed his neck and chin and shifted his feet. "Don't figure You've had much to do with me, God—since You took away my eyes—but I sure hope you'll be lookin' out for Cole. An' help his Kathleen through all this. I guess that's a prayer. Sort of. Hope You'll count it so." His tongue rolled across parched lips. "Be watchin' over Rios, too. I hear tell You care about Mexicans. Hope so. He's a good'un. Cole rates him high—an' that's good enough for me." He paused and concluded, "Don't know what You think about Injuns—but I got a feelin' one's headed your way. Treat him kindly, will ya? He was a good man."

Something breathed hot air against Ethan's arm and he jumped away, drawing his pistol and dropping the reins.

"What the . . . !" Then the sensation became known. "It's a cow, you blind fool. It's a cow." His observation was more of a sigh than a statement. "One of them beef Nance told us about. Just came over to say, 'Howdy, Ethan.'" He reassured himself and reached out his hand to find the animal's wet nose. "Sorry, lady, but you bumped into a blind man. Nearly got yourself shot."

After retrieving his lost reins, he resumed his wait. Silence around him was growing closer. Thicker. Night sounds that should have been there were absent. He strained to hear movement but couldn't. Only the hot breath of the cow. It was better to focus on finding Gee. Surely this would be over soon. Strangely, there was no revenge in his heart, only an ache to find his brother.

What if Cole is dead? His mind told him Abe was and he accepted it. He had sent men to their death during the war; they died doing their duties. He knew it was so with Langen and now Abe, even before hearing for certain. Rios might not survive the ride to camp either.

Cole was another matter. Even when he left to continue on the outlaw trail, mostly out of anger at Ethan for settling down, Ethan thought he would return one day. He never believed Cole had been killed in the Nations, or Kansas, or wherever, when the stories came filtering in. He wouldn't believe it now.

"Cole, you stay with me, brother. You hear me?" He spoke aloud and a soft echo brought an encore to his words.

"Did I tell the boys that I wanted Gee alive?" Ethan asked himself, forcing his mind to change the subject. "Damn. I want him alive—so we can ask him about Cole. Him or that fake ranger. That's the one who should know." He stepped away from the cow, hoping it would move on. "I hope DuMonte thinks of that. Should I yell to him?" He didn't wait for his own answer and yelled, "I want Gee alive."

The canyon repeated his message in a wave of overlapping sounds. And it was quiet again. Ethan checked the cinch on his horse. It was fine. Time was long in passing.

Horse's hooves finally broke the silence of his forced wait and he straightened; his hand near his holstered pistol.

Swinging down from the saddle, DuMonte couldn't speak at first. Words couldn't find support within him. A gasp finally broke the wall of hurt. "Abe's . . . Abe's dead. Th-they cut him up. Took some of his teeth even." He slapped the reins in his hand against his worn chaps to push away the retching that wanted out.

Ethan's face became stone. Only his eyelids moved, blinking three times. He turned his head slightly to the right, as if listening to an unheard voice.

"Nobody's there except four dead men. Victorio Gee . . . an' that fake ranger fella . . . an' the rest . . . gone." DuMonte continued, squeezing his eyes to hold back tears that were beginning to take the place of vomiting.

Ethan's head jerked back into place. He looked like someone had hit him in the stomach. He turned and stared up at the canyon's jagged wall as if he could see.

DuMonte looked down at his boots and chaps, both carrying streaks of mud and water. His breathing was uneven but gradually calming.

Finally Ethan asked, "What's Nance got to say about it?"

"I read it that he was surprised as we were," DuMonte said, wringing his hands together. "He even called out to Victorio as we came across the field. Friendly like." The black cowboy motioned in the far end of the small canyon.

"Could've been a prearranged signal that something was wrong," Ethan advised, his voice low and almost soft.

"Thought of that but we combed the area. Boys are double-checking now, Mr. Kerry." DuMonte hitched his gunbelt; he was suddenly aware of how heavy it had become. He was a cowman, not a gunfighter. Yet, most of all, he was Bar K.

"How come nobody saw tracks comin' out?" Ethan's forehead rolled into a frown. He felt for the cigarette makings in his shirt pocket, then changed his mind and let his hand drop to his side.

"Rain would've washed 'em away. An' we weren't looking for 'em either. Didn't even see any of Mrs. Kerry—or Miguel—getting away," DuMonte didn't want to say the last but did. "Abe's our best tracker. Was. I can find beef as good as any, I suppose. Not men."

Again Ethan was quiet. Finally, he spoke slowly and evenly. Whatever concern was lodged in his throat had disappeared. He was once again the leader.

"Alright, Harold, we'll go back to the roundup. Get it started again. All right?" Ethan's hands came up and eased apart like he was a minister blessing the congregation. "We can't track 'em at night—not after this rain."

"You promised the boys they could have a time in town, Mr. Kerry," DuMonte reminded him.

"Oh yeah."

"I don't want to go to town," DuMonte added.

Ethan reached again for the cigarette sack and papers. This time he continued the task, rolling a smoke as he talked. He told DuMonte to let anyone who wanted to go back to Uvalde do so, but to be back in camp by tomorrow night. DuMonte reported the men wanted to bury Abe before they left; they had already started.

"Luther—an' Sotar, if he's willin'—we'll start lookin' for Cole's trail come sunrise." Ethan paused and lit the cigarette just made, then stared unseeing toward the western slope of the interlocking ridges. "His wife said he wasn't with Gee's bunch. Nance'll tell us where he was supposed to be."

Wiping his mouth with his hand to rid the uncertainty, DuMonte said he wanted to go with the Kerrys to find Cole. Ethan acknowledged the request but said he needed DuMonte's leadership at the roundup.

"Where do you want me to go after that? We should be finished in a week or so, if the rain doesn't slow us." DuMonte's eyes showed the compliment of Ethan's trust in his judgement.

"Put the boys out at the line cabins like we planned. You come to the ranch with the regulars," Ethan advised. "We'll return soon after."

"Then we're just going to let them get away?" DuMonte asked.

"They're long gone now, Harold—not likely to come back," Ethan's tone was reassuring. "Tell the boys they did well. That was a damn army we took on and we stung 'em good." He rubbed his chin and asked, "I don't suppose they left our money behind."

DuMonte answered that they hadn't found any and decided it was the best he was going to get from Ethan before more questions came. He remounted, wheeled his horse and kicked it into a lope toward the other end of the canyon.

Smoke encircled Ethan's face, crossing in front of his unseeing eyes. "If Victorio killed my brother . . ." He withdrew the cigarette. "*Ablakela Sunkawakan,*" Ethan said the halfbreed's full Sioux name. "Calm Horse, wasn't it? He was a long way from calm." He chuckled. "Could rattle off swear words better'n any man in the outfit." He replaced the cigarette in his mouth and inhaled. "Cole liked him a lot. I used to get mad at him for puttin' Abe 'way out front of the herd." Ethan took a deep breath. "Reckon Cole knew what he was doin'. We'd have never made it through that God-awful prairie fire without Abe's warnin'."

He moved to his horse, running his hands along its chest to give him a sense of location. "Well, let's get at the buryin'. Rain'll be comin' back soon enough." He placed a boot in the stirrup without hesitation and continued talking to himself, this time about Cole's friendship with Miguel del Rios. A frown followed the observation and the blind rancher was silent again.

He lifted himself into the saddle. "We gotta look for signs of Kiowa. That big red's got a stride like no other horse around here." He tossed the cigarette and countered his own assessment. "Rain took all that away, Ethan."

Nudging the horse forward, he decided his hearing would direct him toward his men. He pulled the brim of his hat lower in anticipation of the coming sadness, remembered the captured outlaw Feril Nance and asked himself, "What about Nance?" His jaw rose and his mouth became a thin streak of meanness. "We're gonna get him to tell us where Gee's gone—then we're gonna hang him."

Chapter 14

Dull streaks of morning surrounded a quiet world of scattered trees and large boulders as Cole Kerry awoke with a start. He was slumped over in his saddle. His bloody right arm and leg were both stiff and straight. His left eye was closed from caked blood that had drained from the wound in his forehead. His body was stiff and screaming its pain.

The rain had stopped in the night, covering the land with a coat of white mist. His bleary right eye told him he was in the high range. The ragged forest encircled him, except for the twenty-foot circle of open space where he stood. A few feet away was a hardy stream. Small patches of fog decorated the ground.

It was a strange looking place with no signs of wildlife, no trails, no sounds. A ghostlike place, he thought. He couldn't remember ever having been here before. The entire opening was ringed with odd-shaped stones, many quite large. He had heard of such places. They were supposedly built by Indians long vanished from the earth. No one knew what these places were used for, or who these ancient people were. A few books mentioned their previous existence. Cole's friend Miguel del Rios had talked of them and said they were among the most ancient of people.

The morning air was as cold as the night's had been. His breath came in short, white bursts. He was feverish and trembling but he was alive. In spite of the cold, and his damp clothes, he was sweating. But he was alive! Vestiges of a dream of being led by someone he didn't know were still with him. His first thoughts were of Kathleen. Then of his brothers. They seemed so far away. They might be. He had no idea where he was. Their great ranch seemed like a dream world.

His mind finally reminded him of the ambush by the ranger. The man must've been an advance scout for Gee and not a real lawman. The new concern ripped through his throbbing head and he gasped. What if Gee's men were waiting for the posse and ambushed them? He was a failure. He'd had one task and couldn't accomplish it: Save his own wife. How would he face Ethan and tell him? His mind swirled away from the thought and settled into throbbing pain and he could think no more.

His fine sorrel was nearing exhaustion. An all-night climb into the roughest country had taken its toll; the bullet wound was crusted over on his right flank and the lead was probably in there. A zigzag pattern of cuts and scrapes on the horse's front legs indicated he had gone through heavy brush and rock. Horse and rider were standing motionless and had been so for several minutes. Kiowa's well-shaped head was down, unmoving. His powerful body was heaving for air that wouldn't enter fast enough. He, too, was sweating in spite of the cold.

A soft whinny stirred Cole and he realized that his great horse needed relief from his burden. He reached out to pat Kiowa's head and was reminded of his binding. Slowly he unwrapped the wet thong from his hands and thighs. Deep white lines marked the back of his hands; even his good hand had no feeling in it. He dismounted as carefully as possible, but collapsed as soon as his legs felt the pressure of the ground. He lay with his knees curled into his stomach, squeezing his eyes shut to turn back the horrible waves of pain triggered by the movement. Convulsions whipped through his body.

Hours later, he awoke again. Standing took minutes as he tried to keep the weight off his injured leg. Shakily, he took the reins of his horse and limped toward the stream. The animal was breathing normally. At the bank, he studied the water while the horse drank. A three-foot waterfall, ten yards away, ushered the water into the stream where he stood. At this point, the water paused to catch its breath from the downward tumble before resuming its descent down the rest of the mountain fifty yards away. Far below Cole's resting place, the stream cascaded into a short, wide fall of spewing water.

Hallucination jerked Cole back to the roundup camp. He tried to call out to Luther and Ethan talking on the other side of the stream. Cole waved his good arm to attract their attention, stumbled and fell near the bank. The noise of his horse slurping brought him back to consciousness. After drinking from the cold stream himself, he bathed his head wound and decided to do the same with the others. Removing his bloody shirt was a combination of jerking, pulling and struggling.

A bullet remained lodged in his arm but he couldn't do anything about removing it. He sat on the bank and eased his stiffened limb into the water, pouring its coolness over the throbbing destruction with his left hand. Another bullet had passed through the flesh and hadn't broken any bone that he could tell. He let the cold water work its way into the black holes in his arm and the red slices across his shoulder. Swirling water removed shirt fragments. Finally he stood and led the horse back to an area where the grazing looked good. His balance could barely handle the walking.

With what strength he had nearly gone, Cole dragged the saddle from his tired horse, letting the tack fall in a heap on the ground. His canteen banged off his right arm. He stopped for a few minutes to let the pain pass. He attempted to rub down the horse with handfuls of dry leaves he could reach without moving too far. The wound on his red horse's flank was cleaned by pouring canteen water over it and rubbing away the crusty blood with his left hand. He could not tell if a bullet remained or not. Probably. But he couldn't trust his left hand with a knife to remove it.

With the point of his blade, he cleaned the sorrel's hooves of the mud and rock from the night's ride. The effort drained his remaining stamina and he could do no more. But it was the least comfort he could provide for the animal that had saved his life, if only for another day. A stomach convulsion brought up nothing; there was nothing left inside him. Kiowa was left to graze without any restriction. There was no reason for the great sorrel to die here, too. A tied horse would eventually have no chance.

His linen duster, tied to the saddle when it had been too warm to wear, would have to do as his bedroll; his sleeping gear was in the chuck wagon. He dragged the garment toward a likely looking resting place. His saddlebags would serve as a pillow. Four times he fell to the ground like some giant invisible hand had shoved him down. Nausea immediately followed each tumble.

A fire would feel wonderful, but he wasn't strong

enough to gather wood. The best he could manage was to put together a bed underneath some large rock outcroppings. They would shield him from the worst of the weather. Through bleary eyes, he studied the ring of rock surrounding him. Even to his barely conscious mind, the place was eerily quiet, like he was the only person to have entered it in many years. A picture of the ranch and Kathleen waiting on the porch floated into his vision. He stopped his already feeble progress and tried to get her attention as she walked around the far edge of the stone circle.

"Kathleen! Kathleen!" he yelled out. His voice was screechy and thin. The words slid away and bounced off of the trees above him. Then he saw young Eli talking with his mother, Claire Kerry. They had joined Kathleen on the porch.

"Eli! Eli, over here! It's me, Uncle Cole. Claire? Kathleen?"

Shaking uncontrollably, Cole Kerry collapsed into sleep under his makeshift bed. The midday sun was warming, even on the mesa. From a careful distance, a wild steer observed the horse and man. Satisfied, it moved to the stream to drink, lifting his head every few seconds to check on them. Then the rangy steer moved on, ready for the solitude of some well-hidden shelter.

Like black magic, a wolf wandered into sight, a sleek coat darker than most. One instant nothing was near Cole's body, and the next the animal was beside him. Snorting and stomping, Kiowa blasted toward the wolf. Surprised by the attack, the dark animal vanished. Yellow eyes surveyed the two from the safety of the thick forest. Concerned, the horse nuzzled the sleeping Cole before returning to his grazing, glancing up occasionally to assure himself that the wolf had truly left.

By mid-afternoon, a chickadee had taken up a permanent residence in a sapling close to Cole. The small bird seemed out of place in such a wild country. On the other side of the sapling was the crumbling skull of a longhorn, half buried in the loam created by the stream.

Only the tiny voice of the chickadee and grass chomping of Cole's horse broke into this hilltop cathedral, encircled by stands of live oak, cottonwood and pine. The forest closed in, absorbing sound and transforming light into a gray coat. Overhead, an eagle floated across the treeline in search of food, once diving so swiftly no eye could follow. A hungry bobcat could not force the evacuation of the chickadee, creating only its brief spurt to higher safety, followed by a severe scolding.

By nightfall, Cole had not stirred from his slumber, in spite of the growing cold. Frost settled lightly about him. His horse moved to a position next to his unmoving body. The sorrel was uneasy about the encroaching night sounds breaking into the silence of the forest opening. There was comfort in the closeness of Cole. From somewhere within the ring of pines, the unblinking eyes of a mountain lion brought a stomp of Kiowa's front hooves and a vicious tossing of his red head. Cole slept on without notice.

Cole awoke on the morning of the second day since the ambush, the first time he had been fully conscious. Disoriented, he had no idea of where he was, or what day it was. He was weak, dizzy when he tried to stand—and very hungry. His wounded leg wouldn't move and it was impossible to move his right arm. But warmer winds had pushed the cold away, at least for the moment. His body wasn't as chilled as it had been either but he wondered where his shirt had gone.

After a few minutes of clouded contemplation, of

trying to get his mind focused, Cole finally hobbled again to the stream, dragging his wounded leg. It was the only decision his mind would settle on. At the water, he saw his crumpled shirt, little more than a red rag, and was puzzled at how it got there. With his one working hand, he poured water once more over his wounds. He laid the side of his head down into the stream to let the cooling water heal the reddened mark. His pants were more blood-covered than not.

For the first time since Kiowa brought him to the forbidden mesa, he noticed his gunbelt and the two Colts there. Both ivory handles were crusted with mud. He tried to clean them with his right hand but it wouldn't cooperate and he lost interest.

Someone told him to strip and cleanse his whole body, to let the medicine of the mesa water flow in and around him completely. He looked up and it was a Comanche warrior dressed in ancient garb. Cole didn't know him but nodded agreement at the suggestion. He looked back and the warrior was gone.

Taking off his pants, gunbelt and boots was not an easy task in his weakened condition. But it did make sense to bathe. His pants were in better shape than his shirt, except for the long tear on the left trouser. He stared at the crumpled gunbelt at his feet, trying to remember if the weapons were loaded or not, then not caring enough to check them. Instead, he slid his naked frame into the cold water and his nerves screamed from the shock. Pinkish swirls seeped from his wounds. With a burst of bravado, he submerged himself. First came invigoration and then a sudden draining of his limited energy. He emerged, gasing for breath and lunging for the bank. Darkness returned to his eyes, he swallowed repeatedly to hold back the urge to vomit.

He could not remember getting out of the stream.

His knees and forearms were muddy and bloody. He washed them clean again, as best he could, without reentering. His body began to shake uncontrollably and he struggled to retain his balance. He turned to run away from the awful trembling and fell as his leg gave way. When he awoke, it was colder; his naked body was blue. He struggled to his saddlebags. From his limited gear came a rolled-up shirt and long johns, which he put on. His old pants and long coat added another layer of clothing. But nothing could make him warm.

Dizziness forced him to sit. From this position, he emptied the saddlebags to see what food might be there. A trailing concern came immediately: What happened to the posse coming behind him? *Did they make it? Why is my forehead sweating when the rest of my body is so cold? How could I have let Bartlyn do this to me? Did Victorio Gee get away with Kathleen? Oh God, what will they do to her? I have to find her. I have to . . .*

He shook his head and the pain drove away any more thought, of any kind. After a few minutes, he returned to his saddlebag search. He lifted two boxes of bullets from Ethan, more leather strips and three buttons. Remembering his gunbelt, he stared at the stream. The guns lay near the bank; he couldn't recall how they got there. He frowned and returned to his task.

Foodwise, his gear yielded a small piece of licorice, three potatoes, some jerky, a little sack of coffee, a handful of corn dodgers, more nuts and a sack of dried beans. He also found a cigar, a tin cup, a closed pouch of tinder and matches. Food from trail scavenging—an old habit from his outlaw days—included a handful of Indian potato roots, cattails for food and medicine and a few bee plants to eat.

In the pile were other things of little value now, like cleaning materials for his weapons and a flattened roll of heavy string with a fish hook embedded in the ball. A blackened tin plate lay across the string. A small flask of whiskey caught his eye and he drank deeply of it. He choked on the fiery liquid and almost vomited.

For several minutes, he sat looking at his things without comprehending what was there. Cole's drunken father put a hand on his shoulder to show the boy something in their house. His mother smiled at him from the kitchen; she was making stew in a huge kettle. All three windows were open and sunlight made the small house bright. His father disappeared before Cole could turn to see what he wanted to show him. His mother held her hand to her mouth to hold back tears. Kathleen appeared to comfort her; then came his two brothers.

Cole didn't remember falling asleep on top of his food and gear. He tried to stand but things under him kept moving. His left leg wouldn't hold him. Then Kathleen helped him to his feet again. Before he could say thanks, she left to talk with two strange-looking Indians at the far end of the opening in the forest. They were standing beside a tepee with unknown markings decorating its sides. His father and mother joined them. Cole yelled at the group to come and help him, but they didn't hear his plea.

The hallucinations spun him into sleep again.

Chapter 15

As hungry as he was, food was quite hard to keep down after his nap. He drank from the canteen, refilled from the stream. This time he remembered to bring back his gunbelt, but it was heavy. So heavy. Taking an hour to prepare, a small fire warmed his torn body; so did the coffee that followed.

He curled up to rest for a few minutes before going for more firewood. But Cole Kerry sank again into an exhausted sleep. The sun of the new day was caring but he didn't know of it.

Over the next several hours, curious animals paused by his camp. A wildcat and three deer were among the larger visitors. Ground squirrels and agitated jays scurried in and out. Once, his red horse walked over to nudge Cole's body with his nose and get assurance of the man's continued breathing. Another day passed with Cole repeating this ritual of eating a little, bathing and returning to sleep. His saddlebag food supply was soon gone. During one of his lucid times, his mind clicked onto ideas for survival beyond his body healing.

Should I try to ride? Could I get Kiowa to head for the roundup—to get men? Or town? I have to go after Gee's gang; they have my Kathleen. Oh God, Kathleen!

His mind told him that he wouldn't make it five feet, even if Kiowa could carry him. Thoughts about being tracked wandered into his consciousness. A good tracker would be able to follow him over the mountain rocks where his horse went. Unless the rain took all evidence of his passage away. Maybe Gee was convinced he was dead, or didn't have the time to check. Maybe the posse caught up with them. There wasn't anything he could do about it anyway. If they came, he would die.

Maybe that was best; he couldn't help Kathleen.

Cole Kerry wept.

The cold had probably saved his life, stopping the blood and keeping out infection. Cole placed what moss he could find on his wounds twice, or was it three times? *Where am I? How long have I been here? Does anyone miss me at the roundup? Or town? Or do they think I'm dead, too? Was it all over? Kathleen . . . Kathleen . . . Will I ever see her again?*

Somewhere in the middle of this discussion with himself, Cole fell asleep again. But he had managed to fix a splint of straight sticks, tied with thong, for his right arm. There was some feeling there for the first time since he was shot. Mostly sharp twinges that would pierce his courage and ignite pain in his shoulder, leg and head. Before going to sleep, he managed to gather some more small kindling for his fire.

In the late afternoon, a young mountain lion dragged a deer carcass beside the south edge of the circle of rocks. His yellow teeth tore at his prize to get at the choice vital parts the big cat loved. But he was troubled by the man smell and ate nervously, looking up every few seconds to reconvince himself that all was well. From a scrawny pine branch, the chickadee called the panther names and told him to leave. After devouring the deer's organs and filling his stomach, the beast left the bloody remains and ambled away from this troubling area. He would return when hungry.

Rain began to fall again. A cold hard rain that wanted to turn into sleet but couldn't quite do it. Cole wasn't aware of either the panther or the chilling weather. His deep dreams were disjointed, violent and dark. He lay with a Colt gripped in his left hand; his soaked gunbelt curled like a rattlesnake several feet away. Once in his sleep, he screamed out Kathleen's name into the pounding rain.

After the storm, three riders zigzagged up Ghost Mesa where Cole lay, without knowing what existed far above them. One rider trailed the others, staring unseeing into the land. Their horses were frightened by the unstable rock shelf underfoot, making the men uneasy about the treacherous footing they were encountering. Finally they decided to turn back to the safety of the lower valley. There was no way anyone wounded and on foot could have climbed this high, they agreed. No one could climb the rock ledge above them. No one. Not even Cole Kerry.

Hunger awoke him but his small food supply was long ago used up. In desperation, Cole dragged himself around the area, holding the revolver for reassurance, while looking for vegation that might provide some nourishment. Anything. His stomach was knotted in hunger. He drank long and hard from his canteen, while he rested on one of the circled rocks. Depressed, he was too weak and too dizzy to go on with this. He had found nothing. Although he wouldn't put it down, he was too weak to hold a gun steady long enough even if there was game to shoot at. Besides, the noise might bring enemies.

Then he saw it. Just twenty feet from the outside of the rock circle were the remains of the deer left the day before. He half-limped, half-crawled to the nauseous mass of blood and bones. A coyote ran off with a bloody piece in its teeth as he approached. It was too cold for insects, but Cole knew they wouldn't hurt him anyway. He'd seen Comanches eat them when there was nothing else. He could swallow handfuls now. For the first time in days, he laid down the Colt.

An hour later, he was eating cooked meat from his small fire. A pine tree had also yielded a dozen small cones. After they were charred in his fire, the roasted cone seeds were quite tasty. His hunger satisfied, he decided to take a nap, holding the gun again for its weighty companionship. It was a nap that turned into a deathlike sleep for the rest of the day and through the night. Cole awoke to a rising sun. His vision was blurred worse than usual. The massive pain in his lower back seemed like it was new. He reached around to his lower back, above his left hip, and felt the heavy presence of a bullet. He would have to get to a doctor to have it removed—and soon, before infection set in.

But he couldn't ride; he couldn't even see. And hunger was visiting again. His enthusiastic trip to the deer remains brought a new despair: only a few bones were left. He shut his eyes to squeeze away the depression.

A proud deer showed itself inside the rock circle, then headed toward the stream as if he didn't exist. This was his chance! He tried to level his Colt, disregarding his concern about the sound carrying to enemy ears. Hunger had shoved that worry aside. Many times he had used this revolver with his left hand, but never when so weak. He needed the stopping power of a rifle. There could only be one shot. But his Winchester was in its saddle sheath and his saddle was twenty feet away. If he moved the deer would surely run. His Colt would have to do.

He laid the gun on his lap and opened the cylinder hatch to see if the gun contained live cartridges. Three. Were they wet from earlier rains? The question popped into his mind. It didn't matter. His gunbelt was too far away—and it had been in the rain as well.

The young deer drank unworried. Cole propped the gun atop a flat rock and squinted along the barrel. Forced concentration produced unwanted trembling. He took a deep breath to make this body relax and cocked the weapon. He tried to ignore the increasing pain in his back. He would have to go for the animal's head, even though it was a lower percentage hit, especially with his uneven sight and coordination. A body shot might not put the deer down and there was no way he could follow if it ran away wounded.

Crack! The deer stood at attention, and then bolted into the forest. Cole had missed. Completely. Disgusted at his poor performance, he limped over to the stream and drank. In the water's clear reflection, he saw a dying man. His string and hook, with a little venison bait, was untouched in the water's quiet corner near the far bank. In an undisturbed pocket of the stream, on the far side of the bank, were what appeared to be arrowhead plants, lying like lily pads upon the surface.

If that's what they were, small tubers on the roots would be there, too, under the mud. He had eaten them before; the taste was much like a roasted potato. But he would risk drowning if he went after them in his condition. The icy cold stream would be bad enough, but one had to feel around in the water—

usually with one's feet—to find the tubers, and then dig them out. He wouldn't be able to do all of that and keep his balance. Maybe after he slept, he would feel better. Maybe. Maybe they weren't arrowhead roots at all. Maybe they were just lily pads: Maybe he was a dead man. Maybe he would never see Kathleen again. Or his brothers.

He tried to think. Ethan had told him that thinking was the only thing that separated man from other animals. The ability to think through a problem, instead of simply reacting. At least he was safe from his enemies here. For now. If he could only build up a food supply somehow, he could make it, get strong enough to ride away from this weird mesa. To home. Oh, how sweet that word. To home—and Kathleen.

Maybe after he slept, he would be able to think more clearly. He would find Gee's trail and follow him to the end of the world to get his wife back. She would be all right, he assured himself. They would keep her as something to trade if the posse got close. No, they would rape her. The awful thought ripped through him and he retched. Nothing came up but the blackness of his mind.

The bullet in his back would produce infection soon though. There was no solution. All of the Indian medicines he could remember, if he truly was remembering them, took things he didn't have. Like eggs, frogs, ground buffalo bones, sage, Indian turnips and vinegar. None of this mattered; he was too weak to use them.

He was weak and feverish. Heat was building throughout his body. He laid down beside the steam and rested. There was no way this time. He whispered his death song to the chickadee watching in the sapling. Above him a dead moon now hung. Tiny wings fluttered and the little bird flew away. His head was throbbing again. Throbbing like the roar of a great train.

Pain shot across his right arm and he grabbed for the feeling. The sudden motion brought nausea. He vomited. Dizzy. So dizzy. He was going to die. It would be peaceful. So easy. So easy.

Over there, see? Kathleen was smiling at him. Now she was coming toward him. Oh, how he missed her. *Oh, she had to be alright. Please, God, please . . .* But she disappeared in the growing mist. Something had changed about the clearing that held him safe. Knots of thick fog took birth from the silent ground beneath the encircling rocks. The guardian trees held the ground clouds close. He tried to peer into their hazy whiteness but could see nothing.

Wait! A flicker of light! Then another, and another, and another! Tiny campfires. Hundreds of them in a big circle, all around him! All around the opening where he lay dying. Hundreds of fires! Thousands! The campfires looked endless. As far as he could see into the haze, there were twinkles of campfire light. He closed his eyes and rubbed them. This couldn't be. No one even knew where he was. He was surrounded by an army! A huge army! How could they have sneaked up on him so quietly?

Jerkily, he raised the pistol in his left hand but his thumb wasn't strong enough to pull back the hammer. Yet no shots came at him. Only silence whispered at his ears. He took a deep breath and studied the campfires more closely. Around each one were gathered warriors and women. Indians. Their dress was strange to him. Ancient. Why were they here?

He stood unevenly, intending to go to them and ask what they were doing here. Ten campfires back, he caught a glimpse of Kathleen; she was talking with others, a man and a woman he did not know. She had not seen him yet. She would be happy to see him. The gold glow from the small fire made her face clear to him for an instant, then disappeared into the bleak mist. He began to limp toward where she had been.

"Kathleen! Kathleen!" he called out but his voice had no sound.

As he passed, campfires hissed into icy ashes, food vanished from hands and pouches—and some of the ancient tribesmen froze in their blankets. Cole frantically looked for Kathleen but could not see her anywhere.

At the edge of the forest, Luther was headed his way. With him was Ethan. He tried to yell at them but his mind told him that they, too, were a dream. A deep sigh of resignation took its toll and he collapsed.

Just as Luther sneezed.

Chapter 16

Glittering jewels of morning sunlight adorned the circle of dark green trees. Above, streaks of violet, rose, gray and gold signaled the morning's completed arrival. A dawn fog passed through the open cathedral-like area where Cole lay. The thick mist was reminiscent of the eternal snows on the peaks far to the north from whence it came. A cool breeze danced across the hair on Cole's forehead.

His eyes fluttered open and he saw Luther leaning over him. A few feet away was Ethan, awkwardly staring toward the dawn. Cole sighed and went back to sleep, this time without dreams.

In minutes, he reawoke. His wounds were cleaned and dressed. He struggled with the dead sleep in his head, battling to determine where he was and why. Blankets warmed him as he lay on a soft bed of dry leaves. Instinctively his fingers felt for his Colt. Yes, it was still there in his left hand. The muscles in his right arm tingled; then he moved it without pain!

Smells of a sweet medicine he didn't recognize came

gradually to Cole's attention. He was awake and without the dismay or hunger that had torn at him for over a week. The anger of his wounds was gone. A warmth spread through him like a peaceful song. A small fire crackled rhythmic assurance a few feet away. Next to him was a killed badger; his slit belly emptied of its entrails revealing only congealed blood. Cole could see his face in the reflection from the blood's hard surface. The reflected image looked like he was an old man.

Smiling like a jack-o'-lantern, Luther explained it was a good sign. Cole would live a long time. It was a ritual learned from some Comanches he had befriended years before. Cole didn't really care about the symbolism or where his brother had heard it, only that his brothers had found him.

Cole's wounds were tightly bound with soft white bandages. As he became more aware, he realized the bullet was gone from his back. There was more of that strange smell of medicine underneath the wrappings. Not sweet like cedar or maple syrup; more like the smell of just-cut hay. Near his head was a tin bowl of crushed willow bark, a special medicine to be taken for pain.

On a spit over the fire was a roasting grouse. The delightful smell danced over the odors of the kindling. A filled sack was a few feet away. He couldn't see what was in it. Around him were four slender sticks stuck into the ground. Tied to each stick were buckskin bags of tobacco and willow bark, offerings to the ancients who lived on Ghost Mesa, according to Luther, who immediately professed not to believe in ghosts, but didn't think it would hurt anything either.

Finally, Cole saw his hat not far from his head. He sat up, looked around and saw Luther, comprending for the first time. "A-a-are you real, Luther?"

"Yeah, li'l brother. I is. Yur a hard man to find, ya

know. Took a piece to track ya here. Had me a hunch ol' Kiowa would dun brung ya up here." Luther sniffed and wiped his nose. "We dun come this way onc't, but not near far nuff." He sniffed again and looked away. "Sorta holy place, I reckon. Kinda weird, though. Some boys dun think this here be a way into the spirit world. Don't reckon so now. Only ghosts come an' visit, maybe."

"Well, I don't know about that. Kiowa brought me here. I-I don't even know where I am."

Luther smiled again and Cole looked around at his other brother.

"How is that boy doin'?" Ethan's growl was warm.

"He's damn weak—but I reckon he's gonna make it."

"I-I thought I was going to die, Luther."

"Yep, ya was surefire a'dreamin' when we dun got here. Ya was a'yellin' 'bout Injuns in a circle." Luther stood and stepped back to get Ethan.

"A dream . . . it seemed so real. I would swear they were here. Right around here. It seems so . . . even now."

Luther led Ethan toward the resting Cole. Awkwardly, Ethan grunted, "Well, damn you, Cole. You had us searching all over for you. Set the roundup back at least a week. Got Sotar lookin' for you over east o' here."

Luther pushed on Ethan's arm. "We're mighty glad to find ya, boy. It t'were Rios's idee fer us'n to look fer ya up here. I weren't so sur any hoss could be climbin' ov'r all that thar rock an' stuff. No wounded man fer sur."

"That's Kiowa for you," Cole said weakly.

"Yeah, that's what I kept a'figgerin'."

"Well, I'm damn glad that red hoss's good for somethin'—besides kickin'." Ethan snorted and folded his arms.

"Where's Kathleen? Is she at the ranch?"

Cole's questions slapped the two brothers across their faces and left the mark that was mostly anguish. Luther looked at Ethan, who shook his head.

Ethan spoke. "She's at the ranch, Cole. She's alright. Really worried about you, though. Not sure you're worth all that worryin'."

Luther's expression was one of surprise. His eyes widened and he stepped back involuntarily, nearly stumbling as his spurs crossed.

Cole rolled over and hid his face. Only a low moan indicated he was alive, then his entire body began to shake. Uncontrollably. "Thank you, thank you, thank you." He began to mutter as the joy of hearing his Kathleen was safe rambled through him.

Quietly, Ethan whispered to Luther that he thought it was best not to tell their brother about her condition yet. Or Miguel del Rios. Or Abe, for that matter.

Luther nodded. He was unsure but he understood his brother's thinking and agreed for the time being. Earlier, Ethan thought it was a foolish waste of time to climb Ghost Mesa but Luther thought a wild mustang, like Kiowa, would take his hurt rider into the wilds to protect him. They had turned back once when both Kerrys thought no one could have climbed higher but their lack of success elsewhere brought them back a second time, at Luther's insistence.

The oldest Kerry brother knelt beside Cole to add his own words of comfort about Kathleen. Grimacing, Luther tried to push the images of the distraught Kathleen out of his mind as he touched Cole's shoulder, then lightly touched his youngest brother's face with a rough hand. A flash of yesterday hit his thinking and he saw his own wife and children dead. Oh so dead. He shivered and fell backward. Ethan realized what had happened but didn't know why and stepped awkwardly toward him.

"Be fine, Ethan. Be fine." Luther quickly forced himself upright and returned to caring for Cole.

A day later, the three brothers rode together down the steep incline, headed for the Bar K ranch. Cole lay in a travois, made by Luther, and was dragged behind Luther's horse. The slow-minded wrangler brought the saddled Kiowa along with a rope halter. At first, the fiery horse didn't want to go along but Luther talked and comforted the animal into a state of reluctant understanding.

The descent was difficult and slow, with Luther doing his best to keep the travois from thundering against the rocks. He hadn't objected much to Ethan's insistence on riding his black down the roughest part; Luther was too busy with the travois and Kiowa. He noticed, however, that Ethan was unusually quiet, but figured his brother was concentrating.

Sotar joined them not far from the base of Ghost Mesa. Ethan briefed him quietly about what they told Cole concerning his wife. Sotar's expression didn't change at the news. His mouth a line of rock, he nodded agreement at the approach.

They stopped early in the afternoon and made camp. Cole's clenched teeth were the only indication that he was fighting the weakness in him. He wanted to go on. He wanted to see Kathleen. His ramblings became incoherent as he talked about her, then with her, then with people even Ethan and Luther didn't know.

While Sotar gathered wood for a fire, Luther began to prepare a simple meal. A collection of sticks, and one sizeable branch, was soon a small fire. Under a lone tree, Ethan sat beside Cole lying on the travois and told him what had happened. The Bar K men returning and surprising Gee's gang in town; the posse's ambush; Bartlyn posing as a ranger and shooting him; and the discovery of Gee's hidden canyon with the aid of a captured outlaw. He didn't tell about Abe dying or a badly wounded Rios being at the ranch, or Kathleen's physical and mental state when they found her.

During his recitation, Cole didn't speak; his eyes were closed. Ethan reached over and ran his hand along Cole's right arm until he found his hand and squeezed it. Cole's response was feeble but definite.

Finally, talk turned to cattle. Ethan thought it would help to get his brother's mind on something else. The roundup was going well, although it was behind schedule. One of their cows had given birth to twins. Both little he-bulls. Ethan wished they had been heifers.

"We're short o' cash money." Ethan spit out the assessment. "Reckon most folks 'round here are. Especially since Gee got part of the bank's money." He paused and added, "But I had Claire keep gold in a box at the ranch. So we're better'n most."

Cole opened one eye. "Yeah, I know. Claire told me."

Ethan appeared surprised. "She did? Well, don't that beat all. I never do know what that woman's gonna do."

"She's a good one. You were lucky."

Ethan's mouth curled upward in the right corner. "Lucky? Now, I don't think many folks would use that word for me."

"You know what I meant." Cole choked at the next words. "Y-you h-have the w-woman . . . you love."

Ethan swallowed. "Ah, Eli . . . an' Maggie'll be real glad to see their uncle."

Cole didn't answer.

"So will Kathleen."

Again, no response. Emotion surged through Cole's body like a river suddenly released from its dam. His legs shivered, then his entire body. His eyes watered. He was light-headed. He tried to speak, turned his head away and vomited into the grass.

"Cole, are you all right?" Ethan asked as he heard him vomit again.

"E-Ethan, d-did they . . . ?" Cole struggled to answer, spitting away residue.

It was Ethan's turn to be silent and Cole knew.

"Sh-she's everything . . . to m-me. I-I c-couldn't live without her. I-I w-wouldn't." Cole's voice was hoarse as his head returned to its prone position. "W-when she needed me most . . . I couldn't help her. My God, they . . . they raped her! OhmyGod!" Cole became more agitated as he spoke. "I should'a . . ." His words were gone, continuing only in his head.

Wiping his forehead to remove the sweat beads that had surfaced there, Ethan finally spoke. "You did everything you could, Cole. So did we. It just wasn't to be. But she's safe now, Cole. She's home." He reached into his pocket for his cigarette makings.

"W-will she be . . . ?"

Ethan dropped the tobacco pouch and papers fluttered onto his lap. "I . . . ah . . . Claire says so. Ah, you need to rest, Cole. You were . . . damn near dead when we found you."

"I-I wish I were."

Recovering the pouch and one of his cigarette papers, Ethan fumbled to roll a cigarette while he thought of what to say. "I didn't want to lose my eyes either, Cole. But that's the way it is. You wouldn't let me give up—an' I won't let you. I won't let Kathleen either. You just have to go on. Together."

"I-I know. B-but it hurts. It hurts so much."

Ethan didn't know what to say and concentrated on completing his cigarette. "Would you like a smoke?"

"N-no. I just want to sleep—an' then to go see K-Kathleen."

Parched chaps creaking like they needed soaping

brought a welcomed distraction for Ethan. It was Luther sauntering over to his brothers while Sotar worked a skillet of fried pork and a pot of coffee. Dried mud flittered from Luther's batwing chaps as he stopped in front of Cole's travois.

"Wal, how's our li'l brother a'doin'?" Luther's question was a pushed attempt to sound upbeat.

Ethan withdrew the cigarette from his mouth to reply but Cole answered first with his eyes closed. "Luther, I know what they did to her."

Cole looked like a man being torn apart from the inside out.

Choking on the smoke in his mouth, Ethan sputtered, "I, ah, I told him . . . ah, that Claire said she'd be just fine . . . after awhile. Needs time, that's all. Just time."

Luther's wrinkled face was contorted as his slow-moving mind sought something to say, something that made sense, something that would comfort Cole. All that clashed inside his head with the desire to spit out how badly hurt she was. He stared at his grieving, badly wounded brother and wanted to hold him.

"Ethan's right. Time be what ya need, what y'all need." He finally proclaimed, satisfied that it sounded right.

Partly to change subjects, and partly to follow through on something that was in his mind, Ethan asked Sotar to ride to Rios's ranch and determine the status of things there. None of them thought he had any family close by but they weren't certain.

"We'll need to notify his kin about his being hurt an' all," Ethan concluded. "Maybe you can find some papers or somethin' that will help us know where they are."

"I don't reckon he had no kin," Luther drawled. "Gee dun kilt 'em all. That's what he said."

"Could be, but we owe it to him to find out—and to take care of his place until we do—or he's able again," Ethan said. "I want riders assigned to watchin' his herd, too."

Chapter 17

Late autumn winds were ganging up on the land and biting at the edges of the Bar K ranch as the Kerry brothers approached. Two young cottonwoods within the ranch yard itself were swaying slightly, telling themselves it would not get worse. By the time they reached the Bar K ranch gate, Cole Kerry was sleeping, in spite of the bouncing travois.

"Wal, we're home, boys," Luther said as they rode under the entrance poles with the longhorn skull branded with a Bar K hanging from the center pole.

"Luther, is the skull tilted . . . again?" Ethan asked.

Luther glanced upward. "Nope, she's straight as can be." He looked again to make certain it was hanging as Ethan thought it should be. The oldest Kerrry decided to check it again in the morning. Just to be sure.

A lonely midday sun lay across the array of well-built ranch buildings, sheds and corrals and caressed the large log-and-adobe ranch house with its added-on room for Cole and Kathleen. Dirt was solidly packed around the foundation timbers of all the main structures with trenches dug to lead water away. Mute testimony to the kind of detail Ethan was known for before he was blinded, and insisted upon, after.

Only one of the three corrals was empty. The smallest had a single brown horse with a hurt leg, which stamped its feet and whistled from inside the farthest corral, defying anyone to enter. In the largest pen were a dozen horses in various stages of breaking. Most of their working horses were still at the roundup; some had already been turned out for the winter. Bailarin was alone in the middle pen.

Off to their left was the bunkhouse, also seemingly empty. Or should have been. When they passed the small stone house for storing butter and milk, a lone cowhand in the bunkhouse came out to greet them and get a look at the injured Cole Kerry. Ferguson was limping badly, the result of being kicked by a green horse yesterday. DuMonte and the rest of the hands were finishing the roundup and making sure the line cabins were well stocked with supplies for winter.

"Ferguson, what'er you doin' here?" Luther was only mildly surprised.

The heavyset cowboy pointed at his leg. "Got kicked. Real bad. That new line-back dun Loop was ridin'."

"Sorry to hear that, Ferguson," Ethan said, continuing to ride past the stone-lined well a few feet from the bunkhouse.

"Let's rein up here," Luther said, giving his brother a clue to their location. " 'Side the well. Sur is a purty sight."

"How's the roundup goin', Ferguson?" Ethan asked as he stopped his horse.

"Near finished, I think. I got hit yesterday. Jus' couldn't ride no more."

"When the doc comes to look at Cole an' Rios, we'll have 'im check that leg," Ethan said.

"Thanks, boss. It sure does hurt."

Luther chuckled to himself and glanced back at his unconscious brother. To himself, he mused how silly the cowhand appeared with Cole lying on a travois, Rios lying gunshot in the house and Ferguson crying about a hurt leg. It was like the heavyset man, though, and Luther never had the heart to suggest to Ethan, or Cole, that they should let him go.

From the ranch house burst Eli in full speed before he left the porch. A step behind him was Blue. And two steps behind both came Maggie. Walking ladylike, but just as eager as her older brother. She held a handful of pale-orange and light-yellow leaves as if it were the finest bouquet. It wasn't really in anticipation of her father's return; she had been playing with them and discussing their autumn colors with her mother.

"Dad! Uncle Luther! You're home!" Eli shouted as he drew closer. He skidded to a stop as he realized the significance of the travois behind Luther's horse. "I-is Uncle Cole . . . ?"

Luther's grin was forced. "Yur Uncle Cole's got sum holes in 'im whar thar shouldn't be sum—but he's gonna be fine come spring."

Eli's face lit up and he continued running toward them, glancing back as Claire entered the porch. She dabbed at worried eyes, decorated by well-earned crow's feet, with her apron and hurried down the front steps.

"Howdy, Claire, we dun brought the oth'r half o' the Cole Kerrys to home," Luther hollered.

She pushed a smile onto her face. A glimpse at Cole reinforced the rightness of her decision to let Kathleen continue sleeping. Both she and Rios—and now

Cole—needed rest and time. Their physical wounds would heal; she wasn't certain, however, about Kathleen's emotional wounds. It was enough for now that Cole was home. Alive. It had to be.

"It's so good to have you home," she responded and continued walking toward Ethan. Eli stood beside him, waiting. Blue saw something move beside the bunkhouse and took off to investigate.

The tall rancher slowly dismounted, making certain his left boot cleared the stirrup before releasing his grip on the horse's mane. As soon as Ethan touched the ground, Eli squeezed his father's leg.

"How are you doin', son?" Ethan said, roughing up Eli's hair and reaching out to find the horse's loose reins.

"Jes' fine, Dad. I was worried though." Eli blinked to keep a tear from giving him away.

"So was I, Eli," Ethan said. "Hand me the reins, will ya, son? I don't like leavin' a horse free, even if it will ground-tie."

"The new colt, the red one like Kiowa, is doin' real fine," Eli blurted, handing him the reins. "I call him 'Little Kiowa.'"

"That's a good name. We'll have to get your Uncle Luther helpin' you make him a fit horse."

Excited, Eli patted the horse's nose and added, "Mr. DuMonte let us bring that calf home. He's in the barn. Maggie an' me, we've been feedin' him real good. I think he likes us."

Claire came beside them and told Eli to go and greet his Uncle Luther. As soon as the boy left, she wrapped her arms around Ethan.

"Oh, I missed you so," she whispered in his ear.

Ethan was the only man she had ever loved and that fire burned ever more deeply. After the initial shock of his being blinded, she had worked hard to make him feel—and be—the man he had been.

His impish grin was laced with embarrassment at the attention but he hugged her back, pulling the horse along as he did. "Not as much as I did you, lady. I can see you in my mind—all the time. But I can't hold you, like now."

She whispered something sweet and released him. "Maggie brought you an autumn bouquet." She motioned for Maggie to come forward.

Immediately, the little girl bounced toward them, held out the squeezed leaves and asked her father why they had changed color.

Switching the reins to his left fist, Ethan's right hand reached out and found her small face, pushing away a stray lock of hair. His frown was a result of trying to think of a way to explain why the trees changed their appearance at this time of year. How could he describe the process without using the word "dying"? She was puzzled by his attempted, wandering explanations.

With one arm draped around Eli, and the other holding the reins of his horse and Kiowa's lead rope, Luther bellowed his own answer: "By golly, it be magic, that's what it be."

Maggie's eyes sparkled. "Who does the magic?"

Luther looked first at Claire, then to a slowly grinning Ethan, and back again to Claire, who was biting her lower lip to keep from laughing. He crossed his arms, still holding his horse's reins and Kiowa's lead rope.

"Don't look at me," Ethan said and began to laugh, in spite of himself.

Luther's chuckle followed. He leaned over and made an exaggerated attempt to study the leaves gripped in her little hands and finally asked, "What do yur mothur say 'bout them leaves changin' color?"

"Mommy says God does it—an' he brings the pretty snow—an' the springtime, an' the birds, an' our red colt."

"Well, that dun settles 'er, I reckon."

Smiling, Claire went over to Luther and gave him a quick hug, which Luther returned heartily before stepping back.

"How's your cold, Luther?" she asked, patting his shoulder.

"Oh, she's a'gittin' better. Reckon I keep soundin' like a night train though." He looked toward the house. "How's the li'l missy Kathleen a'doin'?"

Her frown was a preview of her response. "Not real good. She's been battered—but she's one tough woman."

"She sleepin'?"

"Yes. Been fitful spells, calling out for Cole, then screaming 'No, no, no.' Her mind's going through a rough time." Claire's bosom rose and fell as she explained; her frown stayed.

"Cole knows. Ethan dun tolt 'im."

Claire lowered her eyes and brushed an invisible speck from her apron. When she looked up, her gaze was steady.

"He should know," she said. "Cole would hate us if we didn't tell him."

"Maybe so, Claire. Maybe so." Luther rubbed his nose, aware of its need to sneeze again, asked about Rios's condition and then if she had heard about Abe being killed.

She shook her head to indicate that she knew about Abe, but the madness of that happening, combined with the horrible state of Kathleen and Cole, was too much. A quarter turn to the right became a full twist which left her staring at their house with tears flowing down her hardy face. Choking away the emotion, she said Rios was showing signs of healing; she didn't think he had any bullets in him. He was staying in Eli's bed and Eli was sleeping on the sofa.

Eli moved to the travois and stood next to the unmoving Cole. By this time, Blue had given up on the mouse or whatever had showed itself briefly, and returned. The big dog ambled alongside the sleeping Cole and nuzzled his side. Slowly, Eli reached out and touched his uncle's cheek. Maggie was a few steps behind, now eager to be near Cole, too.

"Eli touched Uncle Cole!" Maggie tattled.

"I did not." Eli jerked his hand back and gave her a mean stare.

Claire turned back but Luther had already joined the two children.

"Ya know, I reckon yur uncle be likin' ya two to be touchin' him. Real sweet-like." Luther reached over and laid his hand on Cole's forehead. It was hot. Too hot.

With Luther's encouragement, both children stepped closer to Cole; Eli patted his cheek; Maggie patted his mouth. Blue followed and licked his cheek.

Cole stirred and opened his eyes. "O-oh, my little friends. Are w-we home?" He shut his eyes again and was asleep.

"Ferguson, I gonna be needin' yur strong back to he'p me carry this boy into the house," Luther called out.

The fat-bellied Ferguson pointed at his injured leg and Luther shook his head negatively. "Need yur arms an' back—not yur leg." He grinned and glanced at Ethan and Claire talking quietly.

Luther asked Eli to take their horses, including Kiowa, to the corral and begin unsaddling them, after they lifted Cole from the travois. As he spoke, Luther loosened the bindings that held his injured brother in place. The boy wanted to join in the moving of Cole to the house but reluctantly took the reins and lead rope. He led them away as the two men carried Cole inside. Blue joined him, wagging his long tail. Ethan followed, holding Maggie's little hand with his left hand and grasping Claire's arm with his right.

Inside the warm house, a happy fire in the large blackened-stone fireplace reached out to push away cool edges of the day that had followed them. The house was an intriguing mixture of masculine and feminine, of thick-armed chairs, a large bookshelf filled with books and knickknacks, a powerful-looking rolltop desk and an ornately carved cabinet that had come from the Texas Panhandle, both once belonging to Claire's parents. Here and there were delicate touches of lace and the wonderful aroma of hot coffee from the kitchen. Freshly cleaned oil lamps allowed shadows to play in the dark corners.

Above the desk were framed tintypes of their parents, taken on their separate wedding days, watching the room with youthful sternness. Alongside were photographs of Luther and his late wife, Ethan and Claire on their wedding day, and the newest addition, Cole and Kathleen on theirs.

Shadows jumped to protect the sleeping Kathleen as they entered the room carrying Cole. The bedroom was barely a year old, constructed especially for the newlyweds. It offered some privacy because Claire had insisted on doors throughout the house, even when they couldn't afford them. They decided to make a pallet of folded blankets for Cole on the floor a few feet from the bed and Claire was already preparing it. Ethan had suggested putting Cole in his father's bed and making the older man sleep on the couch for a few months. He completed his idea by saying Clancey was drunk so much of the time he wouldn't know the difference. Luther volunteered his own bed and bedroom, saying he could use one of the empty beds in the bunkhouse. Claire thought having Cole and Kathleen together, even this way, would be helpful to both—and so it was.

A solitary candle tried its best to give the room some brightness but its yellow glow barely reached Kathleen's pale and bruised face and made her auburn hair glisten. Luther couldn't help remembering Cole telling him about her—on their first trail drive together—saying her hair was as beautiful a color as Kiowa's flowing mane and tail. That seemed so long ago right now. And the room itself was more like a funeral parlor than the place where two people had laughed and made love only a few days ago.

"Claire, he's dun got a mean fever . . . gotten worst as we came . . ." A terrible sadness swept through Luther with no warning and he couldn't speak.

Once more, he saw his wife and three children dying of the fevers right in front of his eyes. He spun and ran from the room, gasping for breath. Ferguson staggered backwards trying to get out of his way. His hurt leg buckled slightly and he slammed against the wall.

Claire saw Luther's escape and knew what it was. Luther had joined the Bar K only a few years ago, after his family died and he let his small ranch go back to the bank. She never forgot the awful ache in his rawhide face when he rode in. Or his uncontrollable weeping as Ethan held him. Just to remove any tempation, Ethan had hidden all the guns after Luther finally collapsed.

She said something quietly to Ethan and went after Luther.

Eli tugged on his father's elbow. "Dad, Blue's lying down . . . beside Uncle Cole. Should I move him?"

Smiling thinly, Ethan acknowledged it was fine to leave the dog where it was, that Cole was the only person, besides Eli, that the animal took to. He took a deep breath and suggested they leave.

Eli led his father to the children's bedroom where Rios lay in his bed. Ethan asked his son how the Mexican rancher was doing but Eli wasn't sure. Ethan nodded and turned away, asking his son to lead him.

In the main room, Clancey had encountered Claire comforting Luther. The elder Kerry was well in his liquor, as usual, and knew nothing of what had happened to Cole or Kathleen.

"By the saints of me homeland . . . *hiccup* . . . be the fine roundup over this wee day? All the young lions . . . *hiccup* . . . be back," the old man declared, weaving slightly.

Claire turned to speak but Luther beat her to the response. "Nearly so, papa. Nearly so."

"Good it be then." Clancey nodded and returned to the small den where the ranch's paperwork was done and the whiskey was kept.

"Thank ya, Claire. I be doin' jes' fine now," Luther patted Claire on the arm. "Jes' got 'tacked by sum ghosts, I reckon."

"It's been a hard time for all of us."

"Yeah, so's it be. I reckon I'll go check on Kiowa," Luther said. "He be carryin' a bullet wound, too."

Claire agreed and left for the kitchen to get a wet compress for Cole's head.

Chapter 18

Night was a welcome relief from the day, although it brought a chilling edge to the land. Around the heavy planked table, the Kerrys gathered for supper, along with Ferguson, who had been invited to join them. Clancey had finally dropped off into a drunken stupor, snoring loudly from a stuffed chair in the den.

The men had washed up and left their chaps and belt guns on the front porch, along with their hats and gloves. However, their spurs remained on their boots; Christmas day was the only time Claire insisted on their removal.

A liver roast was greeted with high enthusiasm. Sliced onions, carrots, stewed tomatoes, mixed with flour and cut-up potatoes, were topped with slices of bacon. A fresh loaf of rye bread was a special treat; Eli had helped his mother make butter earlier in the day so there was plenty to apply to thick slices.

Claire's prized white stoneware plates and heavy iron utensils, shipped from a Kansas City firm, made the setting seem grand and less sad. A blue glass vase with a tiny crack trickling down its side was right in the center of the table. Maggie's fistful of dead leaves was its display.

As usual, Luther had difficulty getting his bowed legs to cooperate with the chair and sat with his legs spread widely apart. After grace was said, with Luther mumbling and Ethan and Ferguson sitting silently, they began to pass the food and eat. No one spoke as was the custom among western men in particular. Claire left frequently to check on Cole and Kathleen. Ferguson heaped his plate twice and Luther watched him eat with amazement.

"Maybe all that food will he'p your leg," Luther mused.

With his mouth full, Ferguson nodded and slathered butter on another slice of bread.

Over coffee, talk resumed. Ethan wanted to discuss the roundup status and winter projects that needed doing—anything except what happened with the Gee gang.

Eli was disappointed because he wanted to hear more about the outlaws being killed and captured. He had only heard smatterings of what had occurred but decided he could ask his uncle Luther later for all the details.

Claire brought a fresh apple pie and announced it was the last of the fresh fruit until next spring. She had been canning for several days, preparing stored food for the family and the hands who stayed at the ranch for winter. The trail cook would assist her when he returned from the fall gathering.

Tomorrow Ethan wanted to ride out to the roundup camp and determine progress. Of course, that meant Luther would have to go with him. Ethan was worried they hadn't scoured parts of the range for cattle. He liked to assign outriders with particular knowledge of each piece of land. He felt it got the most out of every man's skills and know-how. Luther reminded him DuMonte knew the men as well as they did. Ethan agreed but wanted firsthand assurance anyway.

When the chuck wagon was finished for the fall, the blind rancher wanted to check out the vehicle thoroughly, especially its wheels, and assess the condition of its permanent contents and equipment for the spring trail drive. Winter was always a time of repair. But only Ethan would worry about such details at this time. Luther had learned it didn't help to counter these ideas. It also meant most of the work repairing harness and cleaning tools in the tool box would be his concern. Unless he could convince some of the hands to help.

"Someone needs to go to town and ask Dr. Hawkinson to come and check on our patients," Claire interjected. She was the only one who could challenge Ethan's plans without annoying him.

Ethan was silent a moment. "Yeah, guess so. We'll go do that—an' then head for the roundup."

"Cole's fever is bad, Ethan. Very bad." She frowned.

"What 'bout the li'l missy?" Luther asked, taking another bite of pie, and watched Ferguson gulp down a second piece in two swallows.

She looked at Eli and Maggie, saw they were finished with their dessert and told them to excuse themselves. She insisted Eli work on his ciphering assignment before doing anything else. Tomorrow was a school day, she reminded.

After the children left, Claire returned to Luther's question. "She will heal on the outside. On the inside . . . I don't know."

Luther's face seemed redder than usual; Ferguson looked totally embarrassed and quickly excused himself, saying he needed to stretch his injured leg.

"Ya be able to ride wi' us tomorry?" Luther asked.

Ferguson couldn't read the intent of the question. "Don't know if I can, Luther. She's mighty stiff an' sore."

"Wal, I reckon ya kin start work on that busted harness in the barn then."

The fat cowboy wanted to object but couldn't think of anything that made sense and just nodded, excused himself and limped to the door. He paused there and turned back. "I do thank you for the fine meal, Mrs. Kerry. Ain't had nothin' so good to eat in a long spell. Reminded me of my maw's cookin'."

"Well, thank you, Mr. Ferguson. I'm glad you enjoyed it," Claire said, smiling warmly. "I hope your leg is better soon."

"Yes, ma'am." He opened and closed the door behind him.

Ethan rolled a cigarette and asked about Rios. Reassured of his recovery over time, he returned the conversation to ranching. "Not sure what we should do about Rios's spread, Luther." Then he proceeded to tell in detail what he thought they should do. "I guess we'd better check with the bank when we're in town. Tell Picklewhite what happened. I think Rios owned that land from the pond south . . ."

"Yeah, to them sand ridges on the west," Luther added. "T'were a part o' Winslow's."

"Sure. We'll watch his herd. Does he have anybody ridin' for him?"

"No, jes' him."

"Might be a loan on his place," Ethan said. "Likely, I reckon. I don't want the bank takin' it. Wonder if Gee's boys got his papers with that other stuff they took."

Luther wanted to remind him that they owned a part of the bank but didn't.

"Doesn't he have family that could take it over until

he's ready?" Claire asked, rose and filled the mugs with steaming black coffee.

Ethan explained what had happened to Rios's family and both Claire and Luther were lost in their own memories. Then he began rambling about needing to talk with the bank president and getting him to get the stolen loans duplicated; Picklewhite would have a record to work from. That should be done before anything else.

After a few moments of awkward silence, Luther asked Claire if she should check on Cole's wounds. He described what they had done on Ghost Mesa when they took the bullet from his back. She bit her lower lip and sought distraction in sipping her coffee.

After the conversation wound down, Luther left to check on their father and Ethan reluctantly agreed to help with drying the dishes while Claire washed. It gave them time to talk. Usually that meant Claire talking. But this time Ethan had much to share about the counterattack in town; finding Kathleen, Cole and Rios; and discovering the fate of Abe, which she had learned initially from DuMonte.

Later, Claire went to the bedroom where Kathleen and Cole lay, checked on the young woman and tried to get her to eat some hot broth made from the liver roast. Blue watched her enter, slowly stood and wandered out of the room, grumbling.

Kathleen took two sips and refused more. "C-Claire . . . is that my C-Cole?" She motioned toward the floor.

"Yes, my dear, they brought him in today." She paused. "He's hurt. Bad, I think, but he'll make it. Luther thinks so."

Kathleen pushed herself up on her elbows with Claire rushing to prop her move with a pillow. The battered young woman stared at the sleeping Cole for a long time. Tears soon found their way from her eyes down her freckled cheeks.

Claire turned to leave but Kathleen asked her to stay. "P-please don't go, Claire. D-does h-he know?"

"He knows you're safe—an' that made him very happy."

"I meant, does he know I've been raped?"

Biting the inside of her cheek, Claire hesitated. Should she tell her that he did? Should she let Kathleen learn that from him? How would she take it if she did tell her?

"H-he does, doesn't he?" Kathleen guessed from Claire's indecision.

"Yes, yes, he does, Kathleen," Claire responded. "An' all he cared about was knowing you were safe. The rest didn't matter."

"Didn't matter? Didn't matter? How can that not matter?" Kathleen glared at Claire.

"Those weren't his words, Kathleen, those were mine." Claire crossed her arms, unsure of how to handle the situation. "He got shot up bad trying to get to you. Ethan and Kerry found him nearly dead up on Ghost Mesa . . . and the first thing he said . . . was to ask about you."

"I-I'm sorry, Claire. I didn't mean . . ."

"No need to apologize." Claire reached out and laid her hand gently on Kathleen's shoulder. "I'm going to check his wounds and clean them. Ethan and Luther are riding for the doctor tomorrow."

"May I help?"

"Of course, you may."

Kathleen hesitated, then pushed away the covers. "How is Miguel?"

"He's mending. It'll be awhile. But there's no lead in him."

"H-he saved me, Claire."

"I know. Miguel's a very brave man—an' a good friend."

Kathleen studied the blanket at her waist. "Claire? First, I thought Cole hadn't tried to come after me. I thought he . . . didn't care . . . that much." She began to cry.

"The only way they could stop him was with a lot of bullets, Kathleen. He was more dead than alive when Ethan and Luther found him."

The teary Kathleen held her lips tightly together and closed her eyes. After helping her from the bed, Claire first checked Cole's forehead. Removing the tight bandage, she again washed the angry marks, one from a blow and the other from a bullet, and applied new ointment and a new bandage made of a torn sheet. Cole didn't stir. She decided not to tell Kathleen about his fever. She rinsed out the wet rag and reapplied it to his head. He was burning up, she told herself. The fever must break soon or he wouldn't recover.

Kathleen stood beside her, a bit wobbly. But Claire thought it was good for her to have something to think about besides her ordeal. Claire cleaned and washed his right arm without removing the splint, this one made by Luther. She was happy to discover the bullet wounds had not seriously torn up arm muscles. Bones would heal faster than muscles. But he wouldn't be able to use it for a long time. Maybe never. His shoulder wounds were red but hadn't become infected. She said a silent prayer for that discovery.

Next, she pulled back the blanket covering Cole, with Kathleen helping. He was naked. His lower back was wrapped with the torn remains of an old shirt, one of Luther's. She could see cuts where Luther had worked to get at the lead. Fierce red, yellow and blue marks flamed from the wound. Dr. Hawkinson would have to examine it tomorrow.

She rebandaged the wound and examined the red crease across his flat stomach. It was shallow but had caused him to lose blood. Now it was healing well. After cleaning the wound, she applied medicine and left it uncovered.

Together, they looked for any additional wounds, finding a nasty hole in his calf. A few inches away was a scar from an earlier bullet wound. Neither mentioned his manhood as they searched, but Claire couldn't help seeing it and smiling to herself. She thought about saying it was good that he hadn't been hurt there, but decided not to. Soon he was fully cleaned, rebandaged and covered over with blankets.

Claire helped Kathleen back into bed. The young woman was exhausted by the simple effort.

"Thank you, Claire . . . for everything. Will C-Cole . . . ?" She asked after sliding under the covers.

"Yes. Yes, he will. He's a Kerry. They're bullheaded but they're tough. We're lucky ladies."

"I wish . . ." Kathleen didn't finish her thought, pushing her face into her pillow instead.

Claire left the room but had already decided to return with water for Cole to drink. Somehow. He needed it to counter the fever. Luther had added two logs to the fire in the fireplace and it was doing a good job of pushing away the cold.

Quietly, she returned with a bowl of water and a spoon. It was the only way she could think of. Kneeling beside Cole, she placed a spoonful of water on his tongue, closed his mouth over it and hoped he would swallow the precious fluid. For an hour, she repeated the process, then refreshed the wet cloth on his forehead. Standing, she studied Kathleen for a moment, saw that she was sleeping and left to check on Rios.

Before dawn, she arose alone and brought more water to Cole, again one spoonful at a time. Then, she went to the kitchen to prepare a breakfast of egg gravy, bacon and hot coffee. After eating, Ethan and Luther left for town in a buckboard wagon; Eli and Blue got to go along.

Chapter 19

It was late afternoon and the Texas sun was becoming more agreeable as the Kerrys entered Uvalde. Salutations sought them from both sides of the street. A loaded freighter rattled past them and both Eli and Blue were fascinated by its size and sound. The boy waved at the driver and he gave a halfhearted return greeting.

Deputy Maynard ran up to them as Luther pulled the wagon in front of Dr. Hawkinson's combined office and drug store.

"How's Cole? His missus?" The young deputy was wide-eyed and a bit intimidated by the Kerrys.

Many were, in spite of Ethan's blindness. Or maybe, because of it. Already, some whispered that he could hear when a man was lying and that he had felt the return of Victorio Gee because his lack of sight had heightened his other senses. The *Uvalde Free Press* had presented the cowboys' counterattack, led by Ethan, as a momentous occasion in the life of the town and had referred to Ethan's war experiences as the reason for his strategic skill.

"Wal, they's both home now," Luther drawled, shoving the wheel brake into place with callused hands. "Cole's dun bin shot up purty bad. His missus, ah, she be fine as a daisy. Didn't lay a hand on 'er. They, ah, let 'er go real quick. Figgered she'd slow 'em down, I reckon."

Ethan eased out of the wagon and stood quietly for a moment to let his legs get reacquainted with the ground, then rolled and lit a cigarette. He hadn't spoken and his silence was unnerving the young deputy.

"Mr. Kerry, sir, we sure do thank you . . . again . . . for what you did . . . for Uvalde," Deputy Maynard said. "Oh, they made me acting marshal."

"Congratulations." Ethan nodded and exhaled smoke. "We came to get Doc for Cole—an' Miguel Rios. Is he in?"

"Well, yes, I think so," the acting marshal answered, crossing his arms, then dropping them to his sides. "Sorry that Victorio Gee got away . . . heard he killed one of your men. Heard that Mexican rancher was hurt, too."

"They killed a good man. His name was *Ablakela Sunkawakan*." Ethan took the cigarette from his mouth. "Miguel del Rios, he's a good friend. Owns the River R spread next to ours. He'll be up an' goin' again soon." Ethan inhaled his cigarette and his jaw pressed forward. "But we were lucky, I reckon. Them lettin' Cole's wife go so fast an' all. I figure they knew we'd stop chasin' 'em if they did. Kept our money though."

"Yes. You know, I'm sure Lainwood would like to write a story about you . . . being a war hero an' all . . . an' leading the cowboy charge . . . an' bein' . . ."

"Blind," Ethan finished the statement. "Tell him to

write about someone else, like *Ablakela Sunkawakan* and Miguel del Rios. They're brave men."

"Yes sir, I will." Acting Marshal Maynard swallowed. "Not sure he will, them being . . . different, you know."

"No, I don't know."

The young lawman didn't know how to respond.

Ethan half-turned toward the wagon. "Eli, you and Blue stay in the wagon. We're not gonna be in town long."

"Can't I go to the general store—just to look?"

"Not this time."

Luther patted Eli on the back, lumbered out of the wagon and draped the reins around the hitching rack.

He smiled at the young lawman with the pimply face. "Looks like the town dun got itself back together real good."

Eagerly, Acting Marshal Maynard returned the greeting. "Yes sir, we've been hard at it."

"That be real fine."

"I'm mighty sorry about Cole. Glad his wife wasn't hurt none," Maynard said. "Cole was . . . a hero, too. My gosh, he was the one that jumped 'em first."

Four couples passed briskly but the last man turned back. "Thanks, Mr. Kerry, for saving our town." The other three men made similar responses but didn't stop.

Ethan nodded. "Acting Marshal Maynard, it's been good to see you but we've got business with Dr. Hawkinson."

As the acting marshal said good-bye, Ethan entered the drugstore, holding on to Luther's arm. Their entrance caused several customers to turn toward them before resuming their purchasing efforts. The small store was packed with rows of patent medicine packages, differently colored bottles, glass jars filled with herbs and pills, pressed soaps and many containers of staple health items like cornstarch, vinegar, castor oil, bitters, calomine lotion, toothache powders, cough syrups. and a long row of different kinds of catarrh medicines for relieving head and chest congestion.

Luther was more fascinated by the shelves of whiskey and brandy than the wildly presented patent medicines with their excessively stated guarantees of cure and frequent presentation of the wonder drugs, opium and cocaine. He told Ethan about them as they passed, both the whiskey and the medicines. The rancher wasn't interested in either.

"Where's Doc?"

"Don't see 'im."

"Well, he's in the back then."

As they walked next to the main counter, Luther touched the stone mortar and pestle resting there. Next to them was a brass balance scale. A heavily side-burned clerk was using it to measure some kind of powder for a woman in a light blue dress. Absent-mindedly, Luther stared at the white powder. She was offended by his apparent interest and huffed. Not realizing he was the target of her disgust, Luther touched the brim of his hat and said, "Hope that thar does the trick fer ya, ma'am."

Her face swelled into crimson. "Well, I never . . ."

The clerk turned toward Luther with a knowing frown on his elongated forehead and pointed at the "Dr. Kylad's 'cure for female diseases' " package.

"Is Doc in thar?" Luther asked, oblivious to the fact the woman was buying feminine hygiene medicine.

"Yes, but he shouldn't be disturbed," the clerk said, continuing his annoyance in the tone of his voice.

Ethan made a half step toward the counter, bumped against it and stepped back. "Get him. Now."

"I said the doctor was with a patient."

"No, you said he shouldn't be disturbed," Ethan growled. "You go in there an' tell him Ethan Kerry is here—an' I need help with Cole—an' our friend, Miguel del Rios."

The clerk's face stretched into an even longer presentation as his mouth wobbled open. The woman in blue studied Ethan as if she were seeing someone very important.

"E-Ethan Kerry. Of course. I'm sorry I didn't . . ."

"Now."

Luther smiled and waved at the scale. "Ya go ahaid an' fix up this here lady's needs first."

"Puleese, sir," she objected.

"I'm sure it'll do the trick, ma'am."

She spun around and stomped away, leaving the clerk wondering what he should do next.

Luther shrugged. "Reckon she didn't want none afterall. Maybe it's sumthin' we kin use. What does it be?"

Glancing around, the clerk leaned over and whispered in Luther's ear.

The grizzled wrangler gulped and his tanned face became a deep crimson.

"What's the matter, Luther?" Ethan asked. "Does the lady want it or not? We need to talk with Doc."

Rubbing his chin to help remove the redness in his face, Luther muttered, "Yeah, yeah, git the doc."

After knocking on the office door, the clerk slipped inside. A few moments later, Dr. Hawkinson appeared. He was an older man with slumping shoulders, a bald head and a thick beard, more brown than gray. His thin voice always sounded less professional than he wanted it to.

"Ethan, Luther. It's good to see you again. Sorry for the reason. How bad is Cole?" Dr. Hawkinson said.

Luther explained about Cole's condition and mentioned the need to tend to Rios as well, then he stepped closer to the old physician, glanced both ways and whispered Kathleen needed his help, too. Understanding his sudden secrecy, Dr. Hawkinson told them he would be ready to leave as soon as he finished with this patient. About twenty minutes, he thought. Ethan told him that they would return after checking on some matters at the bank.

Ethan and Luther's next stop was the bank. Bank President Allen J. Picklewhite greeted them warmly. The three Kerry brothers were among the bank's main stockholders after the previous owner, Sam Winslow, was killed trying to destroy the Kerrys and their herd.

"Good day to you, gentlemen. How can I be of help to the men who saved Uvalde?" Picklewhite said in his most enthusiastic tone. He started and ended his welcome with his mouth open, as usual.

A short, stocky man, his mouth was always agape, it seemed. A longtime habit that made him appear like something was caught in his throat. But he was a thorough man and a good fit for the town, knowing when to press for payment and when to wait. He had only been a resident since the bank's ownership changed. Picklewhite was a friend of one of the other stockholders who had recommended him highly.

"Miguel del Rios has been wounded," Ethan proclaimed, loud enough that two customers at the teller window turned to see who was talking. "Fighting against Victorio Gee."

"I hadn't heard that. I'm very sorry," Picklewhite said. "How is Cole? And his lovely bride. Both all right I hope."

"Yes, she's fine," Ethan declared in the same tone. "They let her go—just outside of town. They were worried about Cole, I reckon. He was comin' after 'em like a bat outta hell." It wasn't the same story he had shared minutes before but the tale came out before he thought about the comparison.

Picklewhite glanced at Luther who nodded agreement. "And Cole? How is . . ."

"Cole's hurt bad." Ethan snapped. "Real bad. Doc's goin' with us to take a look at him. He's back at the ranch now. So is Rios. That's why we came in."

"Ohmygod, that's awful!" Picklewhite's hand went to his opened mouth. "That terrible Victorio Gee. I heard they killed the ranger who was with him—but I never heard . . ."

"That ranger was one of Gee's men," Ethan interrupted. "Sent into town as a scout. Probably was in the bank. Shook your hand, I'll bet."

Picklewhite's gaze went immediately to his right hand and he stared at it as if it might sprout warts. Aware of his action, his hand slid to the gold watch chain decorating his vest, pulled it out, flipped open the lid and checked the time. The small banker apologized, saying it was a bad habit.

With no interest in the habit or the apology, Ethan returned to the subject of Rios and whether or not he had a loan at the bank.

Before answering, Picklewhite thought they should step over somewhere out of the way, where they wouldn't be heard or interrupted. Ethan didn't care but Luther agreed and led his brother to the southeastern corner of the bank, where an old grandfather clock clinked its daily story. In an exaggerated whisper, Picklewhite said Rios, indeed, had a loan; first payment was due this fall after the planned drive to Kansas. He said the Mexican had indicated he would be putting his small herd in with the Bar K's. Ethan acknowledged that was so.

"Do you know if he had any relatives?" Ethan asked. "We know his wife and kids were killed—by Gee—but maybe he's got a brother, sister . . . somebody."

Picklewhite shook his head and his opened jaw wiggled. "No one that I know of, Mr. Kerry. He ran the ranch by himself, you know." He paused. "We turned him down once." His eyes darted back and forth as if assessing whether anyone could hear him. "Then your brother Cole came in. He insisted we loan him the money and co-signed for it. I can show you the note if you like. The outlaws didn't get that one."

"That's not necessary. Why wouldn't you loan him the money in the first place, Picklewhite? Because he's a Mexican?" Ethan's voice was a knife.

"Well, ah, yes." Picklewhite's eyebrows arched in a fixed position of superiority. "We must have our standards, you know."

Ethan listened quietly; crow's feet deepening at the corners of his eyes were the only signs of his growing anger.

"Now, Ethan, don't ya do it." Luther knew the signs well. "He didn't mean nuthin' by it, did ya, Mr. Picklewhite?"

"I won't, Luther. Just this." Ethan's voice was a rattlesnake warning. "Picklewhite, I'm gonna tell you this just once. Don't say that again. I'm a lot nicer than my little brother, Cole. It's a wonder he didn't coldcock you right where you stood."

Picklewhite's eyebrows fled to higher places. "Yes, Mr. Kerry, but I have to answer to the other stockholders as well."

Ethan crossed his arms. "You let me handle that."

"Yes sir." The banker rubbed his chin to push away the fear. "I've been working hard to replace those stolen papers. Got to have documentation, you know. Some folks have already come in on their own. It's going to take a while, though."

Luther spotted the woman in the blue dress walking past the bank and wanted to go apologize to her—without telling Ethan or Picklewhite what he was going to do. "Ah, I'll be ri't back, Ethan. Thar's sumbody I need to say sumthin' to." With that, he hurried away, his spurs creating their distinctive music on the bank floor.

"Where the hell's he goin'?" Ethan asked.

Picklewhite watched Luther bound through the heavy door and shuffle down the street. The woman stopped and turned.

"He's talking to some woman. I believe that's Mrs. Huball; she's a widow. Does sewing an' such."

"Luther an' a woman? Can't be."

"Well, she's gone from frowning to smiling," Picklewhite advised. "An' he's got his hat off."

"Damn."

In a few minutes, Luther returned, grinning widely. "Are ya ready, Ethan? We need to git the doc."

"What's with the lady?" Ethan teased.

Luther blushed. "Oh, nothin'. She were at the doc's a'buyin' sumthin'. I think she dun got mad at us a'comin' in like we did. Jes' apol-o-gized, I did."

"That was very nice of you, Luther. Was she pretty?"

"She were real purty. Smelt good, too."

"Come on, lover boy, let's get the doc."

Returning to the drugstore, they found Dr. Hawkinson waiting outside in his buggy. Ethan quickly explained about Rios's and Cole's gunshot wounds; Luther told him a bullet remained lodged in Cole's chest.

"So you'll have to do some cuttin'," Ethan said, rolling a cigarette.

Dr. Hawkinson frowned at Ethan's description.

Luther noted the negative response. "We sur do thank ya fer comin' with us, Doc. Our li'l brother an' our good friend be needin' yur good help. He sur do."

Dr. Hawkinson's sagging face brightened. "Glad to do it, Luther. Just had to finish treating Mrs. Rosewood. Got a nasty cough." He stopped, realizing he shouldn't be sharing such information. "Believe the last time I was out to your place, Ethan had been . . . hurt." The aging physician studied the blind rancher, now lighting his smoke. "Did you ever check out Dr. Crylan in Kansas City as I recommended?"

"No. Haven't." Ethan didn't like the question. "One of these days, maybe."

"Well, you shouldn't wait, Ethan. He's known for his work on eyes."

"I like Texas doctors."

Not sure how to react, Dr. Hawkinson looked at Luther for direction and the oldest Kerry brother changed the subject. Speaking softly, Luther said, "Doc, we want ya to check on Cole's li'l lady, too. Just don't want folks a'knowin'. We tolt 'em in town she were let go—ri't outside o' town."

"I understand."

Chapter 20

Twilight was flirting with the horizon as the Kerrys pulled into the Bar K ranch yard. Talking to himself, Dr. Hawkinson was a dust cloud behind them in his buggy.

"John Davis be back, Ethan," Luther said, noticing the Missouri cowboy conversing with Ferguson near the biggest corral. John Davis Sotar was pointing at a long-legged bay as he talked.

"Good. We'll talk with him while Doc works."

Sotar immediately moved to intercept the wagon as it neared the corral. Ferguson watched, shifting the weight from his supposed bad leg to his good one.

"Whoa, fellers. That's it." Luther coaxed the horses as they pulled alongside the corrals. He watched with satisfaction as the two heavily muscled horses worked in tandem, just as he had trained them.

When the wagon jerked to a stop, Eli asked if he and Blue could go see Kiowa in the corral; he jumped down before Ethan finished his approval, with the ugly dog joining him eagerly. Without breaking stride, the pair were off on a new adventure that would begin at the farthest corral. Once only holding Bailarin, it now held both Kiowa and Rios's gray stallion. The big red horse whinnied approval of the advancing boy and trotted to the rail to greet him. Bailarin joined the exchange.

"Howdy, John Davis, how's ever'thang at Miguel's?" Luther wrapped the reins around the brake.

With his buckled gunbelt slung over his shoulder, Sotar was eager to share what he had learned at the Mexican rancher's small spread. He told them the small rawhide spread consisted of one corral and a one-room house. An elderly woman was living there. He thought she was Mexican, but wasn't certain. She spoke no English, but through his little Spanish, he gathered she wasn't a relative. Rios had taken her in when she had nowhere else to go. She did the cooking in exchange for staying. When Sotar told her what had happened, she cried for several minutes and then asked what would become of her.

"I promised her that she could stay, boss, until Miguel was up an' around." His statement was more question than declaration.

Luther was the first to respond. "O' course, she can. We'd better check on what kind o' food an' such she's got thar."

"Maybe Sotar already has, Luther," Ethan said.

"I did. She's got the makin's for a week. Maybe more. Looked like a lot of corn flour . . ."

"For tortillas," Luther burst out.

"Reckon so. Some salted meat. Dried vegetables. A few cans from town," Sotar recited. "Looked like plenty of salt, sugar. Could use some more beans and coffee, I reckon."

Sotar said he told the old woman that the Kerrys were planning on watching over Rios's herd and leaving riders there until he could return.

Interrupting his report was the arrival of Dr. Hawkinson. He drove his buggy past them and up to the house, where he unfolded from the vehicle, made a futile attempt to brush off the dust from his suit and looped his reins over the rack. From its drooping head, the dappled gray horse appeared not to have any intentions of moving away, tied or not.

"No need to come up, boys, I know my way," Dr. Hawkinson said, pulling a large bag from the buggy seat.

"Wait a minute, will you, Doc?" Ethan turned in the buckboard seat toward the doctor's voice.

"Ah . . . sure, Ethan. But there's no need to . . ."

"Ferguson, come over here!" Ethan barked loudly.

The heavyset cowhand's entire body jerked in reaction to the command. Rolling his shoulders to remove the surprise, Ferguson lumbered toward the wagon, moving his right leg stiffly.

"Y-yes sir, boss . . . what . . . is it?" Ferguson said, huffing for breath.

"Go over to Doc. I want him to see your leg."

Glancing in the direction of Dr. Hawkinson, the cowhand walked over to the puzzled physician with an exaggerated limp. Dr. Hawkinson stood beside his buggy, watching him approach. Once there, Feguson said nothing and bent over slowly. Unable to reach the bottom of his pants, he finally squatted and drew the trouser away from his leg, revealing a purple bruise. Dr. Hawkinson suppressed a chuckle and went to the sprawled Ferguson.

The old doctor squinted seriously and touched the skin around the mark. "Does that hurt, son?"

"Yeah. Something fierce."

"I see. How'd you get this?"

Ferguson started to explain in detail how the accident happened, beginning with breakfast that day in camp.

From the wagon, Luther interrupted loudly, "Hoss kicked 'im."

"Thought so," Dr. Hawkinson straightened his back. "You were lucky. Just a bruise." He smiled slightly. "I recommend getting back in the saddle." He looked toward the wagon and asked, "Shall I see our two men now?"

"That'd be real fine, Doc," Ethan growled. Without moving his face in the direction of the seated Ferguson, he said, "Ferguson, I want you on your horse and out at the roundup in time for supper. If I hear from DuMonte that you didn't do a full day's work tomorrow, you're fired. Understand?"

Ferguson nodded, fumbled with his pants and awkwardly stood. He looked down at his leg, then at Dr. Hawkinson.

"In that house is my brother, full of bullet holes—an' his friend, the same," Ethan said. "I lost a fine scout—an' a good friend—in Abe. Don't come back with another injury unless your leg is gone."

Ferguson gulped and retreated for the bunkhouse; his hurt leg seemingly miraculously healed as he hurried along.

"Oh, good afternoon, Dr. Hawkinson, it's so good to see you." Claire greeted Dr. Hawkinson warmly from the doorway. "I do hope we can talk you into staying for supper."

"My, that certainly has a good ring to it, Mrs. Kerry. You won't have to twist my arm," Dr. Hawkinson replied with a wide smile, doffing his hat. "Where are the patients?"

"In here, Dr. Hawkinson."

While the doctor went inside, Ethan, Luther and Sotar completed their conversation about Rios's ranch.

Ethan wasn't interested in hearing more about the old woman or the state of her supplies, although

Luther clearly was. Sitting in the wagon, the blind rancher leaned forward on his knees and asked if Sotar had found any evidence of relatives, someone they might notify about Rios's condition.

Galloping hooves distracted Sotar and he turned to see Ferguson spurring his horse away from the ranch.

"No sir, boss. Nothin'," Sotar explained, refocusing on Luther. He was never quite sure if he should look directly at Ethan or not and usually chose to look at the oldest Kerry. "Shoot, hardly looked like anybody even lived there as it was."

"What are we gonna do, Ethan?" Luther asked as he jumped down from the seat and began unharnessing the horses.

Sotar offered to help but Luther motioned him away.

"We're gonna take care of his place 'til he can. Simple as that," Ethan responded.

"Your wife's coming back," Sotar advised, watching Claire walk toward them. He couldn't read what the doctor had discovered from her face.

"Is Doc already finished?" Luther's leathery face was a question.

"No. Just with Cole an' Kathleen. He's gonna be fine. Awful weak, of course. Dr. Hawkinson's a little worried about Cole's right arm, but thinks it will come around—in time." Her own expression blossomed into relief. She smiled and added, "He figures all you Kerry boys are tough as boots anyway."

"No doubt about that," Ethan rejoined and climbed out of the wagon.

Luther studied Claire for a moment before continuing. "What's he be a'sayin' 'bout Kathleen?"

She started to answer but the words slammed against her emotions. She turned away, dabbing at her eyes.

"I'm sorry, Claire . . . I dun didn't . . ."

"No, no, Luther. Something just got caught in my

throat. I'll be fine," Claire said. "There isn't much he can do for her. Says she should be healed any day now. Bruises gone in a couple of weeks. But . . ."

"Not the same with her feelin's."

"Y-yes."

Uncomfortable with the situation, Sotar excused himself, indicating he needed to saddle a new horse and catch up with Ferguson on the way to the roundup. Immediately, Ethan told him to make certain they scoured the north range for cattle. Sotar acknowledged that he would tell DuMonte. Happy to be talking about something else, Luther added that he didn't think it would be necessary to remind the roundup boss of anything. Ethan didn't like the response but reluctantly agreed.

"Soon as the roundup's done, take some of the leftover supplies to that old woman at Rios's, will you?" Ethan said, rubbing his chest.

"Sure. I'd like that, boss," Sotar said and hurried toward the full corral.

Luther watched him and yelled, "John Davis, take that brown wi' the white socks on his front legs. He's a good 'un." He thought for a moment and added, "He'll crowhop a mite. At furst." He returned to the wagon horses and began unharnessing them.

Sotar waved without slowing down.

"What 'bout Miguel? Is Doc lookin' at him now?" Luther turned back to Claire but his nose itched and he rubbed it vigorously. The action didn't help and he turned away to sneeze. "Damn. Sorry, Claire."

She smiled wanly and said she didn't know anything yet about Rios. She didn't add that Dr. Hawkinson had also asked her about Ethan and told her that he should go to the specialist he had recommended. Studying him with appreciation, Claire shook her head, then her hand went to her mouth. "Ethan Kerry, you've got wheel grease on your shirt." She was overreacting after listening to the doctor.

"Where?" He patted his chest.

"Right here," she said, touching his right shirt sleeve.

"Oh. Must've caught the wheel just right gettin' down."

Claire shook her head. "Remind me when we go inside. I'll rub some butter on it before I wash."

"Claire, I do hope we're gonna eat soon. My stomach's bin a'arguin' wi' me all the way from Uvalde. Yassur." Luther stopped with harness in both hands.

Her face was tight but her mouth had pushed into a thin smile. "How does fried venison sound, Luther? And some corn pudding. I made oatmeal bread, too, but it didn't come out very good."

"Dun soundin' like heaven to this ol' hoss thief."

"Good. Dr. Hawkinson is going to join us."

Ethan's grimace was unrelated to her announcement and she knew it. He scuffed his right boot back and forth, leaving a line in the dirt. The tall rancher looked up and away, as if seeing something only he could. Finally, words joined his physical concern.

"What are we supposed to do about . . . Cole's wife?"

Claire wasn't surprised at her husband's stilted reference to Kathleen Kerry. In many ways, he had not accepted her as a part of the family. At least not emotionally. He and Claire hadn't talked about it, but she knew part of the reason was simply being a big brother, actually more of a father, to Cole. No woman would be good enough for his little brother. In a strange way, it was a great compliment from Ethan.

"Dr. Hawkinson wants us to get her involved in the ranch as soon as possible. Give her things to do,"

Claire declared. "Have her help take care of Cole." She pursed her lips and her bosom rose and fell with a prolonged exhalation. "S-she told me . . . she wished they . . . had killed her."

Chapter 21

A colder than usual November morning found Luther in the small corral, working with a red colt. Frost smoke peppered the young animal as Luther talked and stroked its legs and back. Shadows, pushed against the corral poles, watched and shivered. He felt it was important for a horse to be handled early and often, even when it was too young for a saddle. "Hoss touchin'," he called it. Today, like several before, the young sorrel was wearing a saddle blanket to get it used to having something on its back.

From the barn came Eli and Maggie, racing toward their uncle with a tale filling their eyes and frost smoke curling around their red faces.

"Have ya dun fed that calf I asked ya?" Luther looked up from his examination of the colt's right foreleg.

They had brought the orphaned calf from the roundup to bottle-feed until it was old enough to return to the herd. Another calf had finally got the hang of sucking and had been left with its mother.

"Ah . . . not yet," Eli reported. "We . . . need your help."

"My he'p fer what, Eli?"

Maggie answered, her eyes widened. "Willie has . . . manure all over him."

Luther chuckled and rubbed his chin. "All over, huh?"

"Yes, it's on his back and down his legs." Maggie waved her arms to demonstrate the extent of the calf's covering. "Do you think one of the horses did that to him? That wasn't very nice."

"Wal, Eli, ya git some hay an' wipe 'im clean." Luther could barely keep from laughing. His body rippled with the repression as he returned his attention to the colt.

Eli frowned and whispered, "I don't wanna."

"You have to," his sister replied sternly, tugging at his coat.

Luther heard the advancing clank of spurs and looked up. A fully dressed Miguel del Rios was headed for the corral where Bailarin and Kiowa were now kept. His left arm was held in a tight sling; the doctor had been as concerned about Rios's arm as he was about Cole's.

"Wal, look who's up," Luther hollered. "How ya feelin', Miguel?"

"*Si*, I ees *bueno, Señor* Kerry. Et ees time for Miguel to go *mi casa*. Thank you *mucho* for your care," Rios said, glancing around for his saddle and gear.

"I already thank *Señorita* Kerry. She has been *bueno* to me. I no see Ethan." He winced at the use of the word "see."

"Kids, ya come an' give this here red rascal a li'l huggin'." Luther rubbed the back of the young horse. "I be surprised ya got past Claire."

Miguel nodded and kept walking. "*Señorita* Kerry no want me leave—but I must. Work ees waiting."

"But what about Willie?" Maggie asked.

"That dung ain't a'goin' nowhere. 'Sides he dun got it thar hisself, a'layin' in it," Luther said, and turned his attention back to Rios. "But, Miguel, we've been tendin' to your herd. An' Sotar an' Miller are at your place now, keepin' an eye out." Luther opened the gate to let Eli and Maggie inside. Frost smoke popped around their faces as they scurried toward the young horse. "Easy now. Let 'im figger us folks is good fer 'em."

"Yes, Uncle Luther." Maggie giggled.

"We'll be careful," Eli said.

Claire stepped into the doorway with Ethan at her side, holding onto her left arm; she said something to him and they began walking toward the corrals.

"Uh-oh, here dun come the heavy artillery, Miguel," Luther chuckled. "I told ya gittin' past Claire were tough."

"*Si*. She ees fine *señorita*." Rios hesitated, then came to a complete stop.

"Yep, that she is—an' most times, I think she dun run this here place. Don't tell Ethan or Cole, though."

Claire and Ethan strode directly to them. Red-faced, Claire turned to Ethan. "Tell him, Ethan."

Luther chuckled and so did Rios, in spite of himself.

A slow grin worked its way across Ethan's hard face; unseeing eyes blinked against the cold air. "Miguel, where do you think you're going? You're sick. You should be in bed. Your arm hasn't healed yet." His grin finished itself and he turned in the direction of Claire. "Did I get it all?"

Claire frowned. "Ethan, don't be silly. This isn't a game. Mr. Rios, you are too weak to be up—much less trying to go home. Please. Come back inside."

Removing his sombrero with his right hand, Rios bowed slightly. Ends of the silk bandana that covered his head fluttered with the movement. "*Señorita* Kerry, you ees kind to me. But I must go. I weel be *bueno*."

"B-but your arm?" Claire blurted, then softened the question with an observation. "You need to let it heal."

"*Si*, eet ees no working. *Mañana* eet weel be *bueno*," Rios said. "I must go see *mi casa . . . mi ranchero*."

It was Ethan's turn. He folded his arms and reminded Rios that two of their hands, Sotar and Miller, were watching his ranch and that his three riders had returned from the roundup. He said they intended to keep an eye on his herd during the winter, along with Rios's own riders. Food and supplies would be sent over as well. Rios nodded his understanding of the situation and thanked them again for their generosity.

"Naw, we're the ones be thankful, Miguel," Luther said. "Ya dun saved our li'l missy. You an' Abe."

"How ees *Señorita* Cole Kerry?"

Claire pursed her lips. "She is going to be fine. Thanks to you."

"Tell Cole I weel talk weeth heem . . . *mañana. Si?*"

"Ya gonna put leather on that fancy gray—wi' one hand?" Luther asked, leaning against the rail fence from inside the corral.

"*Si*. Eet can be done."

Angrily, Claire told Luther to saddle Rios's horse while she prepared food for him to take. She left immediately for the house. After she was out of earshot, Ethan declared that he and Luther would ride along, then make a swing through their range and see how their herd was getting along as well as check on the men in the line cabins. Primarily, it was a trip to get out of the ranch house and back on a horse. Ethan was eager for his brother to describe the herd. Rarely could he get enough detail to satisfy him. Luther had become better at it than Cole, who usually was too impatient for the task.

A half hour later, the three men rode away, leading a fourth, heavily packed horse carrying supplies for Rios's ranch, at Claire's insistence. At the last minute, Luther decided to ride Kiowa, to give the great sorrel a needed workout. They rode easily, talking cattle and weather. Rios tried to hide his discomfort from returning to the saddle.

Kiowa and Bailarin were both eager to run, having been alone in the corral except for Luther's occasional workouts of the exceptional mounts. Ethan's steady black horse ignored the snorting, blowing and jog-trotting of the other two horses.

The tall rancher appeared unaware of his companions' preoccupation with keeping their horses at a walk. He rolled a cigarette, lit it and asked if their breath was making frost smoke and if the sky looked stormy. Luther was positive about the first; negative about the second. Ethan then wanted to know about the condition of the ponds and the grass. Luther told him what they were seeing in considerable detail.

Rios listened appreciatively, trying to imagine what it would be like to never see again. That popped open a memory about his dead family and he winced.

"Are ya alri't, Miguel?" Luther asked.

"*Si*. Eet ees *bueno* to ride *mi caballo* once more." He noticed Luther was puzzled and added, "Ride ze . . . horse. But I be stiff. That ees all." Rios forced a smile. "How soon weel Cole be—weeth you again?"

"Dunno. Sooner'n most. Like ya be," Luther replied, patting Kiowa on the neck to show his appreciation for the horse settling into a walk.

"Cole ees warrior." Rios studied the wintry land with the enjoyment of a man who had returned from death.

"Reckon he dun come by that natural-like," Luther grinned and rubbed his nose to keep it from running. "His big brother, Ethan, here, dun saw to that."

"*Si.*"

"I wasn't always a damn blind fool," Ethan barked.

· "Rios theenks you see better than most . . . now."

Silence rode with them for several minutes after the Mexican rancher's compliment. Crossing a long crease in the brown hills, their conversation returned as three distant riders cleared the misty hills to their left.

"*Tres hombres* to ze left." Rios pointed with his good arm.

"Wonder who they be? Ya reckon it's cowmen?" Luther squinted and raised his hand to filter the day's already dull sun.

"Are they ridin' together—or are they spreadin' apart?" Ethan asked.

Rios removed the thong from his holstered pistol, hanging from his saddlehorn instead of his shoulder. "Spreading. They have seen us."

"Well, they're either outlaws or rangers," Ethan muttered. "Let's rein here. Luther, you get down with your rifle. I'll hold Kiowa."

"Dun make savvy." Luther whoaed the big sorrel, who responded instantly and stood with its ears alert. "Good boy. Good boy." He climbed down, drew his Winchester from its sheath and handed the reins to Ethan, who closed his opened hand when the leather strands touched it.

"No kickin' now, Kiowa," Ethan said. "Luther, find a spot away from us. Fifteen feet or so."

"Wal, I reckon they dun seed us, Ethan, they's a'comin' this a'way."

"Stretch out where you can shoot. Put your sights on the man in the far left."

"Why him?"

"He doesn't like you." Ethan smiled.

Sunlight reflected from metal on the middle rider's shirt, then found a kindred place on the farthest man's coat lapel.

"*Señor* Kerry, they rangers, I theenk." Rios rested his hand on the ivory pistol grip. "They be wearing ze badge."

"So was the man who shot Cole." Ethan transferred Kiowa's reins to his left hand and reached for his own holstered gun. Rios was suprised by the move. "Rios, can you get down—and shoot?" Ethan asked, drawing the Colt.

"*Si.*"

"Humor a blind man and do it then. To the other side of me." Ethan's voice was low and steady.

Rios got down from his horse, more of a slide than a dismount. He felt light-headed and leaned against Bailarin, hoping the trembling would pass.

"I'll hold your horse," Ethan said.

Rios led the gray horse toward Ethan, bringing him to the same side where Kiowa stood. He wasn't certain how to hand the reins to the tall rancher without offending him.

"How close are they?" Ethan asked.

"A hundred yards, maybe."

Ethan held out his left hand holding all of the reins, including his own. "Put the leather here."

"*Si.*" Rios laid the reins in Ethan's opened hand.

"If there's shootin', I'm countin' on you to take out the man on the far right," Ethan said.

"What about ze man in ze middle?" Rios pulled his revolver from its hanging holster.

Ethan flashed his clenched teeth. "I'll take him."

"But *Señor* Ker . . ."

"He'll be the one talking. Trust me, I'll know where

he is," Ethan explained. "Besides, he won't be expecting me to do anything. That'll buy time if we need it."

Rios couldn't help being impressed with Ethan's cool leadership. Nodding his understanding, he glanced at the sheathed rifle on his saddle but knew he wouldn't be able to handle it with one hand. His handgun would have to do. He walked on wobbly legs toward a finger of rock that looked like a stone giant was trying to free himself from burial.

Halfway there, he realized Ethan couldn't see his reaction, stopped and said, "I weel take ze one on ze right, *Señor* Kerry."

Awkwardly, he knelt behind the shallow rock formation and cocked the revolver. It felt strange and heavy. The advancing riders might well be rangers, but having Rios and Luther dismount and take firing positions was a smart tactical move. At the least, it would make the strangers uneasy—and, at the most, more difficult if they decided to attack.

Hoofbeats drew closer. Ethan pulled Kiowa alongside him; Luther's empty stirrup brushed against his boot. Bailarin was left to move next to Kiowa. Both horses were quiet.

Shifting his legs to get comfortable, Rios studied the oncoming riders. His left arm had no feeling. None. *Would it ever be strong again?* he wondered, and turned his attention to the three strangers, then to the one on the right, a bird-faced man with a stringy mustache and a hat with a pushed-up brim. The rider wasn't wearing a badge or it was covered by his coat with its collar up and tightened around his throat.

"Gentlemen, good day to you. That's close enough." Ethan could just as easily have been commanding troops.

The three riders showed no signs of surprise as each man stopped his horse. They were fifteen yards apart; rifles lay across their saddles. All three were well armed; the shapes of pistol butts evident under their long range coats. A buttoned long coat didn't hide the ranger badge on the middle man's shirt and the rider on the left wore his on a coat lapel.

"Easy, mister. We're rangers," the middle rider announced.

Ethan leaned forward in the saddle, holding the three sets of reins in his left hand and a Colt in his right at his side. "The man who shot my brother made the same claim. He was one of Victorio Gee's. How do we know you ain't the same?"

Wearing a tall, center-creased hat, the middle ranger was as steady as Ethan. Graying hair put him older than his two associates. A lot older. He recognized the movement of men into battle position as an indication they hadn't come upon mere cowhands.

Keeping both hands visible by laying them across his saddle horn and in front of his crossed Winchester, the ranger continued, "I'm Captain Thorne, Andrew Thorne. This is Ranger Heilman—and that's Ranger O'Reilly." He paused and smiled. "I'm guessing you're Ethan Kerry."

"I am that," Ethan said. "This is my brother, Luther; he's got Heilman. And my friend, Miguel del Rios; he's got the Irishman. Both are excellent shots. You're my problem, so you've got a chance. Now, what brings you out this way?"

Captain Thorne's mouth tightened with Ethan's introduction but he went on to explain that they were headed to the Kerry ranch, hoping to get details that might help them find Victorio Gee and his men. Ethan told them what they knew about Gee, which was nothing after losing him and his remaining men outside their canyon hideout two months ago.

"We stung him pretty good in town," Ethan ended. "Figured he's gone on to sweeter places."

Captain Thorne nodded, remembered Ethan was blind, and said, "We've got a pretty good source that says he rounded up some more men and is headed back this way. Haven't cut his trail though."

"Why would he do that?" Ethan's face was taut; a thin ripple of tension slid along his left cheek.

"Gee's a hard man to figure." Captain Thorne raised his arm and rubbed his chin.

"Harder to kill." Ethan's Colt rose, trailing the soft noise of the ranger's movement as if they were connected.

"Hey, easy now, I was just rubbing my chin. That's all." Captain Thorne's eyes sought Luther for agreement.

"Ethan, jes' an itch, that's all it be."

Ethan didn't apologize but his gun returned to his side.

"My hand's going back to the saddle horn," Captain Thorne explained, slowly returning his hand to its original position. "You can tell your men to stand down, Mr. Kerry. You know who we are."

"I'll make that decision . . . Captain Thorne," Ethan said. "I've lost one good man, had my brother—and my friend, Rios, here—all shot up by strangers."

"I understand. I'm sorry we weren't there to help. Been tracking Gee long enough. One of these days we'll get lucky."

"With three of you?" Ethan cocked his head to the side.

Ignoring the comment, Captain Thorne proceeded to say what he had started before, that Gee was difficult to figure and that the rangers thought he might be coming back this way for revenge.

"Revenge?" Ethan straightened his back.

"You boys are the only ones who've put him on the run. The only ones."

Ethan looked like he had been struck in the face.

"Well, there's no reason to ride to your place now. We'll head east and see if we can cut his trail." Captain Thorne motioned to his associates to follow him and turned his horse to the east. "Stay alert, Mr. Kerry. Stay alert."

Chapter 22

Two weeks passed since Ethan and Luther rode with Rios to the Mexican's ranch. Rios appreciated Sotar and Miller staying on. Ethan and Luther had ridden their range twice since then, partly to check on the herd and mostly to look for any signs of a returning Victorio Gee.

Claire and Kathleen were in the kitchen; jars and bowls for canning covered the long counter. Maggie had helped, mostly by snapping green beans into pieces and placing them in one of the bowls. After her work was completed, Claire allowed her to play with her doll.

Displayed on the main table were the results of the women's efforts: canned goods for the winter, yet to be stored. Only Maggie's large bowl of green beans and another of beets remained to complete the canning for the year.

"I can finish this little bit, Kathleen," Claire said. "Why don't you see if Cole wants to go for a walk. Be good for both of you."

"He's sleeping. Besides, I don't think he's strong enough to do that."

"Don't be too sure. I heard him tell Luther that he wanted to go along the next time they checked the range."

Kathleen's face was tight. She, too, had heard the conversation, but had pretended to be asleep.

"What if he doesn't want to?" Kathleen's face was layered with suppressed fear.

"I guess you won't know 'til you ask." Claire patted her forehead with the back of her hand.

Kathleen stood for a moment, staring at the adobe kitchen wall. A tiny tremble at the corner of her mouth gave away what she felt. Claire put down a half-filled jar of beans, wiped her hands on her already soiled apron and said, "Kathleen, I know Cole Kerry. He loves you like there's no tomorrow. Get in there. Now." Her voice was stern.

Kathleen's gaze clicked from despair to anger, with the last emotion aimed at Claire.

"You can't change yesterday." Claire's voice was a little gentler. "What happened to you was awful. Maybe you can't get over it. That's not for me to say. But you've got to try."

Kathleen's eyes flashed. "What do you know about it? I was raped—by outlaws, by Victorio Gee, for God's sake. How can any man . . . want a wife . . . like that?" Tears came and she made no attempt to stop them.

Claire stood without moving. This was the first time Kathleen had cried; the first time she had expressed the venom inside her soul. It was a start, even if the hatred was aimed at her.

Waving her arms, Kathleen described what the outlaws had done to her and that she had prayed for death every day since. Claire didn't want to hear the details but knew she must and made no attempt to stop or console her. Finished with her story of terror, Kathleen's chin dropped and she sobbed quietly.

"I saw you kiss Cole's forehead a few nights ago."

"S-so what?" The anger was not as intense as it had been.

"Do you care about him?"

"Of course I do." Kathleen gurgled and rushed toward Claire. "H-help me, Claire. I'm scared. I-I don't . . ." She buried her head in Claire's shoulder and the older woman held her.

Claire's own tears burned down her tanned face and spilled onto her faded dress collar. Stepping back with her hands holding Kathleen, she declared, "I don't have any answers, Kathleen. You're right, I don't know anything about this. But I know about sadness and I know you have to go on. You have to bring Cole close—unless you want to send him away. If you do, they have won. That evil bastard has won. Is that what you want? Is Victorio Gee that important?" Her own words trembled at the edges.

Kathleen shook her head but no words followed. Her face was whiter than usual; freckles softened by lines of tears; eyes reddened by anguish that had ripped through her body to get out.

Claire was silent; she couldn't think of anything more to say. How could she tell Kathleen not to think about it anymore? How could she say it didn't make any difference—to Cole or anyone else? How could she say everything was going to be all right? But more words did come.

"The blackest time of my life was when the doctor told me Ethan was blind, that he wouldn't see. Ever." Claire's chin rose in defiance of the statement. "I thought our world was over." She motioned with her arms. "This place . . . our wonderful dream . . . would be taken by the bank." A single tear escaped from her right eye and followed a well-lined path down her face. "I prayed." She stopped to inhale. "My prayer was answered. Ethan's youngest brother came back. It was like I looked up—and Cole was there. I can still see that. I knew then we would make it."

She paused and told Kathleen about the day Luther rode in to tell them that his whole family was dead. The rawboned wrangler had wept in Ethan's arms and Ethan had hid every gun because he was fearful of what his older brother might do to himself.

"I-I love Cole."

"I know. Go tell him."

Kathleen's gaze clicked from despair to joy. "Cole Kerry, let's go for a walk," she announced and marched from the kitchen.

Returning to her unfinished canning, Claire prayed the gap between the two young Kerrys would be erased and that they could go on with their lives together. A part of her wanted to pray for revenge against the evil men who had ripped apart their lives but she stopped short of that request.

As Kathleen rounded the corner and stepped into their bedroom, Cole was waiting. He stood, fully dressed; his arm in a sling. An undefinable expression on his faded face. His crutch lay on the floor beside his bedding.

"I was just coming in to see if you wanted to go for a walk," he said, unsure of what she might say. "But if . . ."

"Were you really?"

"Y-yes. I-I miss you, Kathleen."

"I-I love you, Cole." She rushed into his arms.

"I love you, Kathleen. More'n anything."

Nothing mattered for minutes as their emotions cracked and melted together.

From the kitchen, Claire couldn't help but peek at the couple as they walked to the door, hand in hand. She smiled. "That's a good start, isn't it, God. Thank you."

The walk from the house to the corral where Kiowa was kept took a long time. Cole's leg was stiff and his body, weak. Kathleen held around his waist and he held around hers with his good left arm as they advanced. Both tried to talk at the same time and Cole told her to go ahead. As if on a string, her thoughts and fears came forward, one sentence after the other, one concern after the other.

She finished with a question: "Do you still want to be with me?"

Cole looked like he had been slapped in the face. He stopped and turned toward her. "When I was on that mesa, I didn't think I'd ever even get to see you again. I can't believe you were worried . . . about that. Kathleen, oh my Kathleen . . . I love you. I can't live without you at my side."

Her face dawned. He kissed her wet cheek. Her mouth sought his. In the middle of the ranch yard, they kissed and held each other. From the ranch window, Claire watched, smiled and turned back to the kitchen.

After a few minutes, they resumed their stroll; this time, in sweet silence.

In the center of the main corral, the big sorrel glistened in the late-morning sun. Kiowa looked every inch the powerful horse he was. Definitely a descendent of the "Spanish pacers" that roamed the land and could run forever. Great stallions that would rather jump off a cliff than be captured. Great stallions that led herds of horses to freedom. According to the stories, there were four of them—each a different color: white, blue roan, black and gray.

Cole's mind jumped from Kiowa to his friend,

Miguel del Rios. They shared a love of strong horses. He wanted to ride over to see how he was doing. Then his mind wanted to go to Victorio Gee and Ranger Bartlyn—and revenge, but he wouldn't let it. Not today. Not with his Kathleen so close.

Kiowa's welcoming whinny brought him back to the moment. In a flash, the red horse was standing next to them at the corral fence, leaning his head over the railing to receive some attention. Cole laughed and rubbed his face and ears with his left hand.

Kathleen watched their exchange and silently wondered about her husband's unmoving right arm. She bit her lower lip and realized it was the first time that she had truly thought of someone else in a long time.

"You're a good boy, Kiowa. A good boy," Cole said, unaware of his wife's review, and studied the horse's flank for any sign of the bullet wound. "Looks like ol' Luther fixed you up real fine." He turned to Kathleen, who was petting the horse's neck. "You know, Kiowa saved my life." He recalled what he could of the time outside the cave and up to the top of Ghost Mesa.

"Luther's been riding him. About every day, I think," she said.

"Good. But he looks like he's put on some weight," Cole observed. "Getting better care than I give him."

She smiled and ran her hand along the sorrel's long neck and down his chest as far as she could reach. She started to say something but didn't.

"Let's walk some more. All right?" he asked.

"Are you sure you're up to it?"

"Yeah. Feels good to be out."

After saying their good-byes to Kiowa, she took his hand and they strolled on, past the barn and past the shed near it. He tried to hide the stiffness in his leg but she noticed and decided not to say anything. Luther was responsible for the shed's contents now and the inside looked nothing like it had when Ethan knew where everything was because everything was in a special place. Cole laughed when he told Kathleen how Luther tried to keep Ethan from realizing how full of junk the small building had become. She joined him when he said that Ethan knew exactly what the shed was like because he had told him so.

Ten feet from the shed was an immense tree stump, four feet tall and four feet wide. Winds had torn away its majesty long ago. They paused beside its jagged top where names were carefully carved in it: "Ethan Kerry," "Claire Kerry" and "Luther Kerry" were in one tight grouping. "Clancey Kerry," "Elijah Kerry" and "Margaret Kerry" in another. Cole's late mother, "Alice Kerry," was there as were the names of Claire's parents, "William Johnson" and "May Allison Johnson." And off to the left was a wobbly version of "Cole Kerry." Beside it was "Kathleen Kerry," carved in deep, bold letters.

Kathleen fingered Cole's name and then hers. "Who put this here?" She already knew; she had been there when the carving was done, but wanted to hear it again.

"Must've been magic." He smiled.

He traced the origin of each name; Ethan had started the tradition with his name and Claire's. He thought it was Claire herself who had added his name; most had thought Cole was dead, somewhere on the outlaw trail. Claire told him Ethan secretly believed he was alive. He wasn't sure about Luther though.

She smiled. "Claire thinks a lot of you. She told me you were the answer to her prayer, after Ethan was . . . hurt."

"It was her idea that Luther an' I should become partners with Ethan on this ranch. She's a rock. A real rock."

"I know."

Cole fingered the edges of the stump. "Funny how a simple thing like this comes to mean so much. It's like, I don't know, like the tree was supposed to be this." He looked up at her. "Sounds kinda silly, doesn't it?"

"Not to me." She put her hand over his. "Will you put the names of our children here, too?"

Cole couldn't breathe for an instant.

"Y-yes," he finally blurted. "Two boys and two girls."

She giggled and he took her in his arms.

"How well are you, Cole Kerry?" she asked impishly.

"What do you mean? Well, I'm . . ."

"Let's go to the barn."

Chapter 23

A patrol of fat, dark clouds gathered to argue, but that didn't deter Claire from declaring, on a gloomy December 15 morning, that Christmas preparations were under way. "All right, you Kerry boys," she said at the breakfast table, "it's time to start getting ready for Christmas."

Her late parents and grandparents had come from Pennsylvania and she had been brought up with Christmas trees, stockings and Yule logs. Long a Kerry tradition, all hands were invited to Christmas dinner, except for a skeleton crew to watch the herds. Even during the leanest years, it was so. Getting ready had become sort of an expanded celebration all its own, with everyone—including the cowhands—chipping in.

Miguel del Rios and the old woman staying with him had, of course, been invited. This year, Ivan Drako and his wife had also been asked to join them. It was Ethan's suggestion. He was certain they had no one to share the holiday with. Claire had readily agreed.

"Boy howdy, Christmas! That do sound real fine,"

Luther exclaimed. He said almost the same thing every year. "Do I git to fix the beef this year?"

"No, that's Cole's job. He and DuMonte," Claire smiled and patted Luther's hand. "You are in charge of the hands. We're going to need lots of butter churned, cream whipped, potatoes peeled. Oh, and the tables set up." Her smile was warm; her eyes sparkled. "An', of course, I'm counting on you to finish the hams. They were so good last year, remember?"

"By golly, they was, wasn't they!" Luther said, turning his mouth from an exaggerated pout into a grin under his thick mustache. "But, shoot fire, I wanted to do the beef."

"Maybe next year," Claire purred.

Ethan folded his arms and listened. This was Claire's event. Even when he could see, his lady took charge of the holiday.

As usual, Luther was assigned the job of smoking three large hams that had been curing since last Christmas; DuMonte and Cole took on the task of making a side of beef taste even better than their last year's effort. They took two days to get the outside cooking coals at just the right level. Of course, Ethan offered suggestions as to timing and fire intensity. Even wood selection. On Christmas Eve day, a half-dozen chickens would be roasted in the regular stove to add to the feast.

Rommey, the trail cook, assisted in the kitchen, while various cowboys took turns churning butter, peeling potatoes, whipping cream and doing other preparatory tasks. Henderson said it was the only work he liked doing when he wasn't on a horse.

Cream puffs, one of Claire's finest Christmas moments, were early on the cooking list. Made with butter, flour, unbeaten eggs and filled with cream whipped to stiffness, they had quickly become a Christmas favorite. The whipping was a cowboy chore. So was the trip to town for more eggs.

Cream puffs weren't the only sweet item on the Christmas fare. Applesauce cake, vanilla custard and bread pudding completed the selection. She also planned on serving peanut brittle, a candy everyone loved last year, if the sack of peanuts she'd bought was shelled in time. The main meal would also feature dumplings, baked corn, baked beans, sweet apple pickles, plum jam and mounds of mashed potatoes. This year, Claire was trying out a new recipe of cabbage-and-corn salad.

In addition to helping Claire, Kathleen was proving herself quite the bread maker. Her rye bread, in particular, was a favorite of all the Kerry men. Her recipe had come from a Swedish woman in Abilene. Thick slices, smothered with butter, were like eating cake. Although she was of Irish blood, as were the Kerry men, she didn't hold with many superstitions—except she insisted on no one singing or whistling around the bread while it was baking. And the loaf must always be served right-side up.

Kathleen figured that it only made good sense to serve bread that way and that being quiet around baking bread was good insurance against it not rising because of noise.

That was the extent of Kathleen's Irish concerns, it seemed. She didn't believe a loaf of bread overturned in the oven was an omen of a death or that a hollow in a loaf was another symbol of death, since it appeared like a grave. Claire was pleased to discover Kathleen wasn't tied to such behaviors; she had always been glad none of the Kerry boys were superstitious. Clancey was a different matter, but no one listened to him anyway.

Of course, the women had to keep a close eye out

for Luther—and Cole—both. They had become adept at sneaking samples. Their stealth had become an expected effort with Claire pretending not to notice some of the time.

During this festive work period, Claire had started another tradition a few years ago: a huge pot stayed on the stove, filled with cooking meat and juices. Alongside were loaves of bread. When anyone was hungry, he simply tore off a hunk of bread, dipped it in the pot to soak up the juices and ladled pieces of meat on top. The savory snack was washed down with lots of hot coffee. It saved time and effort from cooking regular meals.

Ethan made his rounds, walking with Eli's guidance. Outside at the beef-cooking fire, Ethan stopped and offered an observation. "Boys, I think you need to let that fire set awhile. Let those coals really settle in. Let the beef really cook nice an' slow, you know."

"Get outta here!" Cole laughed. He had quit wearing a sling for his arm because the limb was still weak and his fingers were only slowly refinding their dexterity.

DuMonte chuckled and returned to adding more wood to their rich-orange fire.

After Ethan and Eli continued their stroll, Luther came by and whispered in Cole's ear, then ambled around the side of the house, toward the front. Watching him for a moment, Cole winked at DuMonte and yelled at the house, "Claire and Kathleen, could you two come and take a look at the beef?"

"What's the matter?" Claire's voice rang out from the kitchen.

"Not sure. Just want your opinion and Kathleen's—on the fire."

"Just a minute." Claire looked at Kathleen, who bit her lower lip to keep from laughing. "Sound fishy to you, Kathleen?"

"Oh yes. Mr. Rommey can you stand guard while we go?"

Wearing what appeared to be a new white shirt, William Rommey nodded his responsibility, picked up a large cooking spoon and marched over to the counter where the desserts were being placed.

As the women exited the back door to check on Cole's fire, Luther tiptoed around the corner. Seeing Rommey, he stopped, put his finger against his mouth to ask him to stay quiet and reached for the cream puffs.

"No sir, Mr. Kerry. I've got my orders," Rommey declared, shaking the spoon for emphasis.

"Oh, come on now, Rommey. We've bin a'workin' hard. Need a bit o' sweet, ya know."

"Get out of here—or I'll tell the ladies."

"Oh . . . oh . . . oh, don' do that. I'm a'goin'. I'm a'goin'." Luther sputtered and retreated back around the corner.

Claire and Kathleen returned to the kitchen, laughing and talking at the same time.

"Well, Mr. Rommey, did we have any visitors?" Claire asked.

"Ah, sort of—but I think Luther was just passing through."

Claire smiled and folded her arms. "Luther?" Her voice carried throughout the house.

Standing just out of sight, behind the wall to the kitchen, Luther answered, "Yes, Claire? I . . . were lookin' fer a fork. Ya know, fer the ham."

"You may come and get a cream puff for you, Cole and DuMonte—but don't tell anybody about it or we won't have any for Christmas." Claire glanced at Kathleen, who smiled her agreement.

"Ohmyyes!" Luther declared, hustling into the kitchen in that bowlegged shuffle of his. He picked up three of the closest pastries, paused and asked, "Could I take four? Roper's bin he'pin' me sum."

"Yes, Luther, you may." Claire grinned. "Now scoot." She turned away, then spun back as the wrangler waddled out of the kitchen, holding his treats as if they were precious jewels. "Oh, if you come across Ethan, tell him it's time to bring in the Yule log."

"Yes 'm."

Kathleen giggled. "Do you think the puffs can stay in the cooling house until Christmas?"

Shaking her head, Claire put her hand to her mouth to hold back a laugh. "Maybe. But I don't figure there'll be any left by then. If we have time, we'll do another batch. If not, we'll have plenty of other sweets, won't we, Mr. Rommey?"

Uncomfortable with the conversation, and confused about whether he was really supposed to keep people from taking the treats, Rommey frowned and muttered, "I hope so. I could make some pies."

"Of course," Claire said. "Some mincemeat pies, for sure."

Bringing in the Yule log was an exciting adventure for Eli and Maggie, with Ethan waiting by the fireplace for them to bring the previously cut limb. The log had been kept in a special place in the barn, wrapped in an old blanket. Kathleen had tied colored ribbon around it earlier.

Proudly, they brought it into the house, singing, "Deck the halls with boughs of holly, fa-la-la-la-la-la-la-la-laaa. 'Tis the season to be jolly, fa-la-la-la-la-la-la-la-laaa." Eli didn't know any more words so they sang it over and over until they placed it in the fireplace. They stood back to admire their effort. Ethan stepped toward them instinctively and Maggie hugged him around the leg and Eli followed.

As part of the tradition, an unburnt piece of last

year's log would be used to light the new one. Ashes from last year's log—kept in a box under Ethan's and Claire's bed for luck—would be added to the flame. It was Luther's job to bring the box. The tradition was pure Claire—and not, she assured herself, the same thing as a superstition.

Singing his own version of "Deck the Halls," Luther bounced from the bedroom carrying the box. "Deck the breads with butter an' jelly, fa-la-la-la-la-la-la-la-laaa. 'Tis the season to fill your belly, fa-la-la-la—"

Halfway to the fireplace, he stumbled, crossed his right boot against his left leg and fell with his arms outstretched. Ashes, twigs and pieces of burnt wood flew into the air. Ethan jumped but not quickly enough and his pants were streaked with gray powder. Claire's fine oval braided rug was splattered with ashes and soot from one end to the other.

Lying on the floor, with his nose to the ground, Luther slowly raised his eyes to survey the damage. He didn't move.

"What happened?" Ethan yelled. "Luther?"

Claire and Kathleen came running from the kitchen, halfway thinking it was another stunt by Cole and Luther to get to the desserts. Claire again warned Rommey to stand guard as she left.

"Oh-h-h." Claire stood and looked at the living room rug.

Claire put her hands to her mouth, first in shock and then to suppress a giggle. But not quite. That was enough to trigger an outburst from Kathleen. She stood, shaking and laughing, with tears running down her face. Claire joined her, followed by Ethan, without being absolutely certain what he was laughing at. Eli glanced around at the adults and soon was laughing gaily. Finally Luther joined in, from the floor.

Only Maggie frowned; then her lower lip pushed its

way out from her mouth and tears soon followed. She hid her head against her father's thigh. It took a few moments for Ethan to realize she wasn't laughing. He knelt beside her, trying to find her face to wipe away the wetness.

"What's the matter, Maggie? We can clean it up."

"Now we'll have bad luck."

"Bad luck? Who told you that?" Ethan said.

"Grandpaw," Maggie whimpered. "He said the Yule log ashes had to be kept just right or we would have bad luck."

Ethan was fuming that his father would tell his young daughter such foolishness. Wasn't it enough the old drunk was constantly in the way—and had never come close to providing for his family when the boys were young? Cole's resentment of their father was barely contained; Ethan had worked hard at accepting the man's foolhardy ways, with Claire's guidance. Luther was the only Kerry who was truly gentle with the man.

"Grandpaw didn't mean it that way, sweetheart," Claire was beside them. "He was talking about being careful putting the ashes in the box."

"B-but they aren't in the b-box anymore. Does that mean Uncle Luther will . . ."

"No, Maggie." Claire was trying to keep her own aggravation at Ethan's father from showing. "It doesn't. It just means it'll take a little work before we can all enjoy one of our Christmas traditions. That's all." She smiled and patted Maggie's head. "Maybe you could go get the broom." She looked up at Eli. "Son, we're going to need something flat to sweep the ashes onto."

Reluctantly, Maggie left to get the broom but not before she glanced back at Luther with a worried look on her face. Eli was ahead of her, running to get an old newspaper he had seen on the desk.

The bowlegged wrangler struggled to get to his feet. "I'm plumb sorry, Claire. Got all tangled up lik' sum yearlin'." He stood and stared at the mess. "I'll git it all sweeped up."

"I know you will, Luther. Eli and Maggie will help." With that, Claire returned to the kitchen.

"That's what happens when you eat all those cream puffs," Ethan growled.

Chapter 24

On December 23rd, out of the barn came wide planks and sawhorses to make additional tables, all carefully stored for the annual occasion. Ethan had designed the original arrangement of temporary settings in the house and the layout continued to serve them well, even with the addition of two more tables. Of course, Claire directed the assembly.

"Oh, where'd I put that tablecloth?" Claire stewed. "Maggie, go look in the bottom drawer of . . . no, never mind, I'll get it. I know just where it is." With that, Claire disappeared and returned minutes later with a folded light blue cloth in her arms.

"Hey, that were your maw's t'weren't it?" Luther said, as if seeing it for the first time. Claire smiled; Luther said that every year. "Are ya gonna put out them purty candles too?"

"Yes, we are. Kathleen's going to do that, I believe."

"Boy howdy, this's gonna be some shindig!"

Claire smiled; Luther said that each year as well.

She loved the slow-minded man for his sheer enjoyment of Christmas.

With the tables in place, she turned her attention back to the dinner preparation itself. Ethan and Eli were put in charge of distributing plates and ironware, which really meant Ethan would carry a load in, with Eli guiding him, and Eli would set them in place. Maggie would help her mother and aunt, or think she was.

Last-minute additions were three large prairie grouse shot by a new hand, Orville Whitney. He had joined during the roundup. His work had been solid and DuMonte had recommended giving him a regular job. The additional fowl weren't needed but Claire accepted them graciously.

Christmas Eve day came all too soon and Claire wasn't certain she dared to leave the house for church in the evening but everyone insisted she go. Even stiff-necked Rommey offered to finish the various cooking details—except those that couldn't be done until Christmas morning itself.

With that, the entire Kerry family loaded into the wagon and went to town for church services. Except for Clancey, who was so drunk from giving Christmas toasts to himself he couldn't stand. DuMonte was assigned the task of keeping him out of the kitchen; Rommey had no patience for anyone bothering him.

Frost smoke covered their faces as they laughed and sang songs along the way. Cole and Kathleen insisted on sitting in the back of the wagon with Eli and Maggie. And, of course, Blue. The big, ugly dog curled up beside Cole and went to sleep with its huge nose lying on his leg. When Luther described the scene to Ethan, the rancher couldn't believe it and asked Claire, sitting between them, to verify its truth.

The small church sat alone on a hill outside of town.

A large bell stood nearby, used to signal parishioners to worship—and to send the alarm of approaching Indians, back when that was a problem. A boy was working its rope with enthusiasm. The bell's clanging drowned out the lone tinkling of a piano in town, a haunting solitary sound from one of the saloons.

Cole eased himself off the back end, feeling much weaker than he wanted anyone to know, being careful not to put weight on his right arm. But he turned and took Kathleen with both hands to assist her descent. It took all of his strength. His right arm trembled with the weight.

"Thank you, Mr. Kerry," she said, and curtsied coquettishly.

"You're welcome, little lady." His smile was warm. "Hey, let me help this little lady, too." He reached over and lifted Maggie from the wagon to the ground. This time, he used only his left hand.

She looked up at him. "Thank you, Uncle Cole . . . I'm so glad you are well again."

He glanced at Kathleen and replied, "Well, thank you, sweetheart. So am I."

Kathleen whispered. "Not as glad as I."

Cole blushed and grinned.

Eli shunned any assistance getting out of the wagon and told Blue to stay there. The big dog reluctantly slumped to the buckboard floor. As they walked toward the church, a half-painted structure, an awful sense of despair ran through Kathleen. Out of the corner of her eyes, she tried to see if people were looking at her. Surely, they all knew she had been raped. She would be looked upon with the same disdain as the town whores.

She wobbled and took Cole's arm. He seemed unaware of what she was experiencing. They had talked about it once and he had assured her no one knew, that the story told was she had been released immediately so no one would follow the gang. She wasn't sure the story was believable and now her anxiety about it was galloping through her.

The small church was overflowing with happy people, an even mixture of townspeople and neighboring ranchfolk. Services were conducted by the mayor, whose only claim to religious background was that he had once read the Bible all the way through and liked to talk. R. W. Lovington was a short, well-bellied man with slicked-back hair and a deep voice. His sermon was too long and way too rambling; it even included praise for the Kerry men for saving the town from Victorio Gee.

Upon hearing the words, Kathleen turned pale. For a moment, she thought she might faint. Or run out. Would the mayor say something about her? *Ohmy-God, no!* she muttered to herself. *Please, no.*

". . . and we are so pleased, Lord, that you have seen fit to return Cole Kerry to health . . . and Jeremiah Holder and William Lindsay . . . and we thank you for the safe return of Mrs. Kerry . . . unharmed and untouched by those evil men. Again, thanks to the quick and courageous rescue by the Kerry cowboys." He went on to ask for divine assistance in the recovery of Mrs. Trieson from a fall, and Mr. Liemann from a bad fever.

But Kathleen wasn't listening anymore. Her sigh of relief was mostly swallowed by her hand over her mouth. Echoing through her mind were the phrases "safe return" . . . "unharmed and untouched." *Where had he heard this? Cole had mentioned his brothers but this seemed so forceful, so authoritative*. Her startled survey of the church took in a gray-haired man in the second row. Of course. Dr. Hawkinson. That kind old man must have decided on his own to plant the story that she had not been harmed by the outlaws. She wanted to stand and yell out her thanks. It had to be him reinforcing Ethan's and Luther's explanations.

"Let us join together in the hymn 'It Came Upon a Midnight Clear.'"

"It came upon a midnight clear, that glorious sound of old . . ."

She reached over and grabbed Cole's left hand. He looked at her and his smile indicated he knew what she was thinking. Their voices joined the others. After the service, Kathleen quickly sought Dr. Hawkinson to thank him. The sprightly older man smiled and said he didn't know what she was talking about, then asked how Cole was doing.

Outside the building, Mayor Lovington asked Cole if he might have a word with him. Standing off to the side, the mayor said that there was considerable discussion in town about asking Cole to become the town marshal. No one thought Acting Marshal Maynard was mature enough for the post. Cole thanked him for the compliment but indicated he had no interest. He started to tell him that his right hand wouldn't hold a gun but didn't.

"You know, Cole, there's a story going around . . . about Victorio Gee coming back," the mayor said, his eyebrows rising to support the observation. "Nobody's ever done to him and his gang what you Kerrys did. Fact is, some think he'll storm your place."

"Victorio Gee's gone from here, Mayor," Cole said. "Besides, it's Christmas Eve. We can talk about this some other time."

"Sure. Sure. Right you are. Christmas Eve," the mayor quickly supported. "Merry Christmas to ya."

"Merry Christmas to you."

Cole took several steps away, looking for Kathleen, and saw Jeremy McKeon hurrying toward him. The general store proprietor was wearing a new suit, one of the ready-mades he carried, but his attire was subordinated by the frown shoving down to his eyes.

"Cole, it's so good to see you. Merry Christmas." McKeon shook Cole's hand vigorously. "Heard all about your wounds. My goodness, that was awful. Thank God your brothers found your wife before . . ."

"Yeah, we were lucky. Merry Christmas to you, Jeremy."

Stepping closer, the excitable storekeeper said, "I heard yesterday Gee was coming back this way with more men."

"Who told you that?"

"A stranger passing through. Didn't know him," McKeon said. "Came into the store for some tobacco, I think it was. No, he was looking for a watch. That was it, a watch."

Cole smiled. Only a storekeeper would recite such an unimportant detail as a purchase. But it bothered him that the fake ranger was also someone McKeon didn't know. Surely, any spy of Gee's wouldn't tip his hand about coming this way—unless there was some advantage in it.

"He said his brother told him. Lives south of here. Jay Creek. Heard it from some rangers." McKeon licked his lower lip to rid it of the dryness.

"So why did he think Gee was headed this way?"

"He didn't say."

"An' you didn't ask."

"No. No, I didn't. Guess I should've."

Smiling, Kathleen joined them, wished the storekeeper a "Merry Christmas" and informed Cole that the family was waiting. He excused himself but told McKeon to share what he knew with Acting Marshal Maynard and Mayor Lovington.

From the church, Ivan Drako and his wife, Evangeline, emerged; she was filled with holiday spirit and chatting gaily with everyone; he was trying to smile but it didn't come naturally. After they cleared the church, he withdrew a black cigar and shoved it into his mouth. That brought something closer to a smile. They warmly greeted Ethan and Claire and said they were looking forward to being with them tomorrow. Evangeline Drako said she had baked three pies—two apple and one gooseberry. Claire acknowledged that they would be a wonderful addition and thanked her for the thoughtfulness. Evangeline beamed.

"What is your brother talking about with the young constable and the mayor?" Drako asked, chewing vigorously on his new cigar.

"Didn't know he was, Ivan," Ethan chuckled. "Don't see so good these days."

Drako frowned. "Be foolish talk around . . . of this Victorio Gee coming back. I heard it before church. Have you heard this?"

"No. No one's said anything like that to me."

"Just as well, What foolish nonsense some speak of. You would be thinking they had better things of which to do."

Ethan smiled. "Yeah, well, that's people. You got your herd all ready for winter?"

"Yah, I be guessing so. We do as you say, Ethan. I am to keep them in the valley. There is water and grass."

"Good. Your boys are usin' that old cabin?"

"Yes, it is so. Evangeline want to go there and be putting up . . . curtains and bed spreads. Aye, I talk her away of it."

Ethan roared and slapped his thighs with both hands.

"Oh, be looking like Evangeline has the talk with

everyone," Drako declared. "We see you tomorrow. At two?"

"Sounds good. Merry Christmas, Ivan."

"Yah, and a fine holiday wish I give to you, Ethan Kerry."

The ride home was boisterous, with everyone trying to talk at once, even Ethan, who told a story about one Christmas when the Kerry boys were young. All three boys got a lump of coal for Christmas; their father said it was a useful gift and had pointed at their small stove. Luther and Ethan had dutifully added theirs to the small fire but eight-year-old Cole refused. In spite of his father's admonishments—and Ethan's threats—Cole had taken his piece of coal outside and hidden it. Then he brought in a small box he had decorated with cloth and gave it to his mother.

"You should've seen the look on Clancey's face," Ethan said. "Remember that, Cole? Wonder if that piece of coal is still buried there."

Luther choked, apologized and urged the horses into a trot.

Nestled against Cole in the back of the wagon, Kathleen said, "You must've been a sweet boy. I'll bet all the girls were in love with you."

"Hardly. The only girl I ever looked at was you."

"Oh, Cole Kerry, you sweet-talkin' thing." She kissed his cheek, then leaned over and kissed the reddened cheeks of Eli and Maggie. Something passed across her mind and she became silent. Almost studious, as if working to remember something.

"What are you thinking about, my love? Christmas when you were a child? Tell me," Cole asked.

Kathleen looked up, startled. "What? Oh yes, wonderful memories. Once, my mother made this doll for me. I must have been Maggie's age. Maybe a little younger. It was the most wonderful doll in the world. Wish I still had it."

"You do. In your memories."

"That's very sweet. I love you, Mr. Kerry," she whispered.

"I love you, Mrs. Kerry."

It was Maggie's turn to inform them that the moon was "coming home with her." She pointed at the night sky and the moon sliver that appeared to be moving along with their travel. Eli said that was silly while he rubbed his dog's ears but Kathleen told her that she often thought the moon followed her and that it was good luck, especially on Christmas Eve.

When they got home, Luther and Cole dragged in a pine tree that had been cut down and stood it in the southwest corner of the main room, where all would see it immediately upon entering the house. Eli and Maggie draped it with long strings of dried berries and popped corn already prepared. Claire and Kathleen tied on ribbon bows of red, yellow, blue and white and added some small crocheted white circles upon the sturdier boughs.

"Boy howdy, ain't that purty!" Luther exclaimed. "I do believe that's darn near as purty as a good sunset."

Cole whispered to Kathleen that his brother said the same thing every year.

Claire brought out a treasured, handmade wooden tree, something her mother had made years before. She placed the two-foot-high decoration on a lace cloth on their fireplace mantel and began adding candles to the small holes in the wood outpieces.

A toast of warmed whiskey—and hot cider for the children—followed, and the children each got a stocking and Cole held them in place over the mantel with well-placed books. Somewhat embarrassed, Luther brought out one of his and pushed it under a big book.

Giddy, Eli and Maggie went to bed with the promise of a special story from their mother. The three Kerry men went to the bunkhouse with a large tray of freshly baked doughnuts. Luther brought along the whiskey bottle; at Ethan's suggestion, Cole grabbed a new box of cigars from the desk.

The night was cold. Only the thin sliver of a moon had been brave enough to show itself. Scattered across the black sky were a handful of stars. The three men strolled briskly toward the bunkhouse with Ethan gripping Cole's upper right arm. The youngest Kerry didn't want his brother to know that the grip made his arm tingle.

"Sur beats watchin' beef, boys. 'Tis a fine Christmas," Luther exclaimed joyously.

"Yeah, it is," Cole responded and decided not to share what McKeon had told him. Most likely it was pure windy.

"Are the candles in the windows?" Ethan asked. "Does it look like . . . always?"

Luther nodded. He was doing his best to stay happy. Christmastime was always hard on him when memories came calling to drag him back. He turned back to enjoy the candles Claire and Kathleen had placed in all the ranch house windows. Their glow in the night made him shiver. He swallowed to push back one yesterday, then another. Flickers of shadowed memory that he couldn't handle. Two small children sitting beside a hearth; their mother reading them a story. They looked up at him. He took another step and went to his knees. Some of the doughnuts on the tray spilled onto the dark ground.

"Luther, what's the matter?" Cole stopped so quickly that Ethan lost his balance and grabbed his brother to keep from falling.

"What . . . what happened?" Ethan blurted.

Cole steadied the rancher. "Stand here, Ethan. Luther's hurting."

"Hurting? What'd he do?"

"It's memories, Ethan. Memories."

"Oh, damn."

"Yeah."

He stepped toward his oldest brother and put a hand on his shoulder, holding the cigar box in his other. Luther's body was shaking. "Luther, it's all right." Cole spoke slowly, like a father comforting a child awakening from a nightmare.

Looking up at Cole through bleary eyes, Luther blubbered, "Oh, Cole, they was so li'l, so good. An' my April. Oh God, how . . ."

Ethan was beside Cole. "They're in a good place, Luther. When it's your time, they'll be waitin' for you—an' you'll be together again."

Cole glanced at Ethan, surprised at his brother's comforting statement. He knew Ethan hadn't prayed since he was blinded, deciding God was punishing him—or there wasn't a God, depending on his mood.

"Do ya really think that be so, Ethan?" Luther wiped his long, droopy mustache with his fist. Moonlight slid into the heavy wrinkles on the right side of his face and stayed there.

"Yes, I do."

"Will they be a'knowin' me?"

"'Course they will. They'll come runnin' to you." Ethan's own countenance was rigid, as if holding back raw feelings.

Cole was quiet, unsure of what more to say.

"Remember the time, shortly after you came here," Ethan spoke quietly, staring off toward the bunkhouse, "when you thought you saw them in the woods?"

"I-I 'member. They was a'wavin' at me. B-but when I went ov'r thar, they wasn't . . ."

"They were tellin' you that they were fine an' happy—an' not to worry about them, weren't they?" Ethan's words flowed as if coming from somewhere else. "Weren't they?"

"I . . . I reckon so, Ethan. They dun were smilin'." Slowly, the lumbering man stood. He hugged Cole, then Ethan, surprising his blind brother with his burst of emotion. Lifting his chin, he said, "I'm ready now."

"You're sure?" Cole asked. "We're not in a hurry."

It was Ethan's turn to be silent.

"Nosirree, I be jes' fine. Christmas be a time fer bein' happy 'bout what a feller's got—not what he ain't got." If possible, Luther's clothes were more wrinkled than usual.

"All right, let's go see our boys," Ethan declared.

"Jes' as soon as I pick up these here doughnuts—an' wipe 'em off." Luther chuckled and Cole joined in the regathering.

Inside the bunkhouse, the men gathered around the doughnuts with enthusiasm and the bottle was passed along with stories of the trail and days gone by. In honor of the birth of Christ, DuMonte asked if he could offer a prayer and the men quickly bowed their heads and solemnity took over. When he was finished praying, Cole noticed Ethan's lips were still moving for a few seconds.

"Now, don't forget Christmas dinner is at two," Ethan announced. "If we run out of potatoes, it's all Stovepipe's fault."

That brought back joyous noise and a return to stories. They toasted the memories of Abe and other trailmates who had fallen.

In a soft tenor voice, Stovepipe Henderson began to sing, "Silent night, holy night, all is calm, all is bright . . ." Soon the bunkhouse was filled with song. But the caroling soon evolved into trail songs because no one knew the words to anything except "Silent Night."

Morning found Eli and Maggie excited about their stockings filled with candy, nuts and an apple—and wrapped packages resting in the tree itself. Brown wrappings were enthusiastically torn open to reveal their treasures. For Maggie, a new doll, green ribbons for her hair and a tiny red dress Kathleen had made just for the doll. For Eli, a pocketknife, a book about animals and a blue bandana he put on immmediately.

Barely holding back his excitement, Luther joined them and took down his filled stocking and relished in its treasures of nuts, stick candy, an apple and several squares of tobacco. He shoved a candy stick in his mouth and yelled, "Merry Christmas!" Everyone joined in with enthusiastic greetings.

Cole passed Kathleen, standing near the door, and whispered, "Merry Christmas, my love."

"Merry Christmas to you, Mr. Cole Kerry," she said, smiling. "I have a present for you."

His grin was quick and smooth. "Oh really? I believe I have one for you, too."

She bit her lower lip. "Oh, what is it?"

"Can't tell. I'll give it to you later. When we're alone."

"Oh, I can't wait."

Cole watched her return to the kitchen. A loud noise drew his attention back to the main room. Hungover and unusually gruff, Clancey entered the room. He bellowed something about everyone making too much noise. Luther reminded him that it was Christmas Day and the elder Kerry hesitated, as if trying to determine whether or not his oldest son was telling the truth.

Not particularly interested in anything his father had to say or do, Cole turned away. His gaze passed the window behind him and he saw riders. Specks really. They disappeared behind a long line of hills yellowed by the bright winter sun.

Riders on Christmas Day? Could neighbors be coming to call? Had he imagined it? Victorio Gee?

Chapter 25

"Riders coming," Cole said without taking his eyes from the window.

"Riders?" Ethan straightened his back. "From which direction? Is it our boys? Might be trouble with the cattle."

Cole pointed. "Coming from the south. It's not our men. Too many, anyway. Might be a dozen. Could be twenty. Didn't get that long a look. They slid behind those hills."

"Now how do ye be knowin' that, me lad?" Clancey bellowed. He always seemed to think the louder he spoke, the more authoritative he sounded.

Cole didn't answer.

Luther came to where he stood and peered outside. "I don't see nuthin', Cole. Whar they be?"

"They're beneath the rim right now. Behind those yellow hills. When we see them again, they'll be thirty minutes out."

"Folks comin' to Christmas call?" Luther squinted again.

"No, I think it's Victorio Gee."

The words were a bullwhip into the festive room. In the kitchen, Claire and Kathleen froze.

Ethan's jaw dropped. "Can't be! It's Christmas—an' he . . ."

"McKeon told me in church that he'd heard Gee was heading this way," Cole said.

"How come you didn't say nothin' about it?" Ethan exclaimed.

"Thought it was just talk, Ethan," Cole said.

"You still should'a . . ."

"There isn't time to argue about it. If I'm wrong, we can all laugh," Cole interrupted. "I'll go tell the men in the bunkhouse—and we'll fan out to meet them. Maybe we can turn the surprise around."

Glancing at Ethan, Luther burst out, "Three rangers dun tolt us the same thang. Be a month back, it were. When we dun rode wi' Miguel to his place."

Cole was already moving toward his bedroom. His rifle and guns were there. Kathleen met him at the doorway; her face was pale and she was shaking.

He held her in a quick embrace and kissed her cheek. "We've got to be steady now. We've got to think. Be brave. We've got each other."

"Cole . . . I-I'm s-scared. I-I can't . . ."

"I'm scared, too. But we have to be ready. You help shoot. Can you do that?" He touched her shoulder. "I won't let anything happen to you. I promise."

"They can't do anything worse to me, Cole. I'm worried about you." Kathleen's face had suddenly transformed into an accepting calmness; her voice matched her expression. "Be careful. You and I have Christmas presents to unwrap." She forced a smile.

"Yeah, we do, my love."

She left to help Claire and Luther gather weapons and ammunition. Cole opened the dresser drawer, took the gunbelt and its two holstered Colts with his left hand and flung it over his shoulder. He hurried for his Winchester propped against the wall in the corner of the room. His right hand shivered as he gripped the gun and he grabbed it with his left as well, shifting the gunbelt on his shoulder so it wouldn't fall. Could he lever the gun with his right hand? Could he even hold a revolver?

As he ran toward the front door, Cole pointed at the heavy shutters that served to block the windows in times of emergency; gunholes at the right level were cut through the wood.

"Leave them open—until you start shooting," he said without stopping.

"Make 'em think we're napping, eh? Good idea," Ethan replied. "Get some men on horses, Cole. Hit 'em at their rear."

Cole raced out the door, letting his brother's advice sink in and hearing him direct the defense. Ethan's idea was a good one. If there was enough time. Only DuMonte was awake and dressed when he bolted through the bunkhouse door.

"Merry Christmas, boss!" DuMonte said cheerily. From his bed, Stovepipe Henderson yawned and started to say the same thing.

Cole's response was "Victorio Gee's just over the hills."

DuMonte's smile vanished and a quick prayer followed in his eyes. "You heard him, men. Get up an' get your guns." He turned back to Cole. "Should I send someone to the line cabins for help?"

"No time. We've got, maybe, fifteen minutes before they reach the big gate. This'll be over before anyone could get there an' back."

DuMonte blinked and nodded.

"Harold, keep three men here. Place the rest where

they'll do the most good. I'm going to saddle Kiowa an' hit them from the side when they come over the ridge."

"Mr. Kerry, I'd like to ride with y'all, if y'all will have me." The newest cowhand, Orville Whitney, stepped away from his bed. The bearded, stocky cowboy was fully dressed with a gunbelt strapped on and a rifle in his hands. Cole didn't think he was even awake when he came in.

"Glad to have you. Go an' saddle a good horse."

From the far corner, the young cowboy, Roper, came hopping forward with one boot on and no pants; his shirt was buttoned only with one button and it was in the wrong buttonhole, making him look lopsided.

"I'd like to ride with you, too, Mr. Kerry." His expression was pleading.

The young man would be no safer here than with him, Cole decided. "I would like to have you with me, Roper."

Roper's face lit up like he had been invited to a Sunday dance.

"Got a handgun, Roper?" Old Ben Speakman asked, removing his pipe from his mouth. "You can't lasso 'em, boy." A chuckle followed.

"Ah, no. Got me a Henry, though," Roper said, pulling on his pants. "Ain't so good with a pistol."

Speakman offered his big Walker Colt Dragoon, but Roper declined. "Ben, I'd prob'ly fly off my hoss when I shot that thang."

The one-armed former soldier began to tell about a battle when one of his fellow soldiers did just that but Roper wasn't listening as he tried to find his other boot and hat. No one else was listening either as they scurried for clothes and weapons.

"I'll go with you." Henderson sat on his bed with his

boots on, pulling on his pants. His gloves lay neatly beside him.

"Stovepipe, I'd rather have you in the barn," Cole replied. "I need a good man shooting from the loft."

"I can do that." Henderson was grim; fear in his face quite readable. But Cole knew the lanky cowboy wouldn't break. He had seen him fight in the great trail drive ambush.

"Thanks, Stovepipe," Cole said, then turned to DuMonte. "Put somebody inside the cooling house. It'll give another good angle of fire." He put his hand on DuMonte's shoulder. "Hold until they get close. Let 'em into the yard. They'll think they've surprised us."

"We're not long on cartridges," DuMonte advised. "Maybe a box. Whatever's left over from the town fight."

"Send somebody to the house real quick. We've got more there." Cole spun and left, heading for the corral where Kiowa waited. His saddle and tack were lying next to the main corral post. He had ridden yesterday. It felt strange and his leg was so weak he could barely keep himself positioned in the stirrups. That didn't matter now. He had no choice.

Placing his rifle against the post, he belted on his gunbelt, swinging it from his shoulder. The fingers on his right hand were slow, like a thick dream. Hesitating, he drew the Colt from his sidewinder holster and inserted a sixth bullet. His right hand trembled with the weight. Shifting the gun to his good hand, he shoved it into his belt for use with that hand. The second gun, with its sixth cartridge added, was returned to its regular holster.

Satisfied, he yanked the gear from the ground, entered the corral and called to the sorrel. Kiowa's head was already up; his ears alert. A soft snort was nothing more than an indication of surprise; then the horse trotted toward the advancing Cole.

"Steady, boy. I gotta have your help. Not much time, Kiowa. Stand, boy. Stand." Cole flipped the saddle blanket in place and followed it with the saddle. He stopped for breath; his entire body was screaming. His exhalation was jerky and his light-headedness wanted him to tilt to the left.

Kiowa stood without moving. Head down now.

Shaking his head to clear it, Cole tightened the cinch and slipped on the headstall, mostly using his left hand. His mind was yelling "hurry" but the fingers in his other hand were quaking and his wounded leg felt like it would collapse at any moment. He led the big horse from the corral, retrieved his Winchester with his left hand and swung halfway into the saddle. In midair, he lost his momentum and had to push with all his remaining strength to keep from falling. His rifle barrel awkwardly poked into Kiowa's neck and Cole apologized as soon as he righted himself.

From the other direction came two mounted riders: Whitney and young Roper. Silently, Cole wished Rios, Sotar and Miller were here, instead of at Rios's ranch, but Sotar wasn't due for Christmas dinner until much later in the day, coming with Rios. Miller was staying with the Rios herd.

That made him think of his Mexican friend and anger swelled inside him. Abe, Rios and his Kathleen. Three reasons to kill Gee. His battle-savvy mind reminded him that a vengeful man can make mistakes. This was no moment for anger. Only a cool head. Bar K men would be outnumbered if his estimate of Gee's men was anywhere close.

All four horses were snorting and stutter stepping, eager to run. Especially Kiowa. Cole wished there were time to push them for a while, enough to get their second wind. During the war, cavalry had learned horses performed better in battle that way; it was something learned from the Plains Indians.

"Follow me. We'll head out the back and curl around."

"Hit 'em from the rear?" Whitney smiled and the gleam of coming battle was in his eyes.

"Yeah. My brother Ethan's idea."

As they rode east, a flash of movement indicated a cowboy was headed for the stone cooling house. He looked back again to see someone disappearing through its small but thick door. They might hit the bunkhouse first; he wished that he had warned DuMonte of that possibility. It might be better if there weren't many in there. Firing from the bunkhouse windows offered only a limited field of fire anyway, especially after Gee's men fanned out.

His vision also glimpsed Ferguson returning from the house with his arms holding a large box. Cartridges. Cole couldn't remember seeing the fat cowboy move so fast. He figured Ethan had enouraged the speed.

He wasn't certain how Ethan would direct the family within the house but was confident no one could do it better. Probably Eli and Ethan would load, while Luther, Claire and Kathleen would shoot. If Clancey were sober enough, he might, too. Ethan also might have their father take Maggie into her bedroom to help keep her quiet. He chuckled to himself; it would probably be the other way around, with the little girl calming her grandfather.

Claire could shoot. That was well known. She had even taken third place in the county fair a year ago, against all-male competition. Ethan had encouraged her to enter. He knew Kathleen had been around guns but didn't know if she could—or would—be able to shoot. He could only hope her angst would be directed at Gee's destruction. Luther might be slow-minded but he was braver than most men. Cole shook away the tinge of fear that told him this might be the last Christmas they were all together. If Gee's gang got as far as the ranchhouse, it wouldn't take long for their sheer numbers to overwhelm them.

"Let's go, men. I don't want them seeing our dust."

In minutes, they cleared a low ridge and passed a small spring cut from a rock-strewn draw. Sunlight was confident, taking full control of the trees and putting shadows into retreat. A winter wind snapped at the edges of the cottonwoods and struggling alders. Frost bent the brown willows lining natural stone walls that formed this pocket of crystal clear water, breathing from a spring whose soul lay deep within the earth. A thin layer of ice was almost halfway across its surface. Tracks around the pond indicated animals of every kind and from every direction had sought its cool salvation.

Finally, they reined up along a line of cottonwoods that had attracted smaller brigades of stunted pines and dying underbrush. They could see the ranch yard but wouldn't be seen easily. Cole advised the three to dismount and check their weapons; there was no need to stay on the horses and rile them up. Their dash to this location had released some of their winter energy but Kiowa acted like it had been a walk around the corral. The sorrel pawed the ground with Cole holding the reins. Cole quieted the big animal into standing with its ears cocked for any noise.

Winter's hibernation for cattle and cowboys had settled throughout the land, giving it an ominous emptiness. Whatever feelings about Christmas morning had vanished like a man's breath. Silence strutted across the long valley and to their waiting point. Waiting was the worst part in some ways, Cole thought. And the idea that he had been mistaken pushed its way into his mind. *Maybe I was just seeing things. Maybe it was just the Drakos—or Sotar and Rios—coming early. Maybe.*

His thoughts switched to concern about Kathleen and the rest of his family. *What if Gee and his men rode behind the hills and came up on the back side of the ranch house? Would Ethan anticipate that possibility? Why didn't I think of it before?*

"Shorten your stirrups a little, Roper. You'll be able to stand in the saddle better when you shoot." Whitney's suggestion brought Cole back to the moment.

The young Kerry looked around at the two men ready to join him. Roper was acting on Whitney's observation and unbuckling his left stirrup to pull it up shorter. Whitney himself was sitting crosslegged on the ground with his reins held loosely in his hand. Across his lap was his Henry. He could just as easily have been relaxing before a picnic, except for his long coat buttoned against the chill.

His grin was lopsided, appearing more so as his beard shifted to the right. "I remember one ol' Christmas. Sixty-three, it were. We was somewheres in Tennessee. Dug in. Thick breastworks. Yanks were just across the clearing, dug in just as tight. We'd been shootin' at each other for days." Whitney wiped his mouth. "One o' our guys yelled out, 'Hey, Yanks, it's Christmas. We got some tobaccy an' some real sour mash. Y'all got coffee an' sech?' " He shook his head, chuckling. "Before you could be a'sayin' 'Merry Christmas,' there was blue and gray soldjurs out in the clearin', a'drinking an' a'smokin'—an' a'singin'. That were somethin'. Next day we was all back shootin' at each other. Crazy, huh?"

Cole made himself smile; his attention was on the valley. Gunshots should be coming soon. Unless he was wrong.

To himself, he muttered, "I'll take the ribbing from Ethan any day. Let me be wrong, Lord. Let it be the Drakos coming to wish us good tidings. Or Rios and Sotar."

"I'd think we should be hearin' some shootin by now, don't y'all?" Whitney asked.

"Yeah, I do. Let's ride closer." Cole mounted stiffly with his rifle in his left hand. Silently, he prayed for enough strength to get through the day. His right arm was numb and aching.

"We gonna shoot from our hosses?" Whitney was already in the saddle.

"Not if we have a choice."

"Smart thinkin'."

The three riders galloped to the nearest ridge and reined up. The Bar K ranchyard was a wide spoon of land below and to their left.

"Ain't that the Drako woman gettin' outta that wagon?" Whitney spouted.

"Sure does look like her. Be a fine-lookin' woman," Roper added. "An' that's the old Russian himself. Lookin' all stiff an' proper. Right there, shakin' hands with your brother. Ain't that Luther?"

Cole grinned and shook his head. "Well, boys, looks like this Kerry was seein' things. Pure an' simple. Let's go have Christmas."

Laughing, they spurred their horses toward the ranch. Halfway there, Roper started singing "O Come All Ye Faithful" and Cole and Whitney joined in gustily.

Chapter 26

"Here he comes now, ol' Father Christmas hisself," Luther shouted as Cole and the two cowhands rode through the entrance gate.

Around him were Ethan, Claire, Eli and Maggie, all of the Bar K hands at the ranch, and Ivan and Evangeline Drako. Cole rode up, shaking his head and grinning self-consciously. Whitney and Roper held back chuckles as the assembled group greeted him with a teasing cheer. After climbing down from his horse, Cole shook his head and bowed deeply amid hearty cheering.

"Merry Christmas, Cole!" Drako greeted him, waving a fresh cigar in his hand. "Do not know if I be mad at you or not I should. Do not want I being called Victorio Gee." The portly Russian shoved the cigar into his mouth and folded his arms to look his most authoritative. Then, in a gesture he saw as magnanimous, Drako walked over to Cole and held out his hand. "Did not you to know your brothers rid us of that awful gang?" Drako's whisper was much louder than necessary.

With his arms crossed in silence, Cole stood beside Kiowa and let the man have his moment of fun.

As Drako returned triumphantly to the rest of the gathering, Whitney muttered, loud enough for Cole to hear, "Had me a Cap'n like that. Dumbest peckerhead I ever laid eyes on. Lost us fifty men cuz he figured the Yanks wouldn't know about a road, a road we'd seen Yanks on two days before. Dumb peckerhead."

Skipping toward Cole, Eli immediately asked if he could unsaddle Kiowa. Cole thanked him for the offer and handed him his reins.

"Come on, Kiowa. Come on, Blue." Proudly, the boy led the red horse away. Blue charged along behind. Only Luther noticed the sorrel didn't seem to mind having the dog so close.

Whitney and Roper dismounted and led their horses to the corral too. Immediately, the young cowboy started telling Whitney how he had been working on an overhead throw with only one whirl. The bearded cowhand told him that was called a "California twist" and Roper wanted to know how he knew that. Whitney explained several Mexican cattlemen had showed it to him years before. Roper was crestfallen.

"I'm not sure how one wagon becomes twenty men either," Ethan proclaimed, standing next to Claire, "but I wouldn't be able to tell if it was one wagon—or fifty!"

Claire told him to hush, that it was better to be safe than sorry, but Ethan was enjoying his younger brother's mistake too much to end his teasing just yet.

"Actually, Ivan, my little brother was just trying to miss helping get Christmas dinner ready. Come on in and let's toast this good day. It's going to be a lot better than Cole thought it was." Ethan laughed and slapped his thigh.

At the back of the gathered cowboys, Clancey boomed, "Aye, 'tis a sad day when a son o' Clancey Kerry be seein' the devil in his friends."

DuMonte glowered at him. Stovepipe Henderson grunted and walked away. Another cowboy followed.

Clancey didn't notice the reaction and proclaimed again, "Be it known to all ye men—and ladies fair—no outlaw dares to ride upon this land of ours, this Bar K." He thumped his chest and looked around for approval.

DuMonte joined the rest of the cowboys.

This time Claire didn't wait to hear if her father-in-law was going to continue or not; she took control. "Evangeline, Ivan, please do come inside."

"Oh, I almost forgot in all the excitement," Evangeline Drako said, "I brought three pies. Gooseberry—and two apple."

Claire's smile was warm and her eyes were bright, partly with the joy of the day and, largely, because Cole's alarm had proved to be false.

Drako strolled beside Ethan, who was being guided by Maggie. The rigid man lowered his voice. "I understand you to invite all hired help to this dinner of Christmas. That is nice. I assume the colored man not be coming."

Ethan stopped. "Which one is that?"

Surprised at the question, Drako pulled the cigar from his mouth. "You be knowing, the dark man he is. Smokes the pipe. Be more than one with the Bar K?"

"Oh, you mean Harold DuMonte, our foreman. You met him on the roundup. Best man on the place. I sure hope he's comin'. He didn't say anything about it, did he?" Ethan's face was taut.

"I mean . . ."

"I know what you meant, Drako," Ethan's tone was low but brittle. "DuMonte's welcome in our home Christmas or any other damn day. Gonna have our friend Miguel del Rios here, too. If that bothers you, ride on."

Drako shoved the cigar back into his mouth and bit it forcefully. "No, it be your home, not is mine. Christmas is Christmas."

"Good. Let's go have some whiskey."

They walked on several steps before Drako spoke again. "Ethan, if you be willing, I would to put my herd with yours for the drive this spring. Safer it is. Would that be proper with you? We would to have our own, ah, wagon of chuck. Our supplies would be to keep apart."

"It's fine with me, Ivan—but my brothers'll have to agree. An' DuMonte." Ethan's grin crossed his face and stayed there. "He'll be leadin' the drive for us. Rios is goin', too. Can you handle that?"

They continued toward the house without talking.

"Yes, Ethan, that would to be fine," Drako finally said.

"Well, we'll have to see if my brothers—an' DuMonte—go along with it."

"Yah, I to understand."

Cole looked around, accepting the good-natured ribbing from the cowhands and slaps on the back. He didn't see Kathleen.

Before turning to direct the Drakos inside, Claire got Cole's attention and waved him over.

Frowning, Cole walked to her. "Sorry I got everyone so riled up, Claire. I was sure . . ."

"Don't apologize, Cole," she said. "What if you had been right? We wouldn't have had a chance otherwise."

"Where's Kathleen?"

"That's what I wanted to tell you." Claire's expression was painted with concern. "All this . . . she got real upset. Went to your room."

"Oh. I'll go see her."

"Cole, maybe you should leave her alone for a while. Let her collect herself."

"It's all my fault." Cole lowered his eyes to stare at his boots.

Claire folded her arms. "I don't need any of that, Cole Kerry. It's Christmas day—and we've got even more to be thankful for. See that the men get washed up and bring them to the house. There's plenty of whiskey. Eggnog, too." She studied him and smiled. "Bring that wonderful smile of yours, too, Cole Kerry."

Cole was unsure of what he should do next. In the worst way he wanted to see Kathleen but Claire was usually right about such things. What did he know about women? Kathleen's state of mind was fragile; how could it not be? Fear of Victorio Gee returning—and then the release of that fear—had probably seesawed her mind into reliving that awful time. His own body ached from the tension and the activity; postbattle fatigue was settling around him. His right arm felt like it was dead. He squeezed the fingers of his right hand and they didn't want to move. Sweat trickled down his forehead as he forced them into a fist.

His thoughts retraced the images he saw along the yellow hills. Could they have really been a wagon? A lone wagon? He ran his hand along his neck, inside his shirt collar. It was his best shirt, put on for the day's celebration. Now it was sweated through, even with the coolness of the day.

"Boss, I think this shows we'd better do some work to make sure we're ready if that Son of Satan does come." DuMonte walked up beside Cole.

"What?"

DuMonte explained again that he thought they should spend some time in the next few days setting up better defenses in the barn, on the other side of the ranch yard, even placing extra guns, ammunition and water where men might be placed. The black foreman figured it would be a good idea to post guards, far enough out that they could sound an alarm if need be.

At first, Cole thought he was kidding. DuMonte's expression made him realize he was serious.

"This be a blessing in disguise, boss," DuMonte said. "The good Lord helps those who get themselves ready. We just got a chance to see how we would defend the ranch, if it comes to that, without it being real." He paused and pushed his hat back on his dark forehead. "We would've had a tough time. Even with you hitting them from the rear." He swallowed. "The Lord's telling us to get ready. Yes sir, only a fool would think Victorio Gee wouldn't want his revenge on the Bar K, after what we did to him."

Alongside Cole and DuMonte came Whitney, holding his rifle in one hand and his reins in the other. He was leading his horse. "How come you haven't unsaddled, Orville?" Cole asked.

"I ain't no general, Mr. Kerry, but I be a'thinkin'." Whitney shoved his tongue against his cheek. "What if Gee had a scout close by an' saw us gettin' set?"

"You don't have to be polite, I've already heard it thick. I was seeing things. Too much Christmas, I guess."

"No suh. I'm sayin' what if y'all were right," Whitney said. "Would y'all mind if I took a little ride out thatta way—before settin' down to that fine Christmas dinner I've been a'hearin' all about?"

Cole's eyes studied Whitney, and the ex–Confederate

soldier was uncomfortable as the young Kerry's eyes burned deep; then Cole nodded. "I'd like that. But only tell me—and Harold—what you see."

"Yes suh."

"An' don't be late for dinner. That'll make Claire angry—and nobody wants that." He grinned and added, "Sotar, Rios and the old woman should be coming soon, too."

Whitney went swiftly to his horse, mounted in one motion and galloped away. Both Cole and DuMonte watched him as he cleared the entrance and headed toward the string of low hills where Cole had thought the riders had been.

"I'm not sure what I hope he finds," DuMonte said.

"Me neither. Guess I'd better get up to the house—and let them take a few more shots at me." Cole smiled. "Merry Christmas, Harold. I'm glad you ride with us."

"So am I, boss." DuMonte nodded and watched Cole return to the house.

The black foreman knew he was fortunate to work for men like the Kerrys. His own father and mother, now dead, had been slaves; he didn't know what had happened to his brother and sister. They were separated when he was young. He had been among Ethan's first hires and knew he was as welcome in their home as any man. It had always been so.

Inside the ranch house, holiday cheerfulness had resumed with even greater energy. Evangeline had joined Claire and Rommey in the kitchen while they put the finishing touches on the meal. Eli, Roper and Henderson had offered to help serve, hoping it meant they would be excused from doing dishes afterward.

"Howdy, Cole," Luther exclaimed as Cole entered. "It be a fine Christmas afterall. Ain't that great!"

"It sure is, big brother. It sure is."

"Come have sum o' this here eggnog. Gotta be evil—it's so durn good." Luther took him by the arm and led Cole toward a large glass bowl filled with rich, yellow liquid.

Without asking, Luther poured a coffee mug full, spilling a little on the floor. He handed it to Cole and muttered, "Don't tell nobody. I'll clean it up later."

Cole smiled and held out his glass for Luther to touch it with his own. "Here's to the Bar K."

"To the Bar K—an' good hosses!" Luther grinned, banged his cup against Cole's and drained it in one long swallow.

Cole wasn't paying attention. Kathleen stood in their bedroom doorway, looking pale but determined. Her smile was fixed in place and her eyes were somewhere else.

"Maybe we oughta check out the north herd tomorry, Cole," Luther said, not noticing Cole's focus. "Gotta make sure they don't drift too far. We git a storm and they be trapped down in that valley. No water thar. Not sur the line boys kin handle that by their lonesome. Maybe we should ease thatta way . . ."

Leaving Luther talking to himself, Cole walked toward Kathleen, pausing at the table to pour a cup of eggnog. Smiling and hoping, he presented the drink. She stared at it a moment without moving.

"For you, my lady. Merry Christmas. Our scare is over."

"Is it? Maybe for you. It'll never be over for me, Cole." Kathleen's expression was stoic, almost frozen. She still hadn't moved to receive the eggnog.

"I'm sorry. I thought I saw . . . something."

"It doesn't matter. Nothing matters."

"Don't say that, Kathleen. We're together. That matters," Cole said.

Kathleen's eyes met his and he couldn't read what

they were saying. "After Christmas, maybe it would make sense for me to go away."

Swallowing his feelings, Cole cocked his head to the side. "That's a good idea. The ranch is pretty quiet now. It would be a good time for us to get away for a few days. You always wanted to go to San Antonio."

"I meant me. Alone. And not come back."

"I-I don't understan—"

"No, you couldn't." Kathleen's chin dropped and her eyes followed toward the floor. "It would be better for everyone if I left." She glanced at the crowded room; Luther had returned to where Ethan, Drako and Clancey were talking. Her eyes stayed on Clancey for a moment and her breathing jerked.

Cole shook his head; his forehead furrowed in long frown lines. "It wouldn't be better—for me. I love you, Kathleen."

"This isn't the time to talk about it, Cole." She smiled and it was difficult to do. "This is Christmas. I'm going into the kitchen to help. You go be with the men."

"But . . ."

"No buts . . . just go." Her lower lip fluttered. "I love you, Cole—and I always will."

Cole looked down at the two eggnog cups. "You can't leave me . . . please."

"Shhh." She touched her fingers to his lips and headed toward the kitchen.

Unsure of what to do or say next, Cole watched her rejoin Claire and Rommey. The older Kerry woman gave her a big hug and Kathleen returned it. Cole stared at the eggnog, returned to the table and laid the untouched cups on it. He glanced up to see Rios and the old woman standing in the main doorway, looking for him.

"Miguel! How great to see you. Merry Christmas!" Cole shouted and headed for them.

"*Gracias, amigo. Feliz Navidad,*" Rios replied, waving his good arm. His left arm remained in its sling.

The two men hugged, then Cole greeted the older woman warmly. Only he knew it was Rios's mother. The Mexican rancher had asked that Cole keep it a secret. Why, Cole didn't know but he had honored the request. After a few minutes of conversation, both men talking at once, Cole guided them to the eggnog table and then to the crowd of men.

A tug on Cole's arm broke him away from the merriment. He turned to see a wild-eyed Ben Speakman.

Glancing around to make certain no one was listening, the one-armed cowhand whispered, "Orville's back. He an' DuMonte want to talk with you. Sotar just rode in, too. With Rios." Speakman, removing his pipe, looked in both directions again to assure privacy. "Orville saw tracks. Lots of riders. An' Sotar said he dun saw dust. Had to be more'n a handful, he said. It's just like you said, Captain."

With only Luther and Kathleen noticing, Cole slipped out of the house with the older cowhand and headed to the bunkhouse. As he entered, Sotar, DuMonte and Whitney waited. The others were sitting on their bunks, shaving or putting on their best clothes for dinner.

"Orville's right, boss. At least a dozen riders cut through the back side o' them hills. Sometime today." Sotar rubbed his once-cut ear as he talked.

"Which way were they headed?" Cole asked as the rest of the cowhands gathered around them.

"This'a way."

It was Whitney's turn to report. He said the group stopped while hidden behind the low rim of hills. One rider went forward. Whitney had backtracked this rider to a point where he could have watched the ranch yard. Tracks indicated he returned to the group and they rode on to the south. He thought it meant the scout saw the alerted cowboys and reported back.

"Could'a been some riders from town, lookin' for a place," Ferguson volunteered.

The other cowboys stared at him. Speakman grumbled, "Thinkin' like that got me caught in a Yank ambush."

"Sounds like the feller that ran our outfit, too," Whitney added.

"Ferguson, you might be right," Cole said, looking at the heavyset cowhand. "I hope you are. Lots of folks head for places on Christmas, some of them may not know their directions too well." He grinned that confident grin of his. "Or be too full of Christmas whiskey to pay attention to where they were going."

Laughter popped in the bunkhouse, relieving some of the tension.

Whitney and Sotar both started to object, but Cole waved them off. "But, what if it isn't? What if it is Gee? Contrary to some folk's thinking, it wouldn't take him long to round up more guns—and come back."

The two battle-savvy cowboys nodded their heads in unison. Ferguson watched them and added his own approval. With that, Cole agreed they would start rotating night guards at four points just beyond the view of the ranch house.

"You want me—an' whoever—to go out there now?" Whitney asked. "I've missed a few Christmas dinners in my life. I can miss another'n."

"Thanks, Orville, but I don't think we need to do that," Cole said. "Let's all go enjoy ourselves. We'll start the guarding tonight."

DuMonte immediately took responsibility for assigning guards. They would do it just like it was a trail drive with three shifts during the night. Cole told them not to bring up what they were going to do, or to tell what Sotar and Whitney had found. There was no need to frighten anyone—and they would probably think the cowhands were trying to protect him with a made-up story.

"Now let's have Christmas, boys." Cole added, "There's plenty of everything. Even cream puffs."

Chapter 27

Weariness from too much Christmas brought an early bedtime for everyone. Cole lay in bed trying to decide if he should try once more to go to sleep or just get up. Kathleen was dreaming fitfully next to him. She was already dozing when he finally came to bed. He had gone to sleep quickly, only to be visited by a horrible nightmare.

Greedy flames had attacked the ranch in his black dream. Great fists of smoke slammed into the gray sky, turning a cloud into the face of Victorio Gee. He had ridden close to the burning ruins and tried to slow the big sorrel with a tug on the reins and words. Everything in the animal wanted to continue his wild fury. White clouds blew from his nostrils and his red head shook at the suggestion to stop.

Victorio Gee's men laughed and shot at him as his out-of-control horse ran through the flames, then in circles around the open ranch yard. Only it was more like a town. Not Uvalde. Maybe San Antonio. Lying in the dirt was the longhorn skull branded with a Bar K that had hung from the center pole. All three corrals were empty. Two young cottonwoods were sagging from the intense heat of the nearby bunkhouse. Only the small stone house for storing butter and milk appeared immune to the fiery destruction. But it was bigger than it actually was. Everywhere he looked was flame and desolation. It didn't even seem like the prosperous ranch he had come to love. It wasn't.

He saw no one—except outlaws—and reined in the heaving sorrel and yelled, "Kathleen! Claire! Maggie!" His throat caught, then he yelled again, this time adding his father's name to the pleas. "Clancey! Kathleen! Claire! Eli! Maggie! Ethan! Luther!"

Only Victorio Gee's snarling laugh in the form of crackling flames returned his cries. Cole awoke. He was sweating. Trying to remove the dream wisps, he looked over at Kathleen. She was sleeping. More deeply now. He slid his feet to the edge of the bed and stood.

He put his clothes on as if he were still dreaming. Slowly. Mechanically. Out of habit, he used his left hand more than than his right. He wasn't sure why he was dressing or what he intended to do. Just that he needed to do something. His body ached from weakness and healing bullet wounds sought to remind him of their presence. Glancing at the gunbelt lying on the floor, he walked past and entered the main room. Tables and benches were crowded everywhere, making the Christmas tree look like a lone hostage forced against the wall. The room was quiet. A long way from the happy sounds earlier in the day.

Cole remembered the Drakos finally leaving and the portly rancher teasing Cole one more time as he left, something about this being the Christmas "when Cole Kerry saw his shadow." Clancey had followed that with a long drunken sentence that hadn't made any sense, half of it in Irish. Cole shook his head to clear it and strolled outside. Tired but happy, Rios and his mother had returned to their ranch. Sotar had asked to stay in the bunkhouse tonight with his friends.

It wasn't midnight yet. Roper, Henderson, Whitney and Ferguson took the first watch until then. Reluctantly, the line cabin boys had ridden out after dinner, too. Cole had insisted upon it, surprising Ethan and Luther. The herds were just as likely a target as the ranch house. The hands took food, but not whiskey, for the few riders left with the beef during the day.

Maybe he should go down to the bunkhouse and join the next round of sentries. At least he would be doing something. Better than just wandering around. There weren't many in the bunkhouse with the four gone. All of the line cowboys had ridden back to their cabins. DuMonte, Sotar, Speakman and Joel Hawkins would be the only four there. Joining them on guard duty made sense for him; they would be just as tired as he was.

The velvet night was cold. Very cold. Frost smoke covered his face as he breathed. He felt very alone. Sadness over Kathleen lay on his soul. He stared at the dark sky. Either no stars were left or the clouds had blanketed them. His mind wandered to the well-packed adobe between the logs and split planks and thought of the personal hell his brother, Ethan, must live in. That was far worse than his feeling sorry for himself.

Turning toward the main opened yard, a swelling of thought brought him to his own wedding almost two years ago. He saw Kathleen Shannon, beautiful in a new dress made by Claire, white flowers caressing her red hair. He saw little Maggie holding a bouquet of matching flowers. And Claire Kerry beside his bride as matron of honor. Beaming like it was her own wedding day. Both Ethan and Luther had been his best men.

Their images grabbed at his breath and no more would come.

He forced himself toward the porch railing and stood there with his hands against it, trying not to think. It was quiet. Too quiet, his mind registered. Too quiet. Night sounds that should have been there were absent.

To his far left, gray shadows along the two dark lines of cottonwoods caught his mind. Instinctively, he stepped back into the shadows. He took a deep breath, drawing in cool air, and held his hand over his mouth to dissipate the smoky exhalation. He wiped each hand on his pants, then shielded his eyes with his left, as if to help him pierce the darkness to determine what he had seen. His right arm and hand felt like they were asleep. Was this more of his seeing things that didn't matter? He waited. Less than seventy yards away from his position, shadows reasserted themselves and began slipping closer.

Six? Eight? He wasn't certain. They were on foot. Moonlight washed stingily across a gun barrel. Farther to his left this time.

Struggling sounds in the bunkhouse caught his attention. Cole's right hand instinctively went to his holster, only it wasn't there. His mind told him it was just as well; his hand wouldn't hold a pistol by itself. Fully alert for the first time, he backtracked quickly into the house, grabbed his guns and rifle and returned to the main room. There was no time to awaken others; gunfire would have to do that. Obviously, one of the guards had been killed before he could signal the planned alarm. Or more. Propping his rifle against one of the tables, he buckled on his gunbelt and placed the

Colt from his sidewinder holster into his pants for his left hand.

To test his right arm, he retrieved his Winchester, shoved it against his right shoulder and tried to lever the weapon into readiness. A fierce pain slammed through his limb as he attempted to move the action—and couldn't more than halfway. Moving his fingers from the trigger, he tried squeezing his forefinger. He shook his head in disbelief at his weakness and switched the rifle to his left shoulder and tried cocking it this way. The motion was awkward but it would have to do. He had no choice

Should I light a lamp? It might make them stop for a few minutes. Think we're waiting for them. His answer was to snap a match against his belt buckle and ignite the gas lamp sitting on the fireplace mantel. Yellow glow struggled to push away some of the gray in the room. Maybe there was time to waken Luther.

A muffled sound behind him! His rifle was pointing at the muffled noise as he spun. It was a sleepy-eyed Eli. Blue was beside him.

Cole lowered the gun.

"Uncle Cole, what are you doing?"

"Eli, I need your help." Cole glanced out the opened doorway. "Wake up Uncle Luther and your dad. Tell them Gee's gang is here an'—"

"Uncle Cole, are you seeing things again?" Eli stretched and yawned.

"Eli, do what I told you. Be quick. We've only got minutes. Keep Blue with you, too."

Startled, the boy turned and headed for his parents' bedroom as Cole disappeared out the front door.

Outside, the young Kerry slipped into the darkest shadow nestled against the wall. He crouched and stared into the night, gripping the rifle for left-handed use. Two thoughts rammed into his mind. First, the men in the bunkhouse were already under Gee's control. Or were dead. Their throats cut. He hoped that wasn't true but he had to assume no help would come from there. Second, he must make it appear that the house itself was awake with many men shooting. That would buy some time.

Muffled sounds came from his left. Several of Gee's men must be moving to a new position. They were being cautious, wanting their discovery to be at the absolute last moment for the Kerrys. Everything grew quiet again. A flicker of darker gray against the sky, then another. Cole eased to his right and pushed the rifle stock against his left shoulder. The gun was already cocked. He squinted. Yes, two crouched men were working their way forward. They were thirty yards from the cottonwoods. Crawling on the ground. They didn't see him. Yet. He waited for them to come closer. Both carried Winchesters. One was panting and the other whispered for him to stop. The night held its breath.

Trying to catch his breath, a long-faced man with leather cuffs motioned for the outlaws behind him to advance while he rested for a few moments. Beside him, another outlaw's head was on a swivel, moving back and forth, as he crawled slowly past the first.

As the long-faced outlaw's gaze realized the darker shadow on the porch was Cole, the young gunfighter's rifle barked four times, like a chugging night train chugging uphill, as he worked the lever with his left hand. The man groaned and slumped where he crawled. The long-faced outlaw caught himself with his hand as Cole's first bullet struck. He tried to shoot his own gun, but couldn't as reinforcing lead took away his agility.

Without waiting to determine his accuracy, Cole ran and lept over the porch to his right and knelt beside it.

The jolt of landing rammed pain through his wounded leg so excruciating that he couldn't breathe. Inhaling for relief and air, he didn't move. He couldn't move. Finally, gritting his teeth, he crammed new cartridges into the rifle with his left hand, holding it upside-down to put the chamber opening where he could reach it.

Reloaded, he sprayed fire along the cottonwoods themselves, moving as he fired. He hoped it would look like several men firing. His handling of the gun was still awkward but becoming easier. His right arm ached just from holding the barrel in place. The sickening thump of bullets striking trees, ground and an occasional man filled the darkness. Someone from within the trees screamed an order that was more curse than directive.

Cole limped toward the bunkhouse, stopping halfway and dropping to the ground, again gasping for air. Black clouds momentarily took control of a timid moon. He was thankful for the added darkness. His only advantage was that he had no one in a position to help fight, not yet anyway. So he didn't have to worry about them. On the other hand, the outlaws had to be careful of what they shot at and where. They were definitely unsure of Cole's counterattack or how many were waiting for them in the ranch house. It wasn't much of an advantage, but anything helped.

From the darkness came a string of yelled questions about what was happening. An unknown voice shouted out two names as if they were questions. Cole assumed they were the names of the men assigned to crawl forward. Someone yelled for a charge at the ranch house but none had tried so far.

Orange flame erupted from the ranch house in three different places. Then four. Cole smiled. Eli had done well. That should be enough to make the outlaws wary. It was time to find out what had happened in the bunkhouse. After that, he would try to circle behind the members of the gang now hiding among the cottonwoods on the other side of the yard.

Crouching low, Cole made for the long building, not yet certain what he would do. Wobbly, he almost ran into one of Gee's men standing in the darkness, thirty yards from the bunkhouse. Seeing him at the last moment, Cole stopped. Surely the man had seen or heard his firing earlier? Maybe he thought it was his own men.

The fat-bellied outlaw in a cowhide vest jerked his head toward Cole; his rifle followed. "Who's there?" He took several steps closer, almost stumbling over a rock.

"It's me, ya damn fool. Put that gun down an' keep watchin'. Didn't ya hear me shootin' a minute ago?" Cole growled, hoping it would sound somehow familiar.

"Oh, yeah, figured it was you, Sonny. Did you get any of them Kerrys? I ain't—"

Cole's rifle butt drove into the man's round face, crushing his nose and crumpling him to the ground. The only sounds were a thud, like striking a watermelon, followed by a short groan and the rustling swirls of the man and his rifle hitting underbrush, then earth. Adrenaline was keeping Cole from collapsing and he knew it. His right arm ached so much that he held it against his side. He couldn't stop now no matter how he felt. Looking around, Cole studied the bunkhouse ahead to determine if his movement had been detected. Gunfire from the house and the far trees had covered his attack. That and the shadows.

Ahead, the young gunfighter saw a man leaning against the bunkhouse, next to the door. He recognized the tall, lanky man in a long coat immediately. Ranger Bartlyn! The strange outlaw was talking to himself, jerking his head back and forth in his make-believe conversation.

Taking a deep breath to refill his weakened body with courage, Cole sauntered toward him, hoping his appearance and boldness would get him close. He made certain he didn't look at Bartlyn's eyes.

"See anythang out thar?" Cole tried his fake voice again, stepping from the shadows, only ten yards from Bartlyn.

"No, goddammit, go back to your position." Bartlyn barely looked at him, then looked away. "I told them to stay spread out. I told them."

"Bartlyn, if you move, I'll kill you."

"What? Who . . . what the—?"

"Drop the gun. Do it now."

Bartlyn froze. The left side of his face twitched. He turned to the right and said, "Do what he says." His gun thumped against his leg and his hands slowly raised. Out of the side of his mouth, he muttered, "See, I told you them Kerrys were tough. I told you."

"Now, the gunbelt. Don't make me ask about that gun in your boot."

Bartlyn hurried to comply, dropping the unbuckled pistol belt and pulling a short-nosed revolver from his boot and adding it to the collection of weapons in front of him.

Cole cleared the last shadow quickly, jamming his rifle into Bartlyn's stomach so hard the outlaw winced and groaned. Bartlyn's hands dropped to hold his belly. "I-it's you? My God . . . C-Cole Kerry. Y-you're dead. I-I k-killed you."

"Try again, ranger."

"Hey, I was just doin' what Gee told me to do. Honest." Bartlyn waved one arm in the air, holding his stomach with the other. "He's tellin' the truth. Gee ordered him to do it."

"What's going on inside? You're going in ahead of me—so it better be the truth." Cole pushed the rifle barrel under Bartlyn's chin and forced the outlaw to raise his head.

Bartlyn's face twitched, then his head jerked back and forth, before he was able to control it. "I-I . . . we got your men there. Gee wanted us to keep 'em alive so he could hang them. An' burn them. Like he did your other one, that halfbreed." He shifted his head away and spoke out of the side of his mouth. "Gee hates the Bar K, ya know. That's all he can think of. Getting even."

"Gee's going to die."

"Oh I doubt that, Kerry. Nobody's been able to even catch him." Bartlyn straightened himself and almost smiled. "Some Mex said Gee couldn't be killed. Said he was protected by . . . ghosts or somethin'. Magic. That's why it was so easy to get more guns to ride with us. Gee can't be stopped." He shifted his mouth to the side and added, "Everybody knows that."

"Where is he now?"

"Across the way. He's planning on killin' all you Kerrys himself. With his machete. One at a time," he said and turned his head to the side. "We already hit the town. Got all the bank's money this time."

"What?"

"We got all of it."

"How many of your men inside?"

"Ah, four. Just four," Bartlyn said. "Say, whatever happened to that pretty little wife of yours? Even after Gee, she was somethin'." His face twitched and he spoke from the corner of his mouth. "Yeah, I think she liked it, too."

Cole cocked his rifle barrel to drive it into Bartlyn's face. Just before he released the smashing blow, he stopped. The outlaw's mouth sagged in fear and his eyes rolled toward the top of his head.

"No, you're going to die another way. You're going

to hang," Cole said. "Open the door and step in. Tell 'em it's time to switch guards. Say the wrong thing and your head won't twitch anymore."

"Say, I didn't know you were left-handed."

"There's lots of things you don't know, Bartlyn. Like how to kill a Kerry. You an' Gee just aren't that good." Cole felt a wave of nausea run through him.

"A-alright." Bartlyn took a deep breath and his head moved like a mud-deep wagon wheel to the side. "Say it's time to switch guards. It's time to switch guards."

"Turn around."

Bartlyn complied, his head twitching even more than earlier.

Propping the rifle against the building, Cole drew the Colt shoved into his pants with his left hand, cocking it as the gun cleared. With his right hand, he managed to yank Bartlyn's revolver free of its holster and shove it into his belt where the first gun had been carried. His right hand trembled as he withdrew it. He motioned for Bartlyn to go to the door.

Behind him came hurried sound.

Cole spun to meet it. Blue! The ugly dog was racing toward him, his tail wagging. Without turning around, Cole growled, "Try something, Bartlyn. I'd like that."

Bartlyn's fingers brushed against Cole's arm and stopped. The outlaw's head jerked to the right. "No . . . no . . . don't do that."

Stepping to the side as he turned back around, Cole flashed a toothy grin. "Smart to take your friend's advice." He glanced down at Blue. "Stay here, boy. Stay here."

The dog wagged its tail.

"Let's go, Bartlyn." With Cole's gun against his back, Bartlyn turned around and knocked on the door. "It's Bartlyn, I'm comin' in. I-it's time to switch guards." His face jerked to the right. "That's right. It's time to switch guards."

The outlaw stepped into the gray bunkhouse and was greeted by a man to his right that Cole couldn't see. The young gunfighter wasn't certain but he thought DuMonte was down on the floor, ten feet from the doorway. Sotar and Hawkins were standing against the far wall; their hands at their sides. Cole didn't think they were tied. Speakman wasn't in sight; perhaps he was on the floor, beside the far bed.

Cole shoved Bartlyn forward with both hands; the gun in his left hand slamming against him. Flailing his arms, the twitching outlaw stumbled against the downed DuMonte and fell over him. A snarling mass of teeth, Blue bounded into the room and jumped at an outlaw sitting on a bunk. The startled man yelled as the dog knocked him to the floor, biting his arms and hands as they fell as one. His rifle thudded beside him. He screamed again.

The outlaw beside the door jumped. "What the—"

Cole's left-hand pistol roared twice and stopped the outlaw's question. The outlaw rose on his heels and fell backward.

Another outlaw sprang from the closest bed with his rifle moving into position. Cole fired three more times, missing once. He threw the gun in the direction of the man and drew Bartlyn's pistol and fired again. The outlaw's rifle fluttered by itself for an instant, then slammed to the floor. Jerking from the lead, the man teetered and sprawled backward across the bed.

As he fired, Sotar dove at the outlaw nearest him, tackling him at the waist and driving him into a bunk. Hawkins was right behind Sotar, rushing toward the pile of weapons in the middle of the floor. A Mexican outlaw straddling the guns looked back at the oncoming Hawkins, then at Cole. Shrugging his shoulders, he high-stepped away from the pile, laying his own rifle on top.

"*Señor* Cole Ker-ry, me no *muerte. Si?*" The Mexican made no attempt to surrender the two handguns shoved into his belt. "*Señor* Cole Ker-ry, are you ze ghost?"

"Maybe so."

Chapter 28

Inside the ranch house, Ethan was directing the defense as if he could see. Rommey and Kathleen had been sent to the kitchen to watch for an attack from the back. Both took rifles but only Kathleen looked like she had handled one before. In the front, Luther and Claire did the shooting while Ethan and Eli reloaded.

Still drunk, Clancey was roaring around the house, demanding to know what was going on. Finally, Claire said over her shoulder, "Maggie, take your grandfather back into your bedroom. Keep him there."

"Yes, Mommy. Should I tell him what's going on?" Maggie was composed.

"That's fine," Claire responded and fired through the window shutter gunhole. "Just don't let him out here. He's in the way."

Maggie dutifully went after Clancey. In mid-curse, he stopped as she took his hand. "Gran'paw, let's go to my room. I have something I want to show you."

"Huh? Maggie darlin', I be in a fierce battle against the devil hisself . . ."

"No, Gran'paw, you come with me." She yanked on his hand.

The bear of a man mumbled and coughed and followed the little girl without another word.

Sitting at one of the long tables loading a Winchester, Ethan asked loudly, "Does anybody see Cole? What's happening at the bunkhouse?"

Luther growled, "Don't see nothin'—'cept'n outlaws." He was in his longjohns but had managed to pull on his boots.

"He went toward the bunkhouse, Ethan," Claire said, turning to receive a loaded gun from Eli, exchanging it for her empty one. "Cole shouldn't be out there like that. He's too weak." She peered through the peephole in the window shutter. "I doubt if he can even hold a gun in his right hand."

"He'll use his left. Keep an eye out, in case he gets into trouble there," Ethan said. "They must've hit the bunkhouse first."

Luther fired and growled, "Reckon that's why thar's no shootin' from thar. Ya figger our boys is daid?"

"I reckon that's why Cole's goin' there. To find out," Ethan said. "Eli, where's the box? I can't find the box."

"It's right here, Dad. Next to your elbow."

"Oh, thanks, son."

"Dad?" Eli looked up from shoving another cartridge into the Winchester in front of him.

"Yes?" Ethan's fingers danced around the cartridge box, touched its side and sought a fresh bullet.

"Uncle Cole was right about seeing a gang yesterday, wasn't he?"

A frown penetrated Ethan's forehead as he picked up a second cartridge. This time going directly to the right spot. "Yes, he was."

"Dad?"

"Yes?"

"Are we gonna be all right?" Eli's eyes went to the front windows where his uncle and his mother were shooting.

Bullets from outside thudded against the house and the boy tried to ignore their ominous sounds. All around them were vestiges of yesterday's holiday. A Christmas tree in the corner. Myriad tables. His mother's decoration on the mantel appeared to be close to falling off. It all seemed cockeyed, unreal. How could this be?

Ethan hesitated. "In a fight, the victory usually goes to the one who thinks while he fights—and who never gives up."

"Like Uncle Cole?"

"Like Uncle Cole." Ethan wanted to say something more encouraging but the words wouldn't clear his mouth; instead he yelled out, "Rommey? Ah, Kathleen?"

From the kitchen came a response from Kathleen, and Ethan asked if there were any signs of the gang in the back.

"Not yet," she said.

"They'll be there. Keep watchin'."

At the shuttered kitchen window, Kathleen wanted to respond angrily that she wasn't going to keep looking. *What a stupid remark*, she thought. *Does he think we're not going to watch? Cole would never say anything so obvious. Why does Ethan have to do that?*

Her mind flickered to Cole and she wished he were next to her. If they were going to die, she wanted to be beside him. She would not be taken again. Lying on the counter was a pistol Luther had handed to her earlier, along with the Henry rifle in her hands. If it appeared like they weren't going to be able to hold out, she would use it to kill herself. Her thoughts were black and it was difficult to focus on the open land outside.

"Will Cole and I ever be truly happy again? Wouldn't it better for everyone if I just left, like I said?" She mumbled the words, then glanced over at Rommey, who was staring blankly out of the small hole in the other window. If he heard her, she couldn't tell. It didn't matter.

A flush of heat raced through her without warning. She wanted to live! She wanted to be with Cole, to raise a family. Their family. Beads of sweat blossomed along her forehead and she inhaled slowly, then let the troubled air go again. *Please, God, be with my Cole. Keep him safe.*

Thoughts wandered toward him and the present she had for him, hidden in her small dresser: a book of Tennyson poems, leather-bound with gilded edges. She couldn't wait to give it him and her mind asked what Cole had for her. Through the crack in her thoughts, depression sought control of her mind once more.

Something moved! Something moved outside. She felt it, more than saw it.

Where?

Her mind was taut. She cursed the limited vision from the holes in the shutter. They provided safety for the shooter but not much range of sight. She thought about opening them so she could see better but discarded the notion as quickly as it came.

"Mr. Rommey, they're coming." She heard herself utter the statement and it seemed as if the announcement came from someone else.

"Oh my."

For the first time she realized Rommey wasn't going to be effective. He was going to freeze. She knew it without another word from him or looking at him. The stiff-gestured cook was going to fail them when they needed him most.

"Shoot, Mr. Rommey. Just shoot. Pull the trigger," she yelled, thinking the gunfire might, at least, make the advancing outlaws come her way.

"I-I . . ."

"Shoot, dammit."

He lowered the rifle to his side and stood looking out of the peephole.

"Ethan! They're coming," she screamed, and fired.

A shadow jerked and took another step. She fired again. And again. It felt good to strike back and the sensation eclipsed any sense of fear. The shadow collapsed and she ducked out of instinct. Bullets slammed against her closed window. She glanced at Rommey, who hadn't moved, and forced herself to look again at the dark yard. In the distance she could make out trees and a large boulder, good places to hide behind. She cursed them for being there and fired at the boulder. The ricochet whined through the night.

Everything was still again. She wanted to shoot again. At anything. She fired again at the boulder and again the ricochet answered.

Around the corner came Claire holding a Winchester with both hands. Her sudden appearance surprised Kathleen into spinning in her direction.

"Kathleen, it's me. Are you all right?"

"Yes, yes, I'm fine," Kathleen sputtered. "Mr. Rommey . . . he isn't."

Claire moved quickly to Rommey's window. "Move."

Rommey didn't react.

Without another word, Claire stepped in front of the petrified cook and stared out the shutter hole. She placed the rifle butt against her shoulder, pushed it twice to ensure that it was solidly in place, and fired. A groan sounded close. She fired as quickly as she could lever a new load into the breech. The small kitchen was smothered in acrid gunsmoke.

Rommey looked around bewildered, spotted a forgotten pot of mashed potatoes on the counter, laid his gun against the wall and began searching for a cover for the pot.

At her own window position, Kathleen began firing again at glimpses of movement, imagined and real. She levered the Henry and it jammed. Jammed!

"Claire, the gun, it won't work. What'll I do?" Kathleen said, her voice more calm than her emotions.

"Henrys'll do that," Claire responded without turning away from the window. "Yell for Eli to bring you another gun."

Kathleen stared down at the weapon, tried to complete the levering and ran into the main room. "Eli, Ethan, I need another gun. I—"

"Here's one," Eli said, handing her a reloaded Henry.

Ethan cautioned. "It's a Henry. Got to lever it slow an' easy. Like makin' lo—" He stopped. "Like fryin' meat. It's all we've got. Except for the shotgun. How is it back there?"

"Don't know. Yet. They're back there." Kathleen laid her jammed gun on the table, took Eli's offering, and returned to the kitchen. She barely heard Ethan's repeated caution to lever it carefully.

Claire was now using Rommey's gun while the cook was patting the now covered pot and talking to himself about fixing breakfast. Kathleen slid up against her window and stared out. She could see two bodies about ten or twelve feet from the house. Unmoving. Nothing else.

From somewhere beyond the trees, she saw a tiny orange burst, then another. What was going on? The gunfire looked like it was aimed at the trees, or the outlaws behind them, if there were any. How could that be? Was she seeing things? Was her mind producing wishes? Out of frustration, and not targets, she fired. This time, she made herself lever the gun slowly and carefully. She smiled as it came smoothly into readiness.

"There's one of ours out there," Claire shouted. "See? Back of the treeline. Can't make out who it is—but it's a Bar K man."

"I see."

"He's going to drive them into the open."

"I'm ready."

Rommey looked up, "Shall I start some coffee, Mrs. Kerry? Perhaps some bacon?"

"Sure," Claire responded, fired and fired again. "Whatever you want to do is fine." She fired once more. "Eli! I'm empty!"

"All right, Mom." Eli's reply was crisp and calm, as if he were being asked to pass a dish of potatoes. "Be right there."

In the front yard, Cole yelled at the ranch house that he and Sotar were coming across. It gave away any surprise but it would keep his own family from mistaking them for outlaws. More importantly, he hoped it would make the remaining outlaws think they were outnumbered.

"Luther! Ethan! We've cleared out the bunkhouse. All of Gee's bastards are done there. John Davis and I are headed across—with *eight* men." Cole's statement rang through the night. Stating he had eight men with him would give the outlaws something to think about. He started to tell Blue to remain behind but knew it wasn't worth the effort; the dog was coming with them. Shooting from the house was sporadic. Only one rifle was firing now. Had someone been hurt?

"We'll be a'watchin'. All them bastards in back be on their way to hell." Luther's gravelly pronouncement was a cannon in the darkness.

Cole wondered what had happened to the other shooter. Was it Claire—or Kathleen? His heart jumped at the thought but focused on the trees ahead of them.

"Tell them boys in the trees to dun show theirse'fs," Luther roared again. "*Our eight* guns is a'wantin' somethin' to shoot at."

Chuckling to himself at Luther's responding exaggeration, Cole and the Missouri gunfighter crawled toward the remaining outlaws scattered among the trees. It was one thing to make an announcement about attacking; another to get there alive. Blue inched along with them.

Hawkins stayed in the bunkhouse with the two tied-up outlaws and tended to DuMonte and Speakman; both had been knocked out. No one knew the status of the four night guards. Likely one was dead. Maybe all of them.

A bitter snarl of emotion caught in Cole's throat as he moved. He shivered when a picture of what would eventually happen to the Kerry women and little girl if they weren't successful crawled inside his head. He would die trying to save them. That's what Victorio Gee wanted. That's what he would get. Only Cole intended to take the evil leader with him.

So help me, God, I will kill him. Keep me alive long enough to make that happen. Cole spotted movement and fired.

Impressed with the young Kerry's use of his left hand, Sotar knelt and levered four shots into the same area. In response, three outlaws stood with their hands raised, yelling that they were surrendering. Cole hollered again at the ranch house to alert them. Another outlaw stood with his hands up.

"I hears ya, Cole!" It was Luther. "Ya got 'em all?"

"Don't know yet. Might still be some in the back." He thought Luther's earlier response might have been more bravado than fact. "Haven't found Gee yet."

"Well, like I tolt ya, the womenfolk got that under control," came Luther's impish reply. "Whitney's back thar hissel'f. Came in from them boys' back side, sur nuff."

Kathleen. Kathleen. Cole's mind ran away from the outlaws to find her. He remembered her saying that she must leave and he shuddered. *Please, stay, Kathleen. I love you.* He whispered and forced himself to pay attention to the handful of men coming into the open yard. He heard Sotar bark for Gee's outlaws to get down on the ground. He felt weak all over. His right arm was dead weight and needed rest. He needed rest.

"You hit, Cole?"

Cole didn't respond.

"Cole? Are you hit?" Sotar asked again.

"Huh? Oh, I'm all right." Cole returned to the moment and searched the downed outlaws for one in particular. "Where's Gee? Tell me or I'll start shooting."

A ruddy-faced outlaw with a bleeding cheek raised his head. "H-he rode out. . . ."

"Shuddup, Cloud," the humpbacked man next to him growled.

"He can't hurt you anymore, Cloud. I can," Cole said. "Where is he?"

"He rode out a while ago." The first outlaw pointed toward the ridge where Cole had seen riders before. "We was all set to hit you yesterday," he continued. "Victorio liked the idea of killin' you on Christmas. Thought you'd be easy pickin's." He glanced at the outlaw next to him.

Sotar walked over to the humpbacked man and kicked him in the stomach. "Don't look at him."

Hurrying over to the outlaw, Blue snarled an added warning.

"Bartlyn rode down thisaway, saw you boys movin' around fastlike an' figured you'd spotted us. Most of us thought he was seein' things again but Victorio believed him. Were y'all waitin' for us?" He stared at Cole's intense gaze and gulped. "So we went back an' hit the bank. Nobody was watchin' it. Nobody." He snickered, realized what he had done and swallowed again.

From the doorway, Luther strode down the porch steps and toward them. He always had trouble negotiating any steps with his bowed legs. It looked like a man walking on eggs. "Nobody's dun been hurt inside. Thanks to you, Cole. How's our men be?"

"Harold and Old Ben are down," Cole answered. "Coldcocked them both. Hawkins's with them."

"I'll git Claire." Luther turned back toward the house.

"John Davis, watch these men. I'm going after Gee," Cole said and headed for the corral.

"I'll go with ya."

"I'd like that—but this is mine to do. Stay an' help," Cole said over his shoulder. "We may have guards down." He glanced down and saw Blue a few strides away. "Keep Blue here, too."

"How ya figger I gonna do that?" Sotar said and turned toward the house and yelled, "Eli, come here, boy. Git yur dog, will ya?"

A bewildered chicken crossed Cole's path as he headed for Kiowa. The bird screamed at him and scooted away as Cole approached, flapping its wings. Blue stopped long enough to bark at it, before continuing with the young gunfighter. Seconds later, Cole entered the corral and walked toward the quiet sorrel with his saddle in his arms. His Winchester was reloaded and returned to its boot. The weight was mostly on his left arm but, at least, his right was providing balance.

"Big fella, we've got one more job to do," Cole declared as he laid the saddle blanket and saddle on the big horse's back. "This day we may both die. So will Victorio Gee." Cole tightened the cinch, slipped the bit in place and pulled the bridle over Kiowa's head. He didn't attempt to use his right hand.

Flushed with excitement and fear, Eli ran toward the corral, calling for his dog. "Blue! Come here, boy."

"Somebody's looking for you, boy." Cole rubbed the top of the waiting dog's head. "It's all right. You go with Eli. Go on now."

Blue backed away, not taking his eyes off Cole and Kiowa.

"You were a big help, Blue. Go now. I'll see you later." Cole motioned toward the hurrying boy.

With a flick of his tail, Blue spun and trotted toward Eli standing near the corral gate.

"Where are you going, Uncle Cole?" Eli asked. "Everybody knows you were right all along. I heard my dad say so."

"Your father's a mighty good man, Eli. A brother to look up to. You tell him I said that." Cole clucked to the big sorrel and they galloped from the corral.

While a bewildered Eli watched him ride away, Kathleen hurried over to Ethan inside the house. Swallowing away the depression pushing through her, she talked to him for a few minutes. Claire watched, somewhat surprised.

Luther yelled at Maggie to bring out her grandfather. From the bedroom, Clancey roared that he needed a drink.

Chapter 29

Kiowa was eager to run and Cole let the big red horse have his head. Gee's trail wasn't hard to follow even on hard ground in the predawn light. The outlaw leader was headed south; bits of ground and overturned rocks told of pushing his horse hard. Cole cleared a brotherhood of broken hills and didn't see any marks of Gee's passing in the brown quilt of matted, dying buffalo grass that stretched like carpet in front of him.

Reining Kiowa to an unwanted stop, he swung down and shook away the weariness growing within him and tried to ignore the ache in his leg. His leg was pounding again; lack of sleep was aggravating his barely healed head wounds. He led Kiowa through the thick grass, searching for signs. The matted grass made it difficult to read in the uneven morning. He bent his right arm and flexed his fingers, hoping for more agility. The limb moved slowly and with pain; his fingers would barely make a fist.

From over the hills behind him, Cole saw two riders

against the saddened sky. Dawn was still an hour away. He realized the advancing men were Ethan and Luther. They must go back. This was his to do.

Rifles lay across both brothers' saddles, with Ethan riding next to Luther. Cole knew his oldest brother had not wanted Ethan to come. Strain on their faces revealed an emotion he had already experienced. Luther's was a determined bloodhound with a thick mustache. Ethan's was stone. Like the old days of war.

Luther pulled up next to Cole, and Ethan an instant later. His movements were jerky but confident.

"How come you left your brothers behind?" Ethan growled. "Thought we did things together."

Luther glanced at Ethan and decided not to touch his horse. Something warned him not to assist his blind brother at this moment.

"This is for me to do, Ethan." Cole's voice was cold. "I'm the one who's good with a gun, remember?"

"You forgot who taught you?" Ethan said. "How good you figure to be with your left hand?"

"Victorio Gee raped my wife," Cole said. "He killed Abe an' a bunch of our friends—an' robbed the town bank. I'm going to find him and kill him."

"What kind o' lead do he have? Did ya lose his trail?" Luther's voice was soft, layered with dread as he dismounted and sneezed. And sneezed again.

"Maybe an hour. Maybe less. If his men were telling the truth. But I came over that rise and lost him in this grass," Cole said.

"Look for where it's matted down," Ethan barked.

"That's the problem. It's all matted down."

Ethan nodded. "Sometimes it helps to go to one side and look back."

"That's what I was doing." Cole inhaled and added, "It's all my fault." His statement was almost a sob.

Leading his horse, Luther walked over and put his

hand on his younger brother's shoulder. "What kinda fool talk is that, Cole?"

"He . . . he looked at me. Victorio Gee did. In town. When we were fighting. I knew then . . . he knew who I was. I should'a . . ." Cole inhaled deeply to try to bring in air that wouldn't return fast enough. "I'm going after him." He took another deep breath. "He'll die—or die with me, I swear."

Luther patted Cole's shoulder. "We all be going. Us three brothers."

Ethan's face was cocked into a strange snarl. "Hell, Cole, they gunned down Ferguson. Speakman's dead an' DuMonte's hurtin' bad. Why didn't you tell us you were puttin' out guards?" Ethan licked his lower lip. "Never mind, I know. You figured we'd . . . I'd . . . laugh at you again. Damn, I thought you were tougher than that."

Cole inhaled again to release the anger. What was it in Ethan's nature that made him tear away at the obvious? Why did he require such a hurting? Was it because he was blind? No, he had always been that way. A perfectionist, yes, but much more than that. Ethan Kerry was a success, either because of it or in spite of it. He needed perfection—and control. His blindness cruelly took away both, leaving only the desire.

"Thanks for coming, Ethan. You, too, Luther." Cole resumed his study of the grassy area, looking for an indication of Gee's flight direction. "I'll be going after Gee now. You can ride back to the ranch. DuMonte'll need you."

Ethan looked like he had been struck in the face with a bullwhip. "Cole, I didn't deserve that. Neither did Luther. We came to be with you. That means we're going with you after that sonvabitch. I ain't askin'."

Kneeling on the ground, Cole ran his fingers along a troubled line of dirt under a circle of grass, then saw another similar combination a few feet away. Gee had turned west, using the grass to hide his intention.

Luther noticed his brother used his left hand and was holding his right arm close to his side. Crow's feet erupted around Luther's worried eyes. His brother was far weaker than he let on; Luther cursed himself for not seeing that earlier.

Cole stood and put a boot in his stirrup. "I'm sorry. That wasn't my intent. Having you two come means a lot. I thank you. I just . . ."

"You figure a blind man's gonna slow you down?" Ethan cocked his head to the side. Solemnly, he declared, "I won't. Victorio Gee hurt our Kathleen. We intend to be there when he's sent on to hell."

Cole studied the tall rancher and knew his brother meant it when he said "our"—and that one word made him feel warm inside. Kathleen was a Kerry now. Cole also knew there was no use in further suggesting his brothers not go with him. Having Ethan's savvy at his side would be a plus, in spite of his lack of sight. Having Luther's heart with him was always good. He glanced at his oldest brother, who looked like he might cry. He turned away and wiped his eyes with his shirt sleeves.

"Thank you." No more words could be found.

"Where do you think he'll go?" Ethan changed the subject.

"His tracks turn west. He's pushing his horse hard. It won't last long at that pace," Cole said, swinging into the saddle. "Figures he'd kill a horse to get away. That man sure knows how to protect himself, doesn't he? No wonder the Mexicans think he's a ghost—an' can't be killed."

"We dun found the town's gold packed on some hosses. Reckon Gee were in too big a hurry to brung it along," Luther explained, sniffing back emotion.

"You know the closest ranch west of here?" Ethan pursed his lips. He already knew the answer. "It's your friend's. Miguel's."

"You think he'll go there? For a new horse?" Cole eased Kiowa into a lope.

"Yeah. He knows we'll be comin' for him." Ethan heard the movement and kicked his black horse to follow. "He'll likely kill Miguel." Ethan shoved his boots farther forward to balance him better as they rode.

Cole's grimace was his only response as he let Kiowa launch into a full gallop. "Miller's there—but he'll be with Miguel's herd."

"G'wan, Cole, don't hold 'im for us. We'll be a'-comin'," Luther yelled as the sorrel opened several lengths between them.

Luther glanced at Ethan. "We gotta lay into 'em, Ethan."

"Don't hold back for this blind man, Luther. I don't need to see to ride." To demonstrate his point, Ethan spurred his black into a flat-out run.

Shaking his head, Luther slapped the reins against his horse's flanks and spurred it to catch up with his bolting brother and help guide him—without Ethan knowing it.

Half an hour later, Cole reined up at Rios's simple adobe ranch house, only a small square on the prairie. Smoke from the chimney sought the morning sky. A corral contained brown, black and gray blurs of moving horses. He yanked the rifle free from its sheath and levered a cartridge into the chamber.

A few minutes later, Luther and Ethan came up beside him.

"Hope we're not too late," Cole said.

"Won't know 'til we get there," Ethan challenged.

"Yeah. You two stay here. I'll go on in first," Cole

said. "If he's inside, Gee might show himself—if he thinks it's just me."

"Might start shooting, too, little brother," Ethan growled.

"My big brothers'll come fast then."

Ethan shook his head. "Well, well, Luther, the young'un learned somethin' after all." He jutted out his chin. "Use your Winchester instead of your shotgun. You won't be as quick with your left. Better to have the punch of the rifle. Check it for loads."

Cole smiled and looked at Luther. The oldest brother nodded his understanding: that was just Ethan, saying the obvious. He nudged the sweating Kiowa into a lope, holding the reins with his right hand and the Winchester in his left with the butt against his hip. His right arm ached from the tension of keeping the red horse from running.

Kiowa jerked his head to ask for release and Cole held tightly to the reins, in spite of his arm's weakness. Lowering his head, the sorrel eased into the requested lope, so Cole could concentrate on the adobe ahead.

As Cole advanced, Luther and Ethan rode parallel to the last ridge, seeking cover within two cottonwoods enjoying a small pond that seeped across the land. Luther made the comment that Rios had two good ponds on his land, even though they were small. Ethan observed that Rios had more cattle than the water could handle; he had told him so last summer. They pulled up to wait.

Immediately, Luther sneezed, then again. Ethan waited until his brother had recovered before asking where Cole was now. Luther said their brother was halfway to the house, riding with his rifle across his saddle. Luther figured it was cocked and ready. Ethan thought that was a dangerous way to ride since the gun could go off if the horse stumbled or hit a hole. He also questioned Cole's ability with his left hand and wondered about his brother's right arm.

Luther answered by saying the ride was a dangerous one anyway, that Cole could outshoot most men with his left hand, and that the real fact was he shouldn't even be up and around yet. But none of that mattered; Cole had already gone.

"I don't like waiting, Luther." Ethan felt for the cigarette makings in his shirt pocket, then decided against it. "Is he carryin' it for his left—or his right?"

"Don' much care fer it neither—but Cole's ri't." Luther said. "An' he's usin' his left. His ri't ain't so good. Yet."

"Didn't say he wasn't right."

"Jes' checkin'."

Ethan shook his head. "Keep a sharp eye out. Gee might run out the back—or he might be already hidin' somewhere outside. Waitin'."

"I be doin' that, Ethan. It'd be a he'p if ya'd be quiet so's I kin con-sin-trate."

"Sure."

Ahead, Cole rode steadily toward Rios's front door. When he was a hundred yards away, the door opened slightly. Cole's grip on his Winchester tightened; his gaze sought movement in either front window. The door opened further and the old Mexican woman stepped out and waved.

Cole reined his horse and returned the greeting by waving the Winchester in his left hand, then returning it to his hip. His study of the house continued. He asked Kiowa to walk and the animal smoothly did so. *Was she alone? Where was Miguel? Had Gee come and gone?* Was he wrong about the outlaw leader's direction?

"Mornin' to you, *Señorita* del Rios."

For the first time, he saw her wrinkled, brown face

was stained with tears. Her legs wobbled. Her eyes watered. She was light-headed. She tried to speak, stumbled over to the porch railing and vomited.

Cole jumped down and weariness grabbed at his knees. His wounded leg wanted no part of walking. He knelt for a moment, cradling his rifle, to let his body stabilize. A pain slid across his forehead and ignited more agony in his arm and leg. Knowing he couldn't give in to it, his eyes sought the windows for signs of Gee or Rios or both. None were there.

"*¿Como esta usted?*" he asked as he watched the dazed woman vomit again.

Looking up, she tried hard to smile; deep lines rushed against the corners of her eyes and she replied that she was well.

"Where is Miguel?" Cole's voice wouldn't stay calm and he couldn't think of how to say it in Spanish.

"I ees here, *amigo*."

Cole's gaze shot toward the corner of the house where Rios appeared. The sling was around his neck but his left arm dangled at his side. In his right hand was his pistol belt with its holstered weapon.

"Victorio Gee ees back here." Rios motioned with his head. "Come. See ze great *bandito* for yourself, *amigo*. He weel bother no one no more."

As fast as his wounded leg would allow, Cole led Kiowa to the hitching rack, flipped his reins over the post and headed toward his friend. "You hurt, Miguel?"

"I am *bueno, amigo*."

"What happened?"

Motioning with his gunbelt, Rios told him that Gee had sneaked into the corral before dawn to steal a horse. He picked out Bailarin, but the gray horse didn't like the idea of a strange man saddling him and began to snort and stomp its hooves. Gee decided to pick another mount but Bailarin kept up the noise until Rios awoke and went to investigate. He thought it was wolves; Bailarin had warned him before. When he stepped to the doorway, Gee saw him and started shooting. That startled the rest of the horses and they knocked Gee down with Bailarin leading the way. Rios rushed the corral and shot him three times.

"I'm so happy you are safe." Cole's words rushed ahead of his emotion. "I-I was worried."

"How you know he eez *hier?*"

Cole told him of the attack on the Bar K and the subsequent chase. After waving at his brothers, Cole stepped around the side of the house with Rios leading the way. Rios's mother stayed in front, sobbing softly to herself.

"How is your mother, Miguel?" Cole asked.

"She *mucho* scared. For me. Hear shots. No know what ees happen until I come for her." Rios shook his head as they walked. "Eet ees, how you say, ze nervous."

"Oh, nerves."

"*Si*. Nerves." Rios stared down at the empy sling around his neck, then to his still useless left arm. "She ees afraid of *mucho*. Since *mi* family . . . *muerte*. No even want any to know she ees *mi madre*. You know thees."

"Yeah. She doesn't need to be afraid of me, though."

"She ees not. She call you *mi hermano*."

" 'My brother.' I like that."

"Look, ees Victorio Gee. *Muerte*."

Chapter 30

Walking up to the corral, Cole saw the blood-splattered outlaw leader lying against a wooden water trough, awkwardly propped on his side. His head rested on his chest. His legs were curled beneath him. His silk shirt was mostly red. A sheathed machete was under his body; the sheath shoulder strap itself had slid to his waist. One band of beadwork that had decorated the top of his left black boot dangled lifelessly, halfway torn from the leather. His distinctive brim-pinned hat lay upside down on the hoof-beaten ground. Cole's study went to the necklace of teeth. *Could any of Abe's be there?* He shivered at the thought. Gee's long brown hair was streaked in blood. Double black armbands had worked their way to his elbow and looked like limp rooster tails.

"I keel heem but eet no take away ze ache in *mi* heart, *amigo*." Rios swung the pistol belt in the direction of the downed outlaw.

Five horses milled on the far side of the corral; three bays, a pinto and the magnificent Bailarin. The big gray horse whinnied and Rios returned the greeting with a warm salutation, then told Cole again that Bailarin had been the difference.

"Well, if he went after Bailarin, at least he knew good horseflesh," Cole said.

"Si."

Around the corner came the thumping of boots and jingling of spurs as Luther appeared with Ethan holding on to his upper left arm.

"Damn an' a bad saddle! What the hell dun happened here?" Luther sputtered as they neared the corral. He lowered the rifle in his hands. Ethan held his Winchester in his right hand at his side.

"Miguel shot Gee trying to steal Bailarin." Cole pointed at the body.

"He sur nuff did." Luther leaned against the top rail and squinted.

Standing beside him, Ethan fished his cigarette makings from his shirt pocket and began rolling a smoke. The task never failed to fascinate both Luther and Cole as their brother deftly handled the tobacco sack and papers as well as a sighted man.

Bailarin sought Rios by laying its head over the top rail next to him. The slim Mexican rancher began petting the horse, paying no attention to Ethan's performance.

"Sorry we didn't get here sooner, Miguel." Ethan placed the cigarette in his mouth, struck a match on his belt buckle and inhaled.

"I wanted to kill him myself." Cole stared at the dead outlaw. "For what he did to . . . Kathleen." A strange hurried sound in his throat followed.

Luther frowned and bit his lower lip.

Ethan turned his head to the side as if listening to something no one else heard, moving the rifle into a two-handed grip in front of his chest. "Cole, she left.

She told me she was goin'—after Gee's bunch had surrendered. She doesn't want you followin' her."

"What?" Cole's face was strained agony.

"She made me promise not to tell you until she was long gone. She rode off on that little roan mare you gave her. Claire told me it was a pretty one."

Cole was silent, his head bowed and his eyes shut. Luther hurried to his side as Rios put his good arm around Cole's shoulders.

"That be a hard way to come at it, Ethan," Luther chastised.

"Is there an easy way?"

"No, I reckon not. Still, Lordy . . ." Luther patted Cole's shoulder, searching for words that wouldn't take shape. "I's sorry, Cole. We'un's all thought she were . . . a good lady." He bit his lower lip again and looked away.

"Where'd she go, Ethan?" Cole asked, raising his head and opening his eyes.

"I don't know, Cole. I swear I don't know."

"Does Claire?"

Ethan hesitated. "No, she doesn't. I told her what Kathleen told me—an' Claire said not to stop her."

"Claire said that? I don't believe you." Cole's words were hot as he jerked away from the attempted comfort of the two men.

"I wouldn't lie to you, Cole. You know that."

Luther tried to say something and Cole pushed him back. Luther's Winchester popped from his hands and thumped on his boots. "Get away from me. All of you. I'm going after her."

Rios stepped back, his dark eyes understanding Cole's anguish, but having no words to heal the blackness.

"You're gonna die . . . with me, Cole Kerry."

Behind them came a throaty laugh, followed by a

spit of blood. Propping himself on one arm, Victorio Gee aimed a cocked revolver at Cole.

No one saw the movement as Ethan's Winchester swung into position. He levered and fired. Four times. Five times. His left hand was a blur against the lever; his finger held the trigger against the guard. The first three bullets, and the last, struck their target; the fourth bullet slammed against the trough, drawing a long finger of water that soon became a trickle.

Gee's body shuddered and slumped back once more against the wooden frame. Only this time, the evil outlaw's head lay backward against the edge; his eyes stared unseeing into the sky. His pistol shivered and its bullet ripped across the middle rail and into the morning air. Its death song passed a foot from Cole's stomach.

Whirling around the corral, the horses stomped and snorted their fear. In the center, Bailarin reared and pawed the air. Lowering his pistol, Rios calmed the great horse with reassuring words. The Mexican rancher's dropped pistol belt was nestled at his feet.

"Did I hit him?" Ethan cocked the gun this time.

Luther stood with his jaw opened, the rifle still at his feet. Cole was crouched, an unfired Colt in his left fist. "Yeah."

"*Si.*"

Shaking his head, Luther finally said, leaning over to retrieve his rifle, "How'd ya know'd whar he be?"

"Thought I heard him breathe," Ethan said. "His voice told me where. Didn't figure any of you boys was paying attention."

"Damn." Luther stared first at the dead outlaw, then back at his brother. "Ya sur ya cain't see—jes' a piece?"

Ethan laughed. "Wish that were so. We need to ride. Get that money back to town. There'll be a whole lot of upset folks. Gotta get the rest of Gee's gang to jail. The boys are holdin' 'em at the ranch."

Cole straightened and shoved his gun into his belt. "I'll help you. Then I'll head for San Antonio. That's where she talked about going. Once."

"What if'n she ain't thar?" Luther asked, slowly picking up his rifle.

"Then I'll ride to hell if that's what it takes."

Luther looked at Rios and the Mexican shook his head and said he was going along.

Lowering his Winchester again to his side, Ethan reminded them that they needed to find someone in town who could play "Dixie" for Ben Speakman's burial. Luther thought Andrew Sandquist "had hisse'f a horn."

Dusk found pandemonium entrenched in Uvalde. Bank president Picklewhite had been the first to realize the bank was robbed Christmas night. He had screamed the bad news to the slumbering town. That started the panic. Anger had followed surprise as the townspeople shook off their Christmas fog. Soon, they sought someone to blame as the day itself took shape. Acting Marshal Maynard and Picklewhite were everyone's targets.

A crowd of blistering-hot men and a few women gathered around Maynard and Picklewhite outside the bank as the Kerry brothers with Sotar and Rios rode into town. Along with them were nine well-tied outlaws on horseback, plus another string of six horses carrying strapped-on bodies and two more carrying the bank's money. At the rear was a buckboard with DuMonte resting in it and Whitney driving. A rifle was propped against his leg. The Kerrys insisted on taking the black foreman to town for Dr. Hawkinson to see him. DuMonte didn't think he needed to go but they wouldn't change their minds.

"Looks like sum folks still be Christmasin'," Luther observed.

"Looks more like the front end of a lynching to me." Cole pushed his hat back on his forehead. "Why aren't those boys using all that energy on going after the bank robbers?"

Ethan grinned. "That would take work. Easier to gripe and yell."

"Figger we should tell 'em now?" Luther drawled. "Or jes' let 'em stew sum more."

Ethan answered the question by yelling, "Acting Marshal Maynard . . . Mr. Picklewhite . . . we have the outlaws who robbed the bank." He paused purposely. "An' we have our bank's money, too."

As one voice, the crowd around the lawman and banker gasped with unexpected joy. In response to the noise, three dogs, at the edge of the crowd, added their barking to the enthusiastic outburst. Several men ran to shake hands with the Kerrys; a few more went directly to the horses packing the bank's treasure. Banker Picklewhite didn't move; his body shedding the tension of the last hours.

Coyly, Mrs. Huball, the woman Luther had seen when he and Ethan were last in town, scooted up to him and thanked him. She touched his arm and kept her hand there as she expressed her admiration for his efforts. He tipped his hat, turning deep red and avoiding the eyes of his comrades. After her coquettish exchange, she turned away and walked toward the sidewalk, paused and glanced back. Her smile was an acknowledgement of his continued attention. Satisfied with the encounter, she went on, leaving Luther to watch her disappear among the growing string of people on the sidewalk. He rubbed his unshaven chin and muttered, then looked around to see if anyone was watching him. No one was and he grinned.

Trying to act calm, Acting Marshal Maynard sauntered over to the Kerrys as they pulled in front of the hitching rack at the bank.

"Well, sure looks like you got the rest of 'em," Maynard said, studying the assembly of outlaws, dead and tied. "Now, if we can just catch that sonvabitch Victorio Gee."

Cole glanced at Rios. "He's the fourth one back, Marshal. Miguel del Rios handled him in a gunfight at his ranch."

Maynard's mouth popped open and stayed there. "Really? Victorio Gee? Dead?"

"Eet was not me, Marshal. Eet was *Señor* Ethan Kerry who keeled ze Victorio Gee," Rios corrected, easing out of the saddle.

Maynard stared at him, incredulous, knowing he was the target of a joke. "Oh, come on now, boys. Ethan's . . ."

"I wouldn't complete that sentence, Marshal," Cole advised. "Both of us are telling the truth."

Maynard stared at Ethan, then at Rios, unsure of what he should say.

"Now, where do you want this bunch? Got enough room in your jail?" Cole changed the subject for him.

Maynard's concentration was already on Gee's bloody body with his hat tied to the saddlehorn, along with his sheathed machete and necklace of teeth and fangs. He couldn't get over the idea of a blind man shooting one of the most feared men in the region. He glanced back at Ethan, who was listening to Luther tell him about Mrs. Huball and trying not to chuckle at his oldest brother's obvious infatuation.

"I said, where do you want this bunch, Marshal?" Cole's voice demanded an answer.

"Huh? Oh . . . ah, take 'em over to the jail," Maynard jerked his shoulders as he responded. "Put 'em in the open cells. Only one's taken. Jimmy Dilbert's sleepin' off a drunk. You can let him go, I reckon, if you need the room."

"That's your decision, Marshal."

"Oh, sure. I'll come along, too. Yeah."

"And what about the dead ones?"

"Uh, well, I guess we'd better have Phillips in on this." Maynard hitched at his gunbelt, caught his shirt sleeve on the star on his vest and looked annoyed as he freed the cloth from its tip.

An older man smoking a pipe sauntered over to Victorio Gee's body, lifted up the dangling necklace of teeth and studied it. Releasing the necklace, he took the pipe from his mouth, spat at Gee's head and walked on.

Ethan turned from his exchange with Luther. "Why don't you go find him while we get the money back inside. We'll also keep an eye on this bunch until you get back." He looked up and yelled, "Hey, Picklewhite, where are you?"

"Ah, sure, sure." Maynard took a step in the direction of Virgil Phillips's barber shop, where he also served as the town's dentist and undertaker.

Ethan's command stopped him. "After that, you can check on the reward money on all these bastards. Believe we've earned ourselves a nice Christmas gift. Especially for Miguel del Rios. Ought to be a big one for Gee."

"Ah, oh, of course, Mr. Kerry. Of course," Maynard said, forgetting he should try to act older and authoritative.

"Oh, an' Maynard?"

"Yes sir, Mr. Kerry?"

"A blind man can fight when he has to."

"Yes sir, I know that, sir." Maynard spun around, skipped twice and began to run.

"All right, boys, I don't think you'll be needin' me anymore." Cole reined Kiowa away from the hitching rack. "I've got some riding to do. Wish me luck."

Rios's smile suddenly sprang across his entire face, followed by a similar grin appearing on Luther's, who whispered something to Ethan. A faint smile trailed across the blind rancher's face.

"*Amigo*, I do not theenk you weel have far to ride."

"What do you mean, Miguel?" Cole looked in the direction Rios was pointing.

Silhouetted against the dying sky was Kathleen galloping her horse into view. From the white streaks across its withers and neck, the small mare had been pushed long and hard.

Cole yanked Kiowa away from the group and the horse exploded in her direction.

A fat businessman walked past a muttering Bartlyn, seeking a closer look at the bank money. He stopped and backed up to look at the tied-up Bartlyn, sitting quietly astride a horse. "Hey, you're the guy who said he was a ranger. Led our boys into that ambush."

Bartlyn's face jerked as if his entire expression had been sleeping. "What? Not me. I wouldn't do that." His face twisted to the right. "Tell him I'm not the one."

"Sure you are. I remember you. We oughta hang you right now."

Overhearing the exchange, Ethan growled, "Bartlyn, if either one of you says anything more I'll personally hang you—twice."

Bartlyn swallowed and twisted his head to the side, caught himself and swallowed again.

"John Davis, will you help Mr. Picklewhite get the money back inside?" Ethan asked. "I think Cole's gonna be a while. Whitney and Luther can watch this bunch until Maynard gets back."

"You bet, boss." Sotar swung from the saddle and

flipped the reins over the hitching rack, glancing back at the racing Cole as he did.

Cole couldn't remember jumping down from Kiowa and running toward her. He didn't remember dropping the reins or that, for once, the sorrel remained in place. She had halted her mare, which was heaving so hard the horse's stomach looked like billowing brown-and-white sails. A few steps from her, his mind warned him that she might not be receptive and he skidded to a stop.

"Kathleen?"

"Yes?"

"I love you."

"I know." Her perspiration-moistened face sparkled. "I tried to ride away. I really did. I got as far as that funny little pond. The one where you and I . . . I couldn't imagine living without you. Claire told me where you and your brothers were headed. Can you accept . . ."

"I was coming after you, Kathleen. I wasn't going to stop until I found you—to tell you that I love you. That's all that matters to me."

"Are you ready to go home?" Long tears raced each other down her cheeks.

Cole shook his head and resumed his dash toward her. "Wherever you are is my home."